PSYCHOSIS
BY J. H. KING

ISBN-13: 978-1-4457-6070-4

FOR MY MOTHER,
WHEREVER SHE MAY BE.

SESSION ONE

Howard waited patiently, more patiently than he had ever waited before. He glanced around the waiting area, his eyes dancing and bobbling intelligently in his head. His vision erratic and seemingly uncoordinated, he searched frantically for something interesting to focus on. Finally, he settled on some public information literature neatly arranged in a white metal mesh on the wall. He feigned great interest in all of the pamphlets, deciding upon one, though it was of no actual, or indeed particular, interest to him. As he flitted randomly through the pages, he blinked rapidly revealing further the crow's feet and lines that surrounded his eyes. These were complemented well by the puffy blue-grey bags beneath that made his youngish face seem older than his years. His presentation was neat, but somehow unkempt. His clothes were well-kept, but unironed. His trainers were the current model for the masses to be wearing, but were wrinkling and unclean. His neatly gelled hair, combined with his ashen face and the dark circles under his eyes, caused his mother to often repeat her Michael Aspel joke: 'That he looked like a man who had been up all night having his hair done.'

As Howard selected paragraphs of the pamphlet for scholarly study, he made certain to eyeball carefully anyone and everyone who passed within his designated personal space, which seemed to reach as far as he could see. It was almost as if he could glance at the pamphlet, read in depth one of the crucial and deeply fascinating points of the educational literature, while simultaneously assessing everything that he needed to compute about the passers-by, before they could even observe his presence.

He wiped the sweat from his greasy forehead and looked at his now moist hand. Just as he reached to wipe it on his faded jeans, a voice called out to him: 'Howard? Howard Jones?' He looked up, somewhat startled.

'Er, yeah. Yeah, that's me,' he said. He had not actually properly scrutinised the woman who had called out because he was still caught between the act of disposing of the thick layer of sweat that remained both on his hand and across half of his forehead.

'Would you like to come this way, Mr Jones?' the woman said.

'Er, yeah, I guess so,' Howard replied.

As the woman turned to walk down the corridor, he set about the task of analysing her from behind. He began with her rather large backside that was fighting for air beneath a very tight black pencil skirt. It vibrated from side to side as she toddled along. Despite her dumpy build, her prominent buttocks appealed to him. As he followed her along the economy-saving light green painted walls of the corridor, he began to examine the woman's back. She wore a baggy white blouse that she had attempted to stuff into the restrictive black skirt, the net result of which was a surplus of escaping pleats and folds, which distorted the cut of the otherwise discreet top. He could see her bra straps through the thin cotton, which he made great note of.

They reached the end of the small corridor and the woman led Howard through the cheap door and into a medium-sized office furnished with only a desk and a phone, three chairs and a plant on the windowsill of the only window, through which much needed light pervaded the otherwise gloomy room.

'If you wait here, Dr Morris will be along shortly. Would you like some water or anything?' the mousy-faced woman asked. Howard stared at her blankly for a moment before giving a muffled response.

'Er no, I'm okay thanks,' he said, despite the apparent dryness of his mouth and lips.

'Okay, he shouldn't be long,' she chirped back. Something about the way she left the room left Howard disturbed. Perhaps it was the way she had looked at him before she left, perhaps not?

Howard began inspecting the room as soon as the door had closed. He first looked at the desk with its two chairs opposing each other on either side. One, a fairly plush fake leather rotating office-type, the other a fixed square, cumbersome-looking, sponge-covered thing that, though looked monstrous to him with its faded purple and yellow pattern, did look the more comfortable bet of the two. Another sponge-covered beast sat in the corner by the window. The plant was typical spider plant office fare that dangled down from a bog-standard plastic terracotta-coloured pot, its ends browning in the pleasant dust-filled sunshine that streamed in to meet the insincere and oppressive light of the overhead neon bulbs.

He sat down in what he mentally christened the 'purple people eater'. Hands clasped, he slouched slightly across from the empty executive swiveller behind the desk. He was about to continue his research of the mundane by taking note of the beige-grey plastic touchtone phone when the door opened behind him.

'Ah, hello Mr Jones!' a voice exclaimed confidently.

Howard half turned in his chair to be greeted by the handshake of a fairly tall man with brown plastic glasses and a completely bald, or shaven, head. The man's grip was robust but friendly, and he introduced himself as Dr Raymond Morris before moving to sit behind the desk. Howard, still in the process of shaking the man's hand, was left with his arm slightly extended by the time Dr Morris had sat down. He felt as though he had somehow missed something, as if he'd missed time, or just lost it.

Dr Morris began rustling through some papers and a thin brown folder, looking up only once with a half concerned, half pleasant glance, before he returned to the notes in front of him, which he continued to casually sift through.

'I see you've been seeing Dr Ashraf before you came here,' Dr Morris said while continuing to read the notes. He undid the brown folder and opened it.

'Er, yeah. Yeah, I have,' Howard replied.

'Yes he's very good, quite well-respected in his area, in his field,' Dr Morris continued. 'He's been getting more and more cases like yours and he's had a fair rate of success, thankfully - in controlling the symptoms, I mean.'

'Oh right, I see,' Howard answered slowly.

'Right, well let's have a look here. It says you are on 10mgs of Thioroidizine and 5mgs of the anti-depressants, the Sertraline.'

'Er yeah, yeah 5mgs... and erm, ten of the other one... the erm, the Thioroidizine...' Howard trailed off.

'Well, let's see. How do you feel on it now? Is it getting easier to cope? Are you adjusting to the levels that have been administered to you now? I understand you've come down in dosage considerably in the last month or so. Is that correct?'

'Erm yeah, that's er... right,' Howard mumbled. Dr Morris studied Howard's face for a moment before looking back down at the notes in the file.

'Well Howard, what I need you to talk about is the symptoms a little more. As you're now aware, you've really been quite unwell and when you first went in to see Dr Ashraf you were... well, not entirely *compus mentus* to say the least. You were very incoherent and extremely mistrustful of those around you. The thing, Howard, that concerns us is that you weren't very vocal about what was going on with you, either with those around you before, or with Dr Ashraf. Now, he felt that you made excellent progress under the circumstances and he was satisfied that you have an adequate support network with which you can work, but what I need you to do is to open up a little more and be honest with me, in order that I can make an accurate assessment of your current condition. This is important, Howard, in order that we can assess your progress. Do you see what I mean, Howard?' Howard looked at his hands and down at the floor before answering.

'Yes, yes Doctor. I see what you mean.'

'Now, I'm happy for you to come to these sessions if you feel they'll do you some good, if they'll help with your recovery.'

Howard had begun pondering over the doctor's brown waistcoat. He had on a brown and – what looked to Howard - leather waistcoat. More importantly, he had on a brown leather waistcoat with a mildly pink and white striped shirt. That couldn't be right? *Why would anybody wear a brown waistcoat with a mildly pink and white striped shirt?* he thought. Howard examined the doctor further. He was a well-built, athletic-looking man with a completely bald head. Not just his head, but his face too. The man had no hair anywhere on his head, not even an eyebrow. Howard began to dissect Dr Morris further, when it occurred to him that this man may well be gay. As Howard launched into an internal dialogue about how comfortable or not he felt about this fact, Dr Morris interrupted his train of thought.

'I think for now, Howard, we'll just discuss your immediate needs and go over some of the background to your case. Is that okay with you?' Howard closed his eyes for a second before he answered, licking his lips nervously.

'Erm, oh yeah, that's, that's fine, erm… Doctor…' he trailed off again.

'Dr Morris. I'm Dr Morris.'

'Oh. Yeah, er… sure… Dr Morris,' Howard replied cautiously.

'So, the first thing I'd like to begin with is the medication. You seem a little sluggish and a little unresponsive. I can assure you that's perfectly normal. It happens to everyone who takes the medication; they become a little slower and a bit less responsive to stimuli than they would find otherwise. It's really nothing to worry about, though.' Howard shuffled awkwardly in his purple people eater.

'Er, yeah. I, erm… I do find it's… I mean, I feel a bit slow, a bit slower, you know. It's not as bad as it was, but, erm… I don't feel all that right, you know?' he said.

'Yes, well, as I said that's nothing to worry about and it's something that your system should start to work through. Your body will take time to get used to the drugs, but it will start to respond and perform slightly better than it is now, okay?' Dr Morris went back to reading through his notes again, mulling over any details he might have forgotten. He went on.

'So, maybe we can-' Howard cut him off:

'My, erm…' he began, but Dr Morris interjected.

'Sorry Howard, what did you want to say?' Howard bowed his head.

'Sorry to, erm… Sorry to interrupt you, er, Doctor…' he mumbled.

'No, no that's fine, Howard. You go ahead, say what you have to say,' Dr Morris insisted.

'Well, erm, I've noticed my, erm... my, er... my weight has really increased. I've put a shit load of weight on in the last... well, I'm not sure when, but erm... I'm a lot heavier than I was, Doctor.'

'Yes, er, Howard, that's unfortunately one of the side effects that you're likely to encounter. A lot of people seem to have a fair amount of weight gain. Have you noticed that your breasts have grown substantially? A lot of people find they do.' Howard shifted around more and nodded slowly, but definitely.

'Yeah, erm, yeah they have...' he began. Dr Morris interrupted again.

'Some people really find their breasts just...' Dr Morris cupped his hands over his own breasts and began a slow oozing motion, down and outwards like a schoolboy imitating an enormously fat granny taking off her bra. 'They just kind of bluuuurrrr, they just sort of... bbluuuurrr out... do you know what I mean?'

Howard stared at Dr Morris in disbelief as he continued with his graphic physical description and hand gestures, before responding with a muffled, 'Yeah,' that trailed off quietly.

Dr Morris coughed and went on.

'Well Howard, I think the best thing we can do is go over your case history. Talk a bit about how we got to where we are.'

'Mmm,' Howard murmured.

'Now, I know you went over some of it with Dr Ashraf, but I need to you to explain it to

11

me in order that I can gain a better picture, a fuller picture... an idea of what's been going on. I know it's difficult and probably quite repetitive for you having to go over some of the same old stuff, but it will be of great help to me. Okay Howard?'

'Yes, Doctor,' Howard responded reluctantly.

'Okay, start where you want, Howard. But try to begin with when you first started to get the delusions, the hallucinations. Can you remember?' Howard exhaled deeply through his congested nostrils and looked down at his hands. He rubbed his thumbs together slowly for a moment.

'Well erm... it's, it's er... it's kinda difficult to know where to start, where to begin, Doctor.'

'Yes, Howard it is. But we have to start somewhere, so please... take your time.'

'I think... I think... I think the, erm... first real, erm, hallucination I had was... Christ, years ago, back in my teens.'

'Right,' Dr Morris nodded.

'I mean, it, erm... it was the first time I assume that, erm... I, erm... I hallucinated.'

'And what happened to you then? Can you remember what you... experienced?' Dr Morris said. Howard put his finger across his mouth and made a strange sucking sound as though he was cold.

'I must have been about seventeen,' he said.

'So that's quite some time ago, isn't it?' Dr Morris said.

'Er, yeah, I suppose it is now,' Howard replied.

'You're what now – twenty-six, twenty-seven?'

'Twenty-six,' Howard said as he looked to his left and stared into space as if in deep thought, almost meditatively. There was a brief silence before Howard put his finger back across his mouth and began stroking his lips from top to bottom. He looked sad.

'So tell me what happened, Howard?' Howard refocused back to Dr Morris and said reassuringly,

'It was nothing, really. More like a weird moment.'

'Okay. How was it, erm... weird, Howard?'

'Well, erm, we'd gone to this, erm, party...' Dr Morris interrupted him.

'We?'

'What?' Howard asked, bemused.

'Yes, you said we.'

'Oh right,' Howard smirked somewhat relieved. 'Erm, yeah, me and um, some mates.'

'Okay, go on.'

'Erm, yeah, me and some mates went to this, erm, this party in some, erm, some wine bar somewhere... I forget where, erm...' Dr Morris grew slightly impatient, before composing his manner:

'What did you see, Howard?' he said. Howard bit on his lip, aware of Dr Morris' shifting disposition.

'Yeah, and erm, we went to this party and, erm, well it was alright you know. A lot of girls and erm... well, a lot of, erm, a lot of

13

people, all erm... all squashed into the, er... place.' Dr Morris sat motionless, expressionless, waiting.

'Anyway, we were there and, erm, I went upstairs to the, er... the seat bit, the erm... the loungey bit. And erm, the others... most of the others were downstairs in the dance area, by the decks. Anyway, so I, erm, had a drink... with me, I mean, and I, er, I sat down at this table with the others... who weren't downstairs, I mean, they had got a table and Sprucy and his girl were sitting on the end. Anyway, so I sat next to his missus and, erm... I was just sitting there drinking when, erm... There was another table of people, you know, across from us. And these geeze... these blokes, were all on this table. And, erm, they were like, erm, you know... big men compared to us. There was this big black guy. A big, erm, bald...' Howard glanced at Dr Morris' head for a second before continuing. 'Big bald black geezer and erm, there was this Spanish, you know... Hispanic, I think they call them, you know, like a bandito.'

'A what? I'm sorry,' Dr Morris asked with a slight giggle.

'Erm, a bandito, I mean... oh sorry, I mean er...' Howard paused before suddenly blurting out, 'A Latino. I mean, yeah, a Latin type. He had a pony tail and I think a waistcoat on. Anyway, so there were more than those, erm two, but I only really remember those two.'

'That's alright Howard, go on,' Dr Morris sighed as he spoke.

'Yeah, so erm, the thing was it wasn't really a hallucination... but what happened was, I, er… it all just happened in one go, do you know what I mean?' Howard was now jumping to and forth from being slow and forgetful to being rather excited and animated, depending on what he was talking about.

'What do you mean, Howard?'

'Well, I mean,' Howard was actually speaking quite quickly now. 'One minute I was just sitting there, you know… drinking my drink, the next thing is, it all just took off, you know?'

'How, Howard?' Dr Morris asked sternly.

'Well, everything just speeded up and it was like I was looking at all the right places at all the right times. All the right people at the exact right moment, you know.' Howard was rolling his fingers back and forward like some kind of rapper on speed.

'It was like well… it was like a film, really.' Howard realised that he was sitting forward and was perhaps a little more excited than the situation warranted. He slowly reclined back into his slouch and re-clasped his hands.

'Like a film?' Dr Morris said dryly.

'Erm, yeah…' Howard returned to his slow mumbling.

'Was that it, or did anything else happen?' Dr Morris asked.

'Well…' Howard sighed. 'The thing is, erm, I er… I sort of knew what was going on then…'

'What was going on, Howard?'

'Well, I mean, I just knew what they were all about all of a sudden. Even though they were across the room… I knew what they meant. I could read everything that was going

15

down… I just understood without really knowing, do you know what I mean?'

'I think so,' Dr Morris said slowly, unsure. 'And what was really happening, Howard?'

'Well, erm, you know… they were doing a deal or something. I mean, I didn't get it all. But it was suddenly… all clear to me…' Howard barely finished what he was saying, his voice became so low.

'So they were doing a… a deal, a drug deal?' Dr Morris said confused.

'Yeah, I guess,' Howard replied. Dr Morris pursed his lips and nodded slowly, repetitively.

'Anything else you remember from that time, Howard?'

'Erm, not really from then… not like that, you know.' Howard was not even looking at Dr Morris and was talking into his chest.

'I, er, I can remember other things though,' he said.

'Other things from when, Howard?'

'Well, erm, I, er… I remember something that happened to me… you know, when I was a kid. Before I, er, smoked.'

'Okay, Howard. Is it, erm… is it relevant, Howard? Do *you* think it's relevant?'

'Well, erm…' Howard was starting to sit forward slightly and began to speak with more pace again. 'It's just I remember. When I was kid, I mean, it was er… it was this thing in my head you know, that I couldn't stop it…'

'What do you mean by "thing", Howard?' Dr Morris said curiously. Seeing that he had recaptured Dr Morris' interest, Howard began to sit fully forward again.

'Yeah, I er, I couldn't stop it one day and it really got to me. I was walking in the street one day, when I was like, I don't know, like ten, or maybe nine. Anyway, erm, yeah, I remember the music from Scooby Doo was playing in my head, like playing over and over. At first it was alright, but then it started to get to me, you know. I was like walking along and it wouldn't stop, it just wouldn't stop. It, erm, it got so bad that I started to hold my ears and started to cry. All I could hear was the music and all I could see in my head was... you know, the show. Scooby and Shaggy walking along, it was really weird.' Dr Morris scratched his face gently, just under his glasses below his eye, as if he had nearly caught an eye lash. He paused for a moment and then began writing in his pad.

'Is that all you remember from then, Howard?' he said when he'd finished.

'Er, yeah,' Howard said. It was almost as though he was pleased that Dr Morris had responded the way he had.

'The, erm, the strange thing is, is that...' Howard stopped and began to blink slowly and heavily as though he were drunk or had a painful headache. He reached up to his head and closed his eyes hard. Then he shook his head as if he were trying to shake the effects of a punch off, or a very strong shot of Whisky. He rubbed his forehead.

'Are you okay, Howard?' Dr Morris said, extending his neck slightly, almost peering through his glasses.

'Erm… yeah, yeah I am.' Howard shook his head one final time and sat composed, as if he'd just shaken his contact lens back into a comfortable position.

'What were you about to say?' Dr Morris said.

'Erm, just that I, er…' Howard made the same strange suction noise that he'd made earlier. 'I only, erm, I only remembered that thing, the er… Scooby Doo thing, the other day. I, er, I never knew it before. I mean, I, er… I never remembered it till now.' Howard seemed slightly disorientated.

'That sometimes happens, Howard. Try not to worry about it too much,' Dr Morris reassured him. Howard thought for a moment.

'What was that thing Dr Ashraf gave me? That pill?' he said.

'What pill, Howard?' Dr Morris responded with a touch of the impatience he'd shown earlier. Again, it abated as quickly as it had arisen.

'The one that shrunk my mouth,' Howard asserted.

'The one that shrunk your mouth?' Dr Morris repeated, puzzled.

'Yeah, erm, you know… the one that made my mouth shrink and I couldn't talk.' Dr Morris paused for a while, as a look of concern began to spread across his face. He looked down thoughtfully before suddenly smiling.

'Oh, you mean the one that you were given for your anxiety. What's it called… yes, I know the one,' he chuckled to himself. 'Don't worry about that at all, it's just the side effects.'

Howard couldn't help but remember the feeling. His mouth had literally begun to close, bit by bit. He couldn't control it and his mouth began to shrink. Dr Ashraf was asking all sorts of questions, but he couldn't answer. It was like something from *Alice in Wonderland*. The more questions Dr Ashraf asked him, the more he tried to answer. The more he tried to answer, the more his mouth shrank. It got so bad he thought his mouth was going to eat itself. Eventually he was pacing up and down Dr Ashraf's office with his mouth scrunched up in a tiny ball as though he was about to kiss someone. Dr Ashraf kept telling him to calm down and to not worry. But the more he heard that the more his mouth shrunk and the more anxious he became. It was unbearable.

'I want you to try and recall some of the first times you began to experience the full-blown delusions, when you remember actually having your first hallucinations,' Dr Morris said. Howard smiled to himself.

'Right,' he sighed. 'Well, to be perfectly honest with you, Doctor, it's erm, it's become hard to know when they began.'

'Try to remember, Howard,' Dr Morris said. Howard rubbed his mouth and face as though he had a beard despite not actually having one.

'Well… what I mean is… every time I, er… I think that I remember my first, erm, my first… hallucination, I erm, I seem to start to remember another one before that. To be honest with you, I er… I am not entirely sure about things that have happened in the past, you know.' Dr Morris nodded understandingly.

19

'You mean you're not sure about things from the past, whether they're real or not,' he said. Howard nodded and looked down nervously.

'Right,' he whispered.

'Well Howard, that's what we're trying to help you with. To try and help you understand a bit more about what's... about what's been going on with you.

SESSION TWO

'Hello, erm, I'm here to see Dr Morris,' Howard said, staring long and hard at the receptionist. His eyes were sunken and small, 'piss holes in the snow' as his grandmother used to say. The bags under his eyes were large and purple with small intricate veins appearing sporadically.

'Are you Howard Jones?' the squat figure behind the desk inquired.

'Er, yeah, I'm erm... Howard Jones,' Howard replied.

'Like the singer, eh?' the receptionist joked. Howard stared blankly at the rotund man.

'A little before your time, I suppose. Back in the eighties, what did he sing?' the receptionist said to himself.

'Things Can Only Get Better or something,' Howard answered for him with a small but definite dose of sarcasm. The receptionist's cheerful smile waned slightly and he took on a more formal disposition.

'Yes, that was one of 'em. Can't really remember too many of his others, though,' he said still holding his grin.

'What is Love?' Howard said without hesitation. The receptionist chuckled slightly.

'Yes that was another... get that a lot do you, the old Howard Jones thing?' Howard paused and held his gaze at the portly receptionist. He looked down for a moment and then returned his look, still as blank as ever, as though he were a million miles away, before the distant look diminished and he resumed his attention on the man with a smile.

'Yeah, I get that quite a lot, but erm... more from the older generation... you know, the thirty somethings, they erm... they know who he is... was, you know...' Howard trailed off into a slight mumble. His distant gaze returned without seam. The receptionist looked away as if he were perturbed by Howard's glazed, fixated stare, despite its apparent lack of focus.

'Well, Dr Morris is in with another patient at the moment, but if you take a seat he'll be along shortly,' he said with an air of professionalism. Howard looked down, shuffling his feet.

'Erm, okay, er, thanks,' he said. As he walked towards the waiting area the man called out to him.

'There's water there, in the... whatchamacallit... the water cooler. Please help yourself. There's cups on the side, too.'

Howard turned around. 'Erm, ok, thanks,' he said to the man, who was looking down and writing. He didn't answer or look up.

Slightly bemused, Howard fixed his eyes on the water cooler almost as though its purpose did not fully register with him. He walked passed it and sat down. He sat nervously, ill at ease with himself, as though he were slightly fascinated by everything in the room. His eyes scoped upwards, studying every crack in the ceiling and along the cheaply plastered wall. He re-examined the wall-hanging literature as though he might well indulge in another invigorating read of what was on offer from the plethora of informative health pamphlets, before deciding to just sit and stare some more.

After a while he began to make a clicking sound with his tongue. It was a sort of nervous tutting, as though he should be saying something. He began patting the cushion of the chair intermittently, half tapping out a rhythm. As time slowly passed, Howard thought he heard a voice and strained to hear it again. There was a low mumbling noise coming from somewhere, he just wasn't sure of the direction. It sounded to him like a radio. Then he heard the voice again, still more mumbling. He tried harder to hear what the low voice was saying. He was sure it was a radio. He paused for a moment and heard nothing at all. He waited a while longer, but still heard nothing. Slightly disconcerted, he mentally shrugged it off, recommencing his blank expression and his slow study of the room.

As he glanced towards the window, the low humming noise or voice returned again. He began an auditory search for the direction of the voice or noise. Then he glimpsed from door to door, examining the green plastic door handles and the fake pine doors as he went. He tried to see through the small rectangular wire-meshed windows of the doors to see where it might be coming from, but all the lights in the rooms were off. The low mumbling continued, then silence, then it began again, then it stopped.

'NO!' a voice suddenly exclaimed loudly. It seemed to be coming from one of the rooms, but one further down the corridor and out of sight. The radio noise began again and then stopped. There was another pause before the voice shouted again.

'NO! NO IT'S NOT!' Then more silence. There was the faint sound of another voice, but Howard couldn't work out what it was saying. He was sure it was a radio, or perhaps a television.

'NO, I TELL YOU, IT'S NOT LIKE THAT... I GET UPSET...' The radio interrupted the woman's voice. Howard could hear now that there was definitely a woman shouting.

'NO, BECAUSE I GET ANXIOUS. I GET ANXIOUS AND I CAN'T SLEEP!' Again the radio replied in a low streaming voice or voices. The woman began crying and wailing. She had a South Asian accent, or maybe a Greek accent, it was difficult to tell. Howard was slightly disturbed by the woman's crying and felt he should do something.

'NO, I SWEAR TO YOU IT'S NOT LIKE THAT! I CAN'T GO BACK THERE! I CAN'T FACE IT AGAIN!' the woman sobbed. The radio continued for some time, while the woman cried. Howard felt sure that the woman was in some distress and was quite possibly talking to a radio.

'I AM SCARED! I GET ANXIOUS AND I DON'T SLEEP AND THEN THE FEELINGS COME TO ME! I WON'T BE MISTREATED BY THEM ANYMORE. I JUST CAN'T TAKE IT ANYMORE! I WON'T, I CAN'T! I'M NOT MAD, YOU DON'T BELIEVE ME! I JUST GET ANXIOUS!' the woman cried hysterically.

Howard looked around to see if there was anybody else about. There wasn't, even the receptionist was gone. The woman's shouting and protests continued for more than ten minutes, while the radio conversed with her. The more she protested, the more the radio mumbled on and the more upset she became. Finally, the radio noise became slightly louder and took over as the woman sobbed.

Eventually, Howard stopped listening and sat slumped, waiting for his appointment. He began bouncing his right leg up and down and from side to side. The changes from up and down to left and right seemed important to him as he nervously looked from side to side and, every so often, back at the receptionist, who had returned with a cup of tea and was busily munching on a biscuit. Howard continued to refine his bouncing leg to a smaller, quicker motion while, once in a while, he would bounce both of his legs towards each other and out again, before returning to the smaller up and down movement.

'Mr Jones,' the receptionist said as he walked towards Howard.

'Mmm...' Howard began.

'Mr Jones, Dr Morris is still in with his other patient and might be a while longer. I'm sorry about the wait, but he'll be with you as soon as he can, okay?'

'Erm yeah, okay, no problem,' Howard answered politely. The receptionist waddled back behind the reception area, humming to himself. Howard noted his bald head with greying bits at the back and sides and his old-fashioned, greengrocer-type appearance. The soft shoes, the grey/brown slacks, the subtly checked shirt and the fading green tank top. All that was missing was an aged and frayed apron and he could have been someone that Howard remembered from his childhood, when there were old-fashioned greengrocers just like that, Howard thought perhaps this man once was one. Time passed very slowly and Howard gradually ceased his leg bouncing and returned to his tutting noises. Finally, Dr Morris approached him, files under arm, from the corridor opposite to the one where the distressed woman had been pleading with her radio or someone. There was only silence now.

'Howard, so sorry to have kept you waiting,' Dr Morris said slightly out of breath. He appeared flushed, as though he'd been running. Howard sat up attentively.

'Erm, Dr Morris, hi,' he said.

'Won't you come this way?' Dr Morris said as he smiled briefly and then gently ushered Howard along the corridor from which he'd come.

'Let's just see if we can find a suitable room for us,' he said as he looked. Eventually he decided upon a room further up the corridor and held the door open for Howard. As Howard entered, the fluorescent light began flickering on slowly. Eventually the room lit up and Dr Morris closed the door behind him.

'Please, sit down. I'm very sorry about all the delay, but we are running a little behind today.' Dr Morris' voice was soft and calm as he sat down at the desk, which was pushed up against the wall opposite the door. He placed the files on the desk without opening them and turned to face Howard. He gestured for Howard to come closer and they both sat alongside the desk, facing each other. Howard felt nervous of their close proximity, but now had a chance to get a closer look at Dr Morris.

Dr Morris looked smarter today. He had on a clean white shirt and a navy blue tie, as well as some overly-ironed olive green cotton chinos that had faded through washing. Howard looked down and noticed that they were Dockers, and that they were a tad on the tight side for his liking, as well as having grey lines appearing on the seams where the heat of the iron had marked the cotton. He also noticed that he wasn't wearing those horrible plastic glasses.

'So Howard, how are we doing today?' Dr Morris opened a file and nosed through it from time to time, familiarising himself with the case.

'Erm, yeah, you know, I'm okay... surviving, as they say,' Howard said grinning amiably.

'Yes, good,' Dr Morris breezed over the niceties. 'And how are you coping with the medication now?' His voice was gentle, but sure, his manner exact.

'Erm, yeah, yeah, I'm coping with it all right... still feel a bit dopey, but it's getting better, you know.'

'Yes, I think you'll adjust to it more. You'll become more used to it and find that you will probably function quite well eventually... you know, on it.' Dr Morris flicked through some of the papers and wrote something on one of the notes.

'Well, as you know, Howard, we're here to talk... so, erm, why don't we try and pick up where we left off?' Howard's eyes widened momentarily and his pupils dilated as the white light of the overhead neon bulbs streamed into them. He looked worried and ashen-faced.

'Erm, o... okay, erm...' he stammered.

'We were, if I remember correctly, discussing your delusions and, erm, trying to... well, trying to discover their beginning, or perhaps earlier stages of development. Am I right?'

'Yeah, that's it, erm, right,' Howard replied.

'So...' Dr Morris said, reading through the notes some more as though he was looking for something specific. 'So, tell me more about how they started. Last time you told me about something happening at, erm... yes, at a party... erm, can you remember anything else from that time?' Howard clasped his hands together and looked into his lap before looking up at Dr Morris.

'You mean from the party?' he said.

'Well yes, from the party or from that time, from that period in your life.' Dr Morris nodded enthusiastically as he spoke.

'Well, erm... I told you what I can remember from the party, erm... I'm trying to remember, even when that was. You know, it was a long time ago,' Howard explained.

'Yes, yes I realise that Howard, but try, just try... to remember that time in your life. What was going on in your world at that particular point in time?'

Howard sighed deeply and licked his lips. He pursed them together and then gently bit his lower lip nervously.

28

'I, erm...' he sighed again. 'I was at, erm, at college doing my A Levels, I think.'

'Right, so what were you studying?'

'I was doing... erm... A level history and, erm, A level art,' Howard said slightly unsure.

'Did you like them? Were they interesting to you?' Dr Morris asked.

'Yeah, they were alright, you know... I mean, well, I liked history. That was good. Art... well, art, I wasn't much good at it, really. Well, that's, erm... that's what they told me, anyway.' Howard looked hurt as he said it. Dr Morris smiled sympathetically.

'Did you think you were good at it, Howard? Did you think you were good at art?' he said.

'Well, to be honest, I thought I was alright, you know. I thought that, er, I wasn't such a bad drawer. Better than half the others, anyway.'

'Your classmates, you mean.'

'Yeah, I mean... To be honest, Doctor, some of 'em couldn't draw for shit, you know.' Howard smirked as though he was proud of swearing in front Dr Morris. It was as if he was a misbehaving schoolboy again.

'Did you feel hard done by, Howard? By your teachers, or your, your erm... classmates? Did you feel like they were cheating you somehow?' Dr Morris waited patiently with interest for Howard's response.

'Well... in a way, yeah. I mean, some of them, not all of 'em, were complete crap... you know, at drawing. I was definitely better than some of them at least.' Dr Morris raised his hairless right brow ever so slightly.

'Did you feel...?' he began, but Howard cut him off.

'I mean, I know I wasn't the best artist, drawer or whatever, but I wasn't that bad. They didn't have to fail me like that. That was blatant bollocks. I might as well not have come. I think that's what they were saying to me, anyway. Don't bother turning up, mate. You're shite.' Howard was speaking with enthusiasm and authority. Dr Morris cleared his throat.

'So you felt like they didn't understand you... or not...?'

'Well, they told me. He told me that I can't draw 'cos I don't draw what's there in front of me. He told me that I was incapable of sitting down and drawing what was there in front of me.' Howard pointed his finger and prodded it aggressively in mid-air as he spoke.

'Who told you? Your teacher?' Dr Morris asked.

'Yeah, he told me that I might as well not fuckin' bother, 'cos all I do is sit and draw from my head, not what's in front of me. He showed me where the stuff was. You know, all the light and the shadows and all that stuff. He said that's what he wanted from me, not some floating image that had nothing to do with what was sitting in front of me,' Howard replied.

'Were you angry with him, Howard?' Dr Morris said, cocking his head to one side.

'Yeah,' Howard said flippantly. 'I think he thought that I reckoned I was some talented artist who was above petty crap. You know, still life and shit like that. In a way he was right. Not the talented artist bit. I mean the still life stuff. It was boring. I didn't wanna draw some pot of flowers or bowl of fruit. Or some stuffed fuckin' animal, you know.' Howard had tested the waters and it appeared that bad language was to be permitted.

'What did you want to draw?' Dr Morris enquired, while briefly writing some notes. Howard thought for a moment or two before replying.

'Well... I don't know. You know...whatever, but not that.'

'So you found still life boring. Did you find art boring overall?'

'It was alright. I was more interested in some of the girls in the class, anyway.' Dr Morris's eyes widened with a look of interest.

'So you were more interested in the girls... how? In looking at them, or did you talk to them?' Howard looked at Dr Morris as though he were slightly peculiar.

'Well, you know... both,' he said.

'So you found art a bit dull, shall we say.'

'Yeah.'

'What about, erm... history? Did you find that interesting?' Howard nodded slowly.

'Yeah, I liked history, always did.'

'What did you like about history so much, Howard?' Dr Morris phrased the question with a slight air of disinterest.

'I don't know, it's just so good... you know, to hear all those stories.'

'Stories?' Dr Morris said.

'Yeah, you know, you got all these different stories being told by you know, this historian and that historian, and none of 'em can agree. They all reckon they know what really happened. But in between they make up some really good stories, man.'

'You don't think there's such a thing as historical fact, then?' Dr Morris asked thoughtfully.

'Do you?' Howard retorted. Dr Morris smiled and changed his approach.

'Well, Howard, we're not here to discuss what I think. I think it's more important that we focus on what *you* think.'

'I suppose,' Howard shrugged.

'So, you liked history. Do you still like it, history?' Dr Morris said.

'Yeah,' Howard replied genuinely. Dr Morris shifted his weight in his chair and crossed his legs. 'Okay, so you were at university...'

'College... I was at college,' Howard said correcting him.

'You were at college and you were... how were you at that time, socially? How were you getting on with people, do you remember?' Dr Morris said. Howard wobbled his head from side to side slowly.

'Well, alright... you know. I mean, I was social at that time. I got on with people. Some people, anyway.'

'So you were interacting with people at that time?'

'Oh yeah, I mean I had loads of mates and a fit bird and that. You know.'

'So you were having these hallucinations or visions, but you were still having a good social life?'

'Well... I mean... I guess, but they weren't hallucinations...' Howard cut off and thought to himself as Dr Morris wrote in the notes.

'Go on,' Dr Morris said reassuringly.

'Well, they weren't like... hallucinations. I didn't think they were hallucinations at the time, anyway. I thought they were... you know... little freak-outs. You know, didgyness.'

'When you say freak-outs... do you mean... what do you mean?'

'I just thought they were 'cos I was stoned, you know,' Howard said frankly.

'Well, they were, Howard, weren't they?'

Howard stared blankly at Dr Morris for some time, while Dr Morris held his sincere expression.

'Do you see what I mean, Howard?' Dr Morris said softly. Howard hung his head slightly and looked down at the desk leg. 'You do see that those, erm, freak-outs as you called them, were because you were stoned, intoxicated? They were the effects of the drugs you were taking.'

'Yeah,' Howard mumbled slowly, still staring at the leg of the desk.

'So tell me more about them, Howard. Tell me more about the kinds of things you experienced when you were on the drugs.'

'What I mean, Doctor, is... that it wasn't like when I stopped smoking weed. It wasn't like those hallucinations. They were different.'

'How were they different, Howard?'

'They were... well, they were milder... sort of. I don't know how to explain it.'

'You mean they were less pronounced, less frequent, less frightening?'

Howard leaned forward in his chair. 'They were more normal, if you know what I mean. That's why they didn't seem like hallucinations. They were normal,' he said.

'They were normal hallucinations. You mean mundane?' Dr Morris said.

'Yeah, sort of... they were the sort of thing that could happen, you know?'

'Do you mean like, erm, like something somebody would say or do that might occur every day, like everyday occurrences?'

'Yeah, somehow. They were things that suited the situation, things that could easily have happened.' Dr Morris was reading the notes. He looked up again.

'Like a drug deal, for example.'

'Yeah... sort of. I mean, yeah, like that, but... well, anything really. Like... it's hard to think. As I said, it was hard to tell... well, back then I thought it was all real. Well... sort of. What I mean is... I didn't think that what I saw was necessarily true or real. As I said, I'd see things and wonder whether it did happen or not, or whether it was just a little freak-out. But the things that I saw were... or could have been normal enough to have happened. Do you see what I mean, Doctor?'

'Yes,' Dr Morris replied.

'So...' Howard began slowly.

'Can you give me an example, Howard?'

'Of?'

'Of what was happening that could have been normal, but might not have happened.' Dr Morris waited patiently as Howard thought.

Howard shuffled in his seat and continued to look thoughtful, but said nothing.

'Try to think back to what was going through your mind at that time, Howard. Maybe that would be a good place to start.' Howard remained silent for a few moments. Dr Morris observed Howard patiently. The only noise was the sound of a generator coming from outside the building. The faint smell of hospital dinners wafted past the open window, the resonance of which remained in the room.

'Well, what I can remember is not hallucinations, really... well, I'm not sure. It was more like paranoia, really.'

'What were you paranoid about, Howard?'

'Well, er, I remember weird things happening. Like, erm... Like one time I was at a rave and we were getting mash-up and the DJ was chattin' to me.' Dr Morris looked slightly confused.

'Were you worried that he was going to do something to you?' he said. Howard sniggered to himself.

'No, no. I mean he was talking to me from the box, from the decks room. But I was, erm, I was down on the floor, you know.'

'So you were hearing his voice while he was playing his records. Like telepathy, you mean?' Dr Morris said. Howard laughed out loud.

'No,' he chuckled again as he spoke. 'I mean, erm, he was chattin' on the mike, you know, so the whole place could hear.'

'Oh right,' Dr Morris said. 'And, um, what was he saying, to you, I mean?'

'Well, he was, er, he was sort of chattin' to me and about me, you know. Like he was trying to embarrass me.'

'Did you know why he was trying to embarrass you?'

'Erm, no… not really. I mean, I think he wanted me to dance or something and I was just standing with my back to the wall, up against the speaker, you know, smoking a spliff and all that with my mates. But I wasn't dancin' or anything. I think he was, like, trying to make me dance.'

'Was he trying to get you to dance in a nice way or was he being horrible to you?' Dr Morris said.

'Well, a bit of both really. He kept saying something like "Come on mate, let's have it then, show us what you got. You think you're all that, well let's see it then". Stuff like that, really. I think anyway. That's what I mean. It could have happened, Doctor, honestly it really could have just been real. I just can't tell anymore.' Dr Morris tapped his pen lightly on the table.

'Did you think it was real at the time, Howard? Were you sure then?'

'No, I really wasn't, Doctor. It was things like that. That would happen every so often. That's what I mean by a freak-out.'

'Can you give me any different examples, Howard, from that time?' Howard pushed his bottom lip out as he thought carefully. He began shaking his head.

'Not really…' He stared into space, straining to give another example. 'No, it's just that I often thought people were talking about me, or plotting against me.'

'Plotting against you? In what way? To hurt you? Were people out to get you, Howard?'

'Well, yeah, sort of. I mean, they weren't trying to kill me or nothin'. It was more small stuff. Mischievous stuff, you know.'

'Did you feel like people were laughing at you, Howard, or making fun of you?' Dr Morris adjusted his posture and straightened his back.

'Well, they were sometimes. I mean, we all were, making fun of each other, taking the piss and all that.'

'So were you unsure about when they were making fun of you and, erm, when they weren't?' Dr Morris said. Howard rubbed his eye as though he were trying to fully wake up.

'Yeah, it's about the time that things went a bit weird, a bit weirder than normal,' he said.

'You felt weird at that time?' Dr Morris said. Howard sighed.

'Yeah, I felt weird at that time. I felt weird anyway. But it got... I don't know, weirder. It's when I got a glimpse of how people could be.' Howard began staring into space again. This time he looked slightly lost, as though he were upset. Dr Morris pushed the files to one side and leaned forward in his chair. His posture still straight, with his hands clasped between his legs. His trouser legs slid up to reveal his striped red and purple socks. Howard homed in on them with a vague sense of disgust.

'When you say how people could be.' Dr Morris spoke softly, almost kindly, with a look of sincerity on his face. 'Do you mean how people can be nasty to one another?' Howard mentally moved himself and his chair back away from Dr Morris, but did not actually move at all.

'Yeah... that... but, erm...' He didn't finish.

'What else do you mean, Howard?'

'I saw a glimpse of the other side of people.' Howard seemed reluctant to speak.

'Can you elaborate a little bit more?' Dr Morris said gently.

'Erm.' Howard seemed uncomfortable, almost embarrassed. 'I saw the silvery side of people.' His voice grew quieter as he spoke the words.

'The silvery side of people... erm, what does that mean?' Dr Morris asked. Howard grew more uncomfortable and a bit annoyed.

'Well, erm... it's like the devilish side, you know.' He seemed as though he was holding back as he spoke. Like he was revealing something that maybe he shouldn't.

'You mean... do you mean? Is silverish an, erm, expression, you know, like street slang?' Dr Morris said trying to understand what Howard was saying.

'No,' Howard said half sniggering to himself. 'No, erm, it's how I explain it. It's how it seems to me.'

'Do you mean silverish as a way of describing their mood or behaviour?' Dr Morris said. Howard shook his head.

'No, I mean... it's like in *Cocoon*.'

'What?' Dr Morris spat out in confusion. 'Do you mean they are in a silver cocoon? I'm sorry, Howard, you've lost me.'

'No, it's like in the film *Cocoon*,' Howard explained.

'The film about the old people and aliens or something?'

'Yes,' Howard replied.

'Sorry, you'll have to explain what you mean, Howard.'

'It's nothing really, just like, you know the bit in the film when they pull their eye down and they're all shiny and silvery underneath their skin?' Howard said. Dr Morris reached for the file.

'So you thought that they were silvery underneath their skin?' he said, pen ready to write.

'No, erm, it's more like... I dunno. It's more just that sort of effect, not under their skin, but sort of coming from inside them, from inside around their eyes, and around them,' Howard said. Dr Morris began writing in the file. He wrote a small paragraph and some related comments. He turned to face Howard.

'So, did you think they were aliens, like in the film *Cocoon*, Howard?'

'Not aliens, no.'

'What did you think it was, then?'

'I wasn't sure,' Howard said thoughtfully. 'But it always came with a cold feeling, a feeling of the cold wind of a dark winter.'

SESSION THREE

The mobile phone rang three times.

'Hello,' Howard mumbled.

'Hello, my name is Anne Roddick. I'm calling from the Foster's mental health unit. Is it possible to speak to Howard Jones, please?'

'Yeah… speaking,' Howard said.

'Good morning, Mr Jones.'

Howard cleared his throat. 'Erm, yeah, good morning.'

'I'm just calling to let you know that Dr Morris is away this week. He's been called away to another centre and won't be able to make your appointment this week. Is that okay, Mr Jones?' Howard was silent for a moment.

'Yeah, that's okay. That's fine,' he said.

'We're really sorry about that, but there's nothing we can do I'm afraid. If you feel as though you need some counselling, or as though you can't wait until the following week, then please feel free to tell us and we'll see if we can get you a replacement.'

'No, no that's okay. I'll be alright till then.'

'Okay, Mr Jones. As I said, Dr Morris will be back next week and so you can attend the session then, unless we contact you to tell you otherwise.'

'Okay then,' Howard replied.

'Sorry about that, Mr Jones.'

'That's alright.'

'Okay, bye then.'

'Yeah, bye.' Howard put the phone down and sat back in the large and moulded indentation of his armchair.

SESSION FOUR

'Right, Howard. Sorry about last week. I got called away to another centre in Devon to deal with an old case that I knew the history to, so sorry about us not being able to have our last session,' Dr Morris said.

Howard smiled vaguely. His look was less sharp than usual, his physical presence less rigid and firm. His demeanour was soft and his disposition weaker than normal. He looked as though he'd been in solitary confinement for a week and was ready to talk, about anything.

'That's, erm, that's alright, Doctor.' Howard's voice was low, almost a whisper.

'How have you been coping, Howard, since I last saw you?' Dr Morris said. Howard smiled. The crow's feet spread out on either side of his deeply-sunken eyes. The bags beneath them were a violent shade of violet and blue. His face was pale and his pores open. Sweat covered his sleepless body.

'I, er, I haven't had a lot of sleep, really,' he answered.

'I see. Have you been taking your medication?'

'Yeah.'

'Regularly?' Dr Morris said sternly.

'Yeah,' Howard said raggedly. He blinked very slowly and rubbed his eyes. He blinked more, slowly, as though he was trying to focus and to overcome the trailers that accompanied his vision of things.

'So, Howard, why haven't you been sleeping properly then, eh?' Dr Morris seemed brasher than before. He appeared very pleased with himself. As though he'd received some good news or had achieved something that had given his manner a slight swagger, a swagger that was detracting him from his usual persona and considerate approach.

'Well, erm, I don't know really...' Howard began.

'It's just that the medication should help you sleep better, really.'

'Erm, yeah, yeah I know. It's just that, well... sometimes I get a bit, erm, out of sorts really.'

'What do you mean? Anxious and worried?' Dr Morris said. Howard nodded slowly. He was leaning forward in his chair and looking at the floor, without looking up at Dr Morris as he spoke.

'That, but more, erm, more like I get mixed up. My sleeping pattern, you know.'

'So you get out of sorts with your sleeping pattern, do you? You mean you stay up too late and then get up too late as well?' Dr Morris said jollily.

'Yeah, at first, but then I stay up all the time. I erm... I stop sleeping.'

'Right, I see. How long do you go without sleep, Howard?'

'Well, maybe three, four days or so.'

'Without any sleep at all?' Dr Morris exclaimed. Howard continued to talk to the floor.

'Yeah, sometimes. Sometimes, I, er... catch a couple of hours in the afternoon when I'm exhausted.'

'Well, Howard, that won't do really. One of the main things you need is an adequate amount of sleep in order that you are fully rested and are not overly affected by sleep deprivation. I think I should recommend some sleeping tablets for you.' Dr Morris began writing on the notes in front of him and then pulled out a prescription pad from inside the brown file.

'No,' Howard said firmly. Dr Morris looked up in surprise.

'I don't want to take sleeping pills, Doctor.'

'Well, why not Howard? You need to sleep. It's very important that you sleep.'

'Yeah, I know, but, erm, I don't like taking so many pills and stuff, you know.'

'Yes, but Howard, it's not normal or healthy for anyone to go without sleep for three or four nights in a row. So, you're saying you get no sleep at all?' Dr Morris was growing less cheerful by the minute.

'Well, you know… usually two or three nights not sleeping, but I might get a couple of hours in the afternoon, before I get woken up.'

'Who wakes you up? Your mum?'

'Er, no, no she isn't staying over with me anymore.'

'Well, who's with you now, Howard? Is anyone staying with you now?'

'Er, no, not anymore. I mean, erm, they were before, but they have to work, you know.' Howard said. Dr Morris let out a sigh.

'Yes, Howard, but we were under the impression that you had a good support network around you and that's why we were content to not keep you in the centre for longer. We need to know that you're okay, Howard, and that you're not alone too much of the time.'

'Yeah, but I mean they come over a lot, they just don't stay with me anymore. But I have my flatmate at night, when she comes back from work. They just don't need to babysit me all day anymore. I mean, I come here on my own now. I go shopping by myself. I'm not completely useless, you know.' Howard looked up at Dr Morris. 'I just haven't had much sleep, that's all.'

'So who woke you up? Your flatmate?'

'What?'

'You said someone woke you up.'

'Erm, no, erm... *She* did, upstairs.'

'The woman upstairs woke you up?' Dr Morris said. Howard looked down again.

'Yeah,' he replied. Dr Morris leaned forward to see if he could catch a glimpse of Howard's face.

'What did she do? Knock on the door or something?' he said.

'No,' Howard replied.

'Is she very noisy then?' Dr Morris asked. Howard didn't answer.

'Is your neighbour a noisy person?' Dr Morris persisted.

'No, she's not very noisy,' Howard answered reluctantly.

'I'm confused, Howard. How did the woman upstairs from you wake you up, then?' Howard sat silently, with his head bowed forward. His hands clasped before him, he continuously rubbed his thumbs together as though he were extremely agitated.

'Well...' Howard said, continuing to rub his thumbs. 'It's, erm, it's difficult to explain really, Doctor...' he said. Dr Morris clasped his chin.

'Yes, Howard, it's all rather difficult really, I know that. But you have to try and open up a little. I can assure you nothing you tell me is going to shock me. And I'm not going to judge you by the things you tell me. I'm here to help you, Howard. I really am.' Howard looked at Dr Morris wearily, before looking down once more and rubbing his hands together vigorously.

'I, erm, I erm... I sometimes get woken up by the woman upstairs sort of having sex with me.' Howard's voice was all but a whisper. He glanced at Dr Morris with a look of great concern before looking back down at the floor. Fretfully he began rubbing his forehead.

'What do you mean, sort of having sex with you?' Dr Morris said. Howard's look became almost terrified. 'I, er, I mean she sort of has sex with me... but not actually, you know,' he said very quietly.

'Do you mean you masturbate about her, Howard, and she masturbates too? Is that what you're trying to tell me, Howard?' Dr Morris wrote a sentence in his notes, then stopped writing and gave Howard a frank smile. 'If it's embarrassing... well, don't worry, just tell me what happens.' Howard half smiled back nervously.

'No, erm...' His voice was still very low, as though afraid that someone might hear what he was saying.

'It's not like masturbating… it's different. It's more like sex,' he said. Dr Morris frowned slightly.

'Like sex, but not actually sex,' he said.

'Yeah,' Howard replied.

'What is it like, Howard?' Dr Morris said softly and slowly.

'It's, erm, it's like actual sex, except that… well, we're not actually together.' Howard sighed heavily as though a burden had both been lifted then replaced almost immediately.

'So your neighbour is not, er, actually in the room with you?'

'No.'

'So she's where, upstairs?'

'Yeah.'

'In her flat?'

'Yeah.' Howard seemed utterly ashamed.

'And this woke you up… how?' Dr Morris was writing as he spoke.

'She, er… she just, erm, she just takes me. She imposes herself on me.'

'How, does she appear before you and simply… well, you know. How does she impose herself on you?' Dr Morris said slightly bemused.

'No. I, er, I don't see her. I only feel her,' Howard replied informatively.

'So she, she comes and attacks you, or…?' Dr Morris said licking his lips.

'Not exactly… she, erm… I, er, I penetrate her… I mean, she takes me while I sleep and it wakes me up… you know, startled like.' Howard was studying Dr Morris very

46

carefully, trying to read his response. As he spoke he became more comfortable with the subject, as though he were less self-conscious and more concerned with explaining the details.

'How do you know it's your neighbour, Howard, and not someone else if you can't see her?'

'I don't know, Doctor, I just know it's her. As well as the noises she makes. You know, I, er, I hear the noises from upstairs.'

'So you hear her, what, make sexual noises?'

'Yeah, sometimes, but usually she tries to hide it. So I just hear the odd noise here and there. Sometimes it's hard to know whether I actually heard it, you know.' Dr Morris nodded.

'Yes, I see,' he said. Howard leaned forward, his shoulders hunched and his palms pressed together.

'I know you're not supposed to talk about it, are you?' he whispered. Dr Morris paused for a moment to think.

'Why not?' he half whispered back.

'Well, you know. It's one of those things, isn't it?' Howard said, his voice still very low. Dr Morris cleared his throat and raised his voice slightly.

'One of what things, Howard?'

'You know, one of life's strange things. It goes on, but no one dares talk about it. Everyone does it, but wants to leave it alone. Nobody wants to go there,' Howard said as though it were a matter of fact.

'And why is that, Howard?' Dr Morris said. Howard looked blankly at him.

47

'I, er... I don't really know,' he said. Dr Morris breathed deeply and pursed his lips.

'I think maybe we should increase the dosage of your medication a bit,' he said. Howard looked mortified. 'Why?' he exclaimed.

'Well, if you're still having these hallucinations then obviously your medication dosage is not high enough. You shouldn't really be having such strong delusions on the amount that you're taking now,' Dr Morris said. Howard grew annoyed.

'So that's it, is it? I tell you stuff and you dose me up 'cos I said something I shouldn't have. Bent the rules, have I?' Dr Morris put his hands up to gesture for Howard to calm down.

'No, it's not like that, Howard. But if you're having hallucinations like that, then you need to take a stronger dosage of your medication.'

'But it's not...' Howard stopped dead.

'It's not what?' Dr Morris said calmly.

It's... it's real, Doctor, come on. I'm sorry I spoke about it. I knew I shouldn't have spoken about it. It won't happen again. Honestly,' Howard pleaded apologetically.

'Howard, you have to realise that I'm here to help you with your illness. It's not that you can't talk about things. It's just... well. Perhaps you need to trust me a bit when I suggest to you that something is not actually real.'

'Yes, Doctor, I understand,' Howard nodded knowingly.

'You have to understand, that people cannot have sex with each other without them both being present, together. Do you see what

I'm saying to you?' Howard remained silent as though he wasn't sure what the correct answer was.

'Can you understand that it's not physically possible, Howard?' Howard could contain himself no longer:

'Yes! Yes, physically that's right, Doctor, but mentally they can.'

'Yes, Howard, in their minds they can, but it's not actually real or happening. It's only in their minds, in their imaginations.'

'Yes, Doctor, I agree. But there's more to it than that.'

'Is there, Howard?' Dr Morris said sarcastically.

'Yes,' Howard said firmly.

'Howard, surely if that were true then people would talk about it. They would say something. It would come up somewhere along the line. Why wouldn't they talk about it? People talk about their experiences, don't they?' Howard pushed his hands up into a prayer position and bounced them up and down as he spoke, as though he were praying for Dr Morris to give him a fair hearing.

'Yeah, they do, but there's…' Howard lowered his voice and looked around the room with wide eyes: 'There's a lot going on that can't be said right now. There always has been.'

'Look Howard, how could it be? How can two people have sex without actual physical contact? It can only be done through fantasising. And fantasy is not reality.'

'It's because we're all connected, Doctor… everything is,' Howard said certainly.

49

'Yes, Howard. We all have various relationships that connect us, but I am telling you that it is not possible to have sex, actually have sex with someone else through the power of your mind alone.' Dr Morris realised he was beginning to raise his voice and began to breathe deeply and gather his composure.

'But no, Doctor, I'm telling you it happens every day. It's not just me, Doctor, I see it everywhere I go. I feel it.'

'You may feel it, Howard, but that does not necessarily make it real. What you experience is illusion. You do see that you suffer from delusions, Howard? That's why you are given medication.'

'Yes, I know I have problems, but I know what I see. I know what I hear and I know what I feel. So don't you sit there and tell me otherwise, do you hear me!' Howard was out of his seat and pointing his finger at Dr Morris.

'Sit down, Howard. Please sit down.' Howard sat down.

'Okay, but don't tell me about it. If you want to live with your head in the sand, then carry on. But don't have a go at me for not wanting to do the same,' he said irately.

'I'm not burying my head in the sand, Howard, I'm trying to help you. I'm trying to explain to you that you are ill and that this particular issue is very much a part of that illness,' Dr Morris said with authority.

'It can't just be me, Doctor. I see others doing it all the time.'

'So, you see others having sex with each other mentally. How does that work? Come on Howard.'

'I can explain it to you, Doctor, if you'd just let me.'

'Okay, Howard, explain it to me. Explain how it works then,' Dr Morris said in exasperation as he sat back heavily in his chair.

'It works like electromagnetic energy or something.'

'Or something,' Dr Morris said derisively.

'Yeah,' Howard asserted. 'Noise interferes with it, especially the television, or the radio and music.'

'Really, Howard?'

'Sound waves are affected by it. I guess they collide.'

'Howard, don't you see that this is your illness speaking? The things you are talking about are not real,' Dr Morris said sitting forward, urging Howard to see reason.

'So, you're telling me that electromagnetism doesn't exist? That sound waves and radio waves don't exist, oh really Doctor?' Dr Morris smiled slightly.

'No, I'm not saying that, Howard. What I'm saying is that there is no such thing as this… what do you call it?'

'Sexual energy,' Howard said confidently.

'As sexual energy,' Dr Morris went on.

'So you're telling me there's no such thing as sexual energy, Doctor?'

'Well, no, I'm not saying that, Howard. Of course there's such a thing as sexual energy, but it doesn't work like that. Not in the way that you're saying.'

'So how does it work, Doctor?'

'Well… I suppose it, er… it works on a biochemical level.

'Like chemistry,' Howard said mockingly.

'Yes, like chemistry, Howard. But the point is that there is no evidence to suggest that it works in the way that you're saying it does.' Dr Morris seemed uncomfortable, as though he were in slightly uncharted waters.

'What about transcendental sex?' Howard said. Dr Morris looked puzzled. 'What about transcendentalism and out of body experiences?'

'Well, Howard, I don't think we should go into that now, should we?'

'Why not, Dr Morris?'

'Because we're discussing your illness and not religious beliefs.'

'What if my religious beliefs tell me that transcendentalism exists?' Howard said defiantly.

'Well, maybe they…' Dr Morris shifted uncomfortably in his chair. 'Is that part of your religious belief, Howard? What religion do you believe in?' Howard smiled.

'I didn't say I had any religious belief. What I am saying is, what if my religious beliefs were that transcendental sex is possible?' Dr Morris grew irritated, but hid it quite well.

'Is that what you believe, Howard? That people can have transcendental sex? What religion is that from, Howard? Do you know?'

'I haven't got a fuckin' clue, mate. But what I am asking you is what if my religion said that this was possible? Are you telling me that my religion is not true, Doctor?'

'I think we have to end the session there, Howard. We're out of time. I'm sorry. We can pick up this next week, okay?'

SESSION FIVE

Howard sat staring at the desk and his file. He wanted to know what it said, what this clever prick was writing, but he was also terrified. He was terrified of what it might say. Of how he might have got it all wrong. It stood to reason that this wanker was probably getting it all wrong, didn't have a clue, and probably didn't care. After all, this was more than likely just another stepping stone case study until he got to Broadmoor or wherever the hell he was trying to get to. Until he saw the important freaks who had made their mark on the world. The ones who'd carved people up and said and acted upon the thoughts and beliefs they had. Or maybe his file told him things he wasn't supposed to know. Maybe he was a part of something bigger. Maybe he wasn't the only one.

'Sorry about that, Howard,' Dr Morris said with a smile. 'It's just that they've put your case and another client's back to back with each other, but at completely opposite ends of the building, and each time I run across here I'm totally out of breath,' Dr Morris said sipping on his plastic cup of water. Howard looked up at Dr Morris and gave a cheesy grin.

'That's alright, Doctor,' he said, continuing his goofy smile. His eyes looked slightly glazed. He had the self-pleased look of a stoned teenager who was suddenly put in a formal situation and could do nothing but smile and agree with everything said.

'So, how are we getting along today?' Dr Morris said opening the file and placing his plastic cup of water to one side on the desk. 'Let's see… so we put you back up in dosage a little last week, didn't we? Nothing too drastic, but just enough to help you along a bit.'

'Yeah,' Howard said with a slight snigger. His watery eyes fixed on Dr Morris.

'How have you been feeling on that, Howard? Okay?' Dr Morris said in a business-like fashion.

'Yeah, fine erm…' Howard trailed off, his stupid grin returned as he eased back into his chair and continued to maintain eye contact with Dr Morris. Dr Morris glanced at Howard for a moment and smiled back.

'Well, let's see where we were last time, Howard. I do believe you were slightly upset and were explaining the workings of, erm… let's see, what did you call it? Ah yes, transcendental sex. Yes, transcendental sex and the power of sexual energy. Perhaps you'd like to pick up from where you left off and just clarify a bit more clearly what you meant.' Dr Morris sat back in his chair and clasped his hands together. Howard sat staring at Dr Morris. He could not remove the grin from his face and was nodding almost in approval of Dr Morris' newly-adopted approach.

'Well, erm,' he laughed as he attempted to speak. 'What, erm, what do you want to know… Doc?' he asked as he tried to feign sincerity. Dr Morris' irritation grew apparent as he leaned forward in his chair, placing Howard's file open on his lap.

'I want you to explain to me how it all works, Howard.' Dr Morris' voice was stern and slightly aggressive. Howard clasped his hands and pushed them together hard, trying to crack his joints, with only minor success.

'Okay, Dr Morris, if that's what you want, then...' Howard had stopped smiling and was looking right into Dr Morris' eyes. His expression was also unyielding. 'Where shall I begin?'

'Wherever you see fit, Howard. Where you left off. You were having, erm, transcendental sex with your neighbour. Start there.' Howard shifted slightly in his chair and made himself comfortable.

'Okay, Doctor. Like I said, she usually wakes me up with a good morning surprise or good afternoon, whatever. Her favourite thing is to wake me up with it and take me by surprise. I think she likes to hear me wake up with a yelp, anyway.'

'Go on Howard,' Dr Morris said slightly taken back by Howard's change in demeanour.

'Well, what do you want me to say?' Howard said somewhat bewildered.

'Howard, last time you were explaining to me how it works. I'd like to know more about that process, what goes on, what you do and how?' Howard rubbed his chin and thought for a moment.

'Right. Well, erm, I suppose...' he stopped talking and looked as though he was struggling to find the words. He looked baffled as he stared into space.

'Take your time, Howard, there's no hurry. Just tell me about the whole thing. Tell me what happens with your neighbour.' Howard concentrated and looked at Dr Morris.

'Well, the thing is, it's not always when I'm asleep. It's just often she starts it up when I'm asleep. Sometimes she just... you know... gets me going while I'm asleep. Anyway, it works in layers.'

'In layers? What do you mean, in layers?'

'Well, I mean, you have to realise that I'm young and I've been trying to work it out for myself, you know. But as far as I can tell it has a sort of layers system to it.' Dr Morris shook his head slowly and gave a sympathetic smile.

'Look, it starts with... well, I can feel her, you know, fanny on my, er, penis.'

'But she isn't near you is she, Howard?'

'No, no she isn't near me. Well, she can be, but my neighbour isn't. She's upstairs, you know, in her flat. Sometimes I feel the energy.'

'The sexual energy?' Dr Morris enquired.

'Yeah, the sexual energy. Like a sort of electrical pulse I guess, but slightly different. It's, well, hard to explain. Anyway, I sort of get the feeling that we're gonna cross channels or whatever and link up.'

'What do you mean when you say cross channels, Howard?'

'Well, I was trying to work out what it was, how it worked. I figured that there were channels or tunnels of sexual energy that are set out. A bit like ley lines, you know, in the earth where they built all the old churches.'

'I'm not sure I'm familiar with what you're talking about, Howard?'

'Well, you know there's this theory that all the ancient religious sites of worship and significance were placed wherever these ley lines of energy would cross? When Christianity came along, they wanted to usurp the pagan religions so they replaced all the religious holy sites by building churches on them. What they didn't know – or maybe they did – is that they'd built them on these great channels of natural energy and at the points where these cross-streams of energy met.'

'Right... I see. So what does that have to do with the sexual energy?' Dr Morris looked genuinely confused.

'Well, nothing really. I was... erm... offering you a metaphor.'

'Ah okay. Well, go on.'

'So, I'm guessing that this energy is like channels of energy, such as ley lines. The only other theory I can come up with is that the energy is part of another dimension that we can tap into – a bit like wormholes.'

'You're not talking about worms in the garden are you, Howard?'

'No, you know, wormholes in the fabric of space and time. Parts of other dimensions that may or may not interact with our own space in time and possibly allow time travel. You know, like in physics.' Dr Morris nodded in resignation.

'I mean, I'm not saying that they are the same as either ley lines or wormholes. I'm merely offering possible explanations and comparisons with which I might explain better to you what it is I've been observing.'

'Right, okay,' Dr Morris said, unable to contain a wry smile.

'You see, my reasoning is that as we do not continually have these... er... unions, then it stands to reason that they are intermittent for a reason. Of course, we wouldn't be able to function properly if all we did was exercise this ability. Therefore, it seems to me that what we are in fact doing is tapping into channels or tunnels, you know, like tubes or pipes of energy, sexual energy, that we are all connected to and hence connect us to each other at a level other than the conventional or physical world that we all understand, or not, on an everyday basis.'

'But you can't see these, erm, these pipes, can you, Howard?'

'No, Doctor, I haven't actually seen them. However, that doesn't necessarily mean that they can't be seen. I mean, I'm very aware of them through my senses. I can feel them - or, more realistically, I can perceive them, but I haven't actually seen them yet. I think I am training myself to be more sensitive to such phenomenon and may actually be able to see them at some point in the future. The thing is that every day I become aware of things that I wasn't previously able to see or even perceive. The other worlds are opening up to me all the time. It's not that they don't exist. It's a matter of whether you can tap into them.'

Dr Morris slid round and put Howard's file on the desk. He began writing various notes and paragraphs. After several moments he turned to Howard with a more interested look.

'Please continue, Howard,' he said. Howard was totally immersed in what he was saying.

'So, anyway, these sexual energy channels allow us to feel or share a sort of sexual union when both parties tune into the same, er, frequency, so to speak.'

'So you're saying that when this tube or channel is shared, then sexual pleasure can be shared?'

'That's exactly what I'm saying, Doctor. I mean, don't get me wrong, it's not so clear-cut that it's just a case of a guy and a girl choose a channel and Bob's you're uncle. It's not that straightforward and there are… well, millions, billions. I'm not sure how many really, but they do get confused and they do compete for control of them.'

'So people are competing for the channels?'

'Yeah, they are. And it can be quite a nasty business sometimes.'

'You said there were layers, Howard. What did you mean?'

'Right, yeah. The thing is, it's not just a matter of tuning into one channel and that's it. No, you have to tune into channel after channel and undo a puzzle. In other words, as soon as you've found one channel you both have to tune into the next one to get to the next level, the next layer. You see, it starts off slowly and gently. You can't feel it so strongly, which means you're only in a lesser layer. You also have to remember that I have no idea what this is like for a woman as I'm not one. My guess is that it's not totally different. I mean, men and women are superficially different, but fundamentally we're the same species, just two sorts of variations. And obviously the sexual organs are different, but the clitoris and the penis are fairly similar, biologically speaking.'

'So you are both trying to tune into the same channels?'

'That's right, Doctor. You both have to keep up and tune into the same channels at the same time. I usually let the woman lead so I know how fast she wants to go, but I've seen some guys really try to force the pace, and it happens too. Hey, what can I say, each to their own. The thing is, we are all playing this game all the time. It's like a game. We do it when we're bored, when we're waiting for a bus. In fact, from what I can tell we have to play it all the time. I mean, those who opt out get depressed, they fall out of the game and get left behind in society.'

'But surely, Howard, people wouldn't have sex... er, this transcendental sex, all the time when we have to do things? We have to get on with our lives as well.'

'Yes, true exactly, and it's not only that. This is just part of the bigger game. That's why it's so hard because we have to contend with this energy shit all the time. You see people cracking up from it. Some days you're too tired to play the game so you get left behind. Sometimes I've said "no fuck it, I'm not playing today", but then you become vulnerable. We need the energy, I guess, for survival. It's part of what makes the world go round.'

'I see,' Dr Morris said, continuing to write as they spoke.

'The thing is that it gets done in layers. Like the girl will lay the feeling of her, erm...' Howard coughed and cleared his throat. 'You know, her vagina, on you... on your, erm, genitals, and that way you know she's interested. But to be honest a lot of it's unconscious. We just do it at the lesser level without knowing it. The channels tune in automatically and interact with us as we interact with each other. To be honest, Doctor, it's very difficult to explain. I mean, it all happens so normally and, you know, it's such a rudimentary part of what we do. It all just happens. Chopping and changing all the time. One minute you're sort of engaging lightly with some girl on the bus or in the shop, and then some other guy comes along and takes it away. Only to find a few minutes later you're back at it with each other again.'

'So you said this is going on all the time,' Dr Morris said as he stopped writing.

'Yeah, well, most of the time. We can't help it, you know. It's part of the way things work.' Howard was sincere, but slightly frustrated at his ineptitude in explaining what he meant. What he knew to be true.

'Is it happening now, Howard?' Howard stared momentarily at Dr Morris.

'I don't know... well, maybe. For you it might be. Not for me. Not from you anyway. I mean, I'm not gay. I mean, at least I don't think so. I don't know exactly what it's like for, you know... homosexuals. I mean, I think I've felt the beginning of it, but I'm not, you know... gay, so I don't experiment with it,' he said. Dr Morris smiled, almost to himself.

'So how far does this sexual energy reach? Through the walls of a single room? How far?'

'Well, personally I think that it can reach as far as the power of the two individuals will allow and just how well tuned in they are at any given moment,' Howard replied. 'I have definitely done it through walls and, erm… well, across houses and stuff, but it becomes confusing and you have to concentrate more. You have to understand that the further you try to do it the more cross-channels and conflicting interests you have to deal with, so it becomes more complicated and you can really get sucked out there into the ether.'

Dr Morris had really begun to take notice of what Howard was saying. He was no longer writing and was paying perfect attention to the things that were being said.

'So, could people do this across different countries or continents, even?'

'Yeah, I reckon so. I think it's difficult, but I've managed it before.' Howard looked slightly uncomfortable at the mention of this, but his discomfort subsided fairly quickly.

'So, who have you done this with, Howard?' Dr Morris said slowly and deliberately. Howard squirmed in his chair and rearranged himself until he found a position that suited him.

'Well, erm… you know, just girls that I've, er, met or been out with, you know.' Howard now looked visibly embarrassed.

'Okay, but how did you know it was them? How could you be so sure who it was, without seeing them?' Dr Morris said. Howard looked a bit puzzled as he thought over his answer:

'It's kinda weird. I don't really know how, but it's linked to the telepathic part of things.'

Dr Morris paused for a moment and then swiftly turned to the desk and began writing further notes and passages in Howard's file. He then turned back to face Howard.

'What do you mean by the telepathic side of things, Howard?' he said seriously and a little bemused. He looked concerned.

'Well, you know. As your communicating in the sexual way with the channels, or whatever they are, you can also communicate telepathically. I mean, I'm no good at that stuff. To be honest, all I get is confused signals and a lot of static.' Dr Morris leaned forward.

'Static?' he said.

'Well, not actual static or feedback. What I mean by that… sorry to confuse you, is mixed messages. None of it's clear to me. Sometimes I hear someone loud and clear. Other times it's just gobbledegook. But even when it's clear it's never really been that, well, you know, made that much sense. If I try to really focus and get the full transmission or thought, so to speak, then it just fizzles out or becomes repetitive.'

'So who has tried to communicate with you telepathically, Howard?'

'Well, that's a good question, Doctor. As I said, none of it's very clear to me, so I don't really know.'

'Where have you experienced this, Howard?'

'Er… lots of places, really, but often it's on the bus or on the tube, you know. The places where people don't talk to each other very much, but all sit looking at each other and shit, you know.'

'What sort of things do people say to you, Howard?'

'As I said, most of it is just waffle really. I try not to pay too much attention to it. I mean, it really fucks with your head. I don't bother, that shit could send you mad, really. I just try to ignore it.'

'And can you?'

'Often, yeah. It comes and goes, anyway. When I'm stressed out and it's, like, rush hour or something then it can really kick in and people just bombard my brain with their shit. Like I really wanna hear all the crap that they think! To be honest, Doctor, it's more like we are all thinking too loud when there's a lot of stress and we all encroach upon each other's mental space. You know, like everyone is jostling each other physically. Well, it's kind of like mental jostling on a group scale, like in a crowd.'

'Do these people tell you to do anything, Howard? Do they tell you to take any actions at all?' Dr Morris was very interested in the answer to this question and waited almost with baited breath. Howard quickly looked down at the floor. He kept his head hung and gave no answer.

'It's important, Howard. Can you tell me if these voices tell you to do anything? Do they tell you to harm anyone, or to harm yourself?' Howard continued to look down at the floor for several moments before slowly looking up at Dr Morris. He looked uneasy and ashen-faced.

'No,' he answered slowly and quietly.

'Are you sure, Howard? You don't seem sure.' Howard looked away, around the room. He began studying the potted yucca plant that was placed in the corner beneath the window.

'Yeah, I'm sure,' he said definitely, but avoiding any eye contact.

'Okay, Howard. I think we'll leave it there for now. I think we should increase your medication though, just to be on the safe side.' Howard hung his head again and nodded slowly. A peculiar smile spread across his face.

SESSION SIX

Howard stood pressing the buzzer to the hospital. There was no answer. He waited, motionless, wondering what to do. He buzzed again, but still no answer. He took out his mobile phone and selected a number from the menu. He called the number and waited. He waited for thirty seconds or so and could hear the reception phone ringing inside. Then he hung up. He went back to ringing the buzzer. He turned and looked around. All he could see was the grounds to the hospital, the winding path that led to where he stood and the grassy knolls that broke up the path. The grounds were extensive, but there was not a soul in sight.

His rings on the buzzer were polite, not aggressive or impatient. He began ringing at ten second intervals, still nothing. Then he began ringing for longer periods. He seemed conscious to not simply hold down the buzzer and wait. He gave up. He looked back around again to see if he could see anything. Only an ambulance drove past in the distance. There was a medium wind blowing, which gave Howard the slight impression of a western movie when a town is deserted and tumbleweeds blow past. In this case, an empty Tesco bag flew by inches from the ground, swirling and dancing to the wind's command. Howard was just about to leave when the door burst open.

'Sorry, there's no one at reception. I don't know why,' a small, older woman said holding the door open for him.

Howard examined her attire as he passed her by and entered the reception area. She wore faded light green track suit bottoms and a purple sweatshirt with a lace-up V-neck. Her sleeves were rolled up to the elbow and revealed flowery white shirtsleeves that flapped about as she moved. On her feet she had pink Kickers ankle boots and her right trouser leg was pinned tightly by a cycling clip. Howard eyeballed the yellow and orange bum bag she had around her waist. He found it hideous. In her left hand she had a purple and black marl cycling helmet. Her grey hair was short and feathered. From her ears hung long, dangling earrings comprised of a turquoise non-precious stone and a silver patterned square with a plain silver disc placed at the centre.

'I'm not sure where the receptionist is, to be honest,' the woman said earnestly.

'Thanks, er, thanks for letting me in,' Howard said. He glanced around the reception area. The water cooler let out an uncouth burp as an air bubble shot up to the top of the transparent tank.

'Okay,' the woman called out behind her as she hurried off and the door closed behind her. Howard peered around the corner and along the corridor. There was no one in sight. He walked back to the reception desk and looked down at the appointment book. He stood waiting, but no one came. He looked at his watch.

'The Mary fucking Celeste,' he muttered to himself. He waited for a few minutes at the reception desk before sitting down in the waiting area. He got tired of waiting. He had some water from the cooler. He sat back down. He heard a noise from outside and looked through the windows of the entrance doors to see who it was. It was Dr Morris and the fat fucking porter he had seen around the place before. The two stood chatting for a moment before the porter opened the door and entered with Dr Morris.

'Yes, I tried to get in earlier as well and she wasn't around then. Very strange,' Dr Morris said to the porter.

'She's one of the new uns, Doctor, and she's been told before. You should tell them to have a word. I can't keep comin' over 'ere and lettin' all and sundry in now, can I?' the porter said. He was a fifties throwback. His greatly receding grey hair was brill-creamed into a perfect quiff, albeit somewhere in the centre of his head and a mile away from where it once hung, suspended in greasy animation, above his brow. At the back he had the duck's arse finish that he had practised ever since he was fourteen, and which couldn't be undone with a hurricane such was its training. He fingered his lips as he conversed with Dr Morris, revealing a large gold sovereign ring and his matching chunky gold bracelet with name tag intact. His porter's look was composed of a black V-neck jumper, white shirt and grey flannel trousers, perfected completely by his black Reebok Classic trainers.

'Alright Doctor, I'll get back and if I see Mr Gibson then I'll have a word, alright? Cos as I said, it ain't the first time this as 'appened now, is it?'

'Okay Tom, see you later,' Dr Morris called out as he turned and walked towards Howard.

'Hi Howard, how are you? Have you been waiting long?' he said.

'Erm, well not, er, too long, you know,' Howard said as he stood up.

'Having a few problems with the new receptionist. She keeps disappearing. Oh well. Shall we wander down to the usual room?' Dr Morris led Howard down the corridor to the room they had settled on using. Dr Morris had with him the usual brown cardboard file.

'Right, let's get down to it, shall we?' Dr Morris said enthusiastically as they sat down. 'So, how are you doing today? Okay?' he continued. Howard sat on his hands and sighed.

'Yeah, I'm er... I'm okay, you know.'

'Do you feel tired on the new dosage? Ooh, that reminds me, we have to take you off of that medication, I'm afraid.' Howard looked confused.

'Why's that then?' he said.

'Well, it seems that people have been dropping dead from it, I'm sorry to say,' Dr Morris said merrily.

'Oh right... how... what?' Howard spoke softly and slowly.

'Yes, apparently it's going to be withdrawn from the market. But don't worry, it's more old people who have been having heart attacks from it. It shouldn't affect you really.'

'Really?' Howard said in amazement. 'Okay then...' he murmured.

'So, we'll get you onto a newer one called Risperidone and see how that agrees with you. Hopefully, there shouldn't be too much difference. Except this one should be a lot safer.' Dr Morris laughed as he spoke and smiled for a while longer after his laughter finished. Howard simply stared at Dr Morris almost in disbelief.

'Right then, we've been discussing your telepathic episodes and your belief that you can have sex with people through the use of sexual energy and channels. Am I correct, Howard?'

'Er, yeah, that's right,' Howard said. He was slightly taken aback by Dr Morris's clarity on his case.

'So do you think we should continue that discussion or not, Howard?'

'Erm, yeah, we could do. I suppose.'

'Well, what I'm saying is that we can continue to talk about that if you want, but we don't have to. You can talk about other things if you wish, Howard. I don't want you to feel pressured here, okay?'

'No, no we can, erm, we can talk about it more. I, er, I don't mind.' Howard slowly closed his eyes tightly for a moment before opening them and focusing in on Dr Morris. Dr Morris skim-read some of Howard's notes.

'So, you were talking about the everyday occurrence of these sexual channels, I believe you called them.'

Howard rubbed his forehead. 'Er, yeah, you know, they're part of the game.'

'What game is that, Howard?' Dr Morris said casually. Howard seemed impatient and

71

looked from side to side, as though he were uncomfortable and dissatisfied.

'You know, Doctor. The game.'

'I'm not sure what game you mean, Howard. You'll have to elaborate for me.'

'So we're back to that are we, Doctor?'

'Back to what, Howard?' Dr Morris said. Howard moaned in resignation.

'So you're telling me you don't know about the game, Doctor?'

'No, Howard, I'm afraid I don't know. You'll have to tell me. What's it called?'

'Oh, for God's sake!' Howard exclaimed. 'The game, the game of bloody life! I don't know what it's called, do I? If I did I wouldn't be sitting here now, would I? I'd have it all worked out, wouldn't I?' Howard stopped and glared at Dr Morris. Dr Morris blinked as if he would tolerate Howard's tone.

'Remember, Howard, this is your illness and these are your delusions. You'll have to be patient with me as I am not telepathic and...' Dr Morris paused for a moment. 'What I mean to say is, that you can't expect me to understand everything you're saying to me, unless you explain it for me. So that I can further understand what you mean. Okay, Howard?' Howard rolled his eyes.

'Yeah, yeah. I hear ya, Doctor. What I ask of you is that you open your mind a little and perhaps be a little honest with me.'

'Howard, you have to trust me. I am being honest with you. When I tell you that what you are experiencing are delusions, I'm not saying it to get at you or pick on you in any way. I'm trying to make you see how the things that you experience are not necessarily what other people are experiencing – at least, not in the same way as you, anyway.' Howard suddenly stared at Dr Morris, almost in disbelief as he spoke.

'What is it, Howard? Is everything okay?'

Howard smiled and nodded his head. 'That's it, isn't it Doctor?' he said.

'What is, Howard?'

'You really don't see it, do you, Doctor?'

'No, Howard, I really don't. Could you explain it to me, please?'

'You really are a naïve, aren't you?'

'A naïve what, Howard?'

'You're one of the naïves. You really, genuinely don't see it, do you?'

'What do you mean?'

'What I mean, if I'm not mistaken, is that you're not one of the evolved, are you?'

'Not evolved in what sense, Howard?'

'What I mean is, that there are those that are evolved and those that are not.' Dr Morris bit his lip for a moment.

'Are you passing a value judgement, Howard?' he said.

Howard laughed uncontrollably. 'Well, I might be, but that's not what I'm getting at. What I mean is, those that are evolved are aware of this stuff. They are able to sense what's going on, at a conscious level I mean. We're all aware of it to a certain extent, but those that realise that something's going on, those that are evolving the new ability... I mean, it's always been going on, but the new breed are becoming aware of it and are beginning to manipulate it consciously.' Howard then sat back comfortably in his chair.

'You see,' he went on, 'I wasn't sure. At first I couldn't understand why everybody seemed to know what they were doing and why I was like a baby, just starting to understand what was going on. I couldn't conceive what the hell I had only just woken up to. I was utterly baffled as to why I had not been aware of this for all these years, and now was suddenly seeing for the first time.'

'What were you seeing for the first time, Howard?'

'But it makes sense,' Howard said, ignoring Dr Morris. 'Who knows who is aware and who is not and to what extent? I mean, maybe those that have really mastered it are those that are the most successful in life, whether they realise it or not. I mean, maybe they do it consciously, maybe they don't. But they are the best at it regardless and that's why they're where they are. Maybe those that are totally conscious of it are the best at controlling people. Maybe politicians and great influential leaders of history have become so clever at manipulating it that they have risen to power and can control whole groups of people, like Hitler and… I don't know, Tony Blair.'

'So you're saying that those that master control over sexual energy can control people?' Dr Morris said slightly perplexed. Howard smiled sympathetically at Dr Morris's confusion.

'It's more than just sexual energy, Dr Morris. It's the whole game that goes with it, the control of energy and its functions generally.'

'Can you explain more about this energy, Howard?'

'What do you want to know?'

'Well, when did you first see it? Or how did you become aware of it?'

'Well, Doctor, I'm not sure when I first became aware of it. I guess, as I became aware of the whole sexual energy thing I gradually began to pick up on the rest of the picture. A lot of it happens on the bus or the tube.'

'Go on,' Dr Morris encouraged.

'I mean, I hate the tube especially. So many people squashed together. It stands to reason that it's gonna cause problems.'

'What sort of problems, Howard?'

'Well, the game. The energy exchange is gonna be difficult and strained and overly competitive. I mean, everybody's fighting for space anyway so it makes the proximity and the numbers involved all the more intense, doesn't it?'

'Yes, I suppose so,' Dr Morris agreed.

'So, I'll be sitting on the tube, you know, nervous about playing, you know. My heart's not really in it, Doctor, plus I don't know what the rules are. I mean, to be perfectly honest I'm just playing to survive and really only just survivin' as I play.'

'What is it that you are surviving, Howard?'

'Well, there's the balls of energy that get tossed around. That's the toughest to deal with, really, and all the slime too. Not to mention the hideous gasses.'

'So you see all of these things, Howard?'

'Not exactly, Doctor. I perceive them. I am aware of them. They don't entirely work at the visual level. They're not quite of the visual dimension. You experience them. You perceive them to be and you experience their effects.'

'Such as?'

'Such as when some fat fucker blows hideous coloured gasses in your face as a defence mechanism. Some people are really putrid in what they've become and how they defend themselves. There are all sorts of low-life and scum out there.'

'I thought you said it wasn't visual. How can the gasses be coloured if they're not visual, if you can't see them?'

'Well, Doctor, they're coloured in effect, in experience, not necessarily in colour, though sometimes you get a tinge of visibility about them generally. It's just like the energy balls. You can't quite see them, but they have an effect. You can basically experience the effect visually, not the actual phenomenon itself.'

'Oh, right,' Dr Morris said with interest.

'Anyway, I'd usually sit on the tube and tune into a girl I liked, but of course sometimes you can't have a peaceful, erm… connection. You have to compete for her with other guys and she might like them better. I mean, even if she fancies you consciously she might subconsciously like some other guy better, especially if she actually prefers what he's doing more. I see that a lot with girls. They choose you consciously and then get confused because, deep down, their primitive side wants, or rather reacts better, to what some other guy's doing, even if he's a bit of an ape or something. But what I wasn't... what I'm not sure about is how conscious people are of it. Are they totally in control, not at all, or is it a mixture, with varying degrees of understanding? You know, the way most things with people seem to be.'

'You mean like differing abilities? Like in running or maths?' Dr Morris enquired.

'Yeah, exactly,' Howard said, staring at Dr Morris with wonder, a smile creeping across his face. 'So, you're one of the evolutionary diverged species? There are those that see the things you claim not to and those that don't. This is how the species has broken off into two, or more different evolutionary groups of humans. The question, Doctor, is why? What environmental factors have caused this split? Maybe it's drugs? Those who are drug-affected and those that are not. Two differing perceptions, a shift for one group into a drug-affected experience and another that is not.'

'Well, Howard, I'm sure drugs are having an effect on humans, both individually and as a species, but I hardly think that constitutes the development of differing species. It takes more than that. It takes generations of genetic selection over quite a long period of time before a new species emerges,' Dr Morris asserted.

'Well, it's been going on for quite some time, Doctor. It's one of the reasons why a proportion of East Asians can't hold their drink,

Doctor, because their ancestors before them, over many generations, boiled their water instead of allowing it to ferment and become alcohol. We Europeans, on the other hand, loved the old fire water. Still do, really, and hence have a stronger tolerance as a result, by and large,' Howard said smugly.

'Yes, well. I still don't think people have been taking modern drugs long enough to constitute a split in the species,' Dr Morris said impatiently.

'Maybe, maybe not,' replied Howard. 'We have been using and abusing substances for a long time, most of which constitute the same base substances, you know, similar base chemicals once they reach the brain. Who knows what effect the latest editions to this old pastime is having upon our children? I mean, shit, you only have to see how big they're gettin' now compared to, well, just my generation.'

'Yes, but a lot of that is just diet, Howard.'

'Sure it is. Especially in the first five years of life. Did you know that in Brazil scientists are researching sections of the country where people's brains are virtually half the size of the rest of the population, and they are declaring them a different species, just from malnutrition? If that's what food intake can do to you, think what the direct consumption of mind-altering substances can do, direct to the brain on a daily basis, Doctor. Something's gotta give.'

'That's very interesting, Howard.' The room filled with a dusty silence as both men gathered their thoughts for a moment.

'So, you were telling me more about your experiences with sexual energy, Howard.' Dr Morris breathed deeply and without comfort.

'Yeah, er... well, I think it has to do with mirror neurons,' Howard said nodding.

'Mirror neurons?' Dr Morris said with a sigh, looking at Howard with a vague degree of sympathy.

'Yeah, you know about mirror neurons, right?'

'Well, I've heard about them. It's not exactly my area, but...' Howard cut Dr Morris off in mid-sentence:

'You know, that basically the neurons in our brain actually mirror the actions we see in others. We actually mentally carry out exactly the same actions, neurologically speaking, that we observe in others – we just don't command ourselves to carry out the actions physically. It's how we understand the actions of others and maybe how we predict the behaviour and thoughts of others.' Howard sat back in satisfaction.

'Okay, what does that have to do with sexual energy?' Dr Morris asked.

'Well, I'm only guessing here, but I think that's how we learnt how to read each other sexually in the first place. And then it led to an ability to basically have sex without touching, you know, just by utilising the sexual energy we have. From there, it's not a great leap to be able to sense it without actually seeing each other. When you look at each other you carry out movements that symbolise something else neurologically. The observer carries out the same movements neurologically and then reciprocates. It's like when someone knows what someone else is thinking. Or they have a good idea, especially sexually. They're forms of telepathy, reading each other. I think humans are so sophisticated at it now that we have got to the point that we can do it without even seeing each other, through brain waves. I mean, you know, when people sit with each other for long enough and converse, their brain waves begin to fall into unison with each other, or when women live together for a prolonged amount of time their periods begin to happen at the same time. It's because we are all much more connected than we think. It's synchronisation. Maybe it's something to do with some primal instinct, when our common ancestors were insects or frogs or something. It's somehow chemical. My guess is that we've always been able to do it.' Dr Morris had begun looking at Howard with almost open contempt. When Howard had finished speaking he cocked his head slightly to one side and regained his composure.

'I see, Howard. So, erm... when we make movements we are initiating sexual intimacy, are we?'

'Well, yeah. I think we are sexual beings and that all the movements we make have significance, both sexually and otherwise. When we choose to tap into the sexual aspect of it, the movements take on a greater sexual significance and can become full-blown sexual activity,' Howard said. Dr Morris wrote something in Howard's file.

'Howard, can I just ask you, when was the last time you had a sexual partner?' Howard looked stunned. He looked down and his leg began to bounce furiously.

'I, er… erm… well, it's been a while, er, Doctor,' he uttered. Dr Morris smiled almost triumphantly.

'Okay, Howard, well I think we have to leave it there for now. The time is up.'

SESSION SEVEN

'Right Howard, so last time we were, how can I put it? Discussing your sexual activities.' Dr Morris smiled and pulled an 'interested' face. Howard sat motionless, staring at the tacky patterned carpet.

'Would you like to discuss this further or would you care to move onto another topic or area?' Howard snorted in defiance and gave a mumbled, unintelligible reply.

'I'm sorry Howard, I didn't quite catch that,' Dr Morris said. Howard sat forward suddenly.

'I said we can talk about whatever!' he bellowed.

'I see,' Dr Morris replied. 'Well, okay, let's stay on the subject for a bit, shall we? You seem to know an awful lot about it, so please enlighten me some more.'

'I've told you,' Howard snarled.

'Yes, you were saying that people can, erm… what were you saying?' Dr Morris looked over some of the notes. 'That's it, yes, have sex without touching – or, I believe you said, without seeing each other… or something.'

'Yeah, that's right,' Howard snapped.

'Well, okay Howard, tell me more. What else can we do without touching or seeing each other?' Dr Morris said. Howard put his hands in the pockets of his loose-fit jeans and gave a face like a sulking child.

'I need to go to the toilet,' he announced.

'Right, well you know where it is, don't you? Please try not to be too long as we only have, well, less than forty-five minutes now, okay?' Dr Morris said, crossing his legs, his expression emotionless.

Howard got up and shuffled out of the door. He was gone for nearly five minutes. Dr Morris read his case file while he waited. When Howard re-entered the room, his mood seemed different. His look was amiable and attentive.

'All better now, Howard?' Dr Morris said patronisingly.

'Er, yeah, thanks Doctor,' Howard said as he sat down, resembling a schoolboy sent before the headmaster.

'So, where were we? Yes, sexual energy, Howard.'

'Mmm, yeah well… it's erm, you know, all part of the game.'

'Yes, right, you said there's some sort of game going on. On the tube, I think you said.'

'Well, on the tube, or the bus. Wherever there's people, really.'

'Does it happen when you're alone, Howard?'

'Well, yeah, sometimes. Like I said, it happens wherever there are people. I am people aren't I, Doctor?'

'Yes, of course you are, Howard,' Dr Morris said dryly. 'What does this game entail exactly?'

'Well, er, basically it's a ball of energy that gets thrown around,' Howard said.

'I see. And how big is this ball?' Dr Morris said. Howard looked at his hand.

'About half the size of a golf ball… but it has more energy around it that makes it seem slightly bigger. You know, stuff that trails off. It looks like a burning comet or meteorite, whichever one it is. It's a comet when it's in the air, isn't it. Or is that a meteor?'

'I have no idea, Howard.'

'Yeah, I think it's a meteorite when it's hit the ground. Something like that, anyway.'

'Go on,' Dr Morris said steadily.

'Yeah, so it looks like a sort of mini, erm, meteor… but it's, erm, it's more, er, translucent than a… erm, meteor. I told you, didn't I? I'm sure I did. You know that stuff, well it's sort of visible, but not really.'

'What do you mean, Howard?' Dr Morris said unenthusiastically.

'Well, it's visible, but to be honest I don't think that it is actually visible. What I think happens is that your third eye, you know the chakra between your eyes, enables you to see it. So it's seeing it in a sense, but not with your normal eyes, you know.'

'So, it's in your mind essentially, wouldn't you agree, Howard?'

'In a way, yes… but, you know, at the same point that the ancient Indians claim there's a chakra. Your most important chakra, I believe. Well, scientists have shown that that is the part… well, a main part anyway, of where hallucinogenic drugs affect you. It's a gland that causes you to trip out, you know, erm… hallucinate.'

'So you can see why you might be hallucinating then, Howard.'

'What do you mean, Doctor?'

'Well, you just said that that is where you see the things that you see from and not with your eyes.' Dr Morris spoke with a softening voice.

'Yeah, true, but er... I have learnt to see them more with my eyes. It takes time and effort to catch them full on. I mean, I still can't catch it all full on, it's always just passing and I'm never looking in exactly the right place when it comes. That's why I have such a hard time playing. I mean, I just don't know when the next ball's gonna come into play. I don't know where they come from. Are they produced somewhere, or are they always flying about somewhere and then they come your way? It's fuckin' confusin' man, I tell ya.' Howard looked annoyed and frustrated.

'So what, erm, what do you... what do these balls do then, Howard?'

'Well, normally when I see them I'll be sittin' on the tube and the long carriage will be stretched out, with all those people sittin' there and all the suits stood up reading their papers, you know, *Metro* or whatever. Anyway, all of a sudden I'll see one appear from nowhere...'

'A ball?' Dr Morris asked.

'Yeah, a ball. And it'll be hurtlin' down the carriage and I'll see it coming, and then some cunt'll catch it out of mid-air and hide it somewhere. You know, behind their back or in their pocket or whatever. And everybody who's watching or who saw it come will be tryin' like mad to work out where it is, or where it's gonna appear next, and then BAM!' Howard smacked the table extremely hard with the palm of his hand, causing Dr Morris to jump and nearly fall off his seat.

'Please don't do that, Howard,' he said breathing heavily. Howard smiled and sniggered slightly.

'Sorry Doctor. Yeah, so BAM! The game is on. All of a sudden, whoever's got the ball will serve it up proper. A lot of blokes like to sneak it down their trouser leg and slyly onto their foot, and then all of a sudden boot it really hard at someone. When it comes that fast all you can do is protect yourself. You know, like deflect it or something, and it bounces off them in another direction.'

'What happens if it hits you?' Dr Morris asked with genuine interest.

'Well, it just fuckin' whacks you, dunnit?'

'I mean, does it hurt or anything?'

'It doesn't hurt you, well... it's like a surge of energy hits you and gets absorbed into your brain. It sort of freezes you for a second. You know, paralyses you. That's when the world and his brother, or sister – trust me, they're just as fuckin' ruthless – that's when they all jump in, mate.' Howard looked deadly serious.

'What do you mean? They actually jump on you?' Dr Morris seemed concerned.

'Not physically, Doctor, no. They put the metaphoric boot in, don't they? You get a dick in the mouth, up your arse, slime in your face, you name it it'll all come your way, trust me. Like fuckin' hyenas, they are. Pack mentality.'

'What do you mean? You said a dick in your mouth and up your arse. What do you mean by that, Howard?' Dr Morris asked. Howard laughed out loud.

'Sorry Doctor, I forgot you don't know. The balls of energy are male or female.'

'They are?'

'Yeah, you see...' Howard laughed uncontrollably for a moment. 'They...' he laughed again. 'They are smells, Doctor.'

'I'm sorry, Howard, you're losing me.'

'Yeah...' Howard kept interrupting his speech with small chuckles. 'They're male and female smells. You know, sexual smells.'

'So, they are balls of sexual energy that smell either male or female,' Dr Morris clarified.

'Now you're gettin' it. You see, how it works is that these are balls of male or female sexual energy that come from either a di... a penis or a, erm, you know, a fanny, erm... I mean, a... erm, vagina. The thing is, Doctor, what I think is that these things are what animals are sniffing for all the time. It's how they identify each other and how they sniff out who they want to mate with and so on. Well, we as humans think we're above all that sort of thing, but we're not, you know. We are basically bald apes, Doctor, mad bald apes. And we do all the same things that animals do, except that we have now gotten to the point where all the common rough stuff that animals do, like sniff each other's arses and all that, we do sub-consciously from a distance. We are, in fact, very sophisticated at it, but we are not consciously aware of it. We just do it and take it all in. It's part of how we determine how and what social relationships we form. You know, pheromones are just a small part of it all.'

'That's fascinating, Howard.'

'It is, isn't it?' Howard said jubilantly.

'No, really Howard, it is,' Dr Morris said disingenuously. 'You seem to really analyse things. And come up with some amazing conclusions. Unfortunately, modern science doesn't back you up on that one.'

'Not yet they don't, but they discover new things all the time,' Howard said dejected.

'Well, that's as maybe, but for now we'll just have to assume that it's not true, okay Howard?'

'Yeah, well, modern science isn't all it's cracked up to be.'

'Have you been taking your medication, Howard?'

'Yes I have, alright?' Howard said aggressively.

'And have you found you're coping with the drowsiness. I have to say, you seem to have adjusted well. You don't seem too drowsy to me. Not like when you first came here.'

'Yeah, yeah, I'm coping with the drowsiness, okay. They just make you tired and I sleep a lot.'

'Yes, they will do that. It's important that you get enough sleep. It really helps. Have you been going for long spells without sleeping, the way you were before?'

'Are you kiddin' me, Doctor? On this dosage all I do is sleep, eat and shit. It's like being in prison.'

'Have you tried some light exercise? It's very good for you, some stretching or some yoga or something.'

'I was doing some light yoga and, to be honest, it really helped. But most days I just can't be bothered.'

'So what do you do with your days, usually?'

'I just watch TV a lot.'

'Do you read at all?'

'I used to, but not anymore. I can't concentrate.'

'That's understandable, Howard. But try to do a bit of light reading if you can, something fun and uninvolved.'

'Yeah, I'll try.'

'Anything else you'd like to talk about, Howard?'

'Well, I would like to say, just to make it more clear what I was saying...'

'Yes?' Dr Morris said calmly.

'We are a sex-obsessed species. So it stands to reason, you know, why beneath the surface we are so controlled by it. All the movements and little gestures we make have meanings. Not only meanings, but they have functions as well. They serve us in a practical way.'

'Such as?' Dr Morris said.

'Well, like when you just put your hand to your nose there, Doctor. You were actually smelling one of the energy balls.'

'Really, Howard?' Dr Morris said insincerely.

'Yes really. See, you just did it again. We do it all the time. We act like we had an itch or we just made a nervous movement, but we are really on the trail for the right kind of energy collection.'

'Look, Howard, people touch their faces, their noses and lips all the time for a variety of conscious and sub-conscious reasons. Sometimes, it's just because they are nervous, or lying. And sometimes it's just out of habit. There isn't really a great deal more to it than that. Honestly,' Dr Morris said with care and concern.

'Yes, Doctor, we do it when we're nervous, that's when we need to be winning the game more. In fact, often we feel nervous in social situations precisely because we are losing out to the other person in the game. They are collecting more balls of energy than us. You see, we have to process them very rapidly and it's difficult.'

'Howard, what do we do with these balls of sexual energy?'

'We collect them, Doctor. We put them on our own genitalia like prize trophies and the more we have, the more attractive to the opposite sex we are. We are sexual energy headhunters. It's all to boost our chances of copulation. We do it subconsciously, we can't help it. We are only sophisticated monkeys, after all.'

'Howard, it simply isn't true.'

'Look, Doctor. The more sexual energy you have, the more virile you feel. Or, if you're a woman, the more fertile you are. It's why, when you have a partner, the world wants to get into your pants. Because you have a continual back-up of sexual energy from your partner and it makes you more attractive to prospective partners than if you don't have that back-up supply. It's also how people work out whether they're attracted to each other or not. If a girl likes you, she'll give you her own balls of sexual energy. If you like her you'll give her yours. It's an exchange, a swap. It's like marking each other as territory.'

'Yes, but Howard...'

'Have you ever been jealous, Doctor?' Howard interrupted. 'Have you ever been jealous of your partner with some other guy, but you didn't know why? You know she wasn't doing anything in particular. Neither was he. But you just knew. You could feel it.'

'Yes, well of course, but that's just intuition, a gut reaction, Howard. Humans are perceptive creatures and we do pick up on subtle things, I admit. But that doesn't...' Howard interjected once more:

'It's because subconsciously you know exactly what's going on. They are tossing their little orbs around and you're left out in the cold, holding your balls so to speak. They are flirting like mad, exchanging sexual energy, but it all simmers beneath the surface. On the face of it they are being polite and courteous, but down at the nitty-gritty where it counts they have mated and are bringing up the kids. It's a natural, daily chemical, biological, electromagnetic occurrence that goes on all over the planet. It goes on in the supermarket, in the post office, in church. You name it, it's going on there.'

'Howard, do you not see that you are obsessing about small and insignificant gestures and behaviour and creating these huge and grand scenarios that have no basis in reality? Howard, you are a bright young man, but unfortunately your judgement has been severely clouded by the drugs that you have taken. And you are reading into things way more than they warrant.'

'No, Doctor. Why do you think men get on average six erections a night? We do it in our sleep, it's 'cos...' Dr Morris didn't let Howard finish:

'It's important that you begin to realign yourself with reality and societal norms in order that you progress. Otherwise you will not get better. You may well get worse. And I don't want that to happen. So, you're going to have to work with me, Howard. And I think that you're going to have to work very hard at it. It's not going to happen overnight. It's going to take time, Howard, but you have to try. Am I making myself clear to you?'

Howard eyeballed Dr Morris before looking down at his trainers, which he began rubbing together.

'Now, I'm going to up the amount of medication you're on by another 2mg and I want you to really think about what I'm saying to you. This is not a game, Howard. This is serious.'

'Can I go now?' Howard mumbled.

'Yes, we can end the session there for today,' Dr Morris said. Howard got up and sloped through the door.

SESSION EIGHT

Howard walked towards the reception doorway. As he approached, the doors flew open and a lanky man of a similar age strode towards him in an almost marching fashion. His arms swung loosely from side to side in an erratic manner. The man was very tall. It seemed to Howard that this man could be nearly seven feet tall. He was dressed in faded blue jeans that were slightly too short for him and had on a pair of navy blue running shoes. His dark brown, waist-length suede jacket flapped around behind him in the wind like Batman's cape. As he approached Howard, he raised his long gangly arm in the air, his palm facing Howard like an American Indian from a sixties western.

'Give me five, man,' the man sang in a Liverpudlian accent as though he were a Baptist preacher from the southern states of America. Without hesitation, Howard reached up and slapped the man's hand with his own. The man stopped dead in his tracks, a look of sheer amazement in his eyes.

'Th-th-thanks man,' he stuttered. The man swung around with an expression of sheer joy and gratitude as Howard passed him by. Howard said nothing, he just kept walking. He went through the usual routine with whichever receptionist was on duty at the time. They seemed to change from one week to the next. Then he waited for Dr Morris to appear, as he usually did, and they went to the same old room for the weekly interrogation.

'Okay, Howard, I'd like you to continue to relay your experiences to me, if that's okay? Then we can discuss how you're feeling about them and just where we can go from here. I think maybe some sort of plan of action as to how to tackle some of them might be appropriate. And please tell me you have been taking your medication.' Howard snorted defiantly at Dr Morris's suggestion.

'So, would you like to say anything, or are we going to sit here and stare at each other for fifty minutes?' Dr Morris said with a smile. Howard shrugged his shoulders and scrunched his mouth up.

'Howard, if you've just come here to sulk then you're wasting my time. You're using up valuable resources and, most importantly, you're wasting your time.'

'Time, there's a funny thing,' Howard mumbled. Dr Morris put both elbows slowly onto the desk and clasped his hands together.

'Look, Howard. I'm not here to piss about, alright.' Howard looked up at Dr Morris, whose expression was stern and tense. He looked away, uncomfortable at the amount of lasting eye contact Dr Morris was giving him.

'Up until now I feel that I've been very patient with you,' said Dr Morris. 'But my patience has bounds, and it's about time you put some effort into this process.'

'What fucking process?' Howard shrieked.

'This fucking process, Howard. The process of getting you to face your problems, to talk about them and to try and deal with them. To help yourself to get better, instead of indulging in your own little fantasy world.' Dr Morris's face had grown red and his eyes puffed out like a chameleon lizard. Howard began fidgeting uncontrollably in all directions, unable to compute the sudden change of attitude being employed by Dr Morris.

'What do you want from me? You know...' Howard blurted. Dr Morris leaned forward, his back expanding like a king cobra.

'I want for you to open your mind a little to the rest of the bloody world.'

Howard looked visibly frightened, almost childlike. There was silence for several moments before a look of resolve slowly began to spread across Howard's face. He began nodding slowly, his eyes fixed upon Dr Morris's.

'Alright, okay, if that's the way you want it. I'll play your little game, Dr Morris. I'll indulge you, your futile charade, you know, if it'll make ya feel better sort of thing, Doctor.' Dr Morris momentarily seemed as though he was about to explode. He took a deep breath.

'Howard, you are only patronising yourself. I am merely trying to put in place for you a situation where you can come and express yourself, and come to terms with some of the thoughts and ideas about things that you have.'

Howard gritted his teeth and spoke through them as they gnashed. 'Well, you're not doing a very good job of it, are you?' he said. Dr Morris opened his mouth to respond, but Howard continued. 'You know I'm here to be helped, not fucking talked down to and demoralised.'

'Howard, I'm not trying to demoralise you.' Dr Morris's tone softened. 'I'm trying to help you, I really am. But... you don't make it easy.' Dr Morris's voice and expression were both sincere and vulnerable. Howard responded to his candour:

'Look, doc, I know you're trying to help me. But you're not that open-minded yourself, are you?' Howard said with a grin.

'What do you mean?' Dr Morris said defensively.

'Well, I just mean that so far all you've done is disregard my point of view.' Dr Morris looked away and thought for a moment.

'Howard, I don't mean to disregard your point of view. I'm just trying to make you see mine.'

'Yes Doctor, I've noticed,' Howard said frankly. Both men sat staring at each other. Dr Morris looked tired, his face haggard and grey. Howard looked strangely radiant and self-assured.

'Okay then,' Dr Morris said, breaking the silence. 'Well, let's get back to work, shall we?' Dr Morris reread some of Howard's notes.

'So... tut-tut...' he said and turned the page. 'You were talking about this game you play.'

'We play,' Howard insisted. Dr Morris gave Howard a look.

'This game that *we* play. Would you care to continue with this, or would you like to talk about something else?' Dr Morris cocked his head to one side.

'No, no, I believe I'll continue with this subject, if you don't mind,' Howard said, adopting a manner of self-importance. 'The thing is, Doctor, it relates to much more than just a game, because what I realised is that there is no such thing as an individual, or even personal autonomy. We are all one entity. We are all part of the same globule. We are connected and interconnected in ways that beggars belief.'

'In what way are we interconnected?' Dr Morris said with a sigh.

'We all share personalities.'

'What do you mean, Howard?' Dr Morris was openly disinterested.

'We all swap bodies, all the time.'

'Really?'

'For example, while you are playing the game, people jump into your mind and make you do things.' Dr Morris nodded in agreement, but looked concerned.

'It's like to put you off. You know, as we're all telepathic and can read each other's minds to a greater or lesser degree. You know, it depends on ability. Well, just like we can, you know...' Howard looked confused as though he couldn't explain what he meant. Dr Morris raised what would have been his eyebrows, had he any, with a vacant look in his eyes.

'The thing is, Doctor, is that we can put ourselves in each other's minds. You remember I told you about the mirror neurons and how they enable us to, you know, er, have, erm... sex with each other... you know, without being together... Anyway, it works in the same way, the same way that the layers of sexual stuff are put down so they, too, can take control of each other. You mentally mirror the other person and then literally jump into their body or their mind for a moment and make them do things. The thing is that they're doing it as well. In fact, we're all doing it all of the time. To be honest, I think most of it is unconscious, that we just mess with each other without knowing about it half the time.'

'You said we share personalities. What does that mean, Howard?' Dr Morris wrote as he spoke.

'It's not that we don't have our own personality, 'cos we do, but it's just that we are also part of a collective, a collective conscious that connects us all together and is actually just as real and influential as our own individual minds. We're like the components of a machine, little cogs. We're like the neurons of a giant brain, all gelled together. I know we run around and have our own thoughts and all that, but we also serve a greater purpose or are enmeshed in this matrix of collectivity that inhibits us from acting entirely as individuals.'

'When did you first become aware of this, erm... idea?' Dr Morris had calmed himself down fully and was back in professional mode.

'Well, I think it sort of dawned on me bit by bit. As I played the game more and more, I was trying to work out how it worked. What the fucking rules are.'

'What are the rules, Howard?'

Howard laughed at Dr Morris's question. 'Well, that's a good question. I find that a hard one. I'm not sure there are any and, if there are, then they are way out of my league.'

'So when did you realise that we were all one, erm… entity, did you say?'

'Well, I think the first time it really dawned on me was when I went on a trip to France with my sister and her boyfriend. They didn't really want me to come, but they needed the money, you know, my contribution sort of thing. So I'm playing the game, doing my best to hang in there, but it was really getting on top of me – you know, in the heat on the beach and stuff. I was really having a hard time of it. And my sister's boyfriend was way better than me at it, so I was struggling and I started to really wish that I was someone else. You know, if I could just escape my own mind for a little bit. A little reprieve, you know. Suddenly I jumped into someone else's mind, just for a split second, and then I was back in my own mind again. I was me being shit on as usual.'

'So you felt it was better in someone else's mind, better than being in your own?' Dr Morris said with some interest.

'Well, sort of. It was more like buying time, taking a break from myself. Then I realised it when the person swapped back. I could do it again, straight away, and that meant I was suddenly somewhere else for another second. And then another and another. Pretty soon I was surfing minds, and it was confusing the shit out of people. They couldn't find me to lay their shit on me.'

'What do you mean, by that – lay their shit on you?'

'They couldn't play the game properly. They couldn't target me so easily. The thing is that it becomes tiring and after a few hours you start to slow down and then you start to return to your own mind. I mean, ultimately you can't escape your own mind. It's where you are. It's you. I once tried to jump into the mind of a passing low-flying seagull, and then from its mind into my sister's boyfriend's mind, but he just laughed and said "ooh, very dangerous", and shook his head.'

'So you used to talk about it with your sister's boyfriend?' Dr Morris said in surprise. Howard giggled.

'No, no, I mean he told me with his mind, you know, telepathically.'

'Okay, so what happened after that, Howard?'

'Well, as I said, I would get tired and eventually could only swap minds every now and then. A sort of token playing, but not really enthusiastically, you know. So I would carry on suffering till I had some sleep or whatever and then start back in on it.'

'Did your sister or her boyfriend have any idea about what was going on, with you I mean?'

'Well yeah, they were playing the game too, every one is.' Howard gave Dr Morris a slightly disdainful look. 'Anyway, it just carried on and I was getting more and more tired and I couldn't cope with it, to be honest Doctor. I just wanted out after a while.'

'Do you mean you wanted to die, Howard?' Howard looked away and then down at the floor.

'Yeah,' he said slowly. 'I just couldn't keep up with it all. It seemed to get faster and faster and new things seemed to be added on all the time. It was like, if you got to grips with one aspect of it, another part would conspire to fuck you over, you know.'

'Do you get on with your sister and her boyfriend? You said they didn't really want you there. What made you think that?'

'Well, it was just an impression, plus I kept getting telepathic messages from her boyfriend he was daring me to kill myself. All I could hear was his voice saying "Go on, why don't you do it, you've got nothing to lose. You're full of shit, you'll never do it." I used to open the back door of the car when we were driving on the motorway and threaten to jump out if he didn't believe me.'

'Didn't they say anything? Didn't your sister tell you to stop?'

'Yeah, she was the one who would tell me to stop it, but he would keep pushing me and pushing me. It was like a tug of war between them. He wanted me dead and she didn't, but I think she was too afraid of him to really make a stand.'

'Surely they must have realised that you were unwell? You know, that something was wrong,' Dr Morris said slightly disturbed.

'Well, we never actually spoke about it. It was all a mind game at that point and there was a terrible tension between us all. At night...'

'Sorry, wait. I'm confused. Didn't you say that you were opening the door and threatening to jump out? Surely they'd stop the car, Howard?'

'Well, they just kept their eyes up front and he kept driving. I used to jump into his mind and put my foot down on the pedal for a moment, or swerve the steering wheel slightly, just to mess with him, you know, to let him know that I wasn't fuckin' around. I don't play, man. One time he got so tired and I was messin' with him so much that he had to stop the car, you know pull over and take a rest. It was a very tense time, I tell you. That's how most accidents happen, you know, by people messin' with each other like that. Sometimes it's by accident. Sometimes it's more malicious, but people get killed.'

'Did you make any other attempts to take your life at that time, Howard? When was this, by the way?'

'This was about, erm… six, maybe eight months ago.'

'And did you attempt to take your life on other occasions at that time?'

'Erm, yeah, we were camping and at night the whole campsite would engage in either encouraging me to kill myself or telling me not to.'

'What do you mean, the whole campsite?'

'Well, I'd be in my tent at night and I could hear them…'

'Telepathically?' Dr Morris enquired.

'Yeah, telepathically. My sister's boyfriend would lead the way and there would be discussion amongst themselves and chattering like monkeys and vultures as to what was gonna happen.'

'And your sister would be telling you to stop.'

'Yeah and others, mainly women. They tended to be more sympathetic, while the guys tended to see it more as a bit of a joke and taunt you and tease you and dare you to do it.'

'And what did you try to do? To kill yourself, I mean?'

'I had a knife. A sort of pocket knife and I would press it to my wrist. Every time the "yes" words would get to the point where their collective will was winning and I would lose control of my body. The force of all those minds pushing me to do it was too strong and the knife would start to cut my wrist. But, as soon as that would happen, then the collective will of all the others would suddenly pull the knife away and there'd be jeers and boos from the yes camp. Then the process would start all over again. It'd go on all night until gradually people would fall asleep, and when enough had fallen asleep I could resist the mob and get some rest myself.'

'It sounds horrendous, Howard. You must have felt an enormous strain. Did you tell anyone what you were going through?' Howard looked nervous and uncomfortable.

'Yeah, well, I know that rule.'

'What rule is that, Howard?'

'That you don't talk about it.'

'Why not?'

'Well, I dunno, I guess 'cos if you do then something bad will happen. You can just tell that the whole fuckin' deal will come crashing down around you then.'

'That's a strange way to look at it, don't you think? To not talk about strange things that are happening to someone.' Howard thought about Dr Morris's point for a moment.

'It's a risky business, Doctor, knowing who you can trust. There's a lot at stake.'

'There's always a lot at stake when we're dealing with our emotions, but we have to show courage and try to confront these feelings. You can't just bury them and hope that they'll go away. It doesn't work like that, unfortunately.'

'I don't think you understand the full implications, Doctor.'

'Why don't you help me understand the full extent of the matter, Howard?'

'I'm not sure I want to talk about it. It's a sensitive matter. And, without being rude, I'm not sure it's meant for you, anyway.'

Dr Morris smiled reassuringly and reached out and momentarily put his hand on Howard's forearm.

'Well, give it time,' he said softly. 'When you're ready.' It was the first human contact Howard had had in over four months and it stayed with him for the rest of the week.

SESSION NINE

'We had parked outside an all-night restaurant used by motorists and truckers somewhere near Montpellier and it was all getting out of control.'

'What was?' Dr Morris said.

'The game, especially my sister's boyfriend. For some reason, he was at it like a mad man. Every girl we came across he was running rings round them. Literally playing with them like dolls. They would always look at me and smile, but before you knew it he was stinging them all over with dirty moves. They hated it at first, but after a while he was just too good for them. They would buckle and put his energy ball up their skirt or in their pocket. I could see them looking at me to do something, but I was just so slow and clueless. The looks on their faces was like "do something", but I just didn't know what to do. That's when I started to realise what was going on.'

'What was going on, Howard?' Dr Morris's voice and disposition were neutral and detached.

'I slowly started to realise that I was a channel.'

'You were a what, sorry?'

'A channel, you know – a medium, a tool through which he could maximise his success.'

'Through your mind, you mean?' Dr Morris said with glazed interest.

'Yes. I suddenly saw what was going on. That I could tune into it way better than him. But... being a channel I was open, susceptible. He was more ruthless than me. He would tune

105

into my mind and take over. He was using me to get to them.'

'The girls?'

'Yes, he was out of control. No check on his appetite at all. He was making them yelp and all sorts. They were jumping in disbelief at how easily he could penetrate them or turn them on. There were certainly no manners about him or anything gentlemanly. He was like a dog on heat. And I was stuck in the middle, sort of paralysed by the whole process. In fact, I can't... I couldn't shut down my ability to tune into the girls and set up the layers with them and connect the channels, the ley-line things.'

'Did you feel used, Howard, like a pawn?'

'No, I felt powerless... I felt as though I was not fully present. I felt all energy.'

'Go on.'

'It got so bad I could do it by sound. So when we were on the ferry and the tannoy girl came on...'

'You mean, the girl made an announcement over the public announcement...'

'Yes,' Howard interposed. 'She was announcing something and he would tune into me tuning into her. Then he'd start shagging the shit out of her to the point where she couldn't talk anymore and had to temporarily stop the announcement. It was awful, I felt so embarrassed for her. Imagine you're trying to do your job and you have to put up with that. The poor girl had to start stop the message over and over until she could play the game in a way that stopped it happening. I would do my best to not tune into her, but it was difficult not to.'

'So he would shag the shit out of her, as you said, with his mind as well?'

'No, he would tune into our minds and then physically, you know, with his, erm, penis…'

'In front of everyone he would, what, start thrusting away?' Dr Morris said somewhat bemused.

'Sort of, you know, he'd put it into the conversation and then do a little dance and make a joke of it, as if we didn't know what was going down, you know. Or if we were sitting down, he'd bounce his leg up and down, pretending to be all nervous or whatever. Anyway, so we were outside this restaurant in France and he reckoned that he needed to sleep 'cos we'd been driving all night. And I was stone cold awake. I couldn't sleep for love nor money. He was ruthlessly making this girl in a camper van scream all fuckin' night. He was rocking back and forward, pretending he was rocking himself to sleep no doubt. And no one could sleep because of this girl's orgasms, they were going on for hours. My poor sister must have been so embarrassed, but she just seemed so docile and too scared to rock the boat. The weird part was that I was starting to understand French…'

'You were picking it up, or you just started to understand it, all of a sudden sort of thing?'

'Exactly, I would tune into what the French truckers were thinking. But at this point the channelling thing was getting out of control.

Like I wasn't even there anymore, or I was but only as an observer, not really having much say in what was happening. Anyway, I could hear what they were thinking, but their thoughts would literally come out of my mouth, you know, as words…'

'You were actually talking? Is that what you're saying?' Dr Morris said.

'Right, and my sister's boyfriend kept telling me to shut the fuck up 'cos he reckoned he was trying to sleep. And my sister would plead with me to be quiet every so often too. But every time these fuckin' truckers would come by the car, or anybody really, I couldn't help it. I would just pop up, you know, sit bolt upright. I mean, I was trying to sleep too. Anyway, I would pop up and look straight at them as they passed by and would read their minds out loud to them. Needless to say, this would drive them fuckin' crazy. I mean, nobody wants their thoughts read out loud in the middle of the fuckin' night now, do they? They are thinking "Where can I get a hooker round here?" or "Fuck, I need to shit", you know, that kind of crap. And I'm staring right at them, telling them in French, which I don't speak, exactly what they're thinking at that moment. Man, it was a fucked-up night.'

'Did the truckers say anything to you?'

'Yeah, but I couldn't really understand them, it was in French and I don't speak the language very well. I could understand their thoughts no problem, though. Strange really. My sister's boyfriend was French and he said they were calling me an idiot. He said he agreed with them.' Dr Morris held back a smile.

'How long did this go on for, Howard?' he said. Howard looked uneasy.

'Well, we got back to my place and they took off pretty quickly. They hardly said goodbye. But to be honest I was glad to see the back of 'em, especially him. I just needed time to rest. But my sister phoned up to see if I was alright later that night. I knew it was them as soon as I picked up the phone. I could smell his Hugo Boss perfume that he always used to wear, wafting down the telephone, and I knew he just wanted to use me to channel a bit more, so I got off the phone as quickly as possible. You know, fuck him.'

'Was this at the same place that you live now, Howard?'

'Yeah, the same place. I just crashed out on a pile of my washing for about three days. Got up to piss and eat and straight back there, waited till my flatmate had gone to work before I'd get up and eat or go to the toilet. But the channelling was getting worse. I could hear everybody now, all my neighbours, every fucker passing by in the street. They were all chattin' the upmost shit to me, telling me their problems, shagging each other. All I could hear were women screaming with orgasms and my upstairs neighbour, well she just wouldn't leave me alone. She would quite seriously rape me for hours and I got beyond enjoying it. It would keep me awake for hours. Then rest, then back to it and I would be rudely awoken again. It started to get to the point where I felt I was no longer in control of myself, of my own mind. It was too much, all these fuckers intruding on my mental space and using me to channel.

Eventually I started to see my neighbour's shadow dancing on the wall, you know, like at the beginning of James Bond films and that's when I started to hear the voice, his voice.'

'Who's voice, Howard?' Dr Morris said with an air of resignation. Howard's face grew ashen. He licked his lips nervously and began rubbing his face with his hands.

'Who's voice did you hear, Howard?' Dr Morris said gently.

Howard gave Dr Morris a wary look, as if to say 'Tread carefully'.

'Howard, it's okay, honestly. You can trust me. Whose voice did you hear?'

Howard whispered something.

'I'm sorry, Howard, I didn't hear you. Can you say it again?'

'Satan,' Howard murmured.

'Satan!' Dr Morris exclaimed loudly. Howard's eyes grew like saucers, amazed at the reckless abandon of Dr Morris's response.

'And what did Satan say to you, Howard?' Dr Morris said, returning to his formal demeanour. Howard had shielded his eyes from Dr Morris with his hand and was looking down in despair.

'He wanted my soul,' Howard said slowly with an air of hopelessness.

'He wanted your soul, I see. And what was he offering you in return, Howard?'

'I'm not sure. Whatever I wanted, I guess. Peace of mind, anything.' Howard's eyes had grown watery, but no tears fell.

'But I didn't sell, Doctor,' he went on. 'Honestly, I didn't. He says I did. He says on a technicality, that I came close enough to count.

That I wanted to and that was enough, but I didn't say it, Doctor, I swear I didn't say it. I never said yes, not even in my mind. He offered me the dancing woman, he promised me no more problems. I saw his long forked tongue and his long claw wrapped around her dancing in the flames, but I never said yes. I never said yes.' Howard was reaching forward to Dr Morris, appealing for his approval. Dr Morris sat back in his chair and put his pen on the desk.

'That's good, Howard,' he said coldly, as though he were bored somehow. He stared blankly for a moment and then picked up the pen and wrote in silence for several minutes while Howard looked on, a quivering wreck, a broken man.

'Would you like to go and wash your face or anything, Howard?' Dr Morris said, breaking the tension that had been building.

'Er, yeah, yeah I would, if that's alright, Doctor?'

'Yes, of course it is, Howard. Take your time.' Howard left the room. Dr Morris sighed with relief and began checking the text messages on his mobile phone. Howard returned five minutes later.

'So, what happened after that, Howard? After Satan wanted your soul?' Dr Morris asked calmly. Howard took a huge gulp of air.

'I, er, I fell onto the pile of washing again. I couldn't find my personality. I couldn't get back to myself. Someone or something had it and I couldn't get back to me. I desperately needed to get back to me, to sort things out, to make things right. I, er, I lay with my feet up in

111

the air and my face in the corner of my room. Then I realised where my mind was. There was a spider in a web in the corner of my room, about a foot away from my face. I looked at the thing, and it looked back at me. I realised, at that point, that was the level I had fallen to. I was on a par with this fucking arachnid and I was losing the struggle.'

'So you were swapping personalities with a spider?'

'Yeah, somehow in the confusion my mind had been sucked down to such a primordial level that I was able to communicate telepathically with this spider. I moved myself forward towards the thing…'

'Are you afraid of spiders, Howard?' Dr Morris asked.

'Doctor, I'm fucking terrified of the things. I bloody hate them.' Dr Morris smiled at this.

'So, I'm down on my belly, nose to nose with this spider, and all of a sudden I'm there.'

'Where?'

'I'm inside the mind of a spider. Well, it's not really a mind, is it? It's just a feeling, an experience, it's knowing what it's like to be a spider. I mean, it doesn't talk to you or say anything. But it has feelings, Doctor. Not feelings like "Oh, I feel like chicken tonight", or "Why did she leave me, oh woe is me" sort of thing. No, but it has desires, primitive primeval desires. It has instincts and awareness, not self-aware like us, but it's aware of its surroundings. It's aware of its own body and its own capabilities. It knows what it has to do from moment to moment. It's not an unconfident bastard, you know what I mean. I mean, it means business. It's thinking food, like all the fuckin' time. Waiting, waiting in this shitty little web for some poor cunt of a fly to come by and get all tangled up. So for a split second my whole mind is consumed by the spider, I'm down there in the web and it's up here in my body. Looking back, I reckon it must have been as freaked out as me. Anyway, I was like woe, woe, FUCK THAT! And I'm back in my body again. Cool, thank fuck that's over. Then all of a sudden we swap back again. The spider wants a second glance. I'm thinking to myself, no way, so I get the fuck out of the room.'

'Where did you go?' Dr Morris said with fascination.

'I went into the front room and sat on the sofa. You know, trying to pull myself together. I mean, I've been living on a pile of dirty washing for three days.'

'And how were you feeling at that point?'

'Pretty fucking grim, I can tell you.'

'So what did you do?'

'I thought, "Fuck it, I'll sleep on the sofa". You know, no need to go back in there tonight.'

'And did you manage to get some rest?'

'I waited till my flatmate came in from work.'

'Did you tell her what had happened?'

'Fuck no, she was off her head on all sorts anyway. So I just played it cool and watched telly with her.'

'And the spider?'

'In its fucking web, I suppose.'

'But no more, erm, personality swapping?'

'Not a dicky bird.'

'Then what?'

'She went to bed. Called me a slob for sleeping on the sofa and I stayed awake all night, listening to all the orgasmic women.'

'So it wasn't such a bad night then?'

'Well, not great, but I just spoke with my flatmate telepathically and tried not to think about the spider at all.'

'Right,' Dr Morris nodded.

'The next day, after my flatmate went to work, I thought "Right, I'll have some cornflakes for breakfast". I'm sitting there eating them, when all of a sudden I see these huge fuck-off fangs.'

'Where?'

'Where were the fangs?'

'Yes.'

'They were where my fucking mouth should be, snapping open and shut trying to help me with my cornflakes.'

'Oh my god, that's awful,' Dr Morris sympathised.

'I was so scared I dropped my bowl of cornflakes all over the floor. Anyway, I was totally freaked out. For the whole day, every so often I would get these flashes of these fucking great mandibles where my jaw used to be.'

'It must have been terrifying. What on earth did you do?'

'I just stayed in the house, freaking the fuck out. My heart was beating like a drum, I swear I was brickin' it.' Dr Morris wrote some notes briefly.

'How often was it happening, Howard?' he said.

'Well, more and more as the day went on.'

'So you just stayed in the house, suffering with these awful symptoms. You didn't run out into the street or call somebody?'

'How could I? All I could do was breathe in between each time it happened. You know, when my personality, my mind, was back with me, which didn't seem to last very long.'

'It must have been truly terrifying, Howard.'

'Yeah it was, but it got worse, Doctor.'

'Well, I'm afraid we've run out of time, Howard. But we can discuss this further when you come back next week, okay?'

'Okay Doctor.'

'Well, I hope you have a good week and make sure you stay up to speed with your medication, okay? It's very important that you do, okay Howard?'

'Thanks doc,' Howard chirped.

'Okay, see you next week then. Bye for now.'

'Bye,' Howard said as he left the room.

Dr Morris shrank in his chair, his face withered and aged. He put his head in his hands and rested his elbows on the desk. He stayed in this position for nearly twenty minutes. He then gathered himself, closed Howard's file, and left the room.

SESSION TEN

'Yeah, it carried on for the whole day. Then I heard my flatmate coming through the front door and I didn't know what to do, so I ran into my room and shut the door. I stood pressed up against the door with the light off, not knowing what to do. I was sweating like a pig and I knew that that fucking creature was in the room with me. I heard my flatmate go into the kitchen and start cooking. I was truly terrified, I tell ya, Doctor. I turned around slowly and reached for the light switch, but as I did this I could feel something above my head. I looked up, but it was dark and I couldn't see anything, but I knew something was not far from my head. I switched on the light. The room smelt stale and there was shit everywhere.'

'You mean excrement?'

'No, I mean stuff, you know, clothes, books, DVDs, that sort of shit. But I could still feel something above my head and I kept looking up, but every time I looked up the feeling would disappear and there'd be nothing. I looked into the corner where the spider had been. It was gone. The web was still there, but the fucker had disappeared. I knew it was still in the room though. That feeling that something was above me wouldn't go away and I kept looking up all time, but my vision was blurred and seemed confusing, as though I was seeing double or something. Then suddenly the feeling got stronger and I looked up and saw these two great fucking antennae floating way above my head, and then they were gone. They kept flashing in and

116

out. One minute I could feel them sticking out of me, I'd look up and they'd be there, then they wouldn't. My heart would race each time I saw them, then calm down slightly when they'd disappear. I wanted to scream, but didn't want my flatmate to hear me. Every time the antennae would appear I would hear this strange sound, a sort of vacuous windy kinda sound like I was in outer space or something. It was fucking eerie, man. Then I started to get this clicking sound in my ear and I knew the spider was in there somewhere.'

'Why didn't you go and speak to your flatmate?' Dr Morris asked quizzically.

'It's the fucking drug culture, man. You just don't ask for help, you don't talk to people on that level. Anyway, what the fuck could she do about it?' Dr Morris gave a disapproving look, almost to himself.

'After about an hour, I said "Fuck it, I'm going into the front room". So I did. I walked right in there and sat down on the sofa opposite my flatmate, who was eating her dinner.'

'Did she notice your behaviour?'

'At that point I was just playing it cool, pretending like everything was okay.' Dr Morris shook his head in amazement.

'So you're telling me that you sat there holding a conversation with your flatmate while all that was going on?' he said.

'Yes Doctor. I didn't know what I was supposed to do, it was a new situation for me and a new part of the game,' Howard said earnestly.

'But how on earth did you manage to act normally?' Dr Morris asked.

'It was like Zen fucking thinking man, just keep breathing and try and empty your mind.'

'And did it stop?'

'Hell no, it just kept going on and I kept pretending like it wasn't.'

'That's extraordinary, Howard. It really is.'

'She offered me some dinner so I took it, but every time I would try and eat those damn fangs would appear and snap at my hand. I kept dropping the fork, so I just gave up. My flatmate said I had Parkinson's and went to bed.'

'Because you kept dropping the fork?'

'Yeah, anyway I stayed up all night again like that. I kept seeing the ceiling, you know, like flashes of the ceiling, but in sections. Then I realised I was seeing through a spider's eyes, all fucking eight of 'em on my forehead. I kept touching my forehead and wondered why it felt so weird and sensitive. It was at that point that I knew that I had to find the fucking thing. Find it and kill it. It was the only way I was gonna get out of this mess. I looked all night in my room, the hall, the bathroom – everywhere, but nothing.'

'You looked for it all night?'

'Yeah and into the next day, but it was nowhere to be seen.'

'Then what?'

'Well, I knew I had work at the weekend and had to find a way to deal with this. I found

118

a bottle of vodka in the freezer and I drank that.'

'Didn't you have problems with the fangs, though?'

'Well yeah, but after about half a bottle it seemed quite funny and I was laughing at the antennae. When they'd flash in it would crack me up, sort of.'

'So you still intended to go to work? I find that amazing. What were you doing?'

'Well, I was at uni, but it was the summer holidays and I was working as a security guard.'

'Did you go to work?'

'Yeah, I got my flatmate to bring me a shit load of beer from the supermarket and I made sure I was always pissed.'

'Did you find that it helped?'

'Yeah, it numbed me out and I didn't have to play the game quite so much. I guess I just missed lots of what was going on, you know, didn't care too much, like drunk people don't.'

'What was work like? It must have been very difficult. Surely you couldn't go to work drunk?'

'Course you can. I was working nights and loads of the blokes were on the bottle, or draw, or speed – anything really.'

'Really?' Dr Morris said with a hint of sadness.

'It was freaky, though. When I was on the tube people would stand next to me and tune into me and I would laugh as they would react to what was in my head. They would literally jump in fear and move the fuck away from me.'

'Mmm, I can imagine. And how did you cope with work?'

'Well, it was okay later at night, but it was difficult earlier on as I had to deal with the office workers going home or working late. One woman came up to me and she was really cool and would usually stop and have a chat and a little flirt, you know, gentle game play. Well, she came up to me at the reception and said "hi", but as soon as the antennae appeared above her head I saw the look on her face, and she totally freaked.'

'What did she do, Howard?'

'She started talking really fast and all sorts of gobbledegook. Then she made some strange excuse and left pronto. Every time the antennae appeared she would let out a shriek and then laugh as it disappeared and came back to me. Let me tell you, after a couple of nights of that everyone was leaving me the fuck alone, which was cool 'cos I really needed the space at that point.'

'So you worked the whole summer like that?'

'No, eventually I had to call in sick as it started to get worse.' Dr Morris had not written a single note throughout the whole session and suddenly realised this fact. He began scribbling notes down as Howard spoke.

'After a few weeks of it I was starting to flag and I was getting more and more tired. I couldn't bear to be around my flatmate and all we did was glare at each other while passing in the hall. She'd bring mates over and they'd sit there popping Es and liquid MDMA, or doing lines of white, so I'd just stay in my room drinking.'

'So you had no contact with anyone at this point?'

'No, it was just me and the spider battling it out for control of my mind. The thing is that a spider's willpower isn't like a human's and there's no reasoning with it. It doesn't play, it competes to win. I knew it was still in the house because of that clicking sound. Every time I heard that I knew it was nearby. I was battling against something that felt like a machine. Every time I pulled hard, it just methodically dragged me further the other way. I mean, spiders are patient fuckers. Think about it. Imagine if you had to sit in a web and wait for some fly to come your way. They can go over a year without eating a meal. A year of waiting. When you're in that time and space, you know a much quicker one than ours. They are wily and hardy fuckers, let me tell you. You know they've been here way longer than us, like millions of fucking years. They've seen species come and go. Ice ages, the lot, and they're still here going strong. I mean, some of 'em don't bother to build webs; they just run after their prey like a fucking lion would, just run it down and kill it. But this one was a waiter and it was having none of it. After a while, I started to see the body of the spider, you know on my chest and belly, all ribbed and hairy. It was horrific, I can tell you that. Legs sticking out everywhere. Then came the final straw.'

'What was that, Howard?'

'I realised it had caught a fly or something, because it started to feed. That was the worst feeling I've ever had in my life. I could feel it sucking the life blood out of this poor bastard. I could feel it sucking the insides of a fly into its belly. All the juices and innards being pulled out of this creature's crispy frame and down into its now swollen guts. I could see the huge ribbed brown abdomen bursting with fly gizzards and blood, or whatever the fuck they have in them. I have never felt so ill in all my life, Doctor. Every few seconds I would experience this in between looking up at the ceiling with my eight eyes and these fucking antennae floating above my head and the hiss that would come out of my fangs. I was starting to feel what the insides of the spider were like, full of juice squelching around inside me, inside us. It was like my guts were gonna burst. And the taste, the taste was running down my throat. It was like nothing I've ever experienced before. The smell was putrid and the steaming heat of the juices was simply hellish, Doctor.' Dr Morris looked utterly disgusted and yet was listening with a macabre fascination, as though he was almost relishing the ghoulish details.

'Then I was nearly finished, Doctor. What happened next nearly finished me off.'

'What was that, Howard?' said Dr Morris, nodding enthusiastically.

'The fly, or whatever it was, was obviously still alive, just. In a last desperate attempt to save itself, or maybe just to not experience the suffering that it was going through, it pulled a fast one and switched personalities, minds, experience – whatever the fuck insects and alike have, and suddenly I have swapped with the fly. Suddenly, I am this half-eaten fucking fly, with most of its guts being sucked out. I can't fucking move, I am paralysed with venom and wrapped in fucking web and I can't move a fucking muscle. The life is draining out of me and all I can see is this huge pair of fangs stuck right into my guts and sucking the very life blood out of me. But the spider is divided into like a thousand tiny images, all of the same thing, and it's happening in slow motion. I knew I was about to die.'

'My god, Howard, that is absolutely bloody awful.' Dr Morris had dropped any pretence of a professional manner and was listening with great interest. 'What the hell happened next?'

'To be honest with you, I'm really not sure. It was like a kaleidoscope of images and sensations, smells and feelings. I think I passed out. When I woke up or came to my senses, things seemed different, more normal than before.' Dr Morris again realised that he hadn't been taking notes and began scribbling bullet points in a slightly frantic fashion.

'So, so... erm, you were... erm, you were having less hallucinations than before. Had the... er, spider, gone?' he said slightly confused. Howard gave a little smile to himself.

'Well, Doctor, the spider had gone, but I would get these much less frightening images of fur and a nice fresh feeling as though I was in a garden or something. But the horror of the spider and fly was defiantly over.'

'So what do you think happened?'

'I really don't know, Doctor. I was just glad it was over, that's all.'

'Did the newer flashes of hallucinations continue?'

'Yes, Doctor, they did and after a while I realised that I was sharing my mind with a cat and it was a hell of a lot more pleasant, I can tell you. Even the eating a mouse bit was marginally more pleasant.' Dr Morris laughed.

'So I sat cleaning myself and rubbing my paws across my face from time to time.'

'Really?' Dr Morris said in disbelief.

'Yeah, my flatmate caught me a couple of times and said I should audition for Cats,' Howard said with a cheeky grin on his face. Dr Morris frowned and cleared his throat.

'Yes, well, I think we can leave it there for this week, Howard, okay? Unless there's anything you'd like to ask me?'

'Not really, Doctor. Nothing that can't wait, anyway.'

'Okay, I'll see you in a week then, Howard.' Howard got up and walked to the door.

'Howard,' Dr Morris called out as he was leaving. 'Have you ever read Kafka?'

'No, but I saw a couple of plays, you know, based on his stuff.'

Dr Morris paused for a moment. 'Which ones?' he asked.

'*Metamorphosis* and, er, another one... I forget its name.'

'Oh, right. Did you like them?'

'Yeah, they were alright,' Howard said with a smile. Dr Morris smiled back and nodded.

'See you,' he said.

SESSION ELEVEN

Dr Morris closed the door to his red Ford Sierra and walked slowly towards the clinic. The jacket he wore was a black, white, grey wool and cotton mix check that fitted him neatly and went well with his Egyptian cotton white shirt and greyish slacks. His shoes were black patent leather and looked new. They creaked slightly as he walked. A few new creases were beginning to appear around the sides where the toes and foot met. His old satchel-style briefcase was a tan colour and its contents slid around inside as he moved. He pushed the buzzer and looked around the grounds as he waited. He was buzzed in after a few moments and went through into the reception area.

'Hello, how can I help you?' the young girl at reception said breezily.

'I'm Dr Morris,' Dr Morris said with a croaky voice. The girl looked at Dr Morris for a moment, her brain ticking loudly.

'Oh, I see, ooh. Are you supposed to sign in or anything, Doctor...'

'Morris. No, I just thought I'd let you know, that's all. And you are?' Dr Morris's voice was strained and hoarse. A look of discomfort spread across his face as he spoke.

'Oh, erm, yes, I'm Marianne,' Marianne giggled nervously.

'Well, very nice to meet you, Marianne. I'll be in the usual room for my next appointment, which is I believe...?' Marianne stared blankly at Dr Morris for a second before leaping into action and looking for the next appointment in the appointments book.

'Let me see, it's, erm…'

'Howard Jones,' Dr Morris said with a brief smile.

'Oh yes, so it is.' Marianne giggled again, desperately trying to prevent the rush of blood that was filling her cheeks.

'If you could send him straight in that would be marvellous, Marianne.'

'Of course, Dr erm… Morris. That will be no problem at all,' Marianne said with all of her nineteen-year-old professional might.

Dr Morris sat sifting through Howard's file, reading various sections, amending others. He took his jacket off. The weather had turned very humid again, even though it wasn't normally the time of year for it. He rummaged through his briefcase and produced a packet of Strepsils. He popped one from the packaging and began sucking on it profusely. There was a knock at the door.

'Come in,' he rasped. The door was pushed ajar and Howard peeked through into the room.

'Come in, Howard, take a seat.'

'Thanks Doctor,' Howard said pulling up a seat opposite Dr Morris.

'You'll have to bear with me, I'm afraid. I have a very sore throat and it's actually quite painful for me to talk at the moment,' Dr Morris said in discomfort.

'That's, erm, okay Doctor, no problem,' Howard said as though he was not fully sure of the implications.

'Anyway, so how have you been?' Dr Morris said trying to clear his throat, which was followed by the beginning of a dry cough.

'Er, yeah, okay, I guess,' Howard replied, a look of concern on his face.

'Are you still taking the medication?'

'Yes, Doctor, I am still taking the medication.' Dr Morris gave half a smile before returning to his semi-grimace.

'Howard, do you dream a lot? Do you have strong dreams or nightmares, anything of that description?'

'Sometimes, yeah.' Howard rubbed his palms together. A series of rolls of dirt appeared as if by magic and fell to the floor, one by one.

'Do you have any reoccurring dreams at all, anything that you keep coming back to?' Dr Morris asked. Howard considered the matter momentarily before answering.

'Yes, Doctor, I have one, erm, nightmare that, er, reoccurs quite often,' he said.

'Would you tell me about it, Howard?'

'Okay, well, it's erm…' Howard breathed in deeply and then exhaled until his lungs felt empty.

'I'm walking,' he said.

'Where?'

'In the street.'

'Which street, do you know it?' Dr Morris asked. Howard glanced at Dr Morris as if to say 'Don't interrupt'. Dr Morris began gently chewing his lip.

'I'm walking in the street. I don't know the street. It's not relevant. What I mean to say is, that it's not the focus at that point.'

'Go on,' Dr Morris encouraged.

'Oh yeah, the dream is in black and white, almost like an old film, you know. Kinda grainy, but not like really old, you know.'

'Yes,' Dr Morris croaked.

'And the thing is, that I'm a kid.'

'What sort of age are you?'

'Maybe, erm, eleven, twelve, something like that. Anyway, I'm walking along this street and then I turn into...' Dr Morris interrupted.

'Sorry, is the child you as a child? I mean, does it look like you?' Howard thought for a moment.

'No, well, I mean it's me. It feels like me, but it doesn't look like me,' he answered.

'Who does it look like, Howard?'

'I don't know, Doctor. I've never seen him before.'

'What does he... what do you look like in the dream, Howard?' Howard paused for thought again.

'He has a shaved head, like a crew cut. And he's a nice-looking child, but he looks quite gaunt and pale. He looks undernourished. Not starving, but poorly fed, you know. The thing is he's... well, the whole feel of the dream is wartime. You know, Second World War time. My... his clothes are wartime clothes. Long grey schoolboy shorts and a horrible, scratchy, brownish jumper.'

'So what happens in the dream, Howard?' Dr Morris said in a half whisper.

'So I turn from the street into a huge, I mean massive, estate.'

'You mean like a housing estate?'

'Yeah, you know, tower blocks galore. The thing is, the feel of the dream changes slightly at that point.'

'What do you mean, Howard?'

'Well, it's still black and white, but it feels more sort of sixties than wartime now.'

'Have you changed at all, Howard?'

'No, I'm still the same, Doctor. Same clothes, same hair. But the tower blocks are huge. I mean, they are like sky scrapers, all grey and horrible looking. The weird thing is that they all seem to be coming from the same spot. Like I'm in the middle of them, but the space between them is not very big and they sort of, erm, splayed out, if you know what I mean? They seem to become small and, erm, you know, narrow at their root, but huge and menacing the higher they go.'

'Mmm, go on,' Dr Morris said with interest.

'So I, er… I walk through them and they seem to spread out a bit, but the estate is massive and just goes on forever.'

'Is there anybody else there with you, Howard?'

'Not yet.'

'So somebody comes along?' Dr Morris said. Howard gave Dr Morris a 'wait' look.

'So you're walking along.' Dr Morris gave another slight dry cough.

'I'm walking and suddenly I look down and the whole of the floor, the ground, is a mountain of dirty heroin needles. As far as the eye can see, it's just enormous grey tower blocks and piles, I mean mountains, of dirty heroin needles.'

'How are the heroin needles, Howard?'

'What do you mean?'

'I mean, what position are they? How are they placed?'

'Oh right, they're in all different directions. They are random. They're all over the gaff, jagged, pointy, you know. Like they've been poured out of a giant dumpster.'

'And how do you know they're heroin needles?'

'I just know, Doctor. I just know that they're all dirty, diseased, used heroin needles.'

'And what happens then, Howard?'

'So I look down and I'm barefoot. I've got no shoes, or I lost my shoes, I'm not sure. And all these needles are sticking into my feet as I walk.'

'How are you walking? I mean...'

'Very carefully, slowly, and carefully. I'm trying not to step on the needles, you know, the sharp bit. But they keep sticking into my feet as I walk.'

'Is it painful, Howard? Do the needles hurt you?'

'Sort of, but it's more just the sheer horror of the sight of them. The pain isn't that bad. Don't get me wrong, it hurts, but it's more about the disease and... I don't know, it's not that painful anyway. The weird thing is that the needles aren't going right into my feet, just a little bit in, you know, like they're catching my skin and getting pulled along before falling out, or they just stay where they are.'

'I see,' Dr Morris said.

'The worst bit is that they're pulling the skin as I walk. So when I pull away they pull my skin up before they come out. That's what I meant. It's not the pain, it's the way they pull my skin out like that, it's disgusting. I can't stand it.'

'So the feeling is of disgust?'

'Yes, disgust and terrible discomfort. I'm so uncomfortable with the situation. Like I don't know where to tread next, but I know I have to keep walking.'

'So what happens then, Howard?'

'Well, this goes on for some time, but I manage to make it to a road that is very narrow and winds round, away from the tower blocks.'

'Do you go down the road, Howard?'

'Yes, I make my way towards the road and finally get away from the needles and the tower blocks.'

'Where does the road lead to, Howard?' Dr Morris asked with a slight cough.

'It takes me down a dark, winding road that leads to a tow path.'

'A tow path to a canal?'

'Yes. I follow round until I'm on the towpath. There's a canal that is filthy and stagnant and full of junk. You know, old bikes and plastic bottles, that sort of thing, lots of polystyrene floating around.'

'Okay,' Dr Morris said in agreement.

'So I walk along the tow path.'

'Is it day, night?'

'It's dusk. I walk towards a bridge and I start to go under it. It's very dark and smelly and the roof of the bridge is very low, so I have to bend down as I walk.'

'Then what?'

'Well, I have to stop halfway.'

'Why, Howard?'

'Because somebody's throwing stones at me.'

'Who is, Howard? Who's throwing stones at you?'

'Two boys are.'

'Where are the boys?'

'They're on the opposite side of the canal from me.'

'Is that far away, Howard? Or near?'

'It's quite close, not really close, but close enough.'

'Are the stones hitting you, Howard?'

'Not really, I mean occasionally, but I'm really scared and I know sooner or later one of them's gonna hit me flush. Most of them are bouncing off the wall behind me and hitting me that way.'

'Do they hurt you when they hit you, Howard?'

'Yes, they sting, and they shatter as they hit the wall. Bits of them are hitting me. That's what stings, the shards.'

'What do the boys look like, Howard?'

'They look like me.'

'Do you mean they have the same face?'

'No, I mean they are dressed like me, they have the same clothes on.'

'How many of the boys are there?'

'There's two of 'em.'

'What are their expressions like? Are they angry or aggressive, or what?'

133

'They're having a laugh, but they're nasty with it. They're aggressive too.'

'What do you do, Howard?'

'I'm shielding my face with my arms and trying to dodge them as they come.'

'Then what happens, Howard?'

'It becomes almost in slow motion, with the shards of stone flying everywhere and me trying to dodge them and them laughing and shouting at me.'

'Are there a lot of stones?'

'Yes.'

'Where do they get them from?'

'I'm not sure. All I can see is them and flying stones.'

'Then what happens? What do you do?'

'I wake up.'

'How do you wake up, Howard?' Howard didn't answer. 'How do you wake up, Howard? Are you frightened? Do you wake up suddenly?'

'No, I wake up normally, but a bit annoyed, a bit disturbed by it. But nothing more.'

'How many times have you had this dream, Howard?' Dr Morris began coughing dramatically. He patted his chest when he'd finished. 'Ooh sorry about that,' he said, in a slightly camp sort of way.

'About nine times, Doctor, something like that. I don't count, you know.'

'And when was the last time you had this dream, Howard?'

'I'm not sure. About… about five months ago, maybe longer.

'And how do you feel about this dream, Howard?' Howard stared blankly at Dr Morris, almost as if he hadn't understood the question.

'I'm, erm, not sure really. I don't have any strong feelings about it really,' he eventually said.

'Were you bullied at school at all, Howard?'

'Well, a bit, but... erm, not too bad really, you know. I was bullied a bit and I did a bit of bullying, you know.'

'And do you live on a council estate, Howard?'

'Not now, no. I live in a flat, you know, a house flat. But I was brought up on a council estate, but not like that, you know, high rises and all that.' Dr Morris wrote some notes in Howard's file. He finished and chewed the end of his pen for a moment.

'So you say you have no strong feelings at all towards this dream, this reoccurring dream?'

'No.'

'Don't you find that a bit strange, Howard?'

'Not really, maybe that's why it's reoccurring.'

'What do you mean?'

'Well, maybe it's reoccurring because I have no strong feelings about it, you know, towards it.'

'I'm sorry Howard, you've lost me.'

'Well, I'm just saying, maybe it'll keep happening until I do have strong feelings about it. You know, till the feelings that it's trying to make me have... appear, you know, feel, sort of thing.' Dr Morris gave Howard a look of agreement, but his mind seemed elsewhere.

'What do you think, Doctor?' Howard asked.

'Well, I don't want to influence you on this matter by giving you my opinion, Howard.'

'So why did you ask me about it?'

'Well, I just thought you might gain some benefit from talking about it. Maybe it'll help you locate that feeling you're talking about.' Howard could not read Dr Morris's meaning in this. It was simply not clear. He looked away from Dr Morris and around the room. Eventually, he refocused his attention on Dr Morris, who looked remarkably under the weather.

'Well, I think we'll leave it there for now, Howard. I'm not feeling very well and I think we've covered everything for today, okay?'

'Okay,' Howard replied.

'See you next week then. Okay Howard?' Howard looked somewhat dejected.

'Yeah,' he said gloomily.

SESSION TWELVE

'I thought we'd continue last week's theme, if that's alright with you, Howard?' Dr Morris said with a slightly gruff voice. His face was pale and weathered, as though he'd had little sleep. His forehead, coated with sweat, shone under the dreary neon light. His favourite pink shirt was wrinkled and unkempt. Instead of the usual shiny cufflinks to accompany it, the sleeves were rolled up to his elbows in a willy-nilly fashion, and his jeans were soft and saggy at the knees, as though they had been sitting in the washing basket for a week or two.

'I thought we'd discuss your dreams a bit further and see where that gets us. How does that seem to you, Howard?'

'That's fine, Doctor,' Howard said with vague disinterest.

'So last week you told me about a reoccurring dream you have.' Dr Morris flitted back and forth a page of Howard's notes. 'It was quite a sinister or disturbing sort of dream wasn't it, Howard?'

'Yeah, I suppose.'

'Have you had other similar sorts of dreams? You know, nightmares or dreams that upset you?'

'That dream didn't upset me, Doctor.'

'No,' Dr Morris said without fully taking on board what Howard said.

'It's just a dream, innit?' Howard drawled.

'Yes, of course it is...' Dr Morris lost focus of where he was going with his line of questioning.

'So... have you had dreams that *did* upset you, Howard?' Dr Morris tried to shake off the drowsiness of the flu medication he'd taken an hour or so ago.

'Yeah,' Howard responded instantly.

'Would you like to share them, Howard?' Howard's expression said that he did not.

'If you think it'll help, Doctor,' he said.

'Well, it might, it might not. But let's just explore it anyway and see where we find ourselves, eh?' Dr Morris said with a sniff.

'You're the boss, Doctor.'

'Mmm,' Dr Morris said, clearing his throat. 'So what other things have you dreamt about, Howard?'

'Well, er, there was this other dream I had that, er, well it fucking scared me to death, frankly.'

'And what happened in it? What was it about that particular dream that scared you to death, Howard?'

'I was asleep in my bed and I woke up suddenly to find these two huge bastards standing at the end of my bed.'

'Who was standing at the end of your bed, Howard?'

'I'm not sure, really. I think they were from the government or the CIA, but I couldn't be sure.' Dr Morris scribbled something in Howard's notes. Howard looked nervous as he did so.

'So what did these two men do, Howard?'

'Nothing, they just stood there looking at me. They were actually standing on the end of my bed, not on the mattress, but on the, erm, bed frame bit.'

'What did these two men want, Howard? Do you know?'

'Oh, they wanted to kill me,' Howard said without a shadow of a doubt. Dr Morris raised his hairless brow.

'And how do you know this, Howard?' he said.

'It was just apparent, Doctor. It was a threat, a warning.'

'A warning about what, Howard?' Dr Morris said. Howard sat motionless, his expression blank. He said nothing.

'Why would they want to kill you, Howard?' Dr Morris waited patiently. Howard didn't answer.

'So what did you do, Howard?'

'I woke up and screamed out loud for ages. That woke my mate up, who was sleeping on the floor, and he started screaming too. I then looked at him and started screaming again.'

'What did he do then?'

'He started shouting "What? What?" over and over, he was more scared than me. It cracked me up afterwards, I tell ya.' Howard laughed, reliving the moment.

'What happened then?'

'We went back to sleep.'

'Did the dream continue?'

'No.'

'I see.' Dr Morris thought for a few seconds. 'What were the men like, Howard?'

'It was one black geezer and one white geezer. They were both about seven foot tall and they had on clothes for a night op.'

'What do you mean, Howard?'

'You know, they had on dark jeans, dark jumper, bomber jackets, big black boots – standard issue and black fishermen's hats.'

'Do you mean like oilskin hats?' Dr Morris said. Howard chuckled.

'No, you know, like in the films. A black woolly hat like, erm, you know, Charles Bronson in *Death Wish*.'

'Did either of them look like Charles Bronson, Howard?'

'Yeah, the black one,' Howard said sarcastically. Dr Morris forced a smile.

'How did you feel when you realised that they wanted to kill you, Howard?'

'Well, it was weird 'cos they looked friendly, you know. Not friendly, but they had looks on their faces that just said "It's nothing personal. It's just our job." Like it was just another day at the office for them, but you knew they meant business and that once they started you were fucked, you know. Like they'd just take you apart quickly and efficiently, no fuss, no mess, just hardcore wipin' you out like.'

'And you were frightened?'

'You're damn right I was. Wouldn't you be? I was about to die, Doctor.'

'Yes, of course,' Dr Morris said unemotionally.

'My whole body was terrified out of its skin. I couldn't stop shaking for about five minutes after I woke up.'

'Did it ever reoccur, this dream?'

'Nope,' Howard said definitely.

'I see.' Dr Morris mopped his brow with a used tissue he had taken out from his rolled-up sleeve.

'Any other dreams like that, Howard?'

'Not dreams, no.' Dr Morris momentarily gave a puzzled look.

'What do you mean? Have you had similar experiences that you think... you feel weren't dreams, Howard?' Howard folded his arms, his gazed fixed firmly upon Dr Morris.

'You don't want to talk about it, Howard?' Dr Morris asked. Howard did not move, his eyes staring piercingly at Dr Morris's.

'Come on, Howard,' Dr Morris said with a snuffle. 'You can tell me, it's okay.' Howard cocked his head to one side, his expression unchanged.

'Howard, I think you've shared enough of your experiences with me to realise that you can trust me, don't you?' Howard realigned his head and began rubbing his tongue along his front teeth behind his closed lips. His face was deadly serious, his gaze unfazed and defiant. For the first time he cut a bold figure, strong and unflinching.

'Look, Howard. If you're not open and honest with me, then how do you expect things to improve? You need to feel secure here. You need to understand that you are not here to be judged, you shouldn't feel threatened or nervous about telling me what's on your mind. I'm here to help you and, believe you me, I've heard it all.' Howard smiled, but still remained silent.

'Well, we can sit here in silence if you wish, Howard. After all, these are supposed to be your sessions, but it is basically a waste of clinic resources and everybody's time if you're going to just sit here playing the strong silent type, now isn't it?' Dr Morris took out the old tissue he had stuffed into the roll of his shirt sleeve and began blowing his running nose. He put it back when he'd finished. Howard watched with an element of amusement. More time passed.

'Look, Howard...' Dr Morris said finally breaking the silence. His voice grew hoarser and hoarser as he tried to feign genuine anger.

'As I said, Doctor, I'm not really certain that you're the person I should be talking to about such matters,' Howard said finally, cutting across Dr Morris. His voice almost sounded in character, as if he was trying out the lines of some epic great classic.

'Howard,' Dr Morris uttered in exasperation, his body finally succumbing to the illness that he had been battling against all week. 'If you think that you want to see someone else, then you are very much mistaken. It has taken a lot of time and effort to get you referred to this programme. People have gone out of their way to ensure you have been kept under the wing of this borough and the resources and facilities we have to offer. There are plenty of people out there who are not lucky enough to receive the same care and attention that you have been privileged to have been exposed to.'

'Whoop-de-doo,' Howard said, wobbling his head from side to side, mocking Dr Morris in a child-like manner.

'Howard,' Dr Morris said with what little authority he could generate. 'I could quite easily have you removed from this programme and you'd be out on your ear, do you understand me? We are not here to play games. We are here to help you come to terms with your mental health problems. Am I making myself crystal clear to you?' Howard sat with his hands resting in his lap. His defiance waned, but his eye contact remained with a now visibly ill man.

'Yes, Doctor,' Howard said in a monotone voice. Dr Morris began to cough and splutter. The usually large man seemed shrunken and feeble behind the desk.

'Now, let's continue, shall we?' Dr Morris said in a low, but measured voice.

'Doctor, are you sure you want to continue? You look like shit,' Howard said with slight concern. Dr Morris gave a long sigh.

'Yes Howard, I'm fine. I just have a bit of flu, that's all. Now please, we were talking about your dreams. You indicated that you were not sure about some of your dreams. You seemed confused that they may be real. Is that correct?'

'I didn't say that.'

'Well, what did you mean, when you said that it wasn't for me to hear or something? What's going through your mind when... what are you getting at?'

'I just think that it's not the right time to talk about such things, that's all, Doctor,'

Howard said with a shifty look, breaking his eye contact with Dr Morris.

'Well, when is the right time to talk about such things then, Howard? That's what you're here for, specifically to talk about such things.'

'You wouldn't understand, Doctor.'

'Try me, Howard. I'm all ears.'

'You'll think I'm mad,' Howard said loudly and dismissively.

'No Howard, I won't think you're mad. We don't use terms like that here. It has neither relevance nor credence here, Howard, I can promise you that.' Howard had grown nervous, his brave stature now relegated back to its usual mental hideaway.

'Come on, let me in Howard,' Dr Morris said humanely. Howard grew pale and withdrawn. He slouched in his seat and looked down at Dr Morris's shoes under the desk.

'Well, I remember not so long ago... something that happened in the night. Not long after my grandmother died.'

'What was it? Another bad dream?'

'I was asleep and while I was dreaming I saw something slip under the door. It was like a black circle, some kind of vapour, but heavier, thicker. It just eased its way under the door and into the room.'

'So, were you awake or asleep at that point? Or were you not sure?'

'I was still asleep, but only lightly, you know. I was aware of the room as well.'

'It's REM sleep, Howard, where you're most likely to remember your dreams.'

'Yeah, but I was aware of what was going on in the room. I could see it.'

'So you were dreaming that your eyes were open and that you could see this black thing coming under the door?'

'No, Doctor. I was still asleep, but I could see the room with my mind, like I was floating above myself, just a little bit. Not like high up in the room, less than a foot above my body.'

'Okay Howard, go on.'

'So this black thing floats around on the floor for a bit and sort of blends in with the shadows. I've still got my eyes on it, but I'm pretending to be fully asleep.'

'So you're actually looking at it now, are you, Howard?'

'No, I'm still asleep. But as I said, I'm floating up a bit and that me is pretending not to see it.'

'Okay.'

'Then it starts to take on a form. The circle starts to form into a figure, the figure of a man. The thing is, it has no face, no features, no bodily details, just the silhouette of a slender, muscular male physique. You know what it looks like? Kinda like black Spiderman. Have you ever seen black Spiderman, Doctor?'

'No, no I haven't.'

'Well, he's the same as Spiderman, but he's all black, like a shadow of Spiderman.'

'Right,' Dr Morris said trying to concentrate.

'So, this thing is on the floor on all fours at the opposite side of the room, and it starts to slowly, sneakily crawl along the floor towards my bed, but it makes no sound and it almost glides as it moves, like it's not really a physical being, you know. Eventually it's alongside me and my bed. It's lying the same way as I am, but it's on the floor and it waits there for a few minutes. I can see exactly what it's doing, and I think to myself, "You sly bastard", you know. I'm sort of smiling to myself as I think it. Then it very slowly, very sneakily starts to sort of slide and manipulate itself over me. So far it's not touching me, but it is above me. At this point, I've gone right back into my body and am lying at the bottom of my physical self, if that makes sense?'

'Not exactly.'

'Well, if before I was nearly a foot above my body, well now I'm sort of squashed into the bottom half of the whole of my body, 'cos this thing is now nose to nose with me.'

'Okay.'

'It still isn't touching me at this point and I'm still pretending to be asleep. Well, I am still half asleep, but I'm very much beginning to wake up. This thing starts to press down on me very slowly, very precisely and carefully, until it is fully on top of me.'

'Is it heavy, Howard? Like a weight pressing down on you?'

'No, Doctor, it's not heavy at all, it's as light as a feather, you can tell. But it is gradually pressing down on me with a supernatural pressure, not its actual physical weight or strength. The weight of this force becomes heavier and heavier and I feel myself being held down and being pushed into the bed.'

'Do you feel like you can't move at this point, Howard?'

'No, I can't and the feeling is stronger and stronger, it's like I'm being paralysed. Then this creature slowly wraps its hands around my throat and is about to start strangling me. It's being extra careful not to wake me up, but I can see what it's doing. The thing is, I start to realise that if this goes much further then I'm not gonna be able to do anything about it. That this thing, this shadowy little fucker, is going to throttle me. So I try to move, but the force of it is too much. I'm being pushed down into the mattress and it has got a full grip around my throat now. It's going for it. It won't be denied. It's almost as if it was about to become a part of me, or be absorbed into my body. Like it was gonna posses me, you know, take control of my entire body and strangle me at the same time. Either way I'm a gonner, know what I mean?'

'What happened then, Howard?'

'So, I realise that I've got to wake up fully 'cos I'm still half asleep, but I can't move. Then somehow, I don't know how, I force myself up. It takes all the strength I've got, I mean every last ounce. But this thing won't let go. It feels like it's halfway into me so it's gonna go the whole hog. So I'm stood in the middle of the room and I realise that this might be it. That this thing is gonna win. It's gonna overpower me and I'm out of here. I swear, Doctor, the adrenalin rush that I got was like no adrenalin rush I've ever had before. I mean, I've been in some dodgy situations and I've had a few fights in my time, you know, but I know at this point that this is it, it's fight or fucking flight man. Either I take this thing out or it's gonna take me out. I struggle so hard it's like pulling off a giant fucking leech, man. I pull on it so hard that I start to black out. I feel so dizzy and I can't see anymore. All I can feel is the force of this thing sucking into me and me trying to force it the other way.'

Howard paused for a moment.

'What happened then, Howard?' said Dr Morris, who was listening intently.

'I don't know how long this goes on for. It could have been seconds, it could have been minutes. I simply don't know. I just lost moments of my life. The next thing I know, this thing is out of me and it's in my arms. I've got it like WWF wrestling man, one arm is across its groin and the other's across its neck and shoulder. I literally lift it up in the air and slam it across the room in a downwards direction, with all the human strength I have and a little bit more. That little bit more you have when it's life or death. It flies across the room and into the filing cabinet. It bounces off that and onto the floor in a heap and for a moment loses all its form. It becomes a mess, a blob of blackness. Then it regroups, it's back in its human form, but it seems smaller and punier. Then it scurries past me on all fours, across the room and disappears under the door.'

'What did you do then, Howard?'

'I just stood there in my boxer shorts, my entire body shaking. I could feel my heart pounding through my whole body, in every vein, at the tips of my fingers right through to my temples. The blood was pumping around me at a hundred miles an hour. I knew I had just saved my own life. I felt like Russell fucking Crowe in *Gladiator*.'

'What did you do then?'

'Well, I must have stood there for about ten minutes like that. When I eventually began to calm down and was sure that the thing wasn't coming back for another go, I looked around the room. It had been totalled. The whole room was wrecked. The TV and the video that had been on a stand were on different sides of the room. The coffee table was overturned. There were books and papers all over the floor. Everything, man. Everything that could have been disturbed was, and was lying in a different part of the room.'

'Goodness, what did you do after that?'

'I tidied up the room and went back to bed.'

'Did you sleep after that?' Dr Morris said with surprise.

'Not until it was light. Once the sun comes up, it's okay to sleep.'

'Well, it all sounds pretty distressing, Howard. But you know what it is, don't you? It's sleep paralysis. Scientists call it temporal lobe seizure.'

'I have had sleep paralysis before once, when my auntie was talking to me while I was asleep. I woke up and could see her, but I couldn't say anything or move. I tried to and couldn't, but it was funny and it just made me laugh inside as it was happening. This was different. It wasn't any temporal lobe seizure, that's for sure.'

'No, seriously Howard, this is well-documented. Some people, especially in

America, think they've been visited by aliens or they are being violated by aliens and things like that. But the truth is, they are just having full REM sleep and they are trying to wake up sort of at the same time, and it just gives this bizarre effect of being pressed down upon by someone or something. I think the mind just tries to make sense of it and creates a sort of drama around it. It's common. In many cultures they believe a witch has come to suffocate them and so on, but it's honestly nothing more than that.'

'You can say what you like, Doctor, but I know what happened and I know what it was,' Howard said with certainty. Dr Morris smiled sympathetically.

'What was it, Howard? An alien?' Howard swallowed hard and gave Dr Morris a disdainful look.

'It was a demon, Doctor. It was a demon straight from hell,' he said. Dr Morris sort of grinned.

'Now, surely Howard, surely you don't believe in that sort of thing?'

'I know what I saw and I know what I fought off.'

'Look Howard, there has been quite a fair bit of research into this and I can assure you that what happened in that room was not a demon attacking you. It was just a bad dream mixed with sleep paralysis.'

'So why did it carry on fighting me after I woke up? Explain that.'

'You were simply still asleep, Howard. Look, people sleepwalk all the time. They smash up rooms and walk out onto balconies and into traffic, all that sort of thing. It happens. You said something about your grandmother dying. Well, grief is a funny thing, Howard; it can make us feel very strange. Were you very close to your grandmother?'

'Yeah, she basically brought me up.'

'Well, there you go, Howard. That just proves my point. You were obviously upset at the death of your grandmother. Did you take it very hard, Howard?' Howard pulled a look of disapproval as if it were obvious.

'Yeah, I was pretty fucked-up from it, you know.'

'Howard, a lot of people who come through these rooms have lost someone. Some people have lost whole families in accidents and tragedies. They all, like you, go through some sort of crisis and end up in very strange places, mentally and emotionally.' Howard looked thoroughly unconvinced and sat staring at Dr Morris as he spoke, as though he was trying to mentally block out his words.

'Look Howard, our time is up now. But I want you to think about what we've discussed here and we'll pick up on it again next week, okay?'

Howard got up and left the room. Dr Morris sat sealed in his own sweat, his body tired and aching. He longed for the comfort of a hot bath, but he sat and reread Howard's notes.

SESSION THIRTEEN

Dr Morris and Howard sat in their usual room. Dr Morris was pallid and looked as though he'd lost some weight. He was, however, smartly dressed and well-presented. Howard sat opposite him, sullen and uncommunicative. His clothes were unclean and his face was pasty. Of the two men, Howard had the posture and demeanour of the older man, despite the fact that Dr Morris was more than fifteen years his senior.

'Did you ever have any bereavement counselling, Howard? After your grandmother's death?' Dr Morris said. Howard shook his head slowly.

'Mmm, that's a pity. It's often very good at moving you forward through the process. It's a necessary process that we don't fully understand, I'll admit. We used to think that it happened in stages, some said seven stages, but we're now starting to realise that perhaps grieving is different for different people and that pretty much anything goes with it. The process, I mean. It would have been good for you in terms of expressing your feelings. Sometimes, people just say the same things over and over. It can often seem that the same conversation is taking place each time you attend. But, bit by bit, it usually works its way out. We have to verbalise our feelings to someone sometimes, a sympathetic listener. It's very important to some people, that they communicate their inner world and connect it with someone else, or several people even. Did you talk to your family about the death of your grandmother at all, Howard?' Dr Morris's voice was clear and strong, the decrepit sound that he had emitted the previous week had disappeared without a trace.

'No,' Howard said shaking his head again. 'There was no one to talk to, Doctor.' Howard's voice was quiet and mild.

'That's a real shame, Howard. It's often a good time for families to pull together and become closer.'

'No, we were never that close. But after that, it just seemed like no one wanted to talk. And when they did talk they'd just argue, over anything, not even important things.'

'Well, I'm afraid, Howard, that is the other side of the coin. It's all too common that death and bereavement tears those left behind apart. Some people don't speak for years afterwards, sometimes ever again. When did this happen?'

'Erm, about six or seven months ago, something like that.'

'And you never really spoke to anyone about it?'

'No. I, er, I don't really speak to people much, anyway.'

'Did you go to the funeral? That's important, to see people off, pay your respects and go through the ritual of burial, that sort of thing.'

'She was cremated, Doctor.'

'Yes, Howard, it's the same thing. It's the ceremony that's important.'

'Yeah, Neanderthals used to bury their dead and have funerals and stuff,' Howard said with a childlike quality.

'Exactly Howard, very good. So how old was your grandmother? Was she a good old age?'

'Erm...' Howard rolled his eyes up as he tried to remember. 'I think she was in her late eighties, Doctor. I think she was eighty-seven.'

'So, she lived to a ripe old age. Any older and it's all a bit confusing, really,' Dr Morris said with a chuckle. Howard's face was sombre.

'Yes, well, I'm sure she meant the world to you, Howard. You said you were close, didn't you?'

'Yes, Doctor, she brought me up.'

'I see, and why did she bring you up, Howard? Where were your parents?' Howard's eyes grew slightly puppy-like for a moment before hardening with resolve.

'Well, my dad left when I was a baby, so I never really knew him. And mum, well, I don't know. She just went away too, when I was about three. I don't know why.'

'So she left you with your grandmother?'

'Yeah.'

'Your father's mother, or your mother's?'

'My mother's.'

'And your grandmother, your mother's mother, brought you up, until you were how old?'

'Until I was about seventeen.'

'And then what happened? Did you leave home, or did your mother come back?'

'My mother came back with my sister.'

'Is your sister younger than you?'

'Yeah, she's my half-sister.'

'Right, I see. And so you lived with them?'

'Yeah, for about a year, and then I moved out.'

'Did you get your own place, Howard?'

'Yeah, me and my mum didn't really get on.'

'Did you argue a lot, Howard?'

'Yeah, we did.'

'So, it was very different from living with your grandmother?'

'Yeah, my grandmother was great. She cooked for me and looked after me.'

'Did you talk to her, Howard? Could you confide in her?'

'A bit, but she wasn't one for words, really. She was quite blunt, but not in a horrible way. She just said it like it was, you know. No messin'. She was the older generation; they don't analyse things too much, they just get on with it, don't they?'

'What about your grandfather? Was he around?'

'What, my grandmother's husband?'

'Yes.'

'No, he died before I was born. From the mines, you know?'

'The mines?'

'Yeah, he worked down the mines, in Wales.'

'So you're Welsh, Howard?'

'Half, yeah. My dad was Irish, so I'm told.'

'Were you brought up in Wales?'

'No, I was born and bred in London.'

'I was going to say, you don't have much of a Welsh accent,' Dr Morris said with a smile. Howard reciprocated and smiled back. It amused him.

'Did your grandfather die in a mining accident then, Howard?'

'No, he died from cancer, I think. But we all know it was the mines that caused it. You know, the dust and all that.'

'Was he a smoker, your granddad?'

'Dunno.'

'So your grandmother lived in London too?'

'Yeah.'

'So how did you feel at the funeral, Howard? Was it a very emotional time for you?'

'Well, yeah, but it was weird. Sort of surreal.'

'In what way was it surreal, Howard?'

'Well, like it wasn't really happening. I can remember it in my head, but I can't remember...'

'Remember what, Howard?'

'How it felt. It was like I wasn't really there, if that makes sense?'

'Yes, it does. I think it's like that for a lot of people, Howard. Don't worry about that. So, were you having any hallucinations at the time, Howard? At the funeral, or around the time of the funeral?'

'Hallucinations?' Howard said with a glint in his eye, but an expression that was deadly serious. Dr Morris gave a little grin.

'Was there anything untoward, anything strange or out of the ordinary going on at that time?'

156

'Of course, Doctor. They play their little games, don't they?'

'Who does? Your family?'

'Yeah, them too.'

'Who's playing little games, Howard?'

'You know.'

'Well no, Howard, I don't know, that's the problem. Do you mean the energy game and all that malarkey?'

'That's always on, Doctor, I told you. No, not that. It's worse than that, more serious than that.'

'I see, well would you like to tell me about it, Howard?'

'What for?'

'Well, so I can know for one thing. But also to understand what you're going through, for another.'

'What do you want to know?' Howard had grown fidgety and slightly more aggressive in both his body language and speech.

'No need to get agitated, Howard. We're just having a chat, and I'm just asking you a few questions, that's all. Let's not forget that, eh?' Howard settled down, but his expression remained stern.

'Now, why don't you tell me what was going on at your grandmother's funeral?'

'I told you, nothing. I was spaced out and it felt weird, don't you listen?' Howard blurted angrily.

'Okay, okay, calm down. You said that things were not right at that time, either. That you had halluc... that you were...'

'Hallucinations. Just say it Doctor, I know what you're thinking.'

'Okay, Howard. Hallucinations. You were seeing some strange and disturbing things then; not necessarily at the funeral, but around that time. What was going on then, Howard?' The veins on Dr Morris's neck were starting to bulge with rage. He was speaking with force, but not outright aggression.

'After the funeral,' Howard mumbled, retracting from the simmering potential conflict.

'Right, so what happened after the funeral, Howard?' Dr Morris said more calmly, but still with some weight.

'It was on the train home.'

'On the train home?'

'Yes, from Wales.'

'The funeral was in Wales?'

'Yeah, we went down for it there. She went home to be next to my grandfather.'

'Her gravestone?'

'Yes,' Howard said agitated.

'Go on, Howard.'

'Well, they all got the car didn't they? But there was no room for me.'

'Who, your family?'

'Yeah, my mum and her sister, and my sister and her boyfriend. He was driving.'

'Okay.'

'And I had to get the train, didn't I?'

'Were you upset about that, Howard?'

'Yes, I fucking was. Like I can afford the bloody train.'

'Did you feel left out, Howard?'

'No, like I want to be sandwiched between those two old bags.'

'Who, your mum and her sister?'

'Yeah.'

'So it was more about the money was it, Howard?'

'Damn right it was,' Howard spat defiantly.

'Okay, so you took the train and what happened?'

'Well, I got on and sat down. And at first there was no one sitting with me. After a few stops, this bloke gets on and sits down opposite me. He cracks open a can of beer and starts to chat to me.'

'What was he saying to you, Howard?'

'Well, at first he was just chatty, you know, telling me he was travelling on business, you know. He told me he worked for some engineering company, some sort of... well, I don't remember what, but it was industrial, you know, industrially-related. Anyway, he tells me he's a qualified physicist and he's noticed that I'm reading Stephen Hawkins, you know *A Brief History of Time*. Do you know that one, Doctor?'

'I'm aware of it. I haven't read it, but I know what you mean, Howard,' Dr Morris said patiently.

'Anyway, we're talking and he starts saying that those kinds of books are no good, that they're just popular science and that those in the real fields don't take it all too seriously, and all this kind of stuff. He goes to me "Good luck with that one, you're gonna need it". But I notice, when he thinks I'm not looking, he's having a good look at my notes.'

'Your notes?'

'Yeah, my notes on the book sort of thing. Sometimes I write notes if I disagree with the book, or whatever, you know.'

'Did that anger you, Howard?'

'Well, it did and it didn't. I didn't say anything, but I thought "I bet he's nicking my ideas." Anyway, we're still chatting away and he starts going on about government experiments and all that. So I ask him if he's seen *Bad Trip to Edgewood*. Have you seen *Bad Trip to Edgewood*, Doctor?'

'No Howard, I haven't seen that one.'

'It's about the US Military during the Vietnam War doing LSD experiments on their own soldiers, they wanted to see if...'

'Okay, Howard, we don't need to discuss the, erm...'

'*Bad Trip to Edgewood*, it's a documentary.'

'Okay, well we don't need to discuss that, do we?'

'Yeah, but they wanted to see what it would do to them...'

'Alright, Howard...'

'No, but they wanted to see if they could use it on the Vietnamese...'

'Okay, Howard, but it's not important here is...'

'They killed a top US general or something. He committed suicide. He jumped out of the hospital window. It was mad, I tell ya.'

'That's quite enough, Howard. Now get back to what you were saying before, please,' Dr Morris said in primary school mode.

'Erm, yeah.' Howard had the look of an exited infant, his eyes wide with wonder and enthusiasm.

'The man on the train, Howard.'

'Yeah, so erm, he says to me... what did he say to me? Oh yeah, he said "What about the government experiments that are carried out on you that you don't know about?" and he leaned forward and looked me right in the eyes. He looked weird then, I tell ya. He was a weird-looking fucker, anyway. He had these huge, thick glasses on that made his eyes look massive, I tell ya. He was a fat bastard, too.'

'Did that make you feel frightened, Howard?'

'Well, yeah, in a way. It freaked me out, you know, 'cause I've seen all sorts of documentaries about that shit – ICI here, and the syphilis experiments they did on black Americans in the forties, or whenever it was.'

'So what did you do, Howard?'

'I changed the subject a bit. I said I knew about the bacteria experiments that the Conservative government did on the homeless down on the Embankment and on the tube... no one batted a fucking eyelid when that was on the news. What the fuck is that about, Doctor?' Dr Morris smiled sympathetically, but with a touch of condescension about it.

'Yes Howard, and then what happened?'

'Well, at that point a shitload of birds got on the train and a load of other people, some skinny, long-haired geezer. They all sat down in the seats to the side of us. You know, at the other table.'

'I see.'

'They were making shitloads of noise, I mean a real racket. They were on some sort of hen night or something. They all had kiss-me-quick hats on and other weird shit, you know – their costumes for the night out, or whatever. They were as pissed as farts anyway.'

'Did they bother you, Howard?'

'They were noisy and aggressive and rough, know what I mean, Doctor?'

'Yes, I think I understand. So then what?'

'Well, they all start playing the game like mad. I mean, like mad. And me and this skinny lad are getting munched up like Pac Man, they're murdering us. The physicist bloke opposite me just shrank into his seat and went to sleep, but I could tell he wasn't really sleeping. He kept opening one eye at every station, without fail. Anyway, so I play this game that I've learnt, whereby I can hold onto the energy for a long time. In fact, at this point I can hold onto it for as long as I want. I can, to put it bluntly, feel it on my, you know what...'

'Do you mean your penis, Howard?'

'Well, yeah, I mean I can hold it in my hand too. That's what people try to do, me included, and you can get away with it for a while. I think it's designed like that, to give people a little breather. But eventually someone will distract you and your hand will *mysteriously open*,' Howard said sarcastically.

'Okay Howard, go on,' Dr Morris said, humouring Howard.

'Yeah, so I can hold it down there and have the main supply, you know, the main catalyst of energy in the room and eventually things will calm down and everyone will focus on me and will try to disturb me. Try to undo it, sort of. But I know that I can hold onto that position for as long as I'm awake and I'm in control. Nothing much can get to me, except violence.'

'Actual physical violence, Howard?'

'Actual physical violence, Doctor. That changes the game completely. I think that's how it works, to be honest. People, especially men, but increasingly women, become violent when they can't play the game well or when someone is particularly outdoing them, do you see what I mean? That can make you release your hold on the energy. Unless you're willing to fight and then it comes down to who can hold onto the energy and fight at the same time. I've seen two boxers go at it on TV. Both fighting for control of the energy, back and forth it goes, until one is too tired or loses concentration, and then it's good night Irene!' Howard looked exhilarated, his eyes brimming with life and passion.

'So, you hold onto this energy, do you Howard?' Dr Morris said, while writing in Howard's file.

'Yeah, I hold onto this energy and that's when it gets serious. That's when they all turn against me. That's when I realised about the other world. The true nature of life here on good old planet earth, it all came into view. I mean, I'd had my suspicions for some time, but right at that point I knew it was true and, what's more, so did they.'

'Right,' Dr Morris said. 'Well, I'm afraid we're going to have to leave it there, Howard.

SESSION FOURTEEN

'I could see how it was going to pan out, Doctor. I looked up and saw how they were all in on it. How there was a community of people all lost and struggling for survival in this world. How they were all lost and in need of answers. But they were lost in their own depravity, their own problems and weaknesses. The damage that life had inflicted on them had caused them to turn to this. But they were guilty and there was no reasoning with them. I knew at that point that it was on. It was up to me to say the word and it would begin.'

'What would begin, Howard?'

'I looked around the carriage and I saw them all at it. I saw the skinny bastard pulling strings. Those tall, long-haired skinny types are always puppetmasters, it's the type they are. Sneaky, but clever. They're technical, you know.'

'What are you talking about, Howard?'

'You know, the tall skinny type of guy with long hair in a ponytail. They always play the game by pulling your strings, like you're a puppet. They do it when you're not looking and they move you around for ages before you clock on and realise what they're doing.'

'So you think that the man on the train was controlling you? How?'

'As I told you Doctor, we're all interconnected and that's their particular area of expertise. They have you on invisible strings and they move your arms and legs like you're a puppet. So you'll be sitting there, with your arm on the rest, and all of a sudden your arm will slip. Why? Because they had you on a string and they pulled it a bit.'

'Come on Howard, now that's just not true.'

'I saw him, Doctor!' Howard shouted. 'I caught him in the act and he just smiled the way a slave does, when he's caught up to no good.' Howard was wide-eyed and he wagged his finger as he spoke. 'It all became crystal clear at that moment, Doctor, and I knew it was on. Nothing would ever be the same again.'

'What was, Howard? What was on?' Dr Morris said with annoyance. Howard sat back in his chair, adrenalin running through his body, his nostrils flaring. A patronising smile spread across his face.

'I don't know whether you know it or not, Doctor. To be quite honest, I don't know whether you know and play along, or whether you are just an innocent in all this, someone with their head in the sand. I think there are basically two types – which one are you?'

'I'm very sorry Howard, but I haven't the faintest idea what you're talking about, I really don't.' Dr Morris was shaking his head rapidly in confusion. 'What was it you knew at that moment, Howard?'

'I knew that what I had suspected for some time was actually fact.'

'What had you suspected, Howard?'

'That this is actually his realm. He's the boss here and I actually saw what the joint really looks like, how things are here really.'

'And what's that, Howard? What's it really like?'

Howard stared deeply into Dr Morris's eyes. His head was leaning forward and his brow gathered together in the middle of his head, like an owl about to pounce on its prey.

'This is hell on earth,' he said. Dr Morris finally grasped where Howard was going with this.

'So you think that this is hell, do you, Howard?'

'No, not hell itself, but he has annexed the earth. It is his playground right now.'

Dr Morris threw his pen down on the desk in resignation. He blew upwards as though there were imaginary hairs hanging over his forehead.

'So, Satan is among us, is he Howard?'

'That he is, Doctor. That he is.'

'And where does Satan live, Howard? Does he live nearby, or does he have a penthouse in Monte Carlo?' Dr Morris said acerbically. Howard grinned in approval.

'Very good, Doctor, very good. That's more like it – show your true colours, why don't you?'

'Howard, where is this getting us?'

'It's getting us, Doctor, to the pretty unpalatable fact that the lord of fucking darkness is roaming this planet, causing mayhem and spreading his evil doctrine to all and sundry.' Howard had not altered his gaze even for a moment. He was deadly serious. Dr Morris's brain was ticking loudly. He thought carefully before he spoke.

'Okay look, Howard. I don't want to argue with you here...' Howard cut him off, like a falcon swooping down on a small rodent.

'I DON'T GIVE A FUCK WHETHER YOU WANT TO ARGUE WITH ME OR NOT, DR MORRIS!'

Dr Morris gritted his teeth.

'Howard,' he warned. 'You are treading on very thin ice, now kindly conduct yourself in a cordial manner or I will be forced to have you removed. Do you understand? DO YOU UNDERSTAND?' he bellowed. Howard sat staring at Dr Morris as though he were in a trance, as though he was not fully present.

'Yeah, I understand alright,' he said quietly, but firmly.

'Now, I'm not going to argue with you about this. We can sit and discuss this reasonably or not at all, alright?' Howard nodded slowly, his stare still transfixed on Dr Morris. He almost seemed to stare right through him. Dr Morris composed himself before continuing.

'Okay, so you thought that this was hell.'

'Yeah, I thought,' Howard scoffed. Dr Morris gave Howard a warning look.

'I *thought* that this *was* hell on earth, Doctor. An annexation. He *had* given himself planning permission to set up shop here and work it like it's going out of fashion.' Howard spoke slowly, as if spelling out the obvious to a simpleton. Dr Morris's jaw was clamped tight and he began to grind his teeth.

'And why did you think that, Howard?' he murmured through his gritted teeth.

'I had been aware of it for some time, Doctor, but this time I saw it.'

'And what did it look like?' Dr Morris said irritably.

'It looked the same, but more sinister, darker, colder, more eerie.'

'And that made you think that this was hell?'

'It was more than that, Doctor. I just knew, I could tell. The way people looked at me as I got off the train.'

'How were they looking at you, Howard?'

'They just knew. They knew it was time, I had called it and it begun. And they were frightened.'

'What had begun, Howard?' Howard looked at Dr Morris as if he should know. Dr Morris looked back as if he did.

'The countdown to judgement day,' Howard said. Dr Morris breathed deeply.

'And how do you know that judgement day is here, Howard?' Howard smiled like the Cheshire cat.

'Because I called it, Doctor, I called it and it was time. They thought they had more time, they always asked for more. They thought they couldn't be caught up with, like Satan. They thought that time was on their side, just like the song, that it'd keep going. But time is a funny thing, it doesn't actually exist. So I called up the moment because it was already upon us, we were already there. They just couldn't see it, didn't know – well, they did in their hearts, the back of their minds, and that's what terrified them most. And I called it.'

Both men had begun to speak in very low voices. The neon light hummed intrusively above them.

169

'And just how could you decide something like that, Howard?' Dr Morris said. Howard said nothing, his pale face looked alabaster under the cheap neon bulb. The light highlighted every crease and pit in his translucent skin, his bony skull protruded through every feature, pushing tiny little blue and purple veins closer to the surface. The silence continued.

'Eh, Howard?' Dr Morris said finally. He studied Howard's face and saw that he was to get no response. 'So what happened after you got off the train?' he said, trying a different approach. Howard continued his silence for another moment before responding.

'I got off the train and felt the change. I felt the wind blow in and the harsh winter begin. I put on my gloves and woolly hat, threw my bag over my shoulder and marched.'

'Where did you march to?'

'I marched to my sister's, that's where I was staying that night. I looked at each and every face I passed. I looked them all square in the eyes and they parted as I approached, all of them without exception. I was ready.'

'Ready for what, Howard?'

'To face him.'

'To face who, Howard?' Howard looked at Dr Morris, Dr Morris looked back.

'Satan.'

'Why would you want to face Satan, Howard?'

'To defeat him,' Howard said. Dr Morris massaged his bald head and pondered for a moment.

'Okay, so then what did you do?' he said.

'I went to my sister's, but she had stayed at my mum's. Her boyfriend let me in. He went to bed and I was sleeping on the sofa.'

'So what happened to judgement day?'

'I was lying there and I could hear him upstairs, writhing in the bed.'

'Who?'

'My sister's boyfriend. Then I get some full-on game play from all the women in the area, from all the neighbouring houses. They're all moaning and trying to hook-up with me. All the energy is flowing my way, I'm in full control. All of a sudden, my sister's boyfriend upstairs starts to compete with me and it's a full-on competition. He starts to talk to me telepathically, but it's not clear what he's saying to me. Suddenly it's almost as if we're one and the same person, me on the sofa and him upstairs. I can see him and what he sees, and he can see me and what I can see. He's on the bed and there are all these women around him and he's laughing hysterically and they're like maniacs, like they're possessed. They're going mental with sexual ecstasy. The room is all weird too, like it's a cave, and the lighting is all sort of red. Then I'm totally in his mind and I look down at his legs and they are all hairy. I don't mean a bit, I mean like an animal, you know, fur. I look at his feet and they're huge. I look at his toes and they are covered in hair, and he has these huge claws sticking out of 'em.'

'Go on, Howard,' said Dr Morris, as Howard pauses.

'Well, suddenly I'm back in me. I look down at my feet, but they are still his and I realise it's him. So, I slowly stand up and stand in the middle of the room, ready to fight, you know. I know he does the same. We're both connected somehow and he's mirroring what I'm doing. I'm ready to have it out. There's no doubt in my mind that I will win, so I walk towards the front room door and he's walking towards the bedroom door at the same time; we are completely synchronised. I open the door and walk into the hall downstairs and he does the same in the upstairs hall. I stand at the bottom of the stairs and he's stood at the top, but we can't see each other 'cos there's two small flights of stairs on a bend, but I know he's there and he knows that I'm there. I feel like rock, indestructible, and I can feel him shaking like a leaf, all over, uncontrollably. Then I realise that he has taken over my sister's boyfriend's body and is controlling him. I can hear him, terrified, unable to control his own body. He's terrified. He doesn't want to fight me, but he's got no choice. I feel sorry for him at that point, but I have to do what I have to do, know what I mean?' Dr Morris was gravely concerned by now and was writing notes as Howard spoke.

'Then Satan revealed himself. A light came from the top of the stairs; it was a red and fiery glow that lit up the whole of upstairs. I saw his huge shadow cast down over the hall. He was enormous. I could hear the sound of his hoofs on cobbles. The snorting noises were like the roar of a huge beast. Then the whole of his lower body transformed into a horse's body and legs. His upper body was hugely muscled and he had a giant trident in his right arm. There was the massive silhouette of a dead and twisted tree surrounded by mist behind him. His breath was wretched and steamed in the cold air. He reared up on his hind legs, as though he were about to charge. My whole body began to shake with uncontrollable fear and all the blood drained from me. I backed away into the front room. I stood in the middle of the front room, completely consumed with terror. He spoke to me telepathically, but directly and with total clarity. He challenged me there and then. He told me to come and face him, but I couldn't. I just stood there, quaking.'

'What happened then, Howard?' Dr Morris said with concern and sympathy.

'I knew I couldn't face him and he accepted that fact. He tossed something down the stairs, they landed by the door.'

'What were they, Howard?'

'I didn't look. I couldn't move. He commanded me to get dressed, so I did. Then he told me to leave my wallet and keys on the table.'

'Why did he do that?'

'Because I was to have no possessions. I was to walk out into the night and never return. I was to face the demons and torture of the hell out there that awaited me. I was to go directly to the park and face the howling creatures that inhabited it.

'Did you go?'

'Yes, I went. As I passed the bottom of the stairs, I saw what he had thrown down to me. It was three large nails. I knew they were to be my only belongings. I picked them up and put them in my pocket. I stepped out into the night and faced the howling winds. I wandered like a lost soul through the streets, where anarchy was being unleashed. I went to the park under instructions and heard all the minions, all the slaves of Satan howling and shrieking. I could hear his forces flying overhead in helicopters. His protectors came to greet me.'

'Who were they?'

'They were his security forces. They put me in the back of their van and took me in to be dealt with.'

'Is that when you got taken into hospital, Howard?'

'Yes, it is, Doctor.'

'Oh Howard,' Dr Morris said with a sigh. 'Don't you see, Howard? This is all just your illness. It's all your fears and insecurities, all mixed up with the effects of the drugs you've taken. It's all the emotional turmoil you've been through. The trauma of losing your grandmother, the insecurities brought on by your childhood. Do you see what I'm saying to you, Howard?' Howard was looking at Dr Morris with an air of pity, as if he was some poor misguided soul.

'Look, this isn't about Satan and judgement day,' continued Dr Morris, 'it's about you not being able to cope. Not being able to cope with your life, with the everyday stuff that most of us have to go through at one stage or another. You need to start facing some of the things that have been affecting you. You need to try and get back into society. Do you have any friends, Howard?'

'I don't need friends. That's not why I'm here.'

'Howard, we all need people, we can't do it all on our own. We can't just be alone all the time.' Howard gave Dr Morris a sympathetic look.

'I am here as an envoy. That is my mission, my *raison d'être*,' he announced.

'Howard, it's good to have a mission, a meaning in life, you know, a reason to be here. It really does help with the ride, so to speak...'

'No, I am here as a representative of the kingdom of heaven.'

'And what exactly is your mission as this representative, Howard?'

'I told you, to face Satan on the day of judgement.'

'Well, didn't you just tell me that you couldn't face him? That you were afraid to?'

'Yes, that's what I thought too, Doctor. But then I realised that I was being tested. And I passed the test.'

'How did you past the test, Howard?'

'You see, the Devil wants me to resort to violence. He wants the conflict to be lowered to his level, to be reduced to a back ally walk. He wants to draw me into doing what is wrong. He knows that, or he thinks that he can weaken me by causing me to sin. His perverted, twisted logic wants to provoke me into violence against him. He's thoroughly misinterpreted what the apocalypse is about. He doesn't realise that his own debauchery, his own violence, will be his downfall. And that God's strength is compassion and love, not violent conflict. Satan is ultimately wrestling with his own conscience. And his conscience is heavy. Every moment it weighs him down. His fear of the final coming eats at his soul, every single second of every single minute of every single hour. Fear drives men to violence, fear and greed. Greed is ultimately a form of fear, the pathological need to accumulate, even at the expense of others. That's deep-seated primeval, primordial fear. It's part of the evolutionary process. Dominate, accumulate, deprive others. Destroy others in order to maintain more than your share, more than you need. There's no trust there. If I don't do this, then others will do this to me. And they're right – others *are* doing it to them, to each other. That's greed, and greed is the deepest fear of all. This is the Devil's forte. Satan thrives on fear and the spread of its doctrine. But, he doesn't get it. He can't let go of it. And because he can't let go of it, he's born to lose it. He can't win. He knows this. What he fears most he knows is a certainty, and that's a tough burden to carry. That's a heavy hand to play. So he's taking as much down with him as possible. He's throwing women and children behind him as he flees. He's buying time and he knows it. But, like a naughty child who knows he's in trouble when he gets home, he's taking his time about returning to the fold. And we're no different. We, people, are the same. Like infants, we put off the bad part, we just keep eating up all the good bits, and we won't go home, we're afraid to. The funny thing is, though, is that we have no choice. It's simply a matter of time. Sooner or later we all meet our maker.' Dr Morris had put his pen down while Howard spoke and, hand on chin, was listening to his little sermon with interest.

'Are you religious, Howard?' he asked.

'No, I'm not religious, Doctor, but I know it's true. It's not something I can escape from. I don't believe, not for one minute, but it consumes me with its truth.'

'What does? What consumes you, Howard?'

'Not what, Doctor, but *who*?' Howard leaned forward, clasped his hands together and placed his elbows on the desk in front of him. 'God does, just as it permeates everything. I am totally saturated by God.'

'What is God to you, Howard?'

'God is indefinable. Only a fool would try to do so,' Howard said without hesitation. Dr Morris blinked rapidly several times and rubbed his eye with his index finger.

'God is everything you can possibly conceive of and more,' continued Howard. 'Your whole perception of *what is* is merely the tip of a giant iceberg. God is vast. So vast that we simply don't get it. *It* gets *us*. And that point, or tip of that iceberg, is just one of infinite icebergs floating in an infinite ocean on an infinite planet in an infinite galaxy of an infinite universe.'

'That may well be, Howard, but I think we should increase the dosage of your medication, just a little bit more, to be on the safe side, okay?' Howard sat back, straightened his posture and folded his arms.

'Yes Doctor,' he said calmly.

SESSION FIFTEEN

'Right Howard, so how are you feeling on the new dosage? I know it's quite a bit more than you've been on, isn't it? The thing is, as you're probably aware by now, you get used to it. As the months go by, your body adjusts and the effects of the drugs seem less pronounced. Do you see what I'm getting at, Howard?'

Howard sat motionless and expressionless. His clothes were heavily softened through wear and there was not one area of them that was not wrinkled or creased. His black chino Dockers were stained, grey patches were smeared sporadically up and down the legs. His white trainers were caked in black marks and food stains; loose tomato seeds had attached themselves to his laces and dehydrated in suspended animation. His chocolate brown, woollen-acrylic mix jumper had a fluffy aura and bobbles everywhere that required the urgent need of a Remington Fuzz Away.

'Well, I expect you know what I'm getting at, don't you, Howard?' Dr Morris said with a smile. Howard gawped back at him, his mouth half open, dried spittle in both corners. He snorted and began rubbing his running nose on his sleeve, a sliver of mucus snail trailed along his cuff.

'Would you like a tissue, Howard?' Dr Morris said as he rummaged through his jacket pocket. He offered it to Howard, who hardly responded.

'Go on, it's better than using your sleeve there, eh Howard?' he said. Howard snorted in all the mucus he could and swallowed it in one large go. Dr Morris smiled through his vague disgust and put the tissue down on the desk in front of Howard.

'For next time, eh, Howard,' he said prissily. 'So, I suppose we should get down to business. What would you like on the menu today, so to speak?'

Howard eventually shrugged his shoulders and gave Dr Morris a surly look.

'Well Howard, last time you were convinced that judgement day was upon us and that you had to have some sort of contest with Satan himself, no less. Do you still feel that way, Howard? I was hoping the medication would resolve some of those kinds of, erm, how shall we put it... apparitions.' Howard, who had been looking down at the floor, slowly looked up at Dr Morris, raised his right brow and looked away with disinterest.

'Well, do you still feel the need to have it all out with Satan in a big sort of fight sort of thing, Howard?' Howard looked at Dr Morris as though he were stupid.

'I told you, that was a test,' he said softly. 'I passed. And anyway, the situation has changed, as I predicted it would. You never listen, anyway.' Dr Morris ignored Howard's last comment.

'So the situation has changed, has it?' Dr Morris said, holding back a smirk.

'Yeah,' Howard said defiantly with a glare.

'I see, and how has the situation changed, Howard?' Howard looked to the heavens in despair and gave a huge sigh.

'Like you don't know, Doctor. This is like having the same conversation twice.'

'Look Howard, we have not had this conversation before. You always seem to think that I know exactly what's going on in your mind, or as if I'm part of some huge conspiracy. Just explain to me what it is you think is going on and I can, if you like, help you to understand whether it is factual or not, okay?'

'Factual, eh?' Howard said with great interest. Dr Morris held his tongue for a moment. He took a deep breath and exhaled slowly until his lungs were empty.

'You know what I mean, Howard. I'll try to explore the likelihood of it being the case or not.'

'Mmm, interesting,' Howard said mordantly. Dr Morris threw open Howard's file on the desk and pushed the top of his pen down, ready for action.

'Okay Howard, I'm all yours,' he said disingenuously.

'Great,' Howard said, returning the flippancy.

'So, what's changed? You no longer have to face Satan, or has Satan left us for warmer waters?'

'As I told you, "Doctor", that was a test, which I passed and now the obvious is apparent.'

'That being, Howard?'

'Well, it was never Satan I was supposed to face anyway, was it?'

'Was it not?' Dr Morris said sarcastically.

'No,' Howard said ignoring Dr Morris's insincerity. 'That was Satan trying to lure me into a trap. He wanted an ally walk to try and pull a fast one, a distraction. He wants me to avoid facing the Antichrist.'

'I see, so it's the Antichrist that you have to, what, fight?'

'Yes, that's when violence will be acceptable, as that is the sole purpose of the Antichrist – violence and destruction. That's his speciality. Satan is here to trick, to steal souls, to take as many away from God as he can. The Antichrist comes to destroy and wreak havoc.'

'And when will he come, Howard?' Dr Morris said. Howard smiled knowingly and sat back comfortably. He clasped his hands together and rested them in his lap.

'Oh, I see,' Dr Morris said. 'So is he with us already, Howard, is that it?' Howard laughed in a way much older than his years.

'What a surprise, eh Doctor?' he said still grinning.

'Yes Howard, what a surprise,' Dr Morris said playing along. 'So where is this great menace to us all, Howard?'

Howard continued his grin, unable to contain it. 'As if you don't know, Doctor. As if everyone doesn't know.'

'Well, let's just pretend I'm from Mars, eh Howard? And I just landed here on earth and I ask you, "Hey, Howard, who's the Antichrist around here?" What would you say?' Howard laughed uncontrollably for a considerable amount of time.

'You're good, Doctor, you really are,' he said as his laughter died down.

'Am I? That's nice, Howard,' Dr Morris said caustically. Howard licked his dry lips.

'Come on, Doctor. Who do you think it is?' he said quietly.

'Well, Howard, I could hazard a few guesses – my resources manager for one. But it's not for me to guess, now, is it? You're going to have to tell me, I'm afraid.'

Howard sat forward, rested his elbows on his knees and pressed his hands into a pyramid position, as though he were an international statesmen feigning being candid in an interview.

'Who is the most powerful man on earth at this moment, Doctor? Who really calls the shots right now? Who's starting all the wars at the moment?'

Dr Morris smiled.

'Who, Howard?' he asked with vague interest.

'Good old George W, Doctor.'

'So, George Bush is the Antichrist, Howard?'

'As if you didn't know, Doctor. Everyone knows it, but many are too afraid to say it. Some are too afraid to think it. And the rest... well, they are onside anyway, aren't they Doctor?' Howard said his eyes piercing into Dr Morris's. Dr Morris sat back in his swivelling chair and twiddled his pen.

'Well, Howard...' he said with a smirk. 'I'd like to be able to argue with you there, but I might have a tough job on my hands.' Dr Morris continued to smile nervously. 'The thing is, Howard... I can see why you might think that, er, George Bush is the Antichrist. I mean, he's certainly a controversial figure and I can sympathise with your dislike for the man. I'm not particularly a big fan of him myself, but surely you can see that he's just a man, Howard, like you and I? He has no special powers, other than the power of politics and his role as the President of the United States. Do you see what I'm getting at, Howard?'

'Very good speech, Doctor, very good.' Howard gave a little round of applause as he spoke. 'That's just the line I thought you might take, Doctor. But well done, anyway. Very protective of you.'

'Oh, come on, Howard, really. You can't think that I am in any way connected to George bloody Bush. I mean, think about it,' Dr Morris said, almost outraged. Howard raised his eyebrows slightly, but his stare remained transfixed on Dr Morris.

'Okay, okay, Howard. So if he, George Bush, is the Antichrist, then by definition that makes you...?' Howard's expression remained unchanged. 'Howard, do you realise what a psychological cliché it is for you to think that you are Jesus Christ? I mean, it's classic stuff, isn't it? Look, you're an intelligent lad, can't you see the logic? Can't you see that this is textbook? Don't you see how ridiculous it actually is, when you think about it rationally?'

'Why is it, Doctor? What's so ridiculous about it?' Howard replied. Dr Morris was momentarily lost for words, his hands extended out to Howard in appeal.

'It's just... I mean, come on, Howard. Surely you can see that, surely part of you recognises the absurdity of it? I mean, why you?'

'Why not me, Doctor?' Howard said calmly. Dr Morris leaned forward and placed an elbow on the desk. He began rubbing his eyes with his middle finger and his thumb, before placing his palm flat against his forehead and gripping his smooth head with his large fingers. He opened his mouth to speak, but no words came out. He placed his index finger diagonally across his lips and looked at Howard with a desperate desire to reach the young man that sat before him. He shook his head slowly.

'Okay, Howard,' he said with a sigh. 'When did you realise this, er... when did you realise that you were Jesus Christ and that you were sent here to, erm, defeat the Antichrist... George Bush?' Dr Morris spoke softly, his voice low and measured.

'I was lying in bed and, erm, I was sort of surfing women, you know... and, erm, I got really taken in by this woman. I don't know who she was, but she was really strong and powerful with it. She began to take full control of my body and then even got into my mind. She wasn't normal. I mean, she wasn't like a lot of the others; she was really good and seemed to tune into me properly. Anyway, so it gets to the point, like, she's really on top of me, you know, really in the room and I can't seem to move. I get a bit uncomfortable with this, as it seems like she has full control of the situation and I am seeing with her mind. She laughs a lot, but not in a good way. You know, it's disturbing and she's wild, like really crazy.' Dr Morris seemed to half switch off as he listened to Howard. He rested his pen down on the desk.

'So she's riding away and it suddenly seems to be all about her and as though I'm not in control anymore, or we're not sharing control, you know. All I can hear in my head is her laughing. And I realise that I can't move a muscle and that she has gained control of me. Suddenly, I start seeing all the roof tops of the houses around the house and then even further, like right across London. Then I start to hear this breathing sound and the sound of thick-heeled boots hitting concrete and sliding on tiles, you know, on roof tops. I start to realise that she's tuning in on someone else.

'There's someone on the rooftops. Someone is running across roof tops and jumping from roof to roof. I can see what they're seeing, it's dark and cold and the sky is an open panorama above them, black and vast, dotted with thousands of stars. The moon is bright and full and it lights the way for this leaping freak. I look down and see that this creature has woman's hands, old and wrinkly. She has on a long sort of black dress thing, made of like sack material, and there's a sort of cape thing at the back. It's all sort of puffy and baggy. I look down at her running feet and she has these long, old-fashioned lace-up boots with a thick sole and a chunky heel. She's running and then she stops and listens. She's trying to work out where I am, which house. She's miles away, but man can she shift some. She's travelling across London, over the roofs.

I'm talkin' about huge, fucking leaps. I can't see her face though, 'cos I'm seeing through her eyes. She keeps running and jumping, and then stopping and listening out for the other woman's laughter and the sexual moans she's making. When she senses where it's coming from, she starts peggin' it in my direction. I can feel her getting closer and closer. Her breathing is heavy and she makes these weird old woman noises as she scrambles from building to building. I realise she's coming for me, that she's gonna take the place of the other woman, but for real. I can see that my window's open, but I can't get up to close it. I can't move and the other woman is just writhing around on top of me.

'I sense that she's really close, I think she's on the next roof top. The other woman tunes into her fully and just keeps me in check. I see the woman's mind rushing through the window and across the street to the roof opposite mine. The woman's mind speeds towards this figure, huddled over, dressed in black, hanging onto a chimney. As the woman's mind rushes towards her at a hundred miles an hour, the figure turns around slowly and my face rushes towards her. She has long grey hair tied back in a ponytail, and the hood of her cape is bunched up behind her head. She is about ninety years old. She is a like an old prune, with a huge nose and hairs sprouting out of her face. She's fucking hideous, man. Her eyes are deep green and really beady.

'She zooms in on where I am and I know she's coming across for me. I see her run and jump towards my roof top and I hear the thud and the scraping of boots against my roof. I can hear her slowly sliding down the roof, bit by bit. I frantically try to move, but I can't. I know pretty soon she's gonna be coming through the window and she's gonna be the one actually mounting me and then I am bang in trouble. I close my eyes and try and move, try and push this other woman off me, but I can't. I open my eyes and the old hag is standing at the end of my bed. She's taken off her black sack clothing and all she has on is this filthy old nightdress, just white and grubby with some childish pattern on it, My Little Pony or something.'

Dr Morris nodded as though he was listening. He was half staring at Howard's notes, but half into space at the same time.

'So, she starts moving towards me and puts her arms out in front of her. I don't know what to do, as I know she's about to climb onto the bed. I close my eyes in desperation and start to beg God for this not to happen. All of a sudden, I'm thrown out of bed and down onto the floor on my knees. I try to look up, but my head is forced forward. Then my whole body is physically forced down, so that my nose is against the floor and my hands are out before me. I hear a voice and, shit, do I know it's God's. I try to raise my head and speak, but my voice is taken and my whole body is pushed flat against the floor, while I'm still on my knees. My face is squashed up against the floor, really hard like. Then, God's voice is everywhere. I can feel it vibrate through my whole body. I mean, every blood cell to the marrow of every bone, in every hair on my body.' Dr Morris had tuned back into what Howard was saying.

'What did God say to you, Howard?' he said with some interest.

'He said "fear me",' Howard said with trepidation.

'Was that it, Howard?'

'No, then I tried to speak to him, to speak my mind, but he commanded me to fear him and I did. I feared him the way you fear something that could simply annihilate you in a millisecond. I'm talkin' like destroy every last bit of ya, down to your DNA, the lot. I had no choice in the matter. Then he sent me my orders. He told me to live as they do.'

'Who's *they*, Howard?'

'The sinners, Doctor. He told me to live as they do. Assimilate and become one with them and do well. He told me I have to get close to the Antichrist. I have to become an inside member of his inner circle and then wait for my moment. He must believe that I am his closest aid and then, at the very moment he turns to me for ultimate sustenance, the moment when he is about to take earth and the ultimate glory to overthrow God and the kingdom of heaven, then I make my move. I will reveal myself to him and destroy him like a toy, at the very moment that he thinks victory is his. Then I will execute him, like a stuck pig before the eyes of the world.' Howard's words and pronunciation had become very exact and mannered. The venom in his voice was palpable; his physical presence seemed to grow as he spoke.

'Now look, Howard, I'm not sure you realise just how serious what you're saying is. You are talking about killing the president of the United States. Now, I know that you may feel passionately about it, but you have to – you must – understand the fact that you simply cannot go around slaughtering people like pigs. It's just not on, do you hear me? Murder is a very serious thing, and murdering world leaders is an even more serious threat to make. Now, I'm fairly confident that you're not going to murder George Bush are you, Howard? But all this talk of killing anyone is against the law. It's wrong, do you hear me, Howard? Wrong, and if you continue to talk like that you're going to be back on a section before you can blink, and you know what that's like. I think we can both agree that it's not exactly a lot of fun now, is it?' Howard didn't move a hair; he just sat and glowered at Dr Morris, who had placed both hands flatly on the desk and had straightened his posture to reveal just what a large and well-built man he was compared to Howard. Howard's body language was unyielding.

'This is not about sectioning and all that petty little shit you talk about, Doctor. This is about the fate of mankind and the battle to save souls. I know you think that...' Dr Morris cut Howard off in mid-sentence:

'HOWARD!' he boomed. 'That's exactly what this is about. This is about whether or not *I* think that *you* are a danger to yourself and others, Howard. It is about whether you are deemed fit for social interaction or not. Whether you like it or not, it is precisely about whether you walk out of the front door or whether I have you sectioned for three months.' A menacing look had spread across Dr Morris's face. The veins in his neck and temples were protruding to bursting point. The colour in his face had gone from scarlet to purple.

'Yes, Doctor, I know it's about whether I am at liberty or not. I know it's about whether I'm "fit" for society or not. I know it's about you determining whether my values or my thoughts are considered "government approved", or "medically sound", and I am also telling you, quite categorically, that it is about whether Satan has his way with humanity or not. But I think it's quite clear which side of that divide you come down on, isn't it, Dr Morris?'

Howard saw, in Dr Morris's eyes, Dr Morris striking him. Dr Morris saw Howard see this. He also made sure that Howard saw it a second time before he stood up and walked over to the window and looked out at the extensive grass grounds of the hospital. Howard sat back in his chair without looking at Dr Morris. Dr Morris began fiddling with the end of one of the spider plants that was perched on the window sill. He crushed away the dead brown end of a leaf and watched it turn to a powdery dust that slowly floated down to the tawdry carpet. He examined his fingers and thumb, rubbing away the remnant of the dead plant.

'You know, Howard, you're only making it difficult for yourself. I think you know that, anyway,' he said evenly.

'Is that what you think, Doctor? That I say these things to be difficult?'

'Do you really believe that you are Jesus, Howard? Really, in your heart? Do you truly believe that butchering a prat like George Bush is going to save humanity?' Dr Morris turned to face Howard; he sat slightly perched on the window sill, his right leg crossed over his left, his arms folded. Howard folded his arms too, but did not look at Dr Morris. He focused his attention on the pen on Dr Morris's desk instead.

'I mean, Howard, do you really think that all that crap applies in this day and age? It's two thousand and eight, Howard. Do you not find it a bit archaic, the notion that Christ will return and save humanity? I thought you were a man of science, Howard. You spout off about evolution and all that. Isn't that a bit of a contradiction?'

'That's exactly the line I thought you'd come at me from, Doctor, the cool rational scientific approach. It took you longer than I thought, but you finally got there,' Howard said steadily.

'Do you know how many people come through institutions like this one saying the same things that you do, Howard?'

'One hundred and eighty point seven annually,' Howard said derisively. Dr Morris gave a brief smile.

'Oh, I think more than that, Howard. Worldwide, over the years, I'm pretty sure of that. But of course, the stuff that you say just happens to be the truth, doesn't it? By some great miraculous stroke of events you, Howard

Jones, actually happen to be the return of Christ come to save us all from great evil. How wonderful. How simply divine, excuse the pun.'

'You can mock all you want, Doctor...'

'Yes, yes I know, you'll turn the other cheek,' Dr Morris interpolated acerbically.

'Fuck you, Doctor. No pun intended.'

'My, my, such filthy language from the anointed one. That will never do now, will it?'

'Your misconceptions are hysterical, Doctor.'

'Really, and what have you been reading lately, Howard? The *Da Vinci Code*? Decided it was you, did you? Are you Jesus' long-lost offspring? Is that it?'

'Yeah, that's exactly it, Doctor. You hit the nail right on the head, there. Well done, give yourself a round of applause, ten out of ten for originality.' Dr Morris stooped, his head in a mock stage bow.

'Well, Mr Jones, we've pretty much come to the end of today's session. But let me just say this, Howard. I'm letting you walk out of that door simply because I don't believe that you believe that you are Christ, or that you have to kill George Bush either. However, if you do carry on playing these silly games with me and arsing around with these stupid mind games yourself, you may well find yourself in more hot water than I care to mention, mark my words. I want you to think long and hard about the things you've been saying and whether you think that what you've been telling me is one, rational and two, right, I mean morally right. Do you think that the answer to things is to kill people? Because I don't think you do. In fact, I'm counting on it.'

SESSION SIXTEEN

Howard crossed the road and stepped onto the pavement, making his way towards the driveway that led into the hospital grounds. As he approached the drive, something above him caught his eye. He looked up to see what it was. Hanging from the wire, connected to two telegraph poles that ran across the road, was a brand new pair of Adidas trainers. The laces of the trainers were tied together and suspended the spanking-new footwear almost directly in the middle of the wire above the road. Howard stopped in his tracks and paused momentarily in awe. He shook his head, then threw it back in laughter. He turned into the drive and walked towards the hospital.

'Right, Howard, now last time we had quite a frank little chat, didn't we? So have you thought a bit about what we discussed last time? I really hope you have.' Howard's stare said it all; it was stern and unflinching.

'Have you been taking your medication?'

'Yeah,' Howard said coarsely.

'And do you feel it has helped you at all? Do you feel less angry, less pugnacious, less like killing anybody perhaps?' Dr Morris said. Howard scowled and tried to look through the window, but was unable to glimpse anything of interest from the angle that he was positioned in, only passing clouds.

'Come on, Howard, you've got to talk about it. It's no good bottling it all up inside, is it now?'

'What's the fucking point of telling you anyway?'

'What do you mean by that, Howard?'

'Well, you know, nothing I say is what you wanna hear is it, Doctor?' Howard said. Dr Morris cleared his throat.

'Come on Howard, you know it's not about what I want to hear, is it? We're not here to discuss what *I* want to hear. It's about you expressing what's been going on in your mind and us discussing some of these thoughts, and maybe coming to some conclusions about those thoughts and ideas.' Howard folded his arms, shook his head slowly and chuckled quietly to himself.

'So tell me, what's been going through your mind since the last little conversation we had? Are you still determined to kill Mr Bush? Is that it?'

'That's none of your business.'

'Oh, I think you'll find that it's very much my business, Howard. And I'm not going to let it go, either. We will discuss this and work something out, because that route will get you nowhere. In fact, it will get you somewhere very much worse than nowhere. I have to help you with this, Howard. But more than that, you have to help yourself with it, because this particular road is one that I don't want to see you travel. Am I making myself understood, Howard? Am I getting through to you?' Dr Morris searched Howard's eyes for a response, for some glimmer of understanding, for some sort of connection. Howard avoided eye contact, his gaze shifted nervously from side to side, only acknowledging Dr Morris's face momentarily before quickly darting away to something else, anything else.

'So, come on Howard, have you still been considering hurting anyone, anyone at all?' Dr Morris said gently, with concern.

'No,' Howard replied in a muffled voice.

'Are you sure, Howard? It's important... I can't convey to you enough how important it is.'

'NO, ALRIGHT!' Howard exclaimed in annoyance.

'Okay, okay, no need to get irate. I'm just making sure, okay?' Dr Morris said. Howard sat forward and put his hand to his forehead, which he rubbed anxiously while staring intensely at the floor.

'Well, do you still think you're Jesus, Howard?' Howard clenched his teeth. 'Eh, Howard? Do you still think that this is about the apocalypse and all that?' Howard turned his head to one side, as if he couldn't bear to look at Dr Morris, as if Dr Morris's presence was almost intolerable.

'Come on Howard, it's not that bad, is it?' Dr Morris said almost with amusement. Howard turned and faced Dr Morris. As he did so, he stroked both cheeks as though he were examining his face for rogue hairs or pimples, despite the absence of both. His look was half childlike, half wild animal. He sat hunched forward as though he had been struck in the stomach, or as though he might be sick.

'No, it's not that bad,' he said in a semi-whisper.

'Good, good,' Dr Morris said triumphantly.

'I can't help it if you don't see things the same way that I do, can I?' Howard mumbled.

'No, I suppose not, Howard. But we're not here to see things the same way, are we, Howard? Not exactly.'

'Are we not, Doctor?' Howard replied cynically.

'No Howard, far from it.'

'What are we here for then, Doctor? What's the point of all this then?'

'Well, I suppose it's about the way in which you view certain things. Certain things that affect your behaviour and the things that you say to people sometimes, Howard.'

'Such as?'

'Well, for example, you telling me that you have to murder George Bush and that you are Jesus Christ. Things like that, Howard.'

'I never told you I was Jesus Christ, Doctor.'

'Perhaps not, but you inferred it, didn't you?'

'Did I?'

'Yes, Howard, you did,' Dr Morris insisted.

'You came to the conclusion, Doctor.'

'Yes, I came to the conclusion because of the rest of the rub... the rest of the stuff you had told me, Howard. It was not exactly an enormous leap to make, was it now?' Dr Morris said. Howard smirked to himself.

'Perhaps,' he said. 'Anyway, who says I'm not?'

'Oh come on, Howard, we're not back to that are we?'

'Well, you know, Doctor.'

'No, Howard, I don't know. Why the bloody hell would you be Jesus bloomin' Christ?'

'Like I said, why not?'

'Look, Howard, I'm not getting into that with you, alright?'

'Well, that's up to you, Doctor. If you have a hard time accepting certain things then that's your tough shit, isn't it?'

'It's not about *me* accepting certain things, Howard, is it really? It's very much about *you* accepting certain things, certain things such as the fact that you are not Jesus Christ. George Bush is not the fucking Antichrist and that this is not bloody judgement day, *okay*?'

'I see, well I beg to differ, Doctor, I really do. I mean, take a look around you, the world, humanity, the whole shebang. It makes a lot more sense than you think.'

'Does it, Howard? Does it really?'

'Oh yeah, face facts, Doctor. Why don't you? Do you see reality creeping in?'

'What, reality according to Howard Jones?'

'Don't be like that, Doctor. Seriously, how could it be any different?'

'It could be... it *is* a lot different, Howard.'

'Is it Doctor? How is it? Tell me.'

'I told you, Howard, I'm not going to get into it with you, alright?'

'No, it's not alright. Isn't it your job to tell me how it is, Doctor? Just what the hell is going on out there on the magic merry-go-round?'

'As I said, Howard, I'm not getting into it, *okay*?'

'What's wrong, Doc? Can't face the music? Can't face the truth, eh?'

'It's not that at all, Howard, I can assure you.'

'What is it then, eh Doc? What don't you want to get into?'

'You know full well what I mean, Howard. It goes no further.'

'Why won't you enter into a discussion about reality with me, Doctor? What are you afraid of?'

'It's not that I'm afraid, Howard, believe you me. It's that I don't want to influence you. I don't want to project my views onto you. I want you to come to terms with your own views.'

'That's bullshit, Doctor, and you know it. You project your views onto me every time you open your mouth. You just don't want to do it in a straightforward fashion. You want to do it through the techniques they taught you at psychology school, the professional way. You want to bring me round to your way of thinking, to your conclusion of me, by the time we finish this crap. You want me to walk away better than I was when I came in here. You want me to come to terms with what's wrong with me. Would that make it right, Doctor? Would it?'

'What makes you think that that's what I'm trying to do, Howard?'

'You're trying to colonise my mind, that's what humans do, Doctor. You are a human, I take it?' Dr Morris surprised himself with the composure he was managing to maintain.

'There's no need to get personal, Howard,' he said forcing a smile.

'It's all fucking personal, Dr Morris.'

'That it may be, Howard, but that does not detract from the fact that you cannot come to terms with who you are. That may well be why you have adopted this alternative persona, this alter-ego of yours.'

'So you say, Doctor, but I say something very different.'

'Well, I think you'll find you're a lonely voice there, Howard. Not too many others would agree with you, I'm afraid to say.'

'But you said it anyway,' Howard said.

Dr Morris grinned. 'But I said it anyway, yes Howard.'

'Well maybe I'm a lonely voice, maybe I'm not. That's not really the point, is it Doctor?'

'Is it not, Howard? What is then?'

'It's about reality, Doctor.'

'And you're an expert on that are you, Howard?'

'It's about what you know and how.'

'What do you know, Howard?'

'How do you know what your name is, Doctor?' Dr Morris shook his head in resignation. 'What are you on about now, Howard?'

'Because someone told you.'

'Yes, Howard, my dear mother named me. So what?'

'Everything you know was told to you. Okay, so maybe you see some stuff yourself, that's what makes you who you are, it's your take on things, your interpretation. But how much of it was taught to you? Most of it, most of what you know is on the word of others.'

'How does that help you, Howard?'

'It doesn't, but it's closer to the truth or a reality than simply accepting the words of others. Therefore, you are asking me to help cure my delusions by deluding myself, by lying to myself and joining the big lie. Joining a consensus enables me to go against what I feel to be true. You want me to lie to myself to rejoin society and live a lie. How is that true, Doctor? How is that truthful? You want me to delude myself to cure myself of delusion. What kind of logic is that?' Dr Morris clasped his hands together and licked his bottom lip.

'How do you know this, Howard? Someone must have told you this, too. Bit by bit you pieced this together from what you have learnt. Don't you see? Who told you to believe this?'

'God,' Howard answered with authority.

'God?' Dr Morris said flatly.

'Yes Doctor, God.'

'Well, God can mean many things to many different people, Howard.'

'Don't skirt around the issue, Doctor.'

'I'm not skirting around the issue, Howard. I'm merely pointing something out.'

'You don't believe in God do you, Doctor? I can tell.'

'It's not about whether I believe in God or not, Howard.'

'Is it about whether *I* believe in God or not, Doctor?'

Dr Morris rubbed his temples briefly. 'Well, perhaps that's part of it, Howard. I'm really not sure.' Howard laughed for a moment.

'I realised that it is,' he said.

'Well then, maybe it is, Howard. When did you realise this, Howard?'

'When I realised the whole thing, the big picture. When I realised just what the hell was going on, when it all came to me,' Howard said. Dr Morris looked weary.

'What's that, Howard?' he said with mild dread in his voice.

'It's when you realise just how interrelated it all is. How everything's connected in a matrix, a web of infinite complexity. It's when you realise that every action, no matter how small, how seemingly insignificant, has repercussions that are endless. The reactions to your actions go on in a chain, or sequence of events, that is infinite. It's when you realise and understand that, just like the butterfly effect, what seems like a small and insignificant gesture on your part may well be responsible for the crashing of the Asian financial market or the bringing down of a civilisation in a galaxy far, far away. Or it may just piss someone off for ten minutes and ruin their morning. The point is, you just don't know. It's when you realise this fact, this obvious state of affairs, that you become very aware, very cautious of your every move, my friend. Except that you can't even do that, 'cos then you come to the conclusion that...'

Howard stopped short, as if struck by an idea. 'Wait a minute, every single action, every move I make, everything I say, feel, think, chemically produce, is actually only a reaction to some other set of actions equally set in motion by another set, that were in turn set in motion by yet another set of events and so on. It's then, my friend, that you become paralysed with fear. When you realise that it's all just a vicious cycle of cause and effect, effect and cause. From fuckin' Genesis to Armageddon, man, it's the wheel of fuckin' destiny, mate. That's what it is!'

'But how does this help you, Howard? In your life, I mean. How can you live with such a perspective?'

'That's all I fuckin' hear from you. How does all this help me? How does this make my life better? How can I live that way? The answer is, it doesn't, I can't, it doesn't fuckin' help me. It doesn't make things better. It makes things considerably worse, my friend. But the answer is that it's not there to fuckin' help me, it's not there to make things better, it's not about me… it just is. The sad and sorry fucking thing is, is that it just is.'

SESSION SEVENTEEN

'Look Howard, how can I explain it to you? The thing is that those religious parables served particular purposes. They give us – or, should I say, they gave us, or offered us – certain moral codes, a way of living. I don't think they were meant to be taken literally. The stories of Jonah and the whale, Noah's Ark and the others were merely fables created to guide us and structure our societies, our social groups. They are also, I might add, more than two thousand years old, some of them. Do you see where I'm coming from, Howard? Can you understand what I'm trying to relay to you?'

Howard smiled sardonically, as though he was gaining immense pleasure and amusement from Dr Morris's 'Introduction to the philosophy of religion 101'.

'Do you see,' continued Dr Morris, 'that in the twenty-first century such ancient and, dare I say it, primitive, belief systems can only operate or survive as a metaphor, as an allegory to illustrate the human condition.'

'Is that so, Doctor?'

'Yes. In the developed western world, we have moved far away from such apocalyptic and, frankly, hysterical world views. We have made considerable scientific advances in the last century or so and, as such, have simply overcome our superstitious instincts to a certain degree. We simply don't believe that stuff on the whole, Howard.'

'I think perhaps you're speaking for yourself, Doctor.'

'Well, yes, in a way I am. But I think I'm comfortable in saying that, certainly in this country, we are, generally speaking, firm atheists and have, by and large, put our faith in scientific discovery and invention. What I'm trying to say is that, generally speaking, science has circumvented such beliefs.'

'So they'd have us believe, Doctor,' Howard said. Dr Morris rolled his eyes in despair and frustration.

'Howard, this is not some ginormous conspiracy. This is quite simply the history of the western world for the last few hundred years.'

'Yeah, that's part of it, but it goes beyond that, Doctor.'

'Does it, Howard? Does it really?'

'Yes, Doctor, it does.' Dr Morris shrugged his shoulders and put his hands out to Howard in a semi-plea, unable to find the words to express his vexation. Howard sat forward and straightened his posture.

'You can see it in the prophesies of Nostradamus,' said Howard. 'I mean, I know a lot of that shit is questionable, written in cryptic verse in ye olde French, but a lot of it is worrying anyway. The Third World War that would last for twenty-five years. I know a lot of it reflects the fears of sixteenth-century France and the coming of the Muslim hordes. But look how it's panning out. It *is* the West versus Islam. I know they say it isn't, but it is being pushed that way. Nostradamus said "A man with a blue hat would come from the east and there would be a world war for twenty-five years". Look at the leader of India, Manmohan

Singh. His signature is his blue turban, it could be him. I'm telling ya, it's gonna really kick off between India and Pakistan. We're talkin' nuclear. The world is heading towards nuclear feudalism, Doctor! All this business in Iraq and Afghanistan, it's just the warm-up to the bigger conflict. Al Qaeda, nine-eleven, seven-seven and all that is just the start. Don't you find it strange that one of the holiest places on earth, as far as the Bible or the Torah and the Quran are concerned, is in total turmoil? Israel, or Palestine, the conquered land by the Israelites and the very place that Christ was born and supposedly walked the earth...' Howard smirked as he said the words. Dr Morris caught his eye and smiled back, almost with a sense of relief.

'The Israeli Palestinian conflict is the most volatile situation...' Howard continued, 'with the most implications on earth. What's more, it's the model for our future world as we're finding out now. You know, secure zones and guerrilla warfare. Civilians are the casualties; in fact, civilians are the currency. It's gonna be a war of attrition, low-intensity conflict. We live under a constant climate of fear, of insecurity. The problems of the world have come home to roost, for the part we've played and, I might add, continue to play – you know, we have to take notice now. Take a good look at Jerusalem, Doctor, at the Temple Mount, Al Aqsa and the Dome of the Rock where Adam was created, where Mohammed ascended to heaven and where the final conflict will kick off, brother against brother. And Iraq... shit, look at Iraq, it's the same. The original home of Abraham and the cradle of civilization according to science, you know, the birth place of writing, possibly agriculture. The garden of fucking Eden, man, and the Hanging Gardens of Babylon are in total disarray. Original sin has turned paradise on earth to hell on earth. Satan is running amok, and God is watching with great interest. The question is, Doctor, which side are you on? Which lord do you serve? Who is your master? Well, it's hell on earth, so Satan is doing his work well. The joke of it is that all those stupid fuckers who want it all now don't seem to get it. If the scriptures are true, if Armageddon is upon us, then surely they must get the end bit. It's no secret, is it? You know, God wins, Christ returns and fucks the Antichrist up. It's not hard to work out, is it? I mean, if you believe it then it's obvious which way you should go. But people are stupid, impatient and ignorant. The point is, if there is an omnipresent, all powerful God the way the great religions prophesise, then it's all part of God's plan. He's the boss, he is in ultimate control, so it's gonna work out the way he decides. And anyway, what's the difference between prophecy and destiny, or self-fulfilling prophecy? Either way the result is the same. Ultimately they are one and the same, and we, my friend, are fulfilling that criteria.' Dr Morris had begun chewing on his pen, his hazel brown eyes astutely studying Howard as he spoke. He patiently waited until he was sure Howard had finished his own, particular little lecture, before taking his turn.

'Howard, perhaps you should give people more credit. Perhaps they've simply worked out that the church, the great books, and all that stuff, are not the be all and end all of everything. Maybe they've thought about things more than you think and have come to their own, quite rational and logical, conclusions about things. I mean, come on, Nostradamus and all that – its poppycock, Howard, it really is.'

'Maybe it is, maybe it isn't. It's bizarre, though, isn't it? Some of the things he said and some of the things that have happened in history. He predicted the coming of three Antichrists, and Hitler was one of them.'

'I'm afraid that stuff just doesn't wash with me, Howard. It's not remotely convincing. It's just a way people sell books and get poor documentaries commissioned.' Howard looked slightly offended, but hid it as quickly as it had surfaced.

'Are you a complete atheist, Doctor?'

'Yes, Howard, I'm afraid I am. Does that bother you?'

'No, it doesn't bother me. I mean, what can I say, it's your funeral.' Dr Morris began massaging his neck gently, a semi-absent look in his eyes.

'Yes,' he said vaguely.

'Don't you think the world is in great turmoil, Doctor?' Howard said. Dr Morris slowly refocused his mind back into the room.

'Well, yes Howard, the world is in great turmoil, it always has been really. This is just another dirty little chapter in mankind's grubby existence,' said Dr Morris without thinking.

'I couldn't agree more with you, Doctor,' Howard said with interest. Dr Morris realised that he had been speaking far too freely, in a sort of auto-pilot mode.

'Of course, what I mean is that, erm… turmoil and conflict are part of life,' he said returning to his professional disposition. 'The problems that you speak of are simply a normal everyday part of how the world functions, Howard. It's not the great cataclysmic scenario that you seem to think is, erm, upon us, so to speak.'

'So you don't think we're at a different stage of human development? Different to any time we've been before?'

'Well, yes Howard, in a sense we are, but that doesn't automatically mean that this is the end of it all. You know, the big push if you like,' Dr Morris said, struggling to fully engage himself in the conversation.

'So you think this is just another day for mankind?' Howard seemed totally engrossed in the subject and had not picked up on Dr Morris's pensive participation.

'It's always just another day for mankind really, Howard.'

'Don't you see, that we're at a precipice in history? We're at the final hurdle, Doctor, and we're about to go arse over tit.'

'Are we, Howard?' Dr Morris said distantly, slipping back into his glassy-eyed expression.

'Of course we are, Doctor. I mean, look at us, humanity – what a fuckin' joke. Half of the world is starving, or being slaughtered like flies. You see it every day on the news – genocide, ethnic cleansing, war, disaster, poverty, disease, it's fucking endless. An endless stream of famine and pestilence. And what do the rest of us do? We sit and applaud ourselves like mechanical fucking sea lions. We're so happy with our petty little achievements. We live for the next games console, the latest trainers. We're obsessed with ourselves. Our banality fascinates us no end. Big Brother and reality TV, what a load of crap! We know we're going down the swanee and all we care about is gettin' pissed, gettin' high, avin' it and all that shit. You know, we're spiralling towards eco-catastrophe, our leaders run amok, corporations clean up left right and centre, tell us what to buy, what to wear, what to think. The media is one big self-lauding machine, one giant fucking pat on the back to itself, and we just take it. We sit in our little cells and insulate ourselves from reality. The last thing people wanna know about is the state of the world. They just wanna bury their heads in the sand, with their Pop Idol and being famous for fame's sake, it's sickening. Andy Warhol was so right when he said everybody will be famous for fifteen minutes. Everybody's a legend in their own lunchtime. All this bling and excessive wealth juxtaposed with the destitute and the hopeless. The winos in the park, the street children of Rio, it's all an obscenity. The affluent and their adoring admirers bask in the glory of their own making, while the hungry, destitute and damaged tread water or fucking drown. No one gives a fuck!' Dr Morris had begun to take notice again of what Howard was spewing at him.

'But lots of people care, Howard. People go on marches. People work hard in all sorts of jobs to try and make a difference. People still have hope.'

'Yeah, and what good does it do? Look at the march against the Iraq war. Did they give a shit? The politicians, I mean. Did they fuck. They knew they were gonna have their war. They gave the order and the troops went in, just like a thousand fucking years ago. Democracy is a joke, a great big bad joke. We can vote for Big Brother, we can text Dimbleby and tell him we don't want a war, but at the end of the day it doesn't mean a damn thing. They made their decisions behind closed doors and smile for the cameras. They're fucking actors, man. That's why Ronald Reagan was the most popular president ever, 'cos he knew where the cameras were and how to read a fuckin' autocue. You know, sort of! I mean, who votes nowadays? Forty or fifty per cent who give a shit about their mortgages and their ISAs. All the voters do is ratify decisions that are based upon economic criteria. The money men run the world and we nod and bow to their every whim; an economic prison. The system's got to the point where pulling the brakes might well derail us all. But we know that the train is heading for the end of the track at high speed. We are in a lot of fuckin' trouble, Doctor.' Dr Morris widened his eyes at Howard as if he'd just stuck his head out of the window of a moving train. As he pondered what to say next to appease Howard and his political rally, Howard reloaded and circled round for another bout.

'The great triumph of western civilisation is in decay, just like the Holy Roman empire, the Pharaohs, the Venetians, the Byzantine empire and on and on. The party's over, man. I mean shit, look at it, it's not really any different to how it's always been. Starving masses, wars, empires, and we, the children of the empire, what do we do? We go out and eat, drink and be merry for tomorrow we die. You got kids killing kids, rapin' kids terrorising neighbourhoods, while the security forces of the empire chase them around council estates in helicopters. Sodom and fuckin' Gomorrah, man.' Dr Morris shifted uneasily in his chair. He went to hold his chin, but cancelled the movement at the last moment.

'Yes, well Howard, that's erm... that's quite a picture you paint there, erm... I suppose it's a matter of perspective, Howard.'

'PERSPECTIVE MY ARSE, DOCTOR!' Howard bellowed.

'Now, Howard, that's enough. I won't tell you again. You do not shout at me, okay? They do not pay me enough for you to sit there and simply abuse me. Is that understood?' Howard hunched forward, raised his finger and wagged it as he spoke:

'We have reached a new stage of capitalism,' he said, much more softly. 'Beyond high capitalism, beyond anything Marx predicted. We have reached the point where content is irrelevant – it's all about how you look, being seen. It doesn't matter if you go home and rot at the end of the day, just live to consume and perpetuate your image. Doctor, once beauty products were largely sold on the basis of keeping women insecure, but now its men too. It's everyone, everyone living for the

213

image, the look. These images of celebrities enhanced by all that technology can offer are blazed into our subconscious, eating away at the back of our minds. And when the products pop up we instantly respond "yes, that's the answer, that'll stop this sad empty insecure feeling I have in the pit of my stomach". The young ones are the worst, they don't know anything else, or any other time. It's just second nature to them. The next best thing – consume it, consume it, consume it!'

'Are you against capitalism, Howard?' Dr Morris said tentatively.

'Well, yeah, but it's more than that. Capitalism, socialism, the problem is human organisation, human corruption, humans capitalising on other human beings. In a way it's not the systems – I mean, I guess I'm a sort of socialist, but look at how that can be if it goes wrong, if it's deceitful. That's it really; the systems are not fundamentally the problem. The problem is people's greed; the way we run these systems is inequitable and elitist. Humans are ultimately grotesque elitists.' It was Dr Morris's turn to sit forward and disgorge his thoughts on the matter.

'But Howard, people are also kind, generous, helpful, and friendly. Go out into the street – people are getting on with it. They're smiling, they're shopping and having coffee, they're taking their kids to school, they're living life with all its ups and downs. For the most part that is what life is: saying good morning, going to work, communicating, getting by, forming relationships. All the stuff that you see going on every day – that's the norm, Howard, generally speaking.'

'And drinking themselves into a stupor, robbing, raping, killing…' Howard said with disdain.

'All that too, but that's life Howard. That's what it's all about. The glass isn't only half empty, it's also half full,' Dr Morris replied, swiftly and with vigour. 'We are also incredibly creative, resilient, unique – human, in fact. We have created whole bloody civilisations, Howard. We are actually quite a phenomenal species,' he continued driving his point home.

'That's the paradox though, Doctor, of humans. We're so fucking clever. Look at what we've achieved. Look how far we've come. Spaceflight, world domination, sophisticated art, technological breakthroughs, yet we are so stupid. We can even predict how things might go. I mean, it's catastrophically wrong, but we can't fuckin' stop it. We can't give it up and make it work. We're so sophisticated, so truly amazing and yet ultimately we're dumb, bald, idiot monkeys who can't leave the law of the jungle behind us. We can conceive of utopia, but we can't make it materialise, not even close,' Howard remonstrated with exasperation.

Dr Morris was beginning to feel the weight of Howard's words. He could feel himself slipping into Howard's little melancholy bubble. Something was gradually resonating in the depths of Dr Morris's psyche, a mood that he violently compressed to the back of his mind with the determination that this little prick would not undermine his wellbeing with his insalubrious diatribes.

'Well, Howard, maybe that's the long and short of it, eh? Perhaps there's just nothing we can do about it all,' he responded curtly.

'Do me a favour, Doctor. You know, we can give full extensive coverage of famines and massacres. We can organise detailed round-the-clock footage and in-depth journalism, UN investigation, government observers and all of that crap. We can afford to film human beings slipping in and out of death and show their corpses when they're gone. Yes, we can supply all that and more, piped direct into your living room. Infotainment for all, up-to-the-minute images beamed into our subconscious. We can do all that, we can arrange it all with such great quality and speed on a daily basis, yet we can't do anything about it all? We can't stop that shit happening? Leave it out, Doctor. We are a perverse, twisted, evil species, Doctor. We are Satan's little minions. It's our fault, all of us. We all say "it's not my fault, what can I do?" We turn a blind eye and let it continue. If it was our family, our friends, or us, we'd wanna do somethin' about it. As long as it's not us, Doctor, as long as it's not us.' Dr Morris had succumbed to the nauseating gloominess that Howard had subjected him to. He didn't show it, but he could feel his whole day slipping into an abyss of unbridled contempt and dissatisfaction. The usual fire in his belly was beaten and kicked until it remained extinguishing in the pit of his bowls like a breeze block in a bin liner.

'Well, Howard,' he said irately. 'Your take on humanity is a lot like some of the adjectives you've used to describe "us" frankly,' he went on.

'My my,' Howard remarked.

'Well, as you're so interested in telling it like it is, I thought I'd join you in my expression of how I see your little tirades. I mean, basically you should be thankful that you live in a society that allows you the freedoms that it does. You should be grateful for the fact that, rather than being locked in some hovel for your grievances and your ill-health, you are afforded this humble, but nonetheless adequate establishment. That you have a roof over your head and change in your pocket because, as you so eloquently pointed out, there are literally millions out there who do not have such luxuries lavished upon them. I think that you should show some regard for the freedoms that nameless men and women lost to history, who fought valiantly and hard so the likes of you – and I, I might add – can sit here and pontificate on the nature and essence of it all in comfort and relative safety…'

'Speak for yourself,' Howard interjected.

'You know what I mean, Howard,' Dr Morris said, rekindling slightly the rage that he held in the depths of his guts. 'The western world has many faults, Howard, many I agree, but it is also a bastion of culture and sophistication, whether you like it or not. It's a sanctuary of bloody security in an otherwise turbulent and belligerent world and you should thank your lucky stars that you have the privilege of residing in it!' Howard scowled at Dr Morris and offered nothing but derision:

'Western civilisation is a dead and hollow, twisted, spiteful…' Howard struggled to find the words through his acrimonious resentment. 'It is a husk of depravity,' he said, recapturing the surge of his verbal torrent. 'It operates on humiliation and shallow imagery, poses of pointless and degrading mockery. It laughs at itself, but not really. It is like the end of the ultimate Roman orgy, with the fat, gorged and the fucked senseless lying around making banal comments in a slurring stupor of fruitless vulgarity and decadence. It is the last sigh of a hopeless emperor who has raped and pillaged his own royal court and is looking around in disgust at his own putrid trail of destruction. Then it snaps its fingers and demands that it happen all over again.' Howard ranted almost as though he were consumed by demonic possession.

'When did you become filled with such rancour, Howard?' said Dr Morris. Howard looked confused, as if he didn't understand the question.

'Such malice, Howard, such bitterness and resentment. Where did it all come from?' continued Dr Morris with genuine incredulity. Howard eyeballed Dr Morris for a moment before responding to his question:

'Sartre said… I think it was Sartre, or was it Oscar Wilde? Fuck knows, anyway he said "Hell is other people." How right he was, and that's the truth of it. We are each other's biggest problem, which ultimately means we are, as individuals, to blame. As a species we are our own worst enemy. Fuck me.'

SESSION EIGHTEEN

Howard walked across to the seating area of the reception and sat down. Opposite him sat an absolutely huge black man. The man could have been anything from his late thirties to his early fifties, it was not easy to discern. Howard glanced at him quickly before averting his eyes and concentrating his attention elsewhere. Seconds later, he began to sneak further looks at the man, who seemed to fascinate him. Bit by bit, stolen look by stolen look, he scrutinised the enormous man. The man's hair was stuck up and leaned over to the right. His afro was dishevelled and had flecks of grey throughout, especially towards the end of his curls. His face, however, made him look younger than his greying tresses suggested. His cheeks were chubby and fleshy and his skin, though shiny and healthy-looking overall, led down to large patches of white, dry and flaking skin around his mouth. He was not a particularly handsome man, but his facial appearance was pleasant, not unpleasing to the eye. His neck was divided into sections by an excess or rolls of flesh that were demarcated by lines darker than the rest of his complexion.

Howard scoped down and examined the man's attire. He was wearing a parachute of a blue, knitted, acrylic V-neck jumper, which was so big it hung off the giant of a man in a mass of baggy, surplus, acrylic sections, from his sleeves, his chest and down below his waist. The man wore the biggest pair of grey, man-made fibre slacks Howard had ever seen. They reminded him of a pair he had worn in school as a teenager, but only in style, certainly not in cut. Although the trousers were huge, they only just fitted the hulk that wore them. They would not fit over the man's buttocks properly and so the crotch was left as a vacuous pocket hanging down between the man's body and the seams that stitched the garment together. A long piece of string hanging between the man's legs led up towards the waist of his trousers, but disappeared under his circus top jumper.

His slacks scrunched up into fold upon fold around his ankles, and piled up over the battered and scruffy brown leather shoes that he wore. There were large tears and flaps of leather protruding out from the aged and worn footwear. They didn't seem to fit the man particularly well, either, and he had not or could not actually pull the heel of the shoes up and around the whole of each foot. The result was a pair of shoes with completely crushed and useless backs rendering them a rather crude and uncomfortable-looking pair of slippers. He wore no socks.

As the man took out a packet of prawn cocktail-flavoured crisps from an old plastic bag that had been resting on the seat next to him, Howard dared to look the man flush in the face. The man opened the crisps and began munching on them profusely; as he did so, he caught Howard staring at him and suddenly stopped chewing. Howard looked down at the floor quickly with minor consternation, before focusing on the man's gigantic hands, that gently held the packet of crisps in one and a single crisp in the other. They were scaly and gnarled, his nails long and filthy.

'Speak your mind,' the man said softly, kindly, as if giving Howard some friendly advice. His accent was broad and African of some sort. 'Or you lose your voice,' he continued. Howard looked up at the man, whose expression remained blank and emotionless. 'I'm tired now I've run out of things to say,' the man finished.

Howard wanted to say something, but nothing sprang to mind. The man's words reverberated through his brain. Before he could summon a reply, the man slowly stood up. He was, Howard thought, perhaps eight feet tall, maybe more, and must have weighed more than twenty stone. The man turned and gathered up the dirty plastic bag that he had produced the crisps from and leisurely shuffled away from the reception area and out of the front door, leaving behind him the strong aroma of body odour and a hint of the smell of urine.

Dr Morris and Howard sat opposite each other, separated by the large wooden desk that Howard's file lay upon, unopened.

'I mean, life is close to the bone, Doctor. It's a dirty business. You can't say it, especially not to each other, as that would give the game away.' Dr Morris sat unresponsive, statue-like, as though he were posing for a life drawing class.

'But when it comes down to it, it's pretty damn ruthless. I mean, on the streets of Bogotá or Freetown you know about it directly, but in the 'civilised' world we dress it up real good, real fancy, but fundamentally the brutality is the same. Dog eat dog, kill or be killed, survival of the fittest; there's not a great deal of variety about the matter. People screw each other over, wherever you are, fairly consistently.'

'If that's how you look at it, Howard,' Dr Morris responded.

'Well, it's not just how I look at it, Doctor, it's how it is. You know, life is an unfair business, people only give a damn about themselves really don't they, Doctor?'

'No, Howard, I don't think that's true, I really don't. We couldn't get by if that were the case. I don't think that's necessarily where the problem lies. I think perhaps it's part of it, but not the whole thing.'

'I'll tell you what the problem is, Doctor,' Howard declared. 'The problem is prejudice. People are prejudiced against one thing or another. It's part of the human condition. We are prone to it. I don't think we can help it. People never apply the same standards to themselves that they apply to others and the result is prejudice.'

'Are you prejudiced, Howard?' Dr Morris said sternly.

'Of course,' Howard replied.

'What or who are you prejudiced against, Howard?' Howard digested the question for a moment.

'Humanity, I think,' he eventually answered.

'So, you're a misanthrope, Howard?'

'I guess,' Howard said hesitantly.

'So, ultimately you hate yourself?' Dr Morris said. Howard cogitated over Dr Morris' suggestion.

'Maybe,' he said earnestly. 'Although, as I said, it's difficult for us to apply the same standards to ourselves. You know, we make excuses for ourselves or we'd top ourselves... sometimes it gets like that, doesn't it?' Howard's voice became softer, more pensive as he spoke.

'Yes, Howard, it can get like that sometimes, if you let it,' Dr Morris said. Howard had drifted slightly, his mind was elsewhere, though he still heard Dr Morris's words and took on board the gist of what he was saying.

'I'll tell you one thing, Doctor,' Howard said, returning his attention back to the conversation. 'When you die you find out what you really believe in. I found that out when my gran died. I mean, there's no second chance or a dressed rehearsal. You meet your maker head on and see into your own soul. You have to face your worst fears before you fall into the great void. That's what I was doing with the spider. I had a prelude to what was waiting for me. The shiny black eyes, all fuckin' eight of 'em man, the slimy venomous fangs, those jaws waiting to impale me and suck me back into the womb of existence, insides first. Just suck me out until I'm a twisted empty carcass. Just like the way life leaves us, an empty shell, a contorted bled corpse, all hollow-eyed and shrivelled.' Howard looked deep into Dr Morris's eyes with great sincerity.

'I mean it, man. If, deep down, you believe in... whatever. If you're a Catholic then you get a Catholic death. I don't care what it is, what you were brought up to believe, whatever they drilled into you, from birth man, all comes to a head when you die. That's why they say your whole life flashes before your eyes. It does, like a click of your fuckin' fingers, man. Bam... and it's over! Your whole life was a build-up to that deep, dark, fucking moment, man. And Christ do you know about it, it becomes all pervasive. It's suddenly all that matters. It pushes all other pressing engagements to the back of the fuckin' queue, man. It says "here I am... over." In seconds it's all over.'

Dr Morris broke eye contact with Howard momentarily. He glanced down at Howard's file before resuming the frank exchange of looks. His was anxious, but hardy.

'Sometimes, I think I died in that bathroom,' Howard said with a haunted look, his face ashen. 'Like some macabre Levis commercial. Sat in the bath in my jeans, carving knife in hand, bathwater stained red, a pool of claret and me... a contorted, pale, dead man, lying there... helpless, insignificant, of no consequence. Another stat for the home office. Just another suicide for the poor cunts who clean up afterwards like dung beetles. Sometimes I think I died and all this is the afterlife. Or, more likely, my last flickering moments that drag on indefinitely for me, but pass in a moment for those left behind. Maybe I'm in heaven? Or hell? If this place is anything to go by, then hell. Maybe purgatory? Maybe this is what it's like to be a ghost, like Bruce Willis in that fuckin' film, the one where he's dead but don't know it? Maybe I died and I just haven't got it yet. Maybe I never will? Maybe it's my punishment for killing myself?' Howard seemed lost. He stared into space with an ethereal expression of wonder across his face.

'I can assure you, Howard, you are still here. You're still very much alive,' Dr Morris said with a tender smile. Howard searched Dr Morris's eyes for assurance.

'How can you be so sure? What makes you so certain of all this, Doctor? The whole deal.'

'I'm not, Howard,' Dr Morris replied candidly, his usual cat-like stare unguarded and open. 'I'm not... I don't think anyone really is, Howard.' Howard quietly snorted, almost like the grunt of an injured animal.

'The problem with man, with humans, is that we need certainty. We need proof... proof of our faiths. We need to be sure of our own beliefs. We look for that which can confirm our desires and set us free from doubt. The problem with this is that there is no certainty, there are no promises. There is only doubt, only uncertainty. Of this I'm sure, Doctor,' Howard said with both conviction and apprehension.

'Well, perhaps that's the case, Howard, but maybe you don't have to dwell on it.' Dr Morris was fully back in his professional mode now. 'Why don't you try not thinking about it, Howard?' Howard looked at Dr Morris as if he were insane.

'The funny thing is, is whether God unleashes his wrath upon us and obliterates it all, or we do it ourselves, or a fuckin' great comet knocks us off our axis. It all amounts to the same thing. I mean, here on earth things will never be the same. The only thing that'll matter then is the afterlife. Whatever there is, whether there's one or not, is what'll count, or not as the case may be.' Dr Morris looked momentarily preoccupied, before addressing Howard:

'Yes, but Howard, shouldn't you be focusing on living rather than all this morbid fascination with death and the end of the world? Don't you see, that life is for living and enjoying oneself – as much as one can, anyway. I mean, I know it's a difficult old game, but if you don't enjoy the good bits then, well… the bad bits seem so much more relevant, so much more predominant.'

'So you think we should just ignore the shit that's going down in the world every single day, every single moment? Someone dies, Doctor, from preventable diseases, from unsanitary water, from fucking diarrhoea for God's sake, like all the fucking time. People are dropping dead from things that mean fuck all to us, Doctor. You know, if we get diarrhoea we just go down the shops and get some fucking tablets to bung us up. Half the damn planet is living under absolutely horrific conditions, I mean inhuman, and we want to just carry on like nothing's happening. We step over people in the street. If we hear someone scream in the night we roll over and hope that it goes away. They say if you're being attacked you're better off shouting fire 'cos otherwise no fucker'll come runnin'. I mean, think about it Doctor, what does that say about us as a species? It's ·fucking deplorable.' Howard's voice was becoming slightly hoarse.

'Yes, but Howard, don't you see? If you focus on all of this, all of the time, then you will simply go under. You can't take on the whole world all the time, Howard,' Dr Morris asserted with verve.

'I'm not taking on the whole world, Doctor. This is about the survival of the species, this is about the work of Satan, this is about saving your soul. Aren't you afraid for your soul, Doctor? Aren't you afraid to die? Of where you'll go, of what'll happen to you?'

'No, Howard. Well, you know, not particularly. I mean, I just don't think about it that much.' Dr Morris blinked rapidly and profusely as he spoke. He sat back and folded his arms. Howard stared at Dr Morris with disbelief, the blood pumping fiercely through his temples.

'You're telling me that you just don't see it? You've got all these qualifications, you're obviously well-educated, yet you are sitting there telling me that you can't work it all out?' Howard said challenging Dr Morris, daring him.

'See what, Howard?' Dr Morris replied coolly.

'You can't put the pieces together? You can't see how it all fits together, like a giant mosaic? The servitude, the enslavement, the drudgery – don't you feel it? Can't you feel the pressure of his darkness pressing down upon us with great force and severity? We are locked into a system of depravity, powered and propelled by great evil. Can't you feel the speed and intensity gaining momentum? The whole world has gone fuckin' mad, Doctor. Surely you can see that?'

'Look Howard... what you're experiencing is not satanic, erm... satanic domination or prevalence. You are merely living through great and interesting times. Indeed, I believe that that is actually traditionally a Chinese curse, forgive me if I'm wrong, but I believe it goes something like "May you live in interesting times".' Dr Morris laughed heartedly. Howard half smiled, but looked slightly disturbed.

'It is quite a normal response,' continued Dr Morris, 'for human beings to feel something frightening and sort of catastrophic about rapid and dramatic change in their societies. I mean, how do you think people who lived through the industrial revolution felt, or Mao's Cultural Revolution, the Third Reich? Take your pick, Howard. History is full of bizarre and troubling events. The people who lived through them for the most part didn't have a bloomin' clue what was happening. They were too busy going through it, putting up with it all to sit and wonder what the hell it was all about.'

'Yeah, but...' Howard began. Dr Morris gestured to Howard that he hadn't finished.

'So is it any wonder that you are one of the many that are baffled and confused, worried and distressed by it all? Your reaction is completely normal... in many ways, Howard. But to think that this is all part of some satanic plot to overthrow God is frankly ridiculous. I don't want to rain on your parade, Howard, or disregard your thoughts and feelings. I just want you to realise that, historically speaking,

this is not, erm, what do you call it...
Armageddon or whatever.' Howard opened his
mouth to speak, but Dr Morris overruled him
again:

'Take, for example, the catapult. I mean
those enormous great things, not the little Y-
shaped thing that Dennis the Menace had,' Dr
Morris said chuckling to himself. 'No, you know
those huge great ones that blasted holes in the
sides of castles and alike? Well, when they
were first invented people thought "My God,
this is it, this is the end of the bloody world.
We'll never live through this one. This is the
super weapon that'll destroy us all". And did it?'

'No,' Howard murmured.

'No, exactly. Take nuclear weapons –
now there's something that really is a threat to
mankind. You're still a bit young to remember it
all, but my generation remembers alright. We
grew up in the nuclear age, we remember the
Cold War well. And the generation before me,
well they're old enough to remember the
Cuban bloody missile crisis, for God's sake.
That really did nearly finish us all. But Howard,
we are all still here, are we not?' Howard
refused anymore contribution to the primary
school participation game.

'Do you see my point, Howard? It's quite
natural for each generation to think this is it,
when the going gets a bit rough and it all looks
a bit dicey. You know, now it's a giant
meteorite that's going to annihilate us all, or
terrorism, or whatever. The suicide rate
amongst populations very often goes up during
periods of accelerated change and social
upheaval. It's a natural fearful reaction,

Howard. But my advice to you is not to jump to conclusions, do not be too alarmed by it all. Just do your best to get better and have a good life. Do you see what I'm saying to you, Howard?' Howard sat back comfortably in his chair, crossed his legs and folded his arms.

'I see what you're getting at, Doctor, quite clearly,' he said with a knowing, an understanding.

'Good,' Dr Morris said gleefully.

'You want me to join in the big lie, Doctor,' Howard said forcefully. Dr Morris, realising his friendly advice set piece had not had the desired effect, let out a gasp of annoyance. 'You want me to get my head down, pull my neck in, right? You want me to tow the line don't you, Doctor? You want me to be a good little minion, a subordinate little slave, one of the faithful, one of Satan's little helpers, don't you Doctor?'

'No, no, no Howard!' Dr Morris exclaimed with frustration. 'I want you to see that things can be better if you just try, Howard.'

'Try what, Doctor!' Howard screeched venomously.

'IF YOU LISTEN, HOWARD!' Dr Morris roared. 'If you realise that you could help yourself. That you could make things so much better for yourself if you just bloody listened to what I'm saying to you, and if you trusted me a bit more.'

'You're a liar, Dr Morris. You're all liars!'

'We are not all liars... what do you mean, anyway? Who's "we"? I am the only one saying anything to you and I am not lying to you.' Dr Morris clasped his hands and placed them on the desk.

'It's all lies, Doctor. It's all deceit. Governments, corporations, relationships, social interaction. You gotta play the part, haven't you, Doctor? Do what's right, say what's right to get ahead, trick, lie, deceive, manipulate to succeed. Be it big or small, on a little or large basis, it's what we do, it's what humans are about. It's what life on earth is about. Chicanery is the name of the game, Dr Morris!'

Dr Morris banged his hand on the desk as though he were a primary school teacher trying to silence his class.

'No, Howard, it's not only like that. That's just not the only picture,' he insisted.

'It's like that in the animal kingdom,' returned Howard. 'You know, everything is feeding off everything else and people are no different from other life forms. They want power and to consolidate their control. They're like bacteria or ants. Given the chance they will conquer, control and colonise. That's how power structures work. They want to proliferate their particular view or kind. Doesn't matter what they think or what you think about it, good, bad or indifferent, they want to impose it on others one way or another; to control others. Whether it's just your point of view or occupying and exterminating, it's just the way things are. Given a chance, life will expand and take over where it can. It's simply part of its nature!' Howard had become slightly frantic and anxious as he blurted out the words. He began waving his arms about and looking around the room almost in desperation.

'Look Howard, calm down, alright?' Dr Morris said as he got up to physically pacify Howard. At this point, Howard looked terrified and disorientated, as though he wasn't quite sure where he was. Dr Morris held him in a bear hug as he writhed about.

'NURSE!' Dr Morris shouted.

'NURSE! Oh fuck!'

SESSION NINETEEN

'Well, Howard, what can I say? I hope to God you're not going to give us a scare like you did last week. That was pretty darn close, I can tell you. Any more antics like that and you may well find yourself back on a section.'

Howard showed no sign of response. The bedraggled state he had been allowing himself to fall into was beginning to culminate in the attire and appearance of someone living on the streets. His personal hygiene was poor and his normally neatly-gelled hair was matted and protruding in differing directions like a punk first thing in the morning.

'Now, I realise that the dosage of medication you're on now is similar to the amount it was when you first started, so I assume you'll be feeling drowsy and uncoordinated right now, but at least you'll be getting some rest. Sleep, as I've stressed to you before, is a great equaliser when it comes to battling your condition. It really does make quite a bit of difference. I'm sure you can vouch for that, eh Howard?' Howard rubbed his grotty nose like a ragged schoolboy, leaving smudged finger marks on his cheeks as he expanded his nasal massage into a full-blown facial rub.

'Well, I can tell from your appearance that you've been letting yourself go a little, haven't you? It doesn't bode well, Howard. You seemed to be doing so well not that long ago. You were always reasonably hygienic and well-presented. I know that the drugs will make it harder work for you to do some of the

234

mundane, day-to-day things that we normally do, but you really should try to keep it together, you know Howard. Discipline yourself a bit. Start with some light exercise and let that be the basis of your day. I promise you, you will feel much better again before you know it.'

'I don't feel like it,' Howard grunted.

'Well, we all have to do things we don't feel like doing, Howard, don't we?'

'Mmm,' Howard replied apathetically.

'What happened to the yoga? Didn't they teach you some yoga when you were a resident here?' Dr Morris said trying to inject some of his energy into Howard.

'Yeah... they did,' Howard answered vaguely.

'Well, you know it's very good for you, you know. A lot of patients have responded well to it and said how much better they feel after a good yoga session.'

'Yeah,' Howard offered unenthusiastically.

'Will you promise me you'll try to do at least one of the exercises they taught you every morning, or whenever it is you get up?' Howard mustered a nod, his eyes heavy and drowsy.

'So have you been keeping yourself busy at all, or...?' Dr Morris trailed off as Howard fell asleep in front of him, a thread of dribble hung from the corner of his mouth and rested itself surreptitiously on his collar.

SESSION TWENTY

Dr Morris left the usual meeting room and walked down the corridor, out into the reception area and across to the water cooler. He glanced over at the receptionist, who was multi-tasking between her in-depth study of a magazine taking her through the ten easy steps needed to make 'her and her man orgasm simultaneously' and the tricky job of applying nail hardener in an even stroke. She acknowledged Dr Morris with a front of house smile before resuming her duties with the upmost dedication. Dr Morris observed her as he pushed on the small black plastic tap and filled his plastic cup with water. He gave the receptionist, an attractive woman approaching her fifties, a friendly nod and a smile as he walked back across the reception area, up the corridor and back into the meeting room.

He sat down behind the desk, reached down and picked up his leather briefcase. He placed it on his lap and began rummaging around for his AZT medication, which he placed on the desk in front of him. He unscrewed the lid of the Zidovudine container and took the medication dutifully and without thought. He drank the rest of the water once he had consumed the pills, returned the medication hastily to his briefcase, which he placed back on the floor by his chair. Then he sat and waited patiently. Several minutes later, Howard knocked on the door and entered without waiting for a response.

'Ah, come in Howard!' Dr Morris said with great vitality and exuberance as Howard walked across the room and sat down opposite him. 'So, how are we today?'

Howard made himself comfortable. His face was puffy, as though he'd just got out of bed. His clothes were fairly dishevelled, but his hair was gelled in its usual conservative way.

'Yeah, I'm alright,' he replied gruffly.

'Good, glad to hear it. Have you been keeping busy at all?'

'So, so,' Howard replied brusquely. Dr Morris smiled.

'Well, what does that mean, Howard?' Howard paused for a moment, as though Dr Morris had asked him something quite ridiculous.

'What you on about?' Howard demanded aggressively. Dr Morris smiled again.

'It's quite a simple question really, Howard.'

'Is it?' Howard replied with little interest.

'Yes, Howard, it is,' Dr Morris said indignantly. 'It means expand on how you've been. It means converse with me, Howard. Is that so difficult?'

'Sometimes,' Howard retorted immediately.

'I see,' Dr Morris said almost to himself. Howard sat back, stretched his legs out in front of him, one crossed over the other, and put his hands behind his head as though he were on his sofa watching television. Dr Morris stared at him blankly for a few seconds.

'Well, I see you've already adjusted to the medication... you *have* been taking the medication, Howard?' he asked cautiously.

Howard pursed his lips and flicked his hair in defiance, rudely addressing Dr Morris:

'What do you think?' he asked.

'I think you should tell me whether you have or not,' Dr Morris said frankly and steadfastly. Howard thought for a moment, smiled, drew his legs back and sat forward obediently.

'Of course I have, Doctor. What do you think, I'm stupid or somethin'?'

'I didn't say that,' Dr Morris said, pleased at Howard's response. Howard beamed back another cheesy grin, his eyes scrunched up into two tiny slits.

'So, have you taken a rest from the world this week, Howard?'

'What do ya mean?'

'Have you been thinking about anything light-hearted or, dare I say it, jovial, this week at all, Howard?'

'Always,' Howard said ironically.

'Humour, that's good,' Dr Morris sparred back. 'Did you manage to do any yoga, Howard, or any exercise at all?'

'I went for a jog every morning, push-ups and aerobics at night, without fail, plus yoga, down dirty dog, walked the dragon and all that,' Howard said saluting Dr Morris and sitting up to attention.

'Very funny, Howard. But really, have you managed anything at all?'

'No, Doctor, it's a job just to get up and get here,' Howard admitted.

'Okay, well keep at it, you'll get there eventually. Little and often, Howard, little and often, that's the key'. Howard went through the motions of agreeing. He nodded his head and faked an enthusiastic face.

'So have you amended any of your views on humanity recently? Are we getting better coverage than last week, Howard?' Howard's expression shifted from amicable, almost playful, to broody and turbulent without a trace of transition or deliberation. Dr Morris realised his error instantly.

'Erm, well...' he stuttered looking for the right words to return the conversation to its previously blithe nature.

'We're cockaroaches, mang,' Howard said in his best Tony Montana accent.

'We're what? I'm sorry,' Dr Morris said without a clue as to Howard's reference.

'We are cockroaches, Doctor,' he said slowly and clearly.

'No, Howard, we are not cockroaches, we are human beings,' Dr Morris reacted irately.

'We are busy little bugs going about our busy little business,' Howard said with contempt.

'We are nothing like bugs, Howard. We have complicated sophisticated lives. We are not some mindless drove of insects who scratch around in the scrub for leftovers and the scraps of others. We are the most advanced life form on earth. Doesn't that mean anything to you?'

'We are parasites, Doctor,' Howard declared.

'Well, just how do you figure that one, Howard? I know we live off things, but everything does. What could you possibly mean by that?'

'I mean, if you pulled back from humanity, like way back, and magnified in so we're like under a microscope. If you pulled back and then magnified us, our behaviour. What we'd look like would be fuckin' ants, man, insects. If you could pull back far enough we'd look like germs, amoebas, bacteria; patterns would emerge. Patterns that we observe in micro life would apply to us, to all life on earth, in the fuckin' cosmos, man.' Howard had grown animated and excited. Dr Morris put his hand to his forehead and then began massaging his brow, back and forth, as Howard elaborated:

'I mean, we can't see it here. From here we can only see up or down. Things roughly our size seem different to us. If you pulled back as far as we are from insects or bacteria then we'd seem very similar, let me tell you. Our mass migrations, our famines, our wars, our cities, our creations would seem just as insignificant, just as fleeting. If you had a life form relative to us in size that we are to micro life as we observe it, they'd make similar decisions, come to similar conclusions that we do. Maybe they are, man, we simply don't know. It's too far out there for us to see, too big, man. I mean, do you think for one moment ants get the picture when we napalm them or pour boiling water down their fuckin' nest holes? Do they fuck! They just do what they can to survive it. They know they're under threat, they know they're affected, but they have no clue what the hell we're up to. When we make a seemingly insignificant gesture, such as spraying a nest with bug spray, we don't give it much thought. They're just a damn nuisance to us. To them it's the end of the fuckin' world, man. Imagine if some big hairy-arsed entity is spray buggin' us, or whatever. Some huge fuckin' creature is making decisions that affect our very existence, our very world, our solar system, our universe. What's to say that everything we perceive, our known universe, everything we're aware of is not just a droplet of fluid dripping off the forehead of some other life form, down off its shoulder and down the drain of some environment of theirs, or its? I mean, it's perfectly feasible that we are caught somewhere in the middle of some vast expanse that we simply cannot comprehend. And that, as we drip off the forehead of some other entity, it is about the same concern or consequence to that creature as our dripping sweat is to us.' Howard was waving his arms about as he spoke, staring in different directions as he emphasised each and every point. Dr Morris sat with his hand over his mouth, fascinated by both Howard's words and actions.

'Then, what if the smaller you get the same thing applies?' went on Howard. 'It's macrocosm and microcosm, man. There's always someone, something, somewhere bigger than you, and there's always someone, something, somewhere smaller than you. It's a seismic chain, possibly infinite in terms of time and space. Well, where the fuck does that leave all the bullshit that we humans have produced, all the bullshit we think we know and have known for the last hundred and fifty odd thousand years, or six thousand if you prefer the biblical approach? I'll tell you where, Doctor – about the same place as itsy bitsy fuckin' spider in the corner of some fucker's front room somewhere in Surbiton. Do you catch my drift, Doctor? Do you?'

Dr Morris rubbed his lips uncomfortably and was looking down at Howard's file. He declined to look up and make eye contact with Howard. Howard looked satisfied and sat back in his chair, the beating of his pulse so loud it sounded to him almost as if he were underwater. Dr Morris remained silent, stroking his lips.

'You know, Leonardo Da Vinci, he got it, man. He understood. You know, with the image of man on the wheel. His arms and legs circled at different points. Man is the centre of his universe…'

'I think that was something to do with artistic proportions, Howard,' Dr Morris interrupted quietly. Howard completely ignored him:

'You can go as far as you like in any direction – out or in, up or down, diagonally – and you get the same thing: infinity, it just keeps going. The only reason you can't understand infinity is because you, as an entity, do not last forever. If you did, you could travel in any direction you care to imagine, travel space inner and outer and all you'd find is more. It just keeps going. For example, once we perceived what we could see with the naked eye and that was all that was there. Okay, so our imaginations thought up demons and the paranormal – perhaps. Perhaps it's real and we just pick up on it intermittently. The truth is, we just don't know. Plenty think they do, but we simply don't. But apart from our minds, we measured what we could see, hear, smell and feel. We could only see what was in front of us, mountains, the sky and, down there, ants and bugs and shit. Then we developed new technologies that enabled us to see further. Further into the skies and further down there, and we discovered more and newer things that we had previously assumed were not there, and hence did not exist. It's like Brad Pitt in that film…'

Howard clicked his fingers desperately trying to remember the film.

'*Twelve Monkeys*!' he suddenly blurted. 'When he's talkin' about germs and how they were once an imaginary theory of some bloke, whose hypothesis guessed that they existed and that washing your hands before you treat patients makes a difference. Eventually, technology allowed us to see them, but at the time it was just a really mad idea! So now we're seeing whole new galaxies and sub-atomic particles that previously didn't exist. As far as we were concerned, they didn't exist and now all of a sudden they do.' Howard caught Dr Morris's eye. 'Well, maybe psychos and the likes of me are seeing things, are tuning into things that exist.' Dr Morris went to interrupt, but Howard continued.

'Once upon a time the likes of me were taken seriously. The fuckin' Ten Commandments were written by some guy who came down from the mountain. He heard

243

a voice and he wrote it down. Moses has and continues to be taken way more seriously than most fuckers who ever existed. Vast institutions and theories of thought have sprung from one man and people like him. If he were born today he'd be a care in the community case, medicated up, if he ever existed.' Howard ranted, his eyes wild and saucer-like.

'You're not going to tell me you're Moses now, are you, Howard?' Dr Morris jibed dryly, although with a hint of genuine concern.

'Why belittle the point, Doctor?' Howard complained, his eyes returning to their normal size.

'Because, Howard, you are allowing yourself to be carried away,' replied Dr Morris. 'You make A to C equations. You see things because you have damaged your brain with drugs. I can't make it any clearer to you than that. You are in this centre because you suffer from mental illness. You are not Moses coming down from the bloody mountain with tablets of stone. You are Howard Jones of London Town, you are twenty-six years of age and unemployed. You need to get a grip, Howard. So far, all I have heard from you is your lack of empathy with human beings, Howard. You seem to have no understanding of humanity, of what it is to be human.'

'I beg your pardon,' Howard said resentfully.

'Well, what the bloody hell do you expect, comparing us to cockroaches and bacteria,' Dr Morris said continuing his rebuke.

'I was merely making a proportional observation,' Howard countered defensively.

'Yes, and in doing so you lose your humanity. You forget what it is that makes us what we are.'

'And what are we, Doctor? Do tell,' Howard said sarcastically.

'We are homo sapiens, Howard. Human beings, remember those?' Dr Morris said, while Howard smirked and nodded slowly.

'We are way more animal than we care to admit,' he said. Dr Morris looked to the heavens briefly, his palms facing upwards in appeal. He sat back in his chair.

'We are animals, after all. Bald apes,' Howard insisted with a slight plea. 'I mean, we build things, great civilizations, spacecraft, computers, but ultimately we are just sophisticated animals. Most of our lofty ideals and thoughts, our precepts, our philosophies, our religions, our belief systems are basically the mental ramblings of some big-brained monkeys who like to chatter too much. Just as the monkeys in the jungle babble away to each other to make some kind of sense of their experiences of the world, so too do we.'

'Well, in a sense, Howard, yes we are monkeys – well, apes to be more precise. We are advanced primates, the most advanced primate the world has ever seen. We are quite unique in that respect, Howard, and there is a sizable gulf between us and our nearest relatives, you know, the chimps, I'm sure you'd agree.' Howard seized upon Dr Morris's participation in the debate:

'If you want to break it down even further, Doctor, if you want to get down to the nitty gritty of it, we are just biological entities composed of chemicals, chemicals that constantly interact with other chemicals. We are a composite of chemical elements that are part of a giant chemical soup. How we as chemical composites are stimulated by other chemical composites and interactions, and how we in turn stimulate other chemical gatherings and interactions, are the components that result in the sum as our experience. The experience we perceive as consciousness, as reality, is merely one giant fucking Petri dish of chemical reactions. I'm not saying that the experience isn't real. What I'm suggesting is it's as about true as... well, as whatever you like. That's my point – we need order, we crave it. We need to believe that we know what the hell is going on. Some kind of sense of it all; some kind of sense that there's some form of cohesive reality to which we belong. Without it we simply merge back into that chemical soup and disintegrate. Our mental picture simply melts away. We need to fabricate some logical or sensory perspective on it all in order to cope with it. The fact is, without the delusion of some form of security, security of faith, security of belief, we simply disappear, become one with it all again. Like we no longer exist as an individual, like we never did. We become one with the giant soup of chemicals and the ball of energy that keeps it charged. We are simply chemicals charged by electrical and magnetic energy. Everything – us, you name it – are just

246

vibrations of differing frequencies, or ultimately we are a vibration of energy, a sound, a noise.'

The room fell silent. Dr Morris looked exhausted. Howard had the look of a man who wasn't sure if he was actually present or not or, conversely, whether he was actually the only thing present at all. He simply couldn't tell which way the Esherism fell.

'Howard,' Dr Morris said, cutting through the stillness that had cloaked the room like a thin layer of early snow. 'Howard,' he repeated, to which Howard seemed to mentally return to the room, albeit with a somewhat lucent quality. 'You can deconstruct us all you like, the fact remains that you and I are both sitting here, two people in a room holding a conversation. Don't you relate with that? Doesn't that mean anything to you at all? I mean, not in the slightest?'

'Of course it does, Doctor,' Howard said, slowly opening and closing his eyes as if he were trying to squeeze some clarity into his eyeballs.

'Then why do you always drift off into the ether, Howard? Why won't you come back down to earth and try. Just make a start at dealing with reality and facing the world?' Howard blinked furiously as if he wasn't sure of the concept that Dr Morris had just laid out before him. He soon, however, regained his bearings.

'I am facing the world, Doctor. Quite frankly, it's you who has difficulty dealing with the truth. All you do is lecture me about how wrong I am about it all and how right your precious rationality is.'

247

'Well, it's a damn sight better than harking on about judgement day and all that religious clap trap,' Dr Morris said acerbically.

'So I should follow the great scientific ethos, should I?' Howard said caustically, returning the insult.

'Well, frankly, yes you bloody well should. I'm trying to help you here and all I get is religious mania and delusion.'

'Do you know how insulting that is to religion, Doctor?' Howard snapped. Dr Morris paused for a second. He rubbed his chin and gave Howard an equitable look.
'Look Howard, I'm not trying to deride religion,' he said back-pedalling. 'I just want you to see that you are mixing up delusion with religion and religious experience. I'm not denying spirituality. It seems that there two kinds of people, those that have spiritually and those that don't; those that seem to need it as a function in their lives and those that can get by without it. They now call it, erm... VMAT 2! The God gene. It's the loss of normal consciousness. Spirituality has a genetic basis, Howard, but you should also recognise the antiquated aspects of religion, the out-of-date perception of the world that it presents to us in the modern era. Surely you can see that the scientific ethos, as you put it, has surpassed religion in that sense and that religious beliefs of the ilk that you seem so fascinated by are just not feasible in this day and age, or even back then, for that matter.'

'Such religious beliefs were the science of their day, Doctor. They were probably the best fuckin' explanations of the time. Based on what we knew then, they possibly still are. My point is that science is the religion or the cult of its day. It maybe, maybe, the best explanation of things at the moment, or for the last few hundred years; but the fact is, that science, like religion or any other ideology or thought, requires belief. Fundamentally, science requires as much faith as any religion.' Dr Morris openly scoffed at Howard's notion, but Howard was not to be deterred.

'I don't mean old science. I don't mean advanced engineering. They were cutting edge once and, in many ways, still are, but they coexisted alongside religion as far back as you care to go; how do you think they built the fucking pyramids, man? What I mean is, the fundamental questions regarding human, animal, botanical and universal origins and existence are still unanswered, are still a matter of conjecture and speculation. Science is just another set of stabs in the dark about things that we really have no clue about. And that includes the science of psychology, Dr Morris. The human mind is an amazing thing, probably the centre of what we are. That's what Da Vinci was showing us. Man is the centre of his universe, stuck on the wheel of life. The Hindus and the Buddhists knew it two thousand years ago, while science is still trying to catch up with big bang theories, with string theories and alike. The truth is that reality is still just as it's always been, up for grabs.'

SESSION TWENTY-ONE

The buzzer to the front door rang once as though it had been leaned on by mistake. A moment passed and then it rang continuously, held down while its piercingly irritating sound echoed around the reception area. Howard looked over to the front door from the waiting section. His eyes squinted as he tried to see what creature was making the awful sound. He tried to see through the slim, rectangular, wire-meshed window, but there was no one in sight. The abominable noise continued. Howard looked to the reception desk to see where the receptionist had gone. Suddenly, the buzzing stopped. Then it began again, but this time intermittently and in a rhythm of some sort, as though it was an oversized electronic xylophone attempting to karaoke its way into the building. Howard's jaw clenched in response to the aural assault he was being subjected to.

Finally, he leapt up, unable to contain his annoyance any longer. He strode over to the door, glaring at the empty reception as he passed. He pressed the exit button and pulled open the door; there was nobody there, just an empty space and falling rain. He stared at a puddle gathering a couple of feet away from the door and was about to close the door when a girl's face appeared around the side of the door frame. She was a pale, chubby-faced thing aged about ten or eleven years old. Howard looked down at her without saying anything. She took a step to the side and stood right in front of him. She was dressed in a pink,

J-Lo style tracksuit that was covered in dark patches caused by the rain, while her oversized, flabby pot belly stuck out, pushing her tracksuit top up so that it hung off her shoulders as though it was too small for her.

'Any money for cancer?' she warbled in a thick North London accent, holding out a giant, tatty, sodden envelope. Howard stared at her blankly.

'What?' he demanded.

'Any money for cancer? We're collectin' money for cancer,' she said with a beaming smile, her eyes dull and expressionless. Howard thought for a moment before checking his pocket, only to find he had no change except his bus fare home.

'Er, sorry, I… erm, I ain't got no change, sorry love,' he said genuinely. The girl paused for a moment before skipping away. Howard closed the door and sat back down in the waiting area. The receptionist was still nowhere to be seen. The buzzer rang again continuously. Howard sighed angrily and went back to answer the door again. He jerked the door open and the buzzing ceased. A taller, slimmer, mixed-race girl of a similar age stood there in a pale blue, J-Lo style track suit, her hair neatly tied back in a ponytail.

'Any money for cancer?' she piped. Howard wanted to react aggressively, but stopped himself at the last minute.

'Er, no, sorry love,' he answered passively. The girl quickly ran away. Howard went back to his seat again. The buzzer rang yet again. Howard refused to move or even look at the door. The buzzing continued. He ignored it and checked to see if the receptionist was back to do her job yet. She wasn't. Eventually, Howard got up and walked towards the front door as the buzzing persisted. As he reached out to open the door, the buzzing suddenly stopped. He could see the two girls through the drizzle-soaked window. He slowly opened the door.

'Oi, mister, you got a plastic bag, 'cos our envelopes is all wet... look,' the chubby girl said, as the two of them held out their soaked envelopes.

'Er, no... I ain't got nuffin' on me,' Howard said, looking back at the reception area for assistance, but to no avail. The two girls ran up the path and across the grounds, giggling as they went. Howard stood looking out at the rain-drenched trees in the distance.

Dr Morris sat back, crossed his legs and placed his hands behind his head. Howard sat forward and pressed his hands together, almost in a prayer-like position. He gently patted his hands against his slightly pursed lips.

'You see, science is basically pissed at religion because it just won't go away. And, as it sets itself apart from – above and apart from religion – it seeks to refute religion's validity,' he explained.

'Well yes, Howard, naturally,' Dr Morris replied serenely.

'In science, scientists basically prove things or not through refuting something,' Howard elaborated. Dr Morris nodded in agreement. 'Someone comes up with a hypothesis or theory and others attack, discuss and examine the hypothesis or theory until it's pecked to death. If it survives such an onslaught, eventually it's considered to be proven, until the next round of attacks or challenges to it. As long as the hypothesis or theory continues to not be disproved, then it is considered proven. The problem with religion and God is that, ultimately, it cannot be disproved. You either accept it or not, or you remain unsure, regardless of the fact it remains not disproved.' Dr Morris shook his head slowly as Howard went on, but said nothing. 'The corollary of this is that religion and God should be considered proven, and that's why it won't go away. But science considers that, as religion or God cannot be disproved, neither can it be positively proven outside of personal testament. The problem with such logic is that it ignores the huge element of personal testament involved in science.'

'Nonsense!' Dr Morris responded.

'Which is why scientists, just like the devout, can agree on little for very long and are constantly trying to outdo each other.' Dr Morris laughed out loud at Howard's comment.

'My point is that science is based upon a particular set of beliefs and theories that shape the scientist's worldview, just as religion does. Often the two overlap and there's no problem. Fundamentally...' Howard began wagging his finger at Dr Morris as they both grinned. 'Fundamentally, though, they disagree, they differ. Once you get to that point they become mutually exclusive and run into conflict, with one set of beliefs struggling to reign supreme over the other. Of course, this is an oversimplification.' Dr Morris resumed his nodding in agreement.

'There's not one camp that belongs to science and one camp that belongs to religion, with a third overlapping group stuck in the middle. It's all more fragmented and sophisticated than that, but basically it comes down to this issue.'

Dr Morris pondered what Howard was saying for a moment, while Howard paused to gather his own thoughts.

'But science operates in the real world, Howard. It's tangible, it deals with observing real-life phenomenon, not some other spiritual plane,' Dr Morris stressed.

'No Doctor, that's not true... I mean, science spends all its time eliminating reality, eliminating reality from the equation.' Dr Morris looked puzzled by Howard's reasoning.

'Take laboratory conditions, Doctor. On the one hand, they're trying to whittle what they're looking at down to its basics, so they can work out how it works, what's going on. On the other hand, they're removing all the variables, all the factors that whatever they're looking at actually operate in conjunction with. All the unseens they remove from the equation. Basically, they remove the actual conditions, the actual influences that the object or subject exists and behaves with. How the hell does that correlate to reality? Quite frankly, it's the opposite. They examine an abstraction of reality, a protected, altered version and come to some obscured conclusion as to what is occurring,' Howard declared. Dr Morris seemed impressed by what Howard had said.

'Well, it's a fair point I suppose, Howard. But we have to start somewhere and we do gain some good understanding of things under laboratory conditions that we can then reapply to the real world. So, it's only an abstraction in the sense of us understanding the fundamentals of how things work, otherwise you'd be there for ever trying to take absolutely everything into account. You wouldn't know what was affecting what and so on. Do you see what I mean, Howard?'

'Yeah, I see alright, Doctor. I'll tell you another thing about science, and you should be well aware of this. Science operates within frameworks, paradigms, parameters of truth that set out that particular model. The facts may be true according to the outline of the model, but the model itself may be inaccurate. It proves itself to be correct according to its own criteria. How the hell can science give us an accurate overall truth or reality? It can't. It can merely offer us continuous sets of criterion-biased models of the truth. Some are complementary and some are mutually exclusive, but no single model gives us an accurate depiction of the 'truth' or 'reality'. What's more, some neurologists have declared that there is no centre to the brain or mind, no core consciousness, that the brain or mind is merely the sum of its components. Isn't it interesting that scientific theory may be the same thing? A sum of components, not a single entity but a collection of models, just like our collection of synapses. Or maybe science has progressed this way, you know, into compartments – fields, areas, precisely because that's how the brain functions. Or maybe all the models are simply wrong?'

'Well, I hardly think that all of the models are wrong, Howard...'

'So why can't they agree, Doctor? Why do they always argue? Who's right and who's wrong?' Dr Morris paused before giving his answer.

'You see, Howard, it's a matter of personal opinion, of working out which theories you think are correct, which is often – not always, but often – based upon who puts forward the best theories. Which theories sound the most believable and which ideas can be proven the most convincingly.'

'Exactly, Doctor. It's a matter of personal opinion. The choice is yours,' Howard insisted.

'Yes, but Howard, some things are simply more plausible than others and some things have more evidence to suggest that that is what is occurring. That doesn't mean you can't believe whichever theory you like, but you may find yourself in a minority or even standing alone, and there are reasons for that. Some things are just too "out there" to be correct.'

'Like religion?' Howard threw into the mix. Dr Morris rubbed his chin and smirked.

'Well, perhaps, yes, like religion. But the thing is, science and religion operate in very distinct ways. And in recent times they have simply gone their separate ways.' Dr Morris shrugged his shoulders. 'And there we are, Howard.'

'Science, religion it's all the same thing, Doctor. I mean, science in its modern form is merely the latest story or sets of tales handed out by the high priests to convince us they are the purveyors of the truth. It's fundamentally no different to how it was two thousand odd years ago, when the pagans and the Jews and the Christians were arguing the toss and jostling for control of the transmission of knowledge to the masses,' Howard said with an air of certainty.

'Yes, but where it differs now is that we know a lot more about things, about the world, the universe. The discoveries made by modern science are proven, Howard. That's a fundamental difference. Scientists and scientific experts can operate as the high priests to a certain extent, I admit, but the things they are dealing with are proved to be correct or not. Therefore, the knowledge they have is not merely religious tales preached to the people,' Dr Morris retaliated.

'Well, yes, to a certain degree, Doctor, but after engineering it's mostly speculation and theory only. Okay, say they can prove that there's something out in the universe by landing on the moon or sending out a probe, or looking through a powerful lens, but anything beyond that is pure conjecture; they can no more prove it than the religious can prove God. I mean, take the big bang theory or the theory of evolution; I admit they're the best stories we've come up with to date, but we shouldn't lose sight of the fact that that's exactly what they are: stories. More than half of the world doesn't believe it, anyway. Most of the world believes in creationism or some other form of religious explanation for our existence. It's a fucking minority sect that believes in science and evolution and, who knows, maybe they're right, why not? But maybe they're not, maybe the creationists are right,' Howard reasoned sincerely.

'Well, okay Howard, maybe they are, but what I'm saying is that the evidence presented by science is irrefutable... well, less refutable than theories of creationism and alike,' Dr Morris reasoned back.

'Yes, from your perceptive viewpoint, but the perception of many others is that you're wrong and that scientists have got it very wrong, or that they are liars to protect the interests of those that they represent. That they present science as fact when actually it's no truer than religious explanations of the world.' Dr Morris scrunched his face in disapproval at Howard's assertion.

'The notion that we came from apes is an anathema to them – they find it insulting and ridiculous. Or that out of nothing popped a giant bang and we turned up after a bit. What came before that? They can't tell you. All they can say is that it doesn't apply to us, it's not relevant. Well, how convenient. That sounds just like every religious 'God moves in mysterious ways' fob-off I've ever heard. And evolution... well, it's full of holes, it simply doesn't add up, Doctor.'

'Of course it does, Howard,' Dr Morris said arrogantly. 'It's fairly straightforward. It works by natural selection, survival of the fittest. It's no great mystery really.'

'The problem with evolution, Doctor,' replied Howard, 'is not natural selection or survival of the fittest. The problem is in mutation, in a genetic shift from one species to another. Mutations do happen, Doctor. I'm not saying they don't, but most are negative in terms of survival or healthy function. Even assuming that there are positive mutations, in terms of health and survival, the chances of this happening once or twice are extremely unlikely, as are the chances of that species surviving and proliferating, never mind it happening millions and millions of times. Put simply, Doctor, genetic mutation from proteins to humans defies all laws of probability. It is statistically and mathematically impossible. Therefore, if it did happen, then there are or were, quite obviously, millions and millions of miracles happening over and over again. If you believe that then fine, but make no mistake it's as out there as any religious notion of creation, Doctor.'

'I hardly think that's the case, Howard. I mean, after all, it has happened,' Dr Morris said sceptically.

'No seriously, Doctor, it's been proven. The probabilities involved in the evolution of proteins is zero in both their likely random formulation and their left-handed asymmetry, never mind the chance of building a single cell, let alone genes or DNA or even a simple bacteria. So you can forget flat worms, fish, reptiles, mammals, humans, Doctor. You can forget humans because, by its very criteria, the laws of mathematics disprove the theory of evolution. There is simply not enough time in the universe, never mind on earth, for chance and trial and error to produce a single protein molecule, not to mention increasingly complex compilations or the impossibility of genuine transition from species to species. In fact, the amount of lucky coincidences for a single creature to come into being, to survive and then reproduce itself, let alone for this process to happen literally billions and billions of times over a billion years or so, is quite simply miraculous by any given criteria. Something else, some other impetus is at work, Doctor. Something more than random chance, that's for sure. You see either life has always been present, in which case mutations were always going to mutate, and the ones that didn't never were going to because something caused those mutations, not chance. Just because we don't know what caused them to mutate doesn't mean it was down to chance. We cannot keep explaining things that we don't fully understand, like mutations or quantum behaviour, as happening by chance. The entire history of human and animal evolution is based solely upon what we find, which is relatively very little and not in any way on what was actually taking place, a story that we will probably never know. The alternative is that life was created. If it was created by chance, then the miracle is beyond the idea of God, or it is as fantastic as that idea,' Howard lectured powerfully. Dr Morris looked slightly overwhelmed by Howard's words, as though he were a little out of his depth.

'Well, I'm not sure that that's the case, Howard. And even if the details are in dispute, the overall theory is very sound, I can assure you. I mean, think about it. It makes perfect sense. Look at the similarities, the development of species, the spectrum of the evolutionary hierarchy. There is obviously a correlation between the differing species. You can actually see the evolutionary process at work,' he said, regaining his footing.

'I'll tell you what else is fucked-up, Doctor. If evolution is the be all and fucking end all, the basic truth of it, all totally impersonal, just a process we are subject to, then why the fuck is part of that evolutionary process the fact that we, of all creatures, know it, see it, have worked it out? What evolutionary purpose does us, as a species knowing that that is what is occurring, serve? What the fuck is the purpose of it? I mean, shit, what are the fucking odds of it, even by accident? What are the chances? It doesn't really make much sense, whatever way you look at it. It's pretty miraculous, don't you think? That we are the particular formulation of atomic, chemical and biological matter that has, after a hundred and fifty odd thousand years of our species' existence... that, all of a sudden, it all becomes clear what it's all about. And that, if we survive another hundred and fifty odd thousand years, do you really think that it will still be the case? I doubt it, Doctor. Maybe it's just today's bullshit. In actual fact, as a concept it has only been around for a hundred and fifty odd years, never mind thousands. So forgive me if I have some doubts as to its postulated absolute certainty as the meaning of fucking life, Doctor!' Howard finished in a great crescendo. Dr Morris grew slightly agitated.

'Yes, but the fact is, Howard, miraculous or not, it has resulted in our awareness of these matters. We have been able to understand and work out many things, to find the answers to such questions.'

'The simple truth is that nobody knows the answers and everybody's guessing in the dark. And science is based upon that, just as much as religion is or any other new age belief system you care to choose. I mean, we get these laymen-friendly books that take away the hard bit, the maths. As if maths wasn't a man-made invention, a perceptive tool through which we create mental order. Scientists see it everywhere and can apply it to everything. If it doesn't add up then we got the calculations wrong, but we can get it. The correct sums will lead to the correct theory and the Holy bloody Grail bollocks! They're chasing their tales like any bloody obsessive compulsive!' Howard's eyes were wide with excitement.

'Yes, I see your point, Howard. But, as I said, their theories can be proved, unlike religious faith. Not everything, but much of it,' Dr Morris said earnestly.

'That's what they tell us, Doctor, but how do we know? We have to take their word for it. I mean, if we don't actually get the science bit, just the stories, then how are we to know?'

'Well, that's why scientists have dedicated their lives to their particular fields, Howard, to gather data and contribute to the bigger picture. They are specialists who spend their time understanding various areas so that we can put pieces of the puzzle together.'

'That's no different from the religious scholars who dedicate their lives to the partial understanding, the life-long study of religious texts. They know better than us because they are experts. How can we know what's true and what's not until we have gained their knowledge, their perception of reality? If some scientist has dedicated their life to understanding molecules, or moulds, or whatever, how could they possibly understand what the religious scholar does and vice versa? Only those who have explored all the avenues could make a reasoned guess at the truth and we both know that's impossible, Doctor,' Howard said, trying to rest his case.

'But science has given us evidence, Howard.'

'Such as?'

'Look at the archaeological artefacts found, the fossils and so on. Think about it,' Dr Morris implored.

'Yeah, look at the fossil record, the humanoid fossil record. It's a patchy, pithy little collection of locational differing compilations. You know, arms from French humanoids being equated with skulls from East Africa, etc. Ginormous assumptions are being made in order that an eminent theory of what has been going on in the past can be formulated, and we're supposed to swallow this speculation as solid fact. It's a farce really,' Howard said scathingly.

'But Howard, those bones and fossils are evidence. They tell us something about what was happening here before we arrived. They have stories… explanations attached to them. It's up to us to work out what those explanations might be,' Dr Morris said struggling to convey his point.

'Yes, I agree the things found indicate something and certainly, based on what we know about the world today, we can make reasonable guesses. But let's be clear, they are only guesses, conjecture. How could they be anything else? I mean, if you find a couple of bones or an old sword and a goblet, it gives you an idea, but not much more. The point is that we weren't there to know. Christ, people can't even agree about what happened yesterday in the news never mind what things were like ten thousand years ago!' Howard exclaimed.

'What do you mean, we can't agree about what happened on the news?' said Dr Morris indignantly. 'We see the reports. Okay, they're not always totally accurate, but we have a free press here, we're very privileged.'

'Of course we do, Doctor. Our press is free from influence or coercion, isn't it?' Howard said sarcastically. 'Anyway, that's not my reasoning,' he went on. 'For any given item reported on the news, I can give you eighty or more different world views from around the world as to what happened. Take the tsunami, for example. Some say it was an earthquake, you know, plate tectonics, some say act of God. Some say the US knew, some say the CIA set it off, some say that's absurd etc, etc. There are endless opinions as to what's going on and what's not. So, if that's the case for what's occurring today, and I think it is, then how the hell can we determine what was happening all those years ago? Be it the origins of man or the universe, Tutankhamen or whatever.' Howard waved his downward pointing finger up and down, like a prime minister laying down the law to his Cabinet.

'Well, we have documentation, writings, hieroglyphics and so on, that give us lots of insight,' Dr Morris insisted, his voice raising an octave in frustration.

'So if, in four thousand years from now, after our global hierarchy and civilization has collapsed, they turned up the remains of the front page of *The Sun* and it said Elton John was sleeping with rent boys, or Jordan was having a baby, would that give us an accurate picture of the world today?' Howard said provocatively.

'In a way it would, Howard,' Dr Morris said steadily, avoiding Howard's baiting. 'It would tell you that the power of celebrity was important or prominent in our society, for example.' Howard looked unconvinced and pulled a face that said so.

'Well, yeah, it might tell that story, but if it turned up with a bit of a PC keyboard and the foundations of the Tower of London, would they really be able to unravel what the world today was about? I doubt it, Doctor. They could make some guesses, but not much more.'

'You'd be surprised, Howard. We have worked a tremendous amount of things out about the world with very little to go on, sometimes. We're a clever species. Howard, science has reached an unsurpassed period in history. We have broken through barriers previously thought of as science fiction. We know more about... well, everything than we ever have before and that is reflected in our scientific theory and thought,' Dr Morris said somewhat grandiosely.

'The science we produce is like anything else. The institutions and pressures of life, of global capitalism, of state funding or pressure, all weigh down upon it and it leads to certain kinds of research and often certain types of results, and hence certain ways of viewing phenomenon,' Howard retorted, diverting the conversation away from Dr Morris's main premise.

'But science and the scientific method are dedicated to questioning things. That's the point, that's how it works, Howard!' Dr Morris uttered in exasperation.

'That's true,' Howard conceded. 'But scientists and science are a bit like capitalists and capitalism,' he continued. Dr Morris frowned through his confusion at Howard's statement. 'You can argue and compete amongst each other, of course, that's how you get the best results, by pushing the limits. But the golden rule is don't question the system itself. Science and capitalism are liberal domains and there's a lot of scope there, but one thing you don't do is question science or capitalism themselves. No, that goes against the rules. Compete with each other, but unite if the system is threatened. If that happens, then our whole ethos is challenged and that won't do. We're far too busy creating theories or making money. Often, the two go hand in hand.' Howard looked at Dr Morris as if he knew he were onto something.

'Oh come on, Howard. I mean, really... look, I know that science is manipulated by budgets and research funding and so on, but it's hardly the sort of cartel that you seem to think it is. It's a fragmented, frankly, self-interested... I mean, on an individual scientist basis, egotistical rat race to produce results... Often funding directed results I'll admit, but a Marxist conspiracy it is not, Howard,' Dr Morris said almost laughing at the absurdity of Howard's insinuation. Howard looked perturbed by Dr Morris's mocking dismissal of his well-thought-out analysis.

'Anyway, you lot, psychologists, weren't taken seriously, not even considered proper science until fairly recently,' Howard hit back in an almost juvenile manner. 'Not until you became applied, became useful to governments and think tanks... population management... the business community, you know, market research analysts, consumer profilers and all that. Funny, isn't it, that when you were able to make money for companies you were suddenly taken seriously. I mean, shit, you can't even agree amongst yourselves. Is Freud right? No, Jung is! Is it genetic or is it environment? Is it a mix of the two? Hmm maybe... let's write a book about it!' Howard said disparagingly. Dr Morris looked slightly offended, but irate at the same time.

'That's just not true,' he squealed.

'There is no truth, only lies,' Howard proclaimed. 'There is an ongoing battle for the domination of the human narrative. There is no truth, only the fight for believers. Like all good lies, the more truths it contains the more persuasive it sounds. The harbingers of knowledge have always both dominated and unified the group. Whether they be elders in a small tribe or global leaders. The stories we tell shape the perception of others. The ideas, the memes that get passed on, become the crux of human beliefs and shape our actions accordingly. They determine whether we revolt or acquiesce. Even those that seek to dominate human narration are not exempt from this process. If anything, they are in one way or another more affected by it than others, despite sharing one story publicly and another amongst themselves. They still ultimately believe. We are all ultimately believers.'

SESSION TWENTY-TWO

Howard sat, gawping at the telephone. He eyeballed suspiciously the bottom-of-the-range, grey-beige touch-tone standard office model that sat inoffensively on the desk in front of him. Dr Morris re-entered the room and sat down behind the desk. He noticed Howard's bizarre attention to the telephone.

'Did it ring?' he asked. Howard shook his head slowly, but did not remove his frowning glare from its transfixed state on the standard Argos hardware. Dr Morris raised his bare brows slightly and made himself comfortable again in his seat.

'I'm sorry, Howard, what were you saying before? I've lost your, erm, train of thought, so to speak.'

'Doesn't matter,' Howard said, still staring at the phone.

'Okay then, but it did seem rather important to you only a few minutes ago,' Dr Morris replied, growing a bit concerned at Howard's preoccupation with the telephone.

'Can't remember to be honest, doc,' Howard said, breaking his trance-like gaze to glance at Dr Morris, before returning his attention, albeit with less intensity, back to the telephone.

'Is everything, alright, Howard? You seem very interested in the phone all of a sudden,' Dr Morris said with vague concern.

'Yeah... yeah Doctor... erm, no problem,' Howard responded, finally losing interest in the telephone and giving Dr Morris his full attention.

'What are you thinking, Howard? Come on, spill it,' Dr Morris said with a wry smile.

'Oh nothing, Doctor,' Howard replied waiting for Dr Morris to pursue the matter.

'Come on, Howard. I think I know you well enough to know when something's on your mind, and something usually is,' Dr Morris said, willingly following Howard's little bread trail.

'I'm just thinking about evolution, that's all,' Howard said nonchalantly.

'Well, it's an improvement on religious doom and gloom, I'll say that much,' Dr Morris said jollily, pleased at Howard's change of direction.

'Well, if evolution is taking place all the time in a piecemeal fashion, from generation to generation, Doctor...'

'Yes.'

'The question is, how is it happening now?' Dr Morris seemed semi-interested in Howard's question and opened his mouth to speak, but Howard continued.

'What changes have we been going through in recent generations? I mean, we haven't been here for very long, but assuming we're gonna be here for a while longer, how are we changing?' Dr Morris waited to see if Howard had finished. He hadn't. 'Of course, the obvious conclusion is that our brains will continue to evolve, as has been the emphasis of our particular evolution. So what's next for the human brain, the human mind? Where are we going, what will we perceive?' Dr Morris held his breath momentarily, hoping to avoid another outburst on Howard's perceptive abilities.

'Just think how our perception of the world around us, the universe, each other and ourselves, has changed over time, from apes to spacemen and beyond...' Howard said, smiling at Dr Morris, who seemed mildly unsure as to how to respond. 'And don't forget...' Howard said, raising his finger to Dr Morris. 'Evolution works through the divergence of species, Doctor. Mutations, splinter groups and whole new species emerge.' Dr Morris nodded in polite, though slightly patronising, agreement. 'What different directions are we going in? And if survival of the fittest is the order of things, then who won't make it? Who has a future and who doesn't?'

'Well, why don't we let future generations worry about that, eh Howard?' Dr Morris said, attempting to defuse the potentially inflammatory territory that Howard was beginning to encroach upon again.

'Well, I don't think it's too difficult to work out is it, Doctor?' Howard continued, well aware of Dr Morris's reluctance to pursue the matter.

'Is it not?' Dr Morris replied evasively.

'No Doctor, it isn't... Technology is the future, isn't it?' Howard said, goading Dr Morris for a response.

'Well yes, Howard, I suppose technology is the future,' Dr Morris answered reluctantly.

'Yes, but is it our future or is it their future? That's the question, Dr Morris.'

Dr Morris took a deep breath and exhaled slowly. He rubbed his forehead and closed his eyes. His expression was that of a man with an impending migraine. Howard grinned mischievously. Dr Morris opened his eyes in time to catch Howard's malevolent leering, to which he responded with a stern scowl. Howard looked down, avoiding Dr Morris's direct eye contact, but looked back up with a glint in his eye. Dr Morris maintained his uncompromising eye contact and so Howard looked away again.

'Who's "they", Howard?' Dr Morris said harshly, as if he didn't require an answer. Howard smiled.

'Technology, Doctor,' he replied as if it were a matter of fact.

'Technology is not "they", Howard. Technology is "it". Now, can we move on please?' Dr Morris said through gritted teeth.

'Well, I suppose technically you're correct, Doctor. Technology is an "it", but it is alive nonetheless.' Howard's cheesy grin gradually waned as he stared blankly into Dr Morris's eyes, blinking only occasionally.

'Oh, for fuck's sake, Howard!' Dr Morris exploded. 'Get a bloody grip, will you!'

'What!' Howard responded indignantly.

'We're not going off on another of your wild bloody goose chases, okay. Got that?'

'Oh, so the man of science has cracked, has he? Can't take it when his own theories are used against him,' Howard jeered.

'What the hell are you talking about, Howard? You just said that technology is alive. What the fuck are you on about? One advert too many I think, Howard.' Dr Morris reacted angrily and without care and attention as to where he was, or who he was talking to. This registered with Howard, although he didn't show it.

'I'm merely pointing out the next stage of evolution on this planet happens to be technological life, that's all, Doctor. No need to give yourself a hernia,' Howard said, taking the upper hand. Dr Morris had never actually struck anyone in his adult life, but at that moment he was sure that a good beating would resolve this whole situation. He took quick, deep breaths until his breathing resumed to something resembling normality, and wiped his brow, imagining sweat to have materialised when, in fact, it had not.

'Technology is not alive, Howard. End of discussion,' he said firmly.

'Is it not?' Howard said, emulating Dr Morris's earlier response.

'NO!'

'It just depends on how you look at it,' Howard said, trying to provoke Dr Morris further.

'It doesn't matter which way you look at it, Howard, technology is not alive. It is made of wires and metal and alike... Has that telephone been talking to you, Howard? Is that it? Have you been having telepathic communications with the phone, or something?' Dr Morris said in an almost frantic fashion, as though he were at the end of his tether.

'Don't be fuckin' stupid, Doctor,' Howard said condescendingly. 'I was merely speculating as to where evolution on earth might perhaps unfold next. I came to the quite scientifically sound notion that technology is indeed the most likely candidate, Doctor.' Dr

Morris composed himself and gave Howard full and malicious eye contact.

'Been watching the Matrix have we, Howard? Decided we are, erm… oh, what's his name…?' Dr Morris said frustrated at the break in his attempted mocking of Howard's delusions of grandeur.

'Neo… the one,' Howard interjected dryly.

'Yes, yes. So are you Neo Howard, the chosen one?' Dr Morris spat venomously.

'And you want me to get a grip?' Howard countered sardonically.

'Is that a bit too lowbrow for your taste, eh Howard?' Dr Morris said with a sneer.

'It's just a film, Doctor.'

'Mmm,' Dr Morris responded, annoyed at himself for allowing Howard to get the better of him.

'Though it offers a metaphor, Doctor. A metaphor for precisely what I'm talking about,' Howard said informatively. Dr Morris bit his lip.

'So you think that the world will be run by robots do you, Howard? Is it Arnold Swarchenegger and all that?'

'It doesn't work like that, does it, Doctor?' Howard said quite seriously. Dr Morris didn't even want to respond. Indeed, he didn't even want to be in the same room as Howard anymore. He didn't answer. Instead, he just offered a vague smile.

'It's part of the evolutionary process, Doctor, not some Hollywood blockbuster,' Howard continued. Dr Morris glanced at his watch.

'Yes, but it's not alive, Howard... we make it... we control it, Howard. It evolves because we... evolve it,' Dr Morris said trying to close the subject.

'Well, that's true to a certain extent, Doctor. We do evolve, as you put it, but it is very much alive and the evolutionary impetus at work is deeper than you realise, more fundamental than that. We evolve together, to put it more succinctly.'

'Okay, Howard, I see your point. We do evolve together in that sense, but it's not alive, is it? It's made of... well, whatever it's made of, you know, like, erm... plastic,' Dr Morris said glancing at the telephone.

'You have to redefine what you mean by life, Doctor,' Howard said with an air of sophistication.

'Why do I?' Dr Morris replied defiantly.

'In order that you can understand what I mean.'

'I'm not sure I want to understand what you mean, Howard,' Dr Morris said defensively, almost squeamish of Howard's onerous gravitational pull.

'What are you afraid of, Doctor?' Howard said gently.

'I'm not afraid, Howard.'

'It goes like this, Doctor. The problem in searching for the nature or origins of life is one based in the realm of semantics and concepts. If, under conventional scientific definitions, life emerged out of the primordial soup more than a billion years ago, against all odds, under hostile and turbulent conditions, then such a definition infers that, at some point, 'life' was born out of... what?' Howard implored Dr Morris, who shook his head in resignation.

'Basically, a lifeless environment... this belies the fact that the chemical soup that gave birth to single-celled organisms is or are actually the building blocks that comprise it and hence, through evolution, us. This definition equates biological life as being fundamentally chemical compositions. However, of course such a receding chronology does not end there. As biological life can be traced back to its simpler chemical origins, so too can chemical compositions be broken down further into molecules and atoms in order to understand their fundamental properties. This eventually brings us to the input of energy and its sources. Energy is understood to be a vital ingredient in 'life'; whether it's electromagnetic or gas-based, it is assumed to be what allows biological life to perhaps be born and continue living. Furthermore, it would be an error to assume that the story ends with this for, once you have traced back to the chemical, molecular, atomic, and energy-based world, you enter into the realm of the origins of both the earth itself and the universe that gave birth to it. If it is accurate to say that biological life cannot exist without its more basic predecessors – chemicals, molecules, atoms and energy – then it is not too irrational to suggest that, as biological life is fundamentally complex compositions comprising of chemical matter, molecules, atoms and energy, then our composition becomes an expression of complex chemo/energy inter-relations. We don't assume that, because micro-organisms are not mammals, they are not alive; therefore, it is not a huge leap of the imagination to extend such a premise to the next level down and assume that chemicals, molecules, atoms and energy are, too, also alive.'

'Yes, but, Howard...' began Dr Morris, but Howard ignored the interruption.

'Indeed, they demonstrate the fundamental criteria for being alive – behaviour. As they interact they express chemical, molecular, atomic and energy behaviour. It's not humanised or even plant behaviour; it is interaction relative to their states, properties and principles. More importantly, such behaviour led to interaction or culture. The socialisation of chemicals, molecules, atoms and energy was already part of the cosmic evolutionary process that has culminated in us. Therefore, by definition, the areas that we consider or assume to not be alive very much were and are. Once this is understood, then the Holy Grail of searching for the origin or birth of life on earth becomes a complete red herring, for life on earth was present from the very first inception of the planet. Indeed, the planet is merely another aspect of life, born out of the universal cosmic cocktail. The earth itself is alive and is teeming with many other expressions of it or life. The entire universe and everything in it is a chain reaction of events, from the big bang to now and beyond, from everything quantum to the activity of stars. And we, Doctor, we were inherent from the beginning, from the big bang. Forget whether that was the real start, wherever, whenever the start was; we were inherent from that very moment – if indeed there was a beginning. We were destined to evolve out of universal evolution. If the big bang was the beginning, then we weren't only destined to come to fruition, but we were destined to realise it as well, which was also inherent in that moment and point of singularity. This means that the beginning of the big bang, the point of singularity, was inherently intelligent. Intelligence as we understand it was present, however latent. To put it another way, the whole fuckin' universe and everything in it is alive. It is all differing expressions of the same thing – life.'

'Look Howard...' words failed Dr Morris. 'The scientific definitions of life are there for a reason...' He struggled to convey what he understood to be correct, but had not the training or knowledge to explicate.

'Their assumptions are wrong, Doctor. You can't just cut off life at a designated point and deny its underlying influences and forces, to close your eyes to its origins as if they were somehow separate and distinct. It would be foolish to do so. To believe that the earth and everything on it, the great ocean and all that was sitting idle as some dead, lifeless puddle, and the electrical activity of the heavens also designated dead and lifeless... that somehow, when these two collided, 'life' suddenly materialised out of absolutely nothing, is frankly primitive, Doctor. It's Mary Shelly time. I mean, I know they've done something similar – though, not really, if you actually think about it. Nowhere near, in fact. But that aside, they produced 'something' under laboratory conditions, but the fact remains that a process at work, mother nature if you will, did it of her or its own volition, as a natural process or course of universal evolution. Evolution happens incrementally over time. Here on earth, it happens bit by bit over generations, or perhaps it happens in sudden spurts brought on by some sort of critical mass, some turning point. Truthfully, we really don't know; either way, such bursts or gradual changes must be inherent in our genes, genes which have their origins in more basic configurations and proteins. And further back, until you get to even more basic elements, but something was, is, present that enables what we determine life to be to spring forth. This basically means that life exists in everything as potential. If we did evolve from bits of clay, from building blocks comprised of elements of the universe – electricity, water, dirt, whatever – then all these elements, air included, contain latently the property and the ability to produce life, which means that life is present in all, in all universal elements, just in differing stages or states. If biological life on earth is merely the expression of DNA, or genes attempting to out-compete other DNA or genes through replication, then universal life is the expression of atoms and molecules, chemicals and energy trying to out-compete other atoms and molecules, chemicals and energy – if, indeed, competition is the correct assumption for the overall equation.' Howard preached as though his life depended on it.

'Besides, their definitions will change in the future, they always do,' he finished. 'And that's why technology is also alive, Doctor.'

'What?' Dr Morris shrieked in disbelief at what he was hearing.

'Choose something, some kind of technology, anything,' Howard said as if he were some backstreet, card-pedalling confidence trickster. Dr Morris huffed rebelliously.

'Go on,' Howard said, laughing. Dr Morris gave no response. He merely clasped his hands together on the desk and looked out of the window.

'Okay, I'll choose for you. Take this telephone, for example,' said Howard, nodding in its direction. 'This telephone is made of plastic, probably oil-based – a natural resource. The wires inside are made of metal, probably copper. A natural resource, the majority of this phone is comprised of plastic, closely followed by metals of one sort or another. These are straightforward natural resources, processed from the earth by man, right?' Dr Morris began to pull partial gurning faces like some bored child as he looked out across the hospital grounds, while Howard continued his theorising.

'Now, granted, these environmental resources are not alive in the biological sense, but if you break down what they are to a microscopic level you will find that there's plenty of activity going on there. At the atomic level, they are a haven of hyperactivity, of chemical reactions going about their daily business. There is also a life cycle involved

280

with these chemicals and their interaction with the environment; rust, for example, is part of the decaying process of metal, just as biological life eventually ages and rots over time. Plastic is a little different and has an amazing, if not environmentally degrading, shelf life. Plastic molecules last for... well, a long bloody time, anyway. My point is that, basically, at a certain point, for example the atomic level, we and our environment are fundamentally the same thing, or similar things in differing compositions. After all, according to scientists, we are truly children of the stars. Exploding stars dispersed carbon all over the place and the carbon in our carbon-based bodies is a direct by-product of the death of great burning balls of energy, atomic energy. Well, so too is everything else on this planet – in fact, the planet itself is an even larger by-product of the magical, mystical explosion we call the big bang. The whole universe is dispersed energy and matter that has been scattered in a zillion different directions and has ended up as planets, stars, moons, oceans, mountains, trees, geraniums, humans, zebras, staplers, Skodas, roller skates, TVs, telephones – whatever you like, all through the process of evolution, universal evolution. You name it, it all came out of the cosmic explosion. Now, just because we put ourselves at the centre of this cosmic expanse and designate ourselves through conceptual semantics devised by the lump of fat, proteins, acids and sugars we call a brain, to be alive. And just because we determine that things similar to us in configuration are also alive and that everything else on earth and in the known universe to be basically dead or, more precisely, not alive, does not actually or necessarily make it so, Doctor.' Dr Morris looked grey in comparison to the divine light that impelled Howard to emit his celestial wisdom in all its idiosyncratic eccentricity.

'Therefore...' Howard continued, as Dr Morris struggled to remain conscious. 'If by redefinition all things in the universe and on planet earth are fundamentally alive, it logically follows that technology such as this here telephone is also alive and kicking in the molecular and atomic sense,' Howard declared in attempted zenith to his conceived conceptual brainchild.

'Yes, but the telephone is not alive, is it, Howard? In any real sense of the word,' Dr Morris replied in a half-interested mumble.

'That telephone, Doctor, is part of the largest technological life form on earth. The telephone network is the most complex technological organism in existence today,' Howard insisted.

'But it's not fucking alive, is it, Howard! It doesn't do anything until I pick it up and push its bloody buttons!' Dr Morris said in a highly irritated tone.

'I return to my previously stated definition of what life is, Doctor. Life is the interaction of atoms and molecules, chemicals and energy, driven by the laws of physics – whatever they may be. In that sense, the telephone is like an atomic molecular creature waiting to interact with you, another atomic molecular creature, and the surge of electricity you provide it with every time you use it, or feed it,' Howard offered from his parallel dimension.

'Yes, but technology is made by us, Howard, and is reliant on us to function. It's hardly independent or demonstrative of any sense of agency,' Dr Morris uttered, almost vibrating with resentment.

'Are we in any sense independent of our environment, Doctor?' Howard retorted in his usual slippery conduct.

'Well, yes, of course we are,' Dr Morris snapped without hesitation.

'How?' Howard asked plainly. Dr Morris strained to muster an answer, but could summon little in the way of an effective reprisal.

'When, at any point in time, are we separated from our environment, whatever that may be? We are always one with it and it with us, Doctor.'

'What the hell has that got to do with technology being alive, Howard?' Dr Morris demanded.

'My point, which I have stated several times now, is simple – that it is all alive, Doctor. Us, our environment, technology – it is all expressions of universal life, interacting and competing in a constant state of cosmic evolution,' Howard maintained quietly, but firmly.

'Well, I think you are out there pissing in the wind with that one, frankly, Howard.'

'Dr Morris, there are people out there... scientists, who not only believe that technology is indeed the next evolutionary step, but some of them feel that it is actually a desirable and inevitable consequence of life on earth. They talk about technology as being alive, and it is, Doctor. It isn't biological life, its mechanical life, just another set of sub-species of non-sentient life. Steven bloody Hawking knows it – he's a straightforward cyborg in the traditional sense of the word.' Howard opened his hands to Dr Morris, expressing his candour and sincerity. Dr Morris did not react.

'As for technology being dependant on us for its survival, well that is currently absolutely correct. But I think you'll also find that we have reached the point whereby we are also just as reliant on technology for our survival, certainly in the west. The global system is completely and utterly entwined with technological evolution and innovation – what the hell do you think the financial markets are? They are digits on stock market computers. If those computers die, then we will pretty soon starve to death. What delivers our food to supermarkets? How do we find out what's holding deliveries up? What sustains us every single day of our lives? Technology of one sort or another – okay, steered by us, but for how long? There is an evolutionary struggle for the dominance of planet earth, Doctor. It has been going on since time immemorial. The battle between sentient and non-sentient life has been the story of all biological beings. The fight to out-compete your environment, or the struggle to not be so manipulated by biological life forms that you, as non-sentient life, become decimated and baron. Our manipulation of resources has culminated in the evolution of non-sentient life from minerals to laptops. This course of evolution is not exclusive to us. It is a two-way process. We adapt and evolve to survive our environment; it selects our genes, for God's sake. Our environment adapts through interaction with us and other biological entities, as well as other non-sentient life.' Howard was speaking in a low, but steady voice. Dr Morris was looking at Howard as if he were a raving lunatic, as if he should tell him this, but he remained silent.

'You can see the evolution of technology right alongside our own, Doctor. Once it was flints. Flints were once the cutting edge, excuse the pun, of technology. I mean, it gave you an advantage over your competitors like you wouldn't believe. Then it was arrows and spear heads, knives, swords, crossbows and catapults, guns and cannons, bombs, missiles... nuclear weapons. Technology has been used to kill us from the word go. Agriculture, engineering, industrialisation, computerisation, biotechnology – we are a cyborg species, Doctor. In the widest sense, to be a cyborg is the culmination of evolving in conjunction with your environment; it is an advanced and sophisticated version of this process. Chimpanzees use weapons, birds make nests, we fly into outer space. All are examples of biological life utilising resources, manipulating the environment, evolving in conjunction with non-sentient life.' Howard was of a serene and tranquil disposition as he relayed to Dr Morris what he understood to be fact.

'If the environment is the main factor in biological evolutionary development, then technology has been the catalyst for human evolution, the ultimate intertwining of man and his environment. But, like a weed wrapped around a tree, its very nature is to strangle and out-compete its accommodating host. Just as a weed may mount a tree to further reach the sun, so too does technology hitch a ride with us to aide its development.'

'You say it as though technology were conscious, Howard, as if it were aware of what it's doing,' Dr Morris scoffed.

'Does a vine know what it's doing, Doctor? It just does it. It's in its make-up, in its nature. Technology, non-sentient life – an extension of our environment finds itself competing with its environment, which includes us. We are slaves to technology, Doctor, we are programmed by it,' Howard assured Dr Morris.

'I hardly think it programs us, Howard. You're getting... how can I put it? Very carried away with your peculiar little metaphors,' Dr Morris said, amusing himself.

'Oh no, Doctor?' Howard responded as if he were challenging a child's assumptions. 'What about time, Doctor? We are slaves to the clock, the mechanical guardian of us all. Our society is organised on the principle of time-keeping monitored by the tick and the tock, or the blip and the bleep. Now such has been the evolution of that little barnacle you wear on your wrist there, Doctor. Time is money, as they say,' Howard said expecting more reaction from Dr Morris than he got.

'We have been transformed, Doctor. We no longer fight like animals, we fight like machines. We no longer ride livestock, instead we are propelled by technology. Some people even suggest we are merely complex and sophisticated machines ourselves, biological programs, but that would be putting the cart before the horse, Doctor, literally. We are not complex machines. Machines are simple duplicates of biological life. We are not machine-like, instead machines are biological-like. Indeed, we design technology in a truly narcissistic fashion. They came from us. They are evolved from us; they are a later species than us. We are backtracking the concept of what it is to be a machine. Machines are our expression of the need to labour-save and reflect such a fact... an orange is not clockwork, Doctor,' Howard said cryptically.

'No,' Dr Morris said drolly.

'But, as I've told you many times before, Doctor, the party is over.'

'How's that, Howard?' Dr Morris said without interest.

'We've been a slave to technology for a long time. First it was animals strapped to ploughs and all that, then we were forced into satanic mills, factories that transformed the way we produce, poisoned the air we breathe. Now we're strapped into cyber worlds that alter our ability to communicate with each other, and hurtle our imaginary riches around the globe at speeds so fast it can undermine whole societies in a single night. Satellites, orbiting litter, bounce light from earth through outer space and back again as we gawp at the

287

impersonal robo-salesman that invades our homes every single night at the touch of a button. Global warming from the toxic emissions of industry, cars and aeroplanes threaten to engulf us in flood, ice, desert or whatever non-sentient onslaught you care to imagine. Technology has created whole new realms, new worlds, the telescope, the microscope; it has enabled us to shift our biological perception of what is. Technology altered our world view and hence our sense of reality and, ultimately, what reality is. The ratchet effect is surely the evolution of diverging species of technological life.' Howard was talking almost to himself as he drifted off into his macabre and catastrophic world scenario.

'Howard... Howard,' Dr Morris said, trying to pull Howard back from his obvious impending spiral into the abyss. 'Howard, I think you're allowing yourself to be carried away again,' he said, pursuing his retrieval of the tranquil Howard that had sat before him only minutes ago. Howard's facial expression metamorphosed as Dr Morris spoke; the belligerence in his eyes flashed like a sweeping forest fire, wiping away any trace of the serenity that had preceded it.

'Technology is destroying us, Doctor!' Howard said furiously.

'No, Howard, it is not,' Dr Morris replied, returning to the established pattern of assertion, denial, assertion, denial that the doctor and his patient had come to rely on.

'Look...' Howard began, his eyes wide and filled with obsessive affliction. 'Technology enables us to stay alive longer. This means that genes that once wouldn't have survived are. This is weakening the gene pool. Technology is weakening us as a species. Genetic engineering will lead to gene pool disasters, as its doing so far, mutants that just won't last. The unseens in genetic modification are endless; just look at Dolly the sheep – collapsed and died because all her organs gave in. In effect, she rejected herself. The corporate scientific agenda, ultimately powered by digits on computers, is pushing genetic engineering at a rapid pace. The casualties will be future generations, experimented on and played God with. They predict super humans, the likely result of which will make the Nazi experiments of Germany and Japan look like quaint little research. And what's at stake is no less than the future survival of our species. Technology is assisting us to lose in the battle for control, for supremacy; technology is out-competing us. Like a weed or a bug living off some other life form, it's carrying its ride to dominance. Today we are mutually dependant, by its very nature it seeks independence. Finally, there are life forms more parasitic than humans themselves!' Howard avowed with a hysterical and slightly frantic laugh.

'Okay, Howard, that's enough. Just calm down,' Dr Morris said in automatic response mode.

'Technology is destroying our capacity to think, to communicate. The MTV generations have shorter attention spans. The generations to come will be largely illiterate. The food we eat becomes more and more processed, more and more synthetic, more and more artificial. The air we breathe is polluted beyond belief. There's more and more urbanisation-destroying, taking over the biological environment by a man-made one, a non-biological one, a non-sentient habitat. Our institutions, our social organisation, has become systematised, mechanised beyond all recognition, speeded up to the point of insanity; it's becoming automated, running away from us, technologically-driven. The market is a gigantic computerised casino, dehumanised, serving only digits stored on microchips, determining whether we live or die. Technosexuals, humans fuckin' machines instead of humans, you name it. They wanna put microchips in our heads, for fuck's sake! Truly interfacing us. Technology is doing more and more for us. It is isolating us, eroding our autonomy. The conditions on earth are ripe for machines, not biological life. We are headed towards cybernation!' Howard proclaimed as if he were some ancient soothsayer.

'Well, Howard...' Dr Morris said, looking at his watch. 'We seem to have run quite a bit over time,' he went on, surprised at his having allowed this to happen. Howard's frenzied expression suddenly faded away and a blank look washed over him.

'Maybe we are winning, after all,' he muttered in quiet contemplation.

SESSION TWENTY-THREE

Howard walked from the bus stop towards the drive that led into the hospital grounds. He strolled across the grass, ignoring the concrete path that wound its way amongst the knolls and wire mesh-covered young trees that were planted sporadically with no seeming pattern or design. He looked up at the sky; it was cloudy, but showed little sign of the rain that had been forecast. As he walked, he began to sing quietly to himself. He hadn't sung for quite some time and the Bob Marley tune 'Waiting in Vain' cheered him slightly, despite its sad lyrics.

As he neared the hospital building, a light-skinned black man with dreadlocks emerged through a side gate that led to another part of the hospital. He was a smallish, wiry man with a striking facial bone structure and a little unkempt goatee beard. His locks were thin, more braids than fully-grown dreadlocks, his black and red leather cap was oversized for his head and was well-worn and softened. Despite the less than warm weather, he wore a baggy, mustard-yellow, teabag vest that hung down between his waist and his knees. His loose-cut jeans had a red detail design on the pocket and he had rolled up the trouser legs that were too long for him; they finished at his pale blue Timberland boots.

The man had seemed to Howard to appear out of nowhere - one minute he was alone, singing to himself, the next the man was walking towards him. Howard's immediate reaction was to cease his singing in slight

291

embarrassment but, as soon as he'd stopped, he began again, as if he were defying his discomfiture at being caught during an assumed private moment; if anything, he raised his voice faintly. The man stopped dead in his tracks and stared directly into Howard's eyes as they were about to pass each other. Howard slowed down considerably, almost to a standstill, but not quite. Both men maintained eye contact which, although intense, was not exactly aggressive or confrontational; it was more perplexity on both parts. As Howard continued his song, unsure of the man's purpose or intent, the man's eyes completely glazed over and he turned away from Howard.

'Robert Nesta Marley,' the man said, as though he were reading from a book or a record sleeve. 'Born sixth of February nineteen forty-five in Nine Miles in the Parish of St Ann, Jamaica. Born of a white father, Norval Sinclair Marley, and a Jamaican mother, Cedella "Ciddy" Malcolm, who lived in Rhoden Hall.' As he spoke, he quickly and, in an extremely jerky and awkward motion, walked away from Howard across the grassy knolls in a different direction from the one he had previously been heading.

'After Bob was born, his father left his mother. When he was five, his father took him to Kingston. Bob saw his mother after a year. Two years later, he and his mother moved to Trench Town because his mother was looking for a job...' the man continued as he walked off into the distance. Howard, who had now completely stopped walking, was puzzled and also, in a peculiar sort of way, amused. He had, however, stopped singing.

Dr Morris looked physically unwell. He was running a temperature and had lost some weight – not a huge amount, but enough to make him seem less robust than usual. He didn't exactly have flu, or even a full-blown cold; he was just extremely rundown, fatigued and weary, which showed on his face, in the lines that always seemed more pronounced when he was under the weather, the way his cheeks lost their colour, and in the way his eyes became more sunken in their sockets. His attire was its usual fair standard of grooming and presentation in his own unique and, sometimes, eccentric collaboration of the very stylish and the downright mistaken.

'Einstein failed because he thought he could take on God, Doctor. He thought he could create a theory of everything, but it's just not possible; we can only ever move towards it. We never, though, actually get there. It is the nature of the beast; it's a journey, not a destination. We are chasing the unattainable, but that need to know is the impetus for us to continue. By chasing probabilities that can never be fully resolved, we surge forward in an evolutionary manner. Without such an impulse we would stagnate and rot,' Howard said in full flight. Dr Morris struggled to offer him any response at all, let alone the discouragement he so desired to imbue in him.

'You see, they argued too much instead of building bridges. Einstein, Plank, Heisenberg – they bickered about general relativity and quantum mechanics, but they're starting to understand that they are just as important and, combined, will bring us closer to where they want to go, unravelling the contradictions, or the paradox is the trick. Hawking is in the same bind as Einstein was, where next? They battle with their egos and all they can find is God. Time and knowledge move on, the nature of all things is change. The universe and everything in it is in a state of perpetual motion. Nothing stays still or remains the same; it's quite simply impossible. Einstein wanted a perfect universe – a predictable universe calculable in a simple equation, but he died a failure. I mean, how could he not, for Christ's sake? The irony is that he didn't realise how close he was. This seeming random, chaotic universe is actually a reliable, stable, ordered set of events that are so complex, so infinite in variables, in input and output, in sequence and consequence that, from our miniscule, transient, enormous, eternal universal viewpoint, we simply cannot comprehend nor predict the order of it all. It is an inextricable web, an inconceivable set of chain reactions that we find ourselves the centre of. There are always unseens, there is always the 'beyond'. If that's the case, then how can we possibly calculate the whole, or even totally accurately the components of that whole? We stumble to predict the results, but we don't have God's insight; God oversees the whole process, *is* the whole process. If quantum theory demonstrates anything, it is our limits as human beings. I mean, it can be applied locally, to create useful applied technology – that may destroy us all, I might add – but they are random estimates resulting in local production. It does have an element of accuracy, but they cannot solve the mysteries of the universe, which serves as a reminder of the elusiveness of reality. Future technology will further show both the extent of the continuous universe in outer space and the continued discovery of more and more miniscule quantum existence, or life. This has been the case from the outset of the telescope and the microscope, you know, and now particle accelerators, if that shit convinces you, and will continue to be as long as the technology and we do. Protons, electrons, neutrons, quarks, gluons – what next? What are quarks comprised of? You know... infinite particles, there is no beginning and there is no end, ultimately 'life' in all its forms goes on forever – birth, death and rebirth. Universes come and universes go. For example, the sun heats up with age, heating our galaxy further. Life on earth under its conventional definition has to evolve according to temperature. If it can cope or even thrive under the temperature provided by the sun, then everything's fine; however, this temperature will fluctuate and so too will life on earth. When life on earth as we know it cannot cope with this increase, it will perish. It is probable that evolution on earth, from single-celled organisms to humans and beyond, and everything in between, will evolve in aggregate over and in time very much according to the constant rise, albeit with interludes, blips in temperature, in congruence with the life cycle of the sun, right up to its death. Hence, the corollary is that this life cycle is applicable elsewhere in our solar system. It is possible that life similar to our own was perhaps once present firstly on Mercury, then Venus, presently earth and tomorrow Mars, which is currently in the deep freeze cryonically, waiting its turn. Following that could be Jupiter, then Saturn, Uranus, Neptune and finally Pluto. It is certainly not guaranteed that life as we currently define it did, or will, 'materialise' – or, more correctly, be brought from latency into activity – but that the conditions for such life forms were, or will be, more prevalent and hence bring forth the likelihood. However, it may be just as probable that "we", meaning earthly biological life, may be the only type to actually come to fruition in this solar system or galaxy at any time in its history. Either way, this overall process is merely a speck of universal life and its cycle of activities. You see, Doctor, 'life' is all about timing.' Howard was sweating with enthusiasm and zeal at his weakened adversary and his opportunity to take the floor, so to speak.

'Erm... do you think that's why we have global warming, Howard?' Dr Morris contributed, in a feeble and truly disinterested attempt to appear to be doing his job.

'We're shortening our time, Doctor. It's like getting under an electric blanket when the central heating is on full whack,' Howard assured him. 'If it's actually anything to do with us in the first place?' he added as an afterthought, almost sidetracking himself.

'Just as atoms are a sort of mini universe, with a nucleus containing extraordinary energy at its centre, so too is the sun the nucleus of our solar system. Our solar system is simply an atom in the universe. Just as we are comprised of atoms, so too is something infinitely larger than ourselves, or our atomic discoveries, comprised of atoms made up of our miniscule solar systems and galaxies. To split the atom, as in nuclear fission or explosion, is in terms of scale relatively equivocal to smashing our solar system with many others and causing an even larger nuclear explosion. Splitting the nucleus of an atom is like exploding our sun with many other stars on impact. To do so is equivalent to cancer in a body; in other words, detrimental. We can either be a cancer in the atoms and cells of a universal body, or we can be and act as a catalyst for good or something positive. The choice is ours, Doctor.' Howard continued to waffle on as though he were a sage or an oracle Dr Morris had consulted on how to rule his imaginary kingdom.

'If you want to understand the origins of the known universe, the so-called big bang, then you need to look at quantum mechanics, at sub-atomic phenomenon, because that is what we are talking about, a sub-atomic compressed mass of explosive energy that, for some reason, exploded or expanded into what we see today. And when you look at quantum phenomenon you quickly realise that compressed units of energy are commonplace and by no means alone. It wasn't a big bang, it was a big collision. It's perfectly possible that the big bang is simply like a large-scale nuclear fission, our known universe exploding out of gigantic atomic collisions. We could be part of even huger sequences of nuclear fission. The big bang that produced us is probably one of an infinite number of big bangs that occur throughout the unknown universe. Possibly the big bang becomes a big crunch. When energy cools, it becomes matter; when matter cools sufficiently, it implodes due to mass or weight and the explosion we know as the "big bang" slows and is eventually dragged back to a single point. However, it doesn't stop there, Doctor. Oh no, it implodes and collapses in on itself until it becomes so condensed that the energy suppressed becomes unimaginably powerful; when it collides with other similar compressed points or nucleuses of energy, the whole big bang nuclear fission starts all over again. Or perhaps it's simply the density of the mass of the big crunch that eventually causes such inconceivable compression to finally explode, due to the immense pressure of the crunch's implosion. And then another big bang occurs, another universe is born, kind of like a multi-dimensional bow tie. Big bangs and big crunches are essentially two sides of the same coin, alternating in sequence, explosion and implosion, each propelled by the other, turning itself inside out, then outside in. These are infinite in number; we, our known universe, are merely a collection of atomic and sub-atomic particles in a constant and infinite number of other similar atomic and sub-atomic collections that form other universes. There are other big bangs and big crunches happening everywhere, all affected by and encroaching on each other, either directly or by infinite proxy. This affects everything in our known universe;

all our laws and events are subject to all the other explosions and implosions, as is ours on all the others. It is a never-ending sequence. Maybe sub-atomic particles explode into existence, like universes do, infinitely smaller and smaller, like microscopic big bangs? Perhaps that's why they seem to appear and disappear, microscopic big bangs and big crunches? Gravity fluctuates between being the weakest force in our known universe to becoming the most powerful, depending on the decreasing temperature of energy from the explosion becoming matter, that eventually collapses in on itself, the nature of which also depends on the impact of other encroaching big bangs and the gravitational pull of other big crunches. Parallel to this are black holes, which may well be mini big crunches that ultimately result in mini big bangs in what would amount to be other dimensions, also probably infinite in number. Maybe all the galaxies are moving further and further apart because we – our entire universe – are actually being sucked into a truly enormous black hole? Maybe we can't see it 'cos it's too big. We – our universe – are actually rotating in orbit around a gigantic event horizon and we, in our time frame, are observing it, living it, without actually knowing. Maybe we've actually been pulled apart by it but haven't received the information yet? If time has slowed more and more, as we get sucked in and ripped apart, it seems to us to have not happened yet, or to be happening but at the rate we experience here and now. But perhaps it would appear, to outside observers, to have happened in a split second? That the original point of singularity is reclaiming us, tearing our very fabric apart, bit by bit. But maybe that's not the end, no... maybe it's just the spinning motion of an enormous – to us, I mean – sub-atomic particle, a proton or an electron in something truly huge, and it is merely the change of direction of the particle. What we experience as being drawn into the ultimate – or perhaps not, as the case may be – black hole, pulling us apart in every direction, is actually only the moment to moment interaction of a universal sub-atomic particle. A particle that seems elementary in another universe, although it's actually all one... universe, I mean, another dimension, that is interacting in a similar fashion to the sub-atomic particles that we observe here on earth. Maybe we are being fired around a particle accelerator of unimaginably enormous proportions, sucked into the black hole and out the other side in the opposite direction... a positive to a negative charge, or vice versa. Like universal synapses – electrical charges in some infinite neural network, our universe is inside a particle inside a particle – ad infinitum. Our universe is spiralling around an enormous singularity or black hole inside a particle spinning one way until it spins another on attraction to another particle of universal proportions. The big bang is actually a big spiral, or the velocity of a particle, emitting waves of attraction and repulsion in conjunction with infinite others. Singularity is the point of contact between particles. Perhaps black holes spiral faster than the speed of light and that's why light can't escape? Maybe they get bigger and bigger as a result, gaining momentum and mass as they do so, maybe? If there was singularity originating in the big bang, then by definition there was a centre of the universe – or still is, even if that single point no longer actually exists as a singularity, but surely exists, detectable or not from our current location and time as the closest density of galaxies in direct contrast to those furthest away. Maybe there was no big bang? Maybe it's all just moving apart due to the black hole sucking us in – no explosion, just spreading us apart. To come from a big bang, from "nothing", is basically a theological concept... I mean, what was it? Nothing? But nothing doesn't exist anywhere in the known universe... large or small, there's always something. So, either before the big bang there was something else, or it was something that doesn't exist here except as a very tricky concept, nothingness, a vacuum. Try and describe it – it doesn't exist outside of philosophy or religion. The point is, that this process is simply ongoing and renders the universe ultimately constant because it is infinite – or, more precisely, it equals a lemniscate, a ribbon – you know, a sideways figure eight, the mathematical symbol, the representative concept that we humans deem to understand such a premise. The formulations are in a constant state of flux of rearrangement and reconfiguring, but the nature of this, the process, is continuous and is by definition permanent. That's why Einstein was right – it *is* fundamentally a stable universe, but quantum physics demonstrates just how complex and seemingly unpredictable it all this is. We can only ever deal in probabilities, to measure it as such because it's infinite and the variables are endless. But Einstein was correct – God does not play dice.' Howard was now ranting uncontrollably and Dr Morris was beyond caring. He simply wanted the session to be over so that he could cancel the rest of his afternoon appointments and go home to bed. Hopefully, he would feel better in the morning and be able to resume his duties as normal.

'It's all about scale, I know it is. There aren't four different energies – electromagnetic, the two nuclear ones and gravity... No, they're all the same thing – the seeming catalyst is scale! Yes! What we observe down there is happening up here and out there, I know it. It just seems different because of scale... one law differing scales. If you can work out how it is down there, then you've worked out how it is up here and out there and vice versa. Particles or waves, or both... or neither? Maybe they're particles emitting waves, a travelling particle, which is why we can only measure position or velocity and not both? It's moving, they all are, constantly. Maybe the particles' velocity is so high... well, maybe only at times, like on repulsion from collision – that they appear as waves, like cine film? A series of images of particles merge, which is why they're observed as both at differing times. Perhaps there are frequencies faster than light but we can't detect them yet, perhaps ever? Sub-atomic particles feed off each other – losing energy on collision, in turn altering the frequency of the particles

302

involved; like gravity is relative to scale or mass, or a conglomeration of matter particles. All of the four universal forces are all the same but are at different frequencies, speed of vibration or sound... loudness or quietness... particles, matter, galaxies affected by it but in different ways, according to scale. Scale or mass affects the forces or force... the force or forces, or frequency, affect different scales or masses differently. The principles are one and the same scale must be the difference, or the number of particles, in differing forms. It seems different in time and space from our scale in time and space... relative... the relativity of scale and velocity or rates of attraction and repulsion... We have abstracted the force into differing things... a spiralling big crunch, resulting in an opposite spiralling big bang... positive and negative charges. The laws we attempt to measure are eternally elusive. Time and space differ according to the scale or size, the velocity, experience and perception of the observer. So, it is possible that the laws may even be the same, but operate at relative speeds and spatial experiences based on the size of phenomenon. We cannot put ourselves as human beings outside of our own time and spatial awareness, however multifaceted that awareness may be. It is limited by our biological perception and our finite presence at any given point in time and space. In the light of an eternal universe, in which we have appeared for a very brief period as a by-product of both miniscule and enormous proportions, it is inconceivable that we might understand, calculate and encapsulate what it all is. The closest we get is religious expression. When scientists talk as though they have truly arrived at "universal theories" that encompass it all, then I'm afraid, Doctor, science is stagnating. Just as it is absurd that we have reached the end of history, as some claim, so too is it ridiculous to suppose that we have reached, or are approaching, the end of science. If that is the conclusion, then science is basically dead in the water. It becomes dogma, theological dogma...'

Howard was at this point talking to himself. Dr Morris sat glassy-eyed in what amounted to a physical depression. His body was simply in overdrive. Warfare of epic proportions was raging throughout his physiology, while his defences were slogging it out like conscripts at Stalingrad.

'I mean, no fuckin' wonder all Einstein could go on about towards the end was God. That's all he kept saying: "It's all God". Did anybody care? Did they fuck,' Howard blustered at Dr Morris, who was currently mentally absent.

'Perhaps that's basically how it works at every level...' Howard said, now ceasing to preach to Dr Morris, but instead almost discussing it with himself. 'Maybe the fabric of space and time... basically the same thing, the latter being a measurement of the former... maybe everything is simply composed of this process. Explosion and implosion, or attraction and repulsion, all interacting with each other, the space in between... no, there is no space in between, it just seems that way. Just slower rates of expansion or compression, or attraction and repulsion, all pushing and pulling against each other, each having the same effect only in reverse, in opposition, all multi-directional, all in every direction possible, all different in size, in scale constantly, continuously, over and over, vibrating, pulsating. The only difference is size and when and where in time and space... all interacting and affecting each other and we are simply observing it all from this present position in time and space... but is there really such a thing as the present, as now? Is it really all just a serious of moments? No past, no future, only now, here and now... but there is no here and now, no moment, there is only the past and the future. The human mind is simply memory and projection, the ability to remember what's happened and the ability to predict, to imagine events that haven't yet materialised... The present is an illusion, this is why living for the moment is so difficult... but we are only ever at a single point at any given moment in time or space, travelling between the point that we were previously to the point that we are about to arrive at... but that's only applicable if time is linear... no beginning no end, just ongoing... The same is true of space, then; the relative point of where "one" is determines where the outer and the inner begin. As this is relative it is not constant, therefore there is no single point at which the inner and the outer begin. It's all just points or particles joined by fields of waves, a matrix or network of points of energy connected by waves of energy, all compressed together at differing frequencies, transmitting each point to the next over infinitely relative huge, average and minute distances, creating varying densities of energy that seem to be joined by surges or particles of condensed waves along waves of travelling surges or stretched elongated particles. It's just what you measure, where you choose or are able to measure and record what amounts to the same thing. This means... this means that they share the same properties... of form and content... what alters them is relativity, the relative point of the "observer", the perceiver or the experiencer. If outer time and space are actually infinite, that means... what does it mean? It means it is infinitely huge; conversely, if inner time and space is infinitely tiny, then it means that they are both, in principle, the same... both are infinite time and space... there is no centre, no core... it's just one great big expanse. Your size simply determines where you are in it, determines where expanse and, and... inspanse? Begin and end for you... our bodies, every drop of sweat, every time we sneeze... whatever... is a million, a billion, even more than that, is an infinite number of universes, not the same as us, as ours, but similar, fundamentally the same, at the very core it's all the same... or is it constantly different? In expression, in composition, it is different, but it's all made of the same stuff... at any point, anywhere, absolutely anywhere is another infinite expanse and... inspance, any point in us, in inner space or outer... Do you realise what that means? It means that no matter where on or in your body you begin, or anywhere or on anything in the universe, how far in or how far out... it's infinite... maybe the universe is all strings, like they say, vibrating strings, like enormous helixes, huge lengths of universal DNA, universal chromosomes... we are living inside truly gigantic universal chromosomes... pulsating, vibrating. We are all made of a vibration, a sound... what about light? Light is actually sound vibrating at high speed, at the speed of light, in fact! Or is it vice versa? Surely it's relative to frequency?' Howard was at this point making no pretence of talking to Dr Morris. This was a private conversation.

'So, you travel in any direction, from any single point on your body or in the universe, which you are merely a part of, not in any way separate. If you go outwards in any direction, it simply keeps going for ever! What's more, if you start at any point on or in your body and travel or explore inwards, down to the atoms that we are comprised of, then it just keeps going too... for ever!' Howard's eyes were wide with awe; all they were missing was a psychedelic vortex of spiralling colours, like a mixed paint tray being poured down a plug hole.

'Space and time are infinite... the universe is infinite... ultimately we are infinite, too. Infinity runs right through us... it's miraculous, it really is! Explosion and implosion, attraction and repulsion, that's all it is. Two forces vying for control – one pushes one way, the other pulls another. We are held together literally by these two forces, the right equilibrium at the right time in the right space... a precarious balance of nature... It's like eating beans and eggs... explosive and binding, the perfect combination!'

Howard finished with a huge grin, directing his attention back to Dr Morris in time to see all the blood drain from his face. He opened his mouth to say something to Howard, but all that emerged was a garbled and nonsensical noise that resembled something that someone in the advanced stages of dementia might attempt.

Dr Morris withered as he produced this sound, flopped forward towards his desk and slithered out of his chair, striking his head with a dull, bone-cracking thud on the edge of the desk as he descended. He slumped to the floor, unconscious, pushing his chair back on its wheels against the wall behind. Howard sat blinking vacantly, unable to process the transition from his internal epiphany to the cold veracity of what had just transpired before him.

'Doctor?' he said in a whisper. Dr Morris did not reply, nor did he even move, as blood trickled from his head and formed little isolated pools on the surface of the impermeable synthetic carpet.

HOW MANY MAGNETONS...?

The post came at twenty-eight minutes past three, the latest it had come all that week, though it had been coming later and later for weeks now. A single letter dropped onto the hall floor of Howard's flat. It was the incentive he had needed to wheedle him out of bed. His bedroom was actually the front room of a converted house. His bed and, indeed, his room, aside from the usual mess of DVDs, books, magazines, clothes and countless dirty dishes with mouldy, half-eaten meals and snacks, was strewn with endless felt-tip pens, permanent markers, pencils, compasses large and small, square and circular cardboard templates, a set-square and graph paper of varying proportions with random squares coloured in differing sequences and elaborate fractals of repetitive numbers and mathematical symbols. Partial and whole successive formations went on and on, from sheet to sheet, of smudged graph paper; each time a single mistake had been made in one tiny part of any of the sequences, Howard had put an enormous black 'X' through it and started all over again.

Amongst all the fractals, were cuttings and leftover sheets of clear Perspex with graph lines photocopied onto them, the waste products of a plethora of three-dimensional models of the numerical chains and fractals that varied in both size and design; from basic cube and spherical creations, to cubes inside spheres inside cubes, and spheres inside cubes inside spheres and so on. Most were marked and labelled in the photocopied graph squares with an array of sequential numbers, equations and mathematical symbols, all different in colour according to the assigned code of that particular model. Each three-dimensional model correlated with the ones already worked out on graph paper; models which, in turn, gave rise to further two-dimensional cycles and paradigms, all comprised of the original series of numbers and symbols.

Without looking, Howard traversed his way through the ocean of Woolworth products that was 'his work', opened the door to his cesspit and picked up the letter that lay in front of the flat's main entrance door, which was adjacent to his bedroom. He ambled dozily along the corridor in his boxer shorts and an old t-shirt, scraping his shoulder occasionally against the cheap woodchip wallpaper, and shuffled into the reception area that he and his flatmate called the front room. He sat on the sofa and tore open the letter.

Dear *Mr Howard James*
I regret to inform you that, due to unforeseen illness, Dr Morris is unable to attend your next appointment. Your next appointment is *Wednesday 19th September 2008* at *3.00pm*. We have, however, arranged a replacement locum psychiatrist to attend on Dr Morris's behalf. We are very sorry for any inconvenience this may cause you, but is due to circumstances beyond our control. If you have any enquiries at all regarding this or any

other matter please do not hesitate to contact us on the above telephone number.

Yours sincerely
Anne Roddick
Administration Co-ordinator

Howard read the letter slowly and thoroughly. When he'd finished, he snorted loudly, scrunched it up and threw it across the room, where it fell against the curtain, rolled onto the floor and into the middle of the room. He picked up the remote control and turned on the television. He sat watching it for ten minutes, changing channels constantly, before getting up and picking up the letter. He sat back down and un-scrunched the letter. He continued to watch television as he sat, slowly stroking the letter until it was reasonably flat and un-creased.

An hour later, he ate a peanut butter sandwich with a cup of tea, then he quickly got dressed, gelled his hair and went out. He marched hurriedly to the end of his road and onto the high street. He rapidly strode towards the tube station, which was approximately eight minutes away, ignoring anybody that he passed. He kept his eyes to the floor, only looking up to ensure he was not going to bump into anyone, avoiding all eye contact as he did so. He bought a one-day travel card from the homeless tout outside the station, who he was able to look straight in the eyes. The tout was unable, or unwilling, to reciprocate the eye contact and looked around uneasily as Howard paid him the pound charge for the scruffy, one to four zone travel card.

As he entered the station, Howard glanced at the Transport for London customer service attendant who had seen him purchase the second-hand travel card. The man was large and well-built, with a pasty puffy face and a day's stubble on his chin. He glowered at Howard momentarily, before turning away and smiling at a buxom peroxide-blonde woman dressed in a tacky pink with black trim business suit and pink stilettos. She wobbled her way through the barrier with an almost fluorescent pink-wheeled suitcase that rattled ungraciously against the sides of the overly-narrow barrier gate.

'Need an 'and, love?' the attendant said, as debonairly as a man reeking of whisky and all-day breakfast could.

'No, thank you,' the woman replied, full of airs and graces as she battled to retrieve her suitcase from the barrier. She caught the man's eye as she finally yanked the case free and waddled off, handbag swinging, as the attendant graphically ogled the woman's ample rear, a salivating sneer spreading across his face.

Howard took it all in as he put his travel card into the barrier and gawked at the attendant, while he waited for the card to return via the exit slot. The attendant turned and scowled at Howard, who quickly retrieved his travel card and hurried towards the escalator, which was out of order, so he followed the signs to the winding emergency stairs. He took the narrower inner section of the old steps in order to by-pass the congested procession of people that was congregating behind an old woman, unable to cope with the turret of an assault course that corkscrewed down before her and out of sight.

Howard sped down the steps, past the young man that had begun assisting the elderly woman in her ordeal, and was soon heading down the tiled passage towards the platform. As he stepped onto the platform, a train hurtled out of the tunnel and halted in front of the crowd of waiting travellers. He quickly negotiated his way through the busy mass of people that were moving forward to board the train and the influx of those that were hastily exiting it, avoiding all eye contact, and continuously avoiding near collisions with the cross-purpose tide of diligent bodies. Eventually, the hordes thinned out as he neared the end of the platform and he boldly stomped onto the carriage, which he found to be strewn with hundreds of pieces of polystyrene, the tiny kind that comes in packaging as a sort of snowdrift cushion. He stared at it momentarily before sitting down in the middle of the row of seats.

He looked opposite to his right, where there sat a man of Mediterranean or Latin American appearance, he couldn't tell. The man, in his early thirties, was fairly small, but quite stocky and was wearing a cheap, non-branded grey tracksuit made of sweatshirt fabric, which clung tightly to his sturdy physique. His hair was cropped short and he had about three days' worth of growth on his chin. His stale body odour and the stench of alcohol engulfed his half of the carriage as he sat, with his arm around an empty, industrial-size cardboard box resting on the seat next to him. Laid out on the two seats next to the box were neat piles of second-hand books, each three or four books high. Howard took interest in the books and mulled over their titles, one by one, as the train pulled out of the station. He glanced at the man as if he might engage him in conversation. The man looked straight back at the friendly-faced Howard, incensed by his actions.

'YOU CAN'T DO THAT!' he yelled with a thick accent of some sort. Howard immediately looked away and faced the window.

'YOU FUCKING BASTARD, WE DON'T ACCEPT THAT!' the man continued to shout. Howard looked increasingly nervous and uncomfortable and began biting his lip, then erratically moving his tongue around in his mouth, over his teeth and up into his gums. The man exploded with rage.

'WE DON'T ACCEPT THAT. THAT IS NOT ACCEPTABLE BEHAVIOUR!' repeated the man. He began waving his arms around furiously as he raved, turning every so often to address the passengers in the neighbouring section of the carriage before returning his fury back to Howard.

'WE DON'T ACCEPT THAT SORT OF BEHAVIOUR AT ALL. SUCKING YOUR GUMS IS NOT ACCEPTED!' the man screamed at Howard, as he grew more nervous and anxious than ever. He could no longer control his mouth and its trembling reactions to this torrent of abuse. In a vain attempt to quell the facial quivering that ensued, he returned to the frantic search of his gums with his tongue.

'YOU SEE, LOOK AT HIM!' the man appealed to the passengers. 'WE DON'T ACCEPT THAT BEHAVIOUR. YOU'RE DOING IT AGAIN AND WE DON'T ACCEPT IT, YOU'RE VERY BAD, SO BAD!' The man was literally having a physical fit, so outraged was he by Howard and his behaviour, and was ranting and waving his arms around, shouting to himself.

'WE DON'T ACCEPT THAT BEHAVIOUR AND WE... WE HAVE TO...' The man mumbled something under his breath that could not be heard, and then drunkenly turned out his trouser pocket as if he were looking for something.

'WE DON'T ACCEPT THAT BEHAVIOUR AND WE HAVE TO KILL YOU FOR IT. CUT YOU UP. WE HAVE TO KILL YOU FOR IT... WE DON'T ACCEPT IT!' The man was now leaning forward and waving his finger at Howard.

Howard looked at him, half terrified, half consumed with discomfort and embarrassment at the amount of attention being directed towards him. He looked opposite to his left; a tall, south Asian man was leaning into the glass panel, reading his paper as though he were trying to be as far as humanly possible away from the ranting man, despite the fact that he was sitting at the complete opposite end of the row of seats. His facial expression was fearful as he attempted to concentrate on reading his paper.

'WE KILL YOU!' the drunken man insisted to Howard. He leaned further and further forward before leaping back into his seat and raving and muttering to himself again, his body language becoming more and more threatening.

'I TELL YOU SOMETHING. WE DON'T ACCEPT IT!' he yelled again.

Howard glanced to his left, where an eastern European-looking man was half turned into the glass panel next to him as though he were somehow invisible, and refused to offer any eye contact to anybody in the carriage. Howard looked directly back at the shouting man and, for a second, a look of anger spread across his face, before the man's continued invective forced him to look away and back to his trembling, nervy, mouth disorder.

'WE KILL YOU!' the man hollered, trying to go through his other pocket. Howard instantly locked his eyes on the man again to see if he was actually producing anything from his pocket which, fortunately, hung empty, inside-out like the other. Finally, after what seemed to Howard like an eternity, the train pulled into the next station. Howard leapt up and stood in front of the doors located in the opposite direction of the man.

'WE DON'T ACCEPT IT! WE WILL NOT!' he called after Howard as he leapt off the train and cut through the waiting travellers. He shook with nervous tension while he climbed the stairs, hurried up the escalator, through the barrier and out into the street. He quickly walked back home, careful not to make any eye contact with anyone, and took refuge in his room.

'Synchronisation,' he muttered to himself as he lay on his bed and covered his eyes with his forearm. He remained there for the rest of the day and the whole night. It was the first time he had been on the underground since beginning his course of medication.

SESSION TWENTY-FOUR

Howard walked across the reception area and sat down. He looked demoralised, depressed; his usual ability to sneak panoramic photographic takes of the entire room in a single glance was absent, unable or unwilling to engage with anything outside of his immediate line of vision, which was people's feet.

There was only one pair of feet sitting in the waiting area and they were opposite him, slightly to his right. The feet in question wore a cheap, tacky and rather vulgar pair of black, mock leather brogues of the typical standard office variety. The hairy ankles were long and in full view due to the negligible length of the truly nasty viscose, cotton-mix silver/grey slacks that could virtually be described as three-quarter length they were cut so short – true ankle swingers. Howard followed the long legs upwards, which sat crossed and bouncing up and down at a tremendous rate. The jacket of the man matched the trousers in colour, design and aesthetic indecency and was complemented well by a matching, ill-fitting shiny charcoal/black shirt and tie that was evidently a ready-made pack variety; a design copy of a design copy, of a design copy.

Howard looked up to examine the face that had created such an ensemble of skilfully arranged ineptitude; he was met with an awaiting grin that beamed across the rough-featured face of a Greek or Spanish-looking man. The man's hair was carefully combed and styled, as if he were about to pose in a photographic shoot for a local barbers in the mid to late-eighties.

'Hi, how are you?' the man said with enthusiastic ardour, before returning to his huge grin of almost perfect front teeth bar one, that jutted out slightly and overlapped the otherwise uniform line-up. Howard stared at the man before he began to blink, as his eyes started to water with the strain of having to look somebody in the face. He gave in and looked down.

'What are you in for?' the man said quietly, conspiratorially, as he sat forward, hands between closed legs, his eyes peered into slits as he leaned in order that Howard could hear him better. Howard immediately glanced back up before looking quickly around the room to see who might be listening.

'Erm, drug, erm… drug-induced psychosis,' he answered in a croaky half-whisper before clearing his throat. 'How about you?' he enquired with genuine interest.

'Me? Oh, I'm here for a job interview,' the man said, his huge grin enlarging to seemingly impossible proportions as he sat back, re-crossed his legs and placed his right arm along the top of the waiting room sofa in great comfort, resuming his furious leg-bouncing. Howard looked as though he were a deer caught in headlights. He wanted to respond with rapier wit but was unable to even look away, which was his second greatest desire at that moment.

'Howard Jones?' a south Asian accent wafted between Howard's startled look and the

319

cat-that-got-the-cream, over-stretched grin opposite.

'No,' the man said reassuringly to the small, grey-haired, cream and dark beige sari-clad woman that stood to his right, clutching a brown file to her chest. She did not respond as she beckoned to Howard to come with her. Howard followed her like a small child lost in a haze of super-skunk fumes.

'Have you been waiting long?' she called out over her shoulder as she proceeded slowly along the corridor. Howard didn't respond; he merely shuffled after her, staring at the floor in confusion.

'This one will do,' she said as she opened the door to a random room. Howard stopped as she did and then allowed her to direct him into the room with a couple of hand gestures. Howard dropped into the chair reserved for patients, while the woman, who was fairly youthful-looking for her age, economically perched herself behind the desk opposite him.

'So…' she said gently, placing a pair of spectacles of the buy-one-get-one-free ilk on the end of her nose and began reading over some of the notes that she had obviously just seen for the first time. Howard looked at her properly for the first time as she did so.

'I see…' she muttered softly to herself as she read with painstaking and thorough scrutiny, albeit at a snail's pace. After nearly five minutes of this, Howard's usual restlessness returned to him as he fully regained his composure.

'Where's Dr Morris?' he demanded finally.

'Hmmm?' the woman responded, as though her husband had just interrupted a good bit of an Agatha Christie novel to offer her an Ovaltine before bedtime. Howard scoffed to himself before repeating the question as though she were slightly deaf.

'Where – is – Dr – Morris?'

'Oh...' she uttered as her concentration was finally broken. She removed her glasses, folded them and placed them on top of the open file. Clasping her hands and leaning forward, despite the dwarfing height of the desk, she smiled.

'My name is Dr Mohneeb,' she said. Howard waited for further information but it was not forthcoming. He gave a look of despondence followed by another of irritation.

'I will be looking after you while Dr Morris is away,' Dr Mohneeb said eventually.

'Well, where has he gone? I mean...'

'Dr Morris is not very well at the moment and that is all you need to know,' she said, cutting him off firmly but without malice.

'Well, how long is he...?'

'That's not important right now. All you need to know is that I will be looking after you for a while and that there's nothing to worry about.' Dr Mohneeb's manner was seductively reassuring but had an undercurrent of rigid authority about it.

'But...' Howard protested.

'Tut tut tut,' Dr Mohneeb replied, shaking her head. 'Now, let us begin your session, shall we?' Dr Mohneeb continued. Howard sat back in frustration.

'Now I'm just trying to familiarise myself with your case, but what would really help me is if you went over your case history with me. It would really save some time and I feel it would be better coming from you, don't you agree?' Dr Mohneeb suggested. Howard sat gawping at her momentarily before sitting forward.

'What I think, Dr Mohneed...'

'Mohneeb, my name is Dr *Mohneeb*,' she interrupted with great emphasis on the 'B.'

'Okay, Dr *Mohneeb*,' Howard said also over emphasising the 'B,' retorting with his usual caustic response to patronisation. 'What I think is that I have done this way too many times for me to start it all over again. In fact, I can't even fucking remember what happened any more. I'm trying to forget all that shit, not fucking remember it, okay?'

'Please...' Dr Mohneeb said, raising a stern finger. 'Please, no swearing, Howard. It is not appropriate.' Her accent grew thicker as she castigated him.

'Oh, for fuck's sake!' Howard reacted immediately.

'I will not tell you again, do you understand?' Dr Mohneeb said harshly, but still in full control. Howard rolled his eyes and, like a schoolboy, deridingly imitated someone suffering from cerebral palsy, with his tongue pushing his lower mouth forward.

'That's it!' Dr Mohneeb said as she sprang to her feet and banged the table with her palm, the sight of which seemed ridiculous to Howard. She reminded him of a television comedy sketch where enormous furniture is built in order to create the illusion of adults being young children. He began to laugh.

'You are an extremely disrespectful young man. It is no wonder you are in the predicament that you are in!' Dr Mohneeb bellowed, the veins in her forehead and wiry forearms swelled as her patience ended. For the tiny and frail-looking woman that she was, the contrast was surprising and Howard ceased his childish giggling.

'Now, if I hear one more bad word from your mouth you will be out of here, do you understand?' she continued with the same authority, but more quietly and composed. Howard snorted in deeply.

'I tell you what, love...' he said condescendingly. 'I'll save you the time, shall I?' Howard got up and stormed out of the room, slamming the door violently behind him.

'CUNTS!' was all Dr Mohneeb heard as he stormed down the corridor.

Howard picked up the letter that was addressed to him from the hospital and peeled open the envelope.

Dear *Howard James*
Thank you for your written apology to Dr Mohneeb, it was much appreciated. You have now gone through the correct procedure for conditional re-admittance on a probationary basis we are pleased to inform you that your next appointment is *Friday 7th December 2008* at *1.00pm* with Dr Morris. If you have any enquiries at all regarding this or any other

matter, please do not hesitate to contact us on the above telephone number.

> Yours sincerely
> *Anne Roddick*
> Administration Co-ordinator

Howard smiled and popped his head around the door of his bedroom. Then he threw the letter into the middle of the cluttered room, where a small pile of hospital letters resided. He could not contain the cheesy grin that spread across his face.

'Welcome back, Dr Morris,' he muttered.

'Welcome back, Raymond!' he exclaimed out loud. He then flopped onto his bed and stared blankly at the wall, his usual melancholic look slowly re-emerging across his face.

SESSION TWENTY-FIVE

Howard entered the room cautiously, gently closing the door behind him. Dr Morris sat calmly waiting for his young client to approach. Unusually, he said nothing; no greeting or great show of bravado or enthusiasm was injected into the meeting. He simply smiled serenely as Howard sat down nervously, awkwardly, as though he were being reunited with an estranged father and was not fully confident of the appropriate demeanour to adopt.

He smiled back at Dr Morris as he re-examined the man he had grown so used to and then had subsequently, week by week, lost the mental image of, as time has a steady habit of accomplishing. Dr Morris seemed significantly smaller than he had appeared before; Howard was certain that this was more than just poor recollection. Dr Morris was not really any shorter, he had simply lost a great deal of weight and looked to have little, or no, body fat left on his now wiry but still muscular physic. Howard noticed the protruding and ugly scar that Dr Morris now sported on the right side of his forehead. It still looked as though it were healing; the stitch marks jutted in different directions like a rough seam along the edges of the main wound, the handiwork of the truly hurried. Dr Morris's normally sparkly eyes were faded and deeply sunken in his skull, his features were weathered and his regularly exfoliated skin was now leathery and slightly saggy in places, as though it no longer entirely fitted his body. In short, he bore the resemblance of a man at least ten years his senior.

'Hello, Howard, long time no see. How are you?' he said gently with an air of fragility about him.

'Hello Dr Morris, erm, fine thank you,' Howard replied as though it would be rude to be any less formal.

'You're looking well,' Dr Morris said, despite the fact that Howard did not look particularly good, though he was positively salubrious in comparison to Dr Morris.

'As you know, I've been away for a while, but I have had a chance to re-familiarise myself with your case,' he said turning the pages to Howard's file. 'I actually have fewer cases to deal with at the moment, which is a good thing really as it gives me more time to devote myself to the ones that I, er... have left,' he finished, as though contemplating the matter.

'Right, I see,' Howard replied gauchely. There was an uneasy silence, which Dr Morris interrupted with a phlegmy cough, followed by a clearing of his throat and a slow drink of water from the plastic cup resting on the desk.

'So, how have you been? What have you been up to, young Howard?' Dr Morris said redirecting the subject swiftly, which was the baton that Howard snatched without hesitation.

'Well, you know not much really. I've pretty much been stuck in the house since the last time I saw you.'

'Apart from the little debacle with our dear Dr Mohneeb. Really, Howard, you should have more respect. She's a lovely woman and a damn fine practitioner,' Dr Morris scolded.

'Oh, her,' Howard responded with a quick roll of the eyes and raising of his eyebrows.

'Howard, she was here to help you. As a result, you forfeit your right to some sessions which, as you know, means that ultimately you're the one who suffers.'

'As long as I don't have to suffer at the hands of imbeciles, Doctor,' Howard said with a brief smile.

'Mmm, I'll take that as a compliment... I think, Howard,' Dr Morris said. Both men seemed to become more at ease with each other than they had been previously. Dr Morris was, through his ill health, more amiable and less domineering than usual, while Howard was more appreciative of a familiar quantity in Dr Morris, besides which he had not held a conversation of more than two sentences with anyone since September and had a great deal on his mind.

'So, Howard, you've been stuck in the house, I believe you said... doing what, exactly? Nothing? Have you sat in the house and done absolutely nothing?'

'Not nothing, Doctor, no... I mean, well, I watch a lot of telly, but I can't stop thinking about things.'

'Things, aye? What sort of things dare I ask, Howard?'

'Well, mostly infinity.'

'Infinity, eh? You've spent more than three months thinking about infinity, Howard?'

'Pretty much. I mean, amongst other things, but mainly infinity,' Howard said without a trace of irony.

'Well, I suppose three months is not such a long time to spend pondering infinity,' Dr Morris said with a chuckle.

'Not at all, Doctor,' Howard sincerely concurred.

'The thing is, Howard, that most people don't really get infinity. What I mean to say is, that... well, most people simply can't quite get their heads around it. It's sort of a non-starter, really. Most people, and I include myself, kind of struggle with the notion of it. You see, everything is born and everything dies, so I'm not sure how it quite fits into the equation. It's simply impossible to get to grips with. Do you see what I mean?'

'No,' Howard said bluntly. Dr Morris paused for a moment and sighed, as though he were very world-weary. He then gave a wry smile, which seemed to lighten the mood he was perhaps otherwise heading for.

'Now, why doesn't that surprise me, Howard? Why, of all people, should you be the only one to get a handle on infinity?'

'Dunno, it just makes sense to me. I don't have a problem with it,' Howard replied in blasé fashion.

'Alright, Howard, explain it to me. I'd love to hear your take on it.' Dr Morris was calm and detached as he spoke, his fading eyes emotionless.

'You see, Doctor, the fact that infinity exists as a concept at all means that anywhere, at any time, in any form or calculation that it is applicable, it then by definition overrides all other finite calculations.' Dr Morris gave a semi-interested look the way a busy mother encourages her child while she is engaged in something else more important.

'Even if it only ever actually applies once in the entire history of universal existence,' continued Howard, 'never mind human experience, then it is there for eternity and cannot be erased. If it is never actually applicable then it was mankind's greatest folly, a false conception, an idea that never came to fruition. The point is, we created it so it exists, even just the once. Pure mathematics and contemporary physics are art, Doctor; they may reflect reality, they may even define it, but they may be nothing more than the inherent beauty we sometimes perceive in nature as people.' Howard nodded in enthusiasm, seeking agreement and approval from Dr Morris. Dr Morris slowly and calculatingly rubbed his mouth before answering:

'Well, Howard, you do seem to have some very interesting and worthy thoughts regarding the matter of infinity. You obviously have some ability to wrestle with the big issues, eh?' Howard was slightly taken aback by Dr Morris's response and, although pleased, seemed slightly unable to accept the compliment. Dr Morris tilted his head back to one side and locked his gaze at Howard.

'Do you see what I'm doing there, Howard?' Howard looked puzzled by the question. 'I'm validating you, Howard. Some people need validation, you see.' The point was wasted on Howard, who was neither particularly enamoured with its connotation nor that interested. He redefined the matter at hand.

'Infinity is the ultimate catalyst,' he said. 'Whatever you apply it to automatically becomes infinite.' Dr Morris grew despondent, but Howard was adamant. 'The whole thing has to be infinite.'

'Does it, does it really, Howard?' Dr Morris said dryly.

'Of course it's infinite, big and small, the universe, superstrings, it is illogical for it to end, but totally logical for it to continue in both directions, tiny and enormous. In fact, if it doesn't continue at both ends then you run into a basic time space problem of illogic, where is it? Everything, if it is yay big and yay small, i.e. technically measurable, technically of specific proportions and dimensions, from the largest measurement out there to the smallest measurement down there, then where is it in space and time? Regardless of shape or dimension, it must be somewhere, in something bigger. If not, you can argue it's not, but then you run into the ancient problem of the void. You know, maybe it is suspended in a void, but technically I'm afraid a void is somewhere, something else, which is hence measurable too, even if the void happens to be infinite. This returns to my original point – it is infinite in time and space – it's impossible for it not to be. The only solution is a force such as God.' Dr Morris gritted his teeth and rolled his eyes to the heavens.

'God would have to obliterate the whole thing from existence so that it no longer existed, which is not logical, but perhaps feasible. Even then, you would still be left with God who would have to obliterate himself/itself in order for there to be non-existence of anything. String theory, the ultimate theory of everything, is theology; its basic tenets or precepts are religious, set in stone, here and no further – you might as well believe in fucking God. At least with God the possibilities are endless; string theory hasn't even fully made up the maths bit yet. I mean, I suppose time and space could just stop, it's not beyond the realms of possibility, but it's unlikely and illogical. It would be designated to the realms of paradox or irrational, closer to the notion of something that is possible but nonsensical, something like the idea of God or a spiritual plane in terms of and in relation to rationality.'

'Oh Howard, you're not going to start prattling on about God, are you?' Dr Morris said in a highly irritated tone. Howard looked slightly perturbed, but managed to regain his train of thought.

'Okay Doctor, have it your way. Up here, out there and down there – it's all the same. It's merely time dilation and Lorentz contraction at work; different scales and speeds, that's all, and the same is true of the four forces. The thing is, if it's infinite down there, then a particle so small may travel at light speed or beyond and still appear minute to us, but humongous to something else's existence. Moreover, if our entire known universe is travelling around something, such as an event horizon approaching light speed or beyond, then the energy and mass of it would have to be expanding in congruence with E equals mc squared. However, conversely, this seemingly enormous set of events that we perceive to be the known universe may well seem as fleeting and minute in the unknown universe out there as sub-atomic particles seem to us. In other words, if the universe is infinite in both enormous and minute proportions, then travelling at the speed of light or beyond may well be possible. In fact, it may actually be occurring on a day to day, minute to minute, second to second basis in realms too large and small for us to observe. If it is all infinite then there is no huge or minute except in relative or comparative terms. Our known universe may well be a particle travelling at light speed or beyond and expanding in mass as a result. The seeming explosion may simply be expansion due to a huge increase in mass as it travels and nothing to do with an explosion or any event horizon.' Howard had begun to slip into his manic mode of talking and expressing himself as Dr Morris had come to recognise he did when he was talking about something that mattered to him passionately. By and large, these were the only times that Howard Jones became animated at all, unless it was to explode in a fit of rage and putrid hostility to notions that challenged his own nuanced world view.

'Yes, but Howard, is all this really important?' Dr Morris said in a semi-plea. Howard briefly took on board Dr Morris's question and responded with an arrogant look of contempt before continuing his tour de force examination of the nature of existence.

'You see, the thing about "zero size", the size of the universe at its so-called origins, is that, from our point in space and time, it seems, from our anthropomorphic experience, to be infinitely tiny or "no size at all", but if as a component of it compressed to such a degree it might seem subjectively as huge, possibly infinitely huge, such is the relativity of scale. Maybe the original point of singularity was a particle travelling at the speed of light, possibly one of many, infinite even, and exploded on impact with another, or merely slowed, and thus the Lorentz contraction is ceasing as the universe slows in velocity and, as a result, from an observer's point of view it seems to expand. Or maybe the point of singularity passed the speed of light, going beyond the laws of physics that we currently understand, perhaps at such a speed that tremendous energy was produced, causing the point to expand in order to generate and or maintain the actual or beyond light speed... maybe it even caused it to explode?' Howard, although manic and excitable, was much more coherent than he had been on similar occasions, which allowed Dr Morris to keep abreast of what he was saying without having a great deal of understanding or interest in what was actually being said.

'That's fascinating, Howard,' he contributed like a bit part actor stepping in for his linking line. Howard remained centre stage.

'But that point of singularity, or what would by now be the densest centre of the current universe, must be the most influential force on space causing it to curve around it.

The centre of the known universe could cause time and space to be roughly spherical, like a bubble or a splatter, depending on the nature of the point of singularity and how its composition caused it to explode or expand in the way that it did, as well as possible collisions with other points of singularity or particles which would, in fact, greatly influence its direction and, hence, shape of splatter, so it could just as conceivably be non-spherical. Whatever shape the bubble or splatter is, it could be one of many that are expanding and growing bigger as it travels, interacting with others and slowing down and this reducing in size. The faster it travels, the more it expands and vice versa. For the universe to be as large as it is, it must be travelling at something approaching light speed. Perhaps it will go beyond? In an infinite universe, in terms of both macro and micro, speed and mass become infinite too, not bound. Mass becomes determined by speed, determined by interaction with other similar splatters or particles. Nothing is ever destroyed, just reduced or increased in size as it speeds up or slows down. It's a constant principle but seems relative based on points of observation, time dilation and Lorentz contraction at work. Interaction is the key.'

'Indeed,' Dr Morris muttered sarcastically, as he observed Howard contract and expand as he realised things and then exploded them into verbal torrents.

'All these universes are actually part of the same thing – components or particles, just like micro activity. It's not that particles emit in

334

all directions before deciding on one in particular; it's that frequencies actually emit in all directions and other "things" or frequencies interfere with them and give the illusion of single point arrivals. Particles are concentrations of waves compressed tightly together; so, for example, electrons seem densely packed to us. Our known universe seems spread apart. Superstrings at a seemingly more fundamental level are the same. If you were small enough to be inside an electron it would seem huge, depending on how small you were in it. It could be as large as our known universe if you were proportionally as small in size; we could relatively be microscopic life that clings to existence on or in the components of particles in the great scheme of things. The trick is scale – if you establish that time and space are infinite, then everything rests on the relativity of scale. Everything is simultaneously enormous, proportionate and minute relative to everything else; black holes and universes become elementary particles, and elementary particles become universes and black holes and so does everything in between. The universe becomes one, one infinite set of scales. Maybe that's why particles seem to appear out of nowhere, because they move unbelievably quickly? Infinite scale would allow this. Perhaps the EPR effect operates so quickly that it seems instantaneous. Its transmission of influence is extraordinarily fast, i.e. light is not the fastest or highest frequency in the universe and, hence, something so unbelievably tiny would, at light speed or beyond, suddenly appear to come into existence, or become detectable to us, through increased mass. But perhaps particles are prevented from increasing even further in size by other particles, so they slow down and remain tiny, but detectable to us, or disappear seemingly without a trace as they reduce back to an undetectable mass. Everything, though, becomes wave-like if you deconstruct it enough, get between the solid mass of the denser areas. Ultimately, this means that everything is composed in this way, including us. It just seems to us that we're solid and tangible; but according to the relativity of scale, we are at a certain level as wave-like as any particle or string. It's just that, for us, reality is very much subject to the anthropic principle.'

Dr Morris had, for the whole session, attempted to take in what Howard was saying for once, but he was finding his theorising tedious and repetitive. What little energy he had left was beginning to exercise itself as displacement activity; he began arranging things on his desk, the pen, the file, the empty cup – all were becoming victims of Dr Morris's newly-acquired obsessive compulsive disorder.

'I mean, it stands to reason that gravity is gonna cause quantum theory problems. Gravity relates to mass and, from our point of view, the more mass there is the easier it is for us to detect its interaction with gravity. But how can we measure the effect of the mass of objects that are undetectable to us, both large and small? Surely their gravitational pull is all part of the equation, but is not there for us to calculate… at the moment.'

'I, er, I just don't know, Howard,' Dr Morris said shaking his head almost in despair.

'In an infinite universe, light may actually slow down or even stop, not remain constant. We simply don't know. If you have infinite time and space to travel through then maybe it does slow down, becomes something else. Maybe that's what other frequencies are like, micro waves and radiation, whatever – slowed light from so far away, further than we could ever detect. Maybe it stops and starts floating around, changes direction. How could you determine that that doesn't eventually happen to light? The only way you could ever be certain would be to travel with it until it slows, or continue with it forever.'

'That's fascinating, Howard. It's true – how could you know?' Dr Morris said without looking at Howard, paying more attention to his detailed pen twiddling.

'Even if string theory is correct, and at the tiniest size it's just strings of energy in varying forms or dimensions, it doesn't at all mean that it ends there. It could quite easily, in fact logically, be an infinite continuous slice of string energy. If you could travel down that far it may well continue for ever as string energy in all its forms. But what is that? What is it comprised of? If you break it down and sub-divide it, surely it can't be constant, but as diverse as the divisions elsewhere. If we could get down there it may fluctuate in temperature, in density, all over the place.' Howard was very exact and precise with the words he was choosing and, although he rarely addressed Dr Morris directly, he was this time very much preaching to him as opposed to some of his more private discussions held in Dr Morris's presence. It was communication of sorts.

'You can have infinite dimensions, there's really no reason why not. The thing about there being more than four dimensions for humans is that they are all we can observe or perceive right now, and I have a feeling that, as you observe or pass through some, you begin to lose others. I would guess that they are fairly relative and subjective. Surely, most common mortal life forms in the universe would only be capable of experiencing a limited number of dimensions at any given moment, even if they were passing from one to another. Only God would be able to see or experience them all at once. Maybe that's what God is? The experience of such phenomenon... is them all, in one.'

'Possibly, Howard,' Dr Morris said quietly.

'Energy, matter, it's all relative expressions of the same thing. We are experiencing here, at this point, six hundred and seventy million miles per hour squared to be the ultimate when, really, that is how it appears to us at this relative point in time. With infinity in the equation – no limit on energy or matter, the same thing – then surely it goes beyond the anthropomorphic? Even if it isn't infinite, which I'm sure it is, we are still detecting what we are able to as it unfolds with our and technologies' evolution.'

Howard paused for breath. Dr Morris glanced up to see if Howard had finished his lecture, to see if he could let it go. Howard understood the look and, for a moment, he really did try to stop, but he could not. His pathological need to thrash out the issues usurped his ability to control the stream of consciousness that flowed through his mind like a freight train. He must reach some kind of finality, some sort of closure on the matter. It was one hundred per cent necessary for his very being. Dr Morris, on some level, recognised this fact and, on resigning to it, was once again able to exhale and release the gross annoyance that Howard's verbal diarrhoea evoked in him. He sat back in his chair.

'They say infinity is not a number, that it's just a concept. But it *is* a number; it's shorthand. It represents a continuum, a series of endless numbers, as if numbers themselves aren't concepts!' Howard said, raising his voice in anger, the first sign of the vile, eruptive side of him that so often suddenly appeared out of left field. Dr Morris shifted uneasily in his seat in dreaded anticipation that he might not have the stamina to cope with the exorcist child that Howard so often became.

'In terms of time and space, to exclude infinity is, one, to deny its existence or possibility, and two, to deny its relation to, or effect, on your equation, existence or space in time. Put simply, it is to exist in a fucking bubble! But, as we know, all who observe a bubble know what lies beyond it… abstractions for locally applied mathematics. Ha!' Howard exclaimed defiantly.

'Infinity is the terrible truth that they flee from. When it arises all they do is mock it, balk at its inherent mystery and unpalatable domineering presence. Mathematicians hate infinity; they smear it away with rules and demonstrate the limits of the language or make up new maths to by-pass it. Physicists are the same – they give you blurred glasses to smear the problems away and say that, because string theory is the fundamental answer, "the ultimate description of the universe", then there is no corrective lens – FUCK OFF! SEMANTICS, CONCEPTUAL CHICANARY! That deliberately avoids, like the big bang, legitimate questions about the physical universe in straightforward materialist terms, never mind the spiritual or the religious, even the fucking abstract! Both theories say here and no further, just like the capitalist system when it observes itself. Calculations that merge general relativity and quantum mechanics result in infinity. They freak and say it's absurd. Then they iron it out. The simple answer stares them in the face and they can't accept it. Hysterical! E equals mc squared is a human expression relating to human experience. Infinity is the realm of God, Doctor! Anyone who knows enough about theoretical physics knows that large elements of it are simply complete speculation, total conjecture, clever and with reason, but nonetheless made-up explanations, hence the name "theoretical physics" to explain rather crucial aspects of astronomy, nuclear physics, quantum mechanics and the origin of the fucking universe, to mention but a few grey areas!'

'But it's a damn sight more plausible than religious explanations, Howard. You know, creationism and all that. Come on!' Dr Morris said, actually engaging for the first time with Howard since the beginning of the session.

'So you believe, Doctor, you "believe" in what the scientists say. You have "faith" that it's true. You don't know whether that it is the case; it may be, but it also may not. In other words, theoretical physics, even fucking evolution, are not written in bloody stone, Doctor, and anybody who says they are is either a believer or a fucking liar!' Howard said adamantly.

'Proof! You talk about scientific proof. I mean, fuck, particle accelerators! The way we observe sub-atomic particles is by chucking things at them, chucking things that we can't see at other things that we can't see and we measure the splatter. Well, how fucking scientific! These mile-long pin ball machines are the closest we get to proving all this micro world exists, yet it leads to some amazing inventions. Don't get me wrong, we still haven't seen a sub-atomic particle, but they know they're there – honest! And string theory, well nobody's ever fucking seen a superstring. String theory is just the latest discovery of a universal frequency, real or imagined. You know, what are the superstrings are comprised of? Why assume they are the fundamental components? Just because they vibrate and bounce us back when we try to observe them, it's just extreme high pressure. They must also be sub-divided like everything else is. It simply goes on and on. That's the thing, we can do – amazing things – and we do have a lot of knowledge. But there's so much we don't know, especially the finer details, you know, like antigravity technology for example; we can do it, but we don't fully understand it, how it works, the physics of it. The battle rallies between classical models, newer usurpers, neoclassical models and so on, they – the string theorists – are just the latest coup and faction to say, finally, "this is it". But, of course, time and history will prove otherwise. If it does not, then physics will truly have become theology, a religious order. I mean, shit, the big bang, an explosion, a flash in the dark. Sounds like reinventing the wheel to me. And God said "Let there be light". It's just another fucking creation story. They say "No it's not, it's an observation". Yeah – an observation followed by a high-tech contemporary genesis story, or genesis with in-depth detail and analysis, but a creation story nonetheless, Doctor!' Dr Morris himself now looked as though he were in purgatory, awaiting a pardon.

'Don't start giving me all that nonsense about God and creationism, Howard. You know full well that science is literally light years apart and ahead of that antiquated old rubbish, and I'm sick and tired of hearing an intelligent lad like yourself even remotely taking it seriously!' Dr Morris spewed with all the strength he could muster, the result of which left him coughing and spluttering.

'String theory and the big bang are correct, according to their own parameters or set criteria,' Howard responded in kind to Dr Morris's ejection of frustration. 'Well, creationism is also correct according to its own parameters and set criteria, Doctor. Both are mutually exclusive, both are abstractions of bigger pictures. Both present problems for the other; hard scientific facts on the one hand and the limits of human inquiry on the other!' Howard paused briefly to allow a response from Dr Morris, but none were forthcoming.

'It's the modern western sickness, Doctor, and it's across the board. The desire to declare contemporary science, politics, social organisation, culture and so on to be the pinnacle of human existence, and to look back with a derisory chuckle as we bask in the glory of the end of everything, history, physics, all of it – we've arrived! It's fucking bullshit, Doctor. It means we are in decline, reverting, like the fucking Taliban destroying all the historical artefacts that preceded them. The Orwellian memory hole seeks to stamp now's hegemony as the final destination of mankind. Never before have we been here and never will we again. It's done. Well done us, we are the fucking champions! We've basically worked it all out so praise it, praise at its altar. BOLLOCKS! We're riding for a fall. Every great civilisation claims it and every one of them ended up spread-eagled eventually. But no, not us. No, we're too clever!' Howard was shaking with pent-up rage, the veins in his forehead throbbing with adrenalin.

'Well, that may well be, Howard, but I'll tell you one thing – religious fervour and delusion will not help us one little bit. It is hysterical mumbo jumbo. It is myth, irrational myth, and that is all there is to it!' Dr Morris said, rattling around in his chair like an angry grandfather who can't abide youth any longer.

'Religion and other seemingly "irrational" beliefs from a logical or evolutionary point of view,' continued Howard, 'may well be a prerequisite for survival of the species, given the nature and state of human history and existence. Without it, we simply may have given up or been overwhelmed in the light of truly insurmountable odds and, more often than not, circumstances that simply did not and, perhaps still, make little or no sense in terms of rationality at all. I mean, what do you think was running through the minds of men and women who, in ancient times, scaled huge mountain ranges and vast oceans in little boats, or basically rafts? How the hell would we, thinking what we think, prepare ourselves for such things? Never mind when the survival of you, your tribe, your gene pool rested on it. What would you tell your children, what would you tell yourself? That the chances are slim and none, and slim's outa town?'

Dr Morris did not answer, but the anger that had surfaced moments ago had subsided. For the second time, he let out a deep breath and relaxed. He could no longer fight this young man and, for that matter, no longer wished to. A smile of content resignation spread across his face.

'Perhaps you're right, Howard,' he said. Howard could hardly believe his ears.

'Really?' he replied.

'Maybe you're right about the whole thing, Howard.'

'Yeah,' Howard said cautiously but with growing conviction. Slightly taken aback, Howard's temper too diminished and his angry posturing gradually began to desist. Calmly and carefully, he began to speak.

'You see, Doctor, all life out there, down there and, most importantly, here with us, is probably an illusion, a trick of the light, the sound, the sense, but more precisely of the frequency. We and everything we experience are differing frequencies experiencing each other. What I have just stated is part of that illusion – a human expression of it, in fact, or not as the case may be. Seemingly wonderfully accurate predictions are in the great scheme of things grossly off target, but just seem to us and our perception of things perfectly as they should be. The notion of classical physics determinism is quite plausible, it's simply that we cannot trace it or predict it. But as I've said before, Doctor, just 'cos we can't see it or perceive it, it don't mean it ain't there. Our arrogance and ignorance astound me sometimes.' Howard paused to see if Dr Morris was actually listening to him, as much as for thought. Dr Morris's smile had not waned; he looked genuinely serene, almost happy to be there.

'Our universe may be a vibrating string in a field of vibrating strings. If we are just sets of vibrations, for all we know our entire universe could simply be a note or a burp coming out of the gob of some enormous thing. Light could easily be vibration of such high frequency that it heats up and we can see it. By its very nature, all the frequencies we

345

experience here and now as humans are gradually changing in form. They have been and will continue to do so. It's not so much that temperature alters them, temperature is it and it fluctuates. As far as we can tell, the whole universe seems to be cooling down. It's one of the reasons why we're here as we are. It is highly probable that whatever we're looking at or measuring, or detecting, whether it be sound, light, electromagnetism and all the others, micro waves, ultrasound, nuclear, whatever, are all simply differing frequencies of the same thing – energy, for want of a better word, infinite in frequency. We are merely able to perceive through our senses, technology, and ultimately our minds, which are basically electrical activity, certain frequencies that we designate as sound, light, electromagnetism, etc. The point is that there are quite likely frequencies so slow, infinitely slower and slower, and at the other end of the spectrum frequencies infinitely quick, beyond light speed, that we can't yet detect them. We are only able to measure a specific number of frequencies at any given space in time. We are, however, seeing more and more as history goes on. The longer we go on detecting, measuring, observing, experiencing such phenomenon of frequency, we will I'm sure perceive newer faster and faster, slower and slower frequencies that we find ourselves part of, more than likely ultimately comprised of. We are basically a particular expression of whatever it is we're perceiving and measuring. The premise, the principle, is infinity, infinite time and space, again two expressions or aspects of the same thing. Some call it God, some call it life itself, while some, Doctor, care to break it down, deconstruct it into a million different categories. The thing is, as long as we can count it all it will continue to be counted. Infinity has no practical application, it cannot be localised for industrial production. It is, however, a fact. If technology enables us to perceive new measurements of scale, of frequency, then in effect technology selects which memes are selected. This is essentially an extension of our environment selecting genes, genes of the mind, perhaps the most important natural selection of them all. Of course, we, technology and our environment evolve together, in conjunction. But the question is, if survival of the fittest is actually the order of the day, then who or what is winning? Our environment was here before us. Humans, our ancestors, were born out of it, but will we really last forever? Highly unlikely, but then what might we become? Reduced to dust and scattered energy? Reverted? Un-evolved? Onto something else? Or is that essentially the same thing? It's all a struggle of oscillation for tessellation of energy, the conflict of which causes certain kinds of interaction, change in frequency and, hence, everything that we perceive and more, so much more. To become uniform, to become one, causes difference, causes change, which in turn constantly reconfigures in an attempt to become one. It's perfectly possible that everything in the universe is attempting, through trial and error, over billions and billions of years, to rearrange itself, trying to reconfigure all that it is, all its components differentiated only by their position and temperature resulting from explosion or expansion, trying to essentially put itself back together like a universal Humpty Dumpty. An explosion or expansion from a point of infinitely condensed, compressed energy that may, at a certain point in its life cycle, have been just a single frequency, and which is, as we observe it subjectively, as a product or component of this process, now a hotchpotch of single energy source scattered into trillions and squillions of differing directions, scrambled in almost utter chaos and is basically trying to reassemble, re-establish the original frequency of energy in a single, ever-compressing point or singularity. It is feasible that all universal behaviour is merely that activity, attempted or successful, a desperate jigsaw of confused energy, a shattered frequency, a sub-set of frequencies all trying to re-establish order. This would mean that all biological life, all human existence and behaviour, basically boil down to this single impetus. All our socialisation, all our organisation, all our creations and destructions reflecting our innate programming, are driven by the desire to return to the source. The higher frequency, the highest power, the most high, God all-fucking mighty. I mean, think about it. We started off worshipping every fucking thing – trees, mountains, spirits, the lot – and we organised and coalesced around such principles. Then we moved towards monotheism, then we tried to impose our shit on others, unify like a giant fucking pyramid, a three-dimensional expression of the widest base up to a single point. Why did we do that?

348

'Cos nature works that way; pyramids are like the most natural way to build a structure. That's why they happened, across the globe. In the natural order of things they make sense, are an expression of this organising principle. Power structures in biological life work like this, as do we. We are emulating the need to conglomerate. Empires, the globalisation process, are a culmination of this. Population growth at an unprecedented height, power structures and networks of communication to socially organise us in a uniform, mono culture, a single human blob merging into the earth combining with her through technology. This will continue for as long as it can, then we'll be broken back down and reabsorbed into the mishmash of scattered matter and buzz of communal energy that we ultimately are, and then it'll try again, another formulation, another attempt to harmonise and unify with the ultimate source, the Godhead. We are, in one sense, a mistake, a working progress, a fucking by-product, a temporary solution to a more permanent problem, but... we are always a part of it. We've always been a part of it. We've always been so and always will be, from God to dust, Doctor, and dust to God.' Dr Morris was still smiling. Howard smiled back.

'All this philosophising and pseudo scientific gobbledegook, Howard. What does it really matter? What possible importance is it to us, to our daily lives?'

'Everything. It means everything to us,' Howard answered politely, but as though the question was nonsensical.

'I fail to see how, really, Howard. I really do. It's all theoretical claptrap that has little to do with our actual existence as human beings.'

'No, Doctor…' Howard said, disturbed by Dr Morris's statement. 'It has everything to do with everything. With the past, the future and right now.'

'I really doubt it somehow, Howard.'

'No, seriously Doctor. I mean, it stands to reason doesn't it, that it governs us all? I mean, we stand here…' Howard held out his left hand. 'And superstrings or sub-atomic particles – take your pick – are here…' Howard held out his right hand. 'And shit, there's a lot in between. I mean, everything we know of, and even more that we don't, sits bang in between us, human existence, human behaviour and it, superstring or sub-atomic particle existence, sub-atomic behaviour… I mean, fuck, you could never ever, not in a squillion light years of human existence, ever predict it, I mean work out even a whiff of the influence of sub-atomic behaviour on our own behaviour. No fuckin' way, man. Not even close. The gulf is simply enormous, almost unfathomable, but it has to at a certain level influence, even control, every fuckin' breath we take, every move we make. The whole evolutionary process is just a part of it; from bacteria, right up to all that we do, it's subject to the same damn laws and, ultimately, the activity that it forces sub-atomic particles to carry out, from nanosecond to nanosecond, I mean literally. And it has to work in reverse too – every fucking flinch we have, to every soul we take, every bloody building we construct or tear down, the whole nine yards is all effecting, influencing, maybe even controlling, too, all that sub-atomic behaviour and existence. It's a two-way street, man. It goes out beyond us to the moon, the stars, the distant galaxies, the fucking dark matter and dark energy we're supposed to believe is out there. You know, like more than half the known fucking universe is missing, but they swear it's there 'cos otherwise the maths don't work, does it? All that shit beyond our atmosphere is influenced by sub-atomic behaviour, too – is basically an expression of it. The known universe presses down on it all and it gyrates, pings and vibrates back at it and we...' Howard began to laugh uncontrollably. 'We are caught somewhere in the middle of it all, dazed and confused, like some fuckin' bimbo at a posh dinner party, you know, pullin' faces and makin' noises, hoping they're the right ones at the right time, knockin' back the champers, hoping that that'll help, not really aware that the universe out there and particles and strings down there don't feel so different. We're all in the same boat. Existence is futile, Doctor. A whirling dervish of non-understanding and confusion, a jostle to the front of the cue like tourists on the London Underground, only to stand there blocking everybody else's way while you try and work out where the fuck you're going and why!'

'Goodness Howard, really,' Dr Morris said, partaking in some mock muddle-headedness. There was no malice intended. 'Well, I do believe we've come to the end of our session, Howard. I'll see you next week, I expect. Take care now.' He spoke abruptly, but with a friendly face.

'Er, yeah… er, Doctor. See you next week then, bye.' Howard called out as he ungainly got up and left the room. The session had gone on for more than twice the usually allocated time, without Howard noticing. It was not because Dr Morris had forgotten the time – the sad truth was that he did not want to go home.

SESSION TWENTY-SIX

Howard had never seen so many people in the waiting area before. He had never seen that many people in the entire clinic at one time. It was like Piccadilly Circus on a Saturday afternoon. He wanted to sit down. There were a couple of spaces available, but he could not bring himself to squeeze in between what seemed to him like hordes of people. Besides, where to choose? He had no desire to sit amongst a group of would-be artists, all sitting fussing and frantically organising their pictures and paintings, nor the woodwork fraternity moping and clinging for dear life to their creations of hideousness, all at the expense of mother nature's own fine craftsmanship. Then there were the crocheting nuts and the fucking Alan Titchmarsh brigade, busy fine-pruning their petunias or whatever the hell it was they did out there in the clinic's grounds. The waiting area was overrun with group therapy plebs on some all-day exhibition of ambassadorial fruit loops and their masterpieces, all nervous and bickering about their great moment of glory. The whole affair was deeply irritating for Howard, who took it as a gross infringement of his right to have the mental health centre all to himself. It was the way he liked it and failed to see why any other scenario should ever come to pass. He had never seen such a ragbag collection of social misfits. He stood scowling in the corner, leaning against the wall, taking meagre refuge behind a large potted plant covered in Christmas decorations that he sincerely hoped did not belong to one of the Ground Force fuckers over there.

There was one person who was particularly grating on his frazzled nerves, despite the racket that was emanating from the day-tripper delegation. She was an auburn-haired woman in a flowery blouse, whose voice was an octave higher than the mob's general din. Every time she called out her son's name – 'Samuel! Samuel!' – her high-pitched, middle-class whining went right through Howard, so much so that it made his teeth clench the way a fork scratching an empty plate or fingernails on a blackboard would. It got to him and made him jump slightly each time she called out to the little shit that was running around the reception area, scaring the hell out of the group therapy clients, like a miniature banshee on coke. The woman kept pleading with her devil child to sit down:

'Oh, Samuel. Sam-u-el, come and sit with Mummy, darling,' to which Samuel replied 'Fuck off, you gay!' Howard literally wanted to hurt the boy and could see no real reason why this should not actually be occurring.

'Samuel, sweetie, please come here. Mummy wants to hug you. Please, my little soldier.' Samuel continued his Red Baron-like tour of the room until the woman got up, took hold of his hand and walked him back to the chair. She sat him on her lap, at which point Samuel began slapping, biting and scratching his mother with all of his nine-year-old strength.

'Oh Samuel, stop that,' she ordered the child with firm authority, but he continued his violent abuse of her.

'Please Samuel, please darling, don't hurt Mummy… you're hurting Mummy, Samuel!' she complained bitterly as he began pulling her hair.

'Samuel, fucki… stop that this instance!' The woman was at this point trying to untangle Samuel's grubby little mitts from her large bush of frizzy hair. Samuel was not to be deterred and began pulling himself up towards his mother by her hair from her lap while in a horizontal position, thus utilising all of his bodyweight as though she were some kind of Moscow State Circus performer and he some deranged midget acrobat. He began to kick and flail his legs as he did so, causing her to stoop forward, at which point he was then able to kick and knee her in the face as well as tug and rip out large chunks of his mother's hair.

Howard stared in amazement. He had never seen anything like it. Much of the room had hushed down as they went through the motions of what they had been doing before, whilst actually paying great interest to the assault and battery taking place.

'SAMUEL!' the woman screamed in pain and anger, but also with huge embarrassment. 'Samuel, please stop, please… I'll give you some sweeties if you stop.'

But Samuel had no intention of giving up his physical attack and increased the intensity and ferocity with which he mangled her. Samuel's mother began trying to release her son's grip on her hair, finger by finger, but her gentle coaxing attempts to release his grip made him release only momentarily before re-grabbing even greater bunches of her locks and literally ripping them out. There was by now hairballs flying around and sticking to the sofa and carpet. Bizarrely, through all this, the woman turned to the bloated motorbike jacket-clad man sitting next to her and began to apologise.

'I'm really sorry,' she said quietly and reasonably calmly under the circumstances. 'He's such a little shit, I just don't know what to do with him anymore,' she continued, almost as though it were happening to someone else.

'YOU'RE A LITTLE SHIT, AREN'T YOU? YOU LITTLE FUCKING BASTARD. I HATE YOU, I HATE YOU SO MUCH!' she yelled at Samuel, on the verge of tears.

The man said nothing. Instead, he just looked away. Howard was mesmerised by the whole spectacle. Mother and son had now become so entangled that it seemed possible that Samuel may have to be cut loose from his mother's web-like mane, as they wrestled with each other like some macabre primary school production of a Greek tragedy.

Finally, Samuel released his hold, untangled himself with a good yank and leapt to freedom from his mother's lap. He sped across the room and hid himself behind the water cooler. He slowly peered around the side and across the room at Howard, who was in the opposite corner glaring back through the tinsel and foliage of the potted plant.

The boy's mother sat between them, her hair in tatters and pulled forward over her face. Her skin had patches that were red raw and she was sporadically scratched and bruised in various places. Holding back the tears, she began trying to redo what was left of her hair and generally regain some kind of composure. As she did so, Howard watched her. She had the expression of a woman who had narrowly avoided being sexually assaulted, or perhaps a medieval woman exposed to a mob that had accused her of witchcraft, but who had been released at the last minute as they found someone else to victimise and had tossed her aside. That's how she seemed to Howard, anyway.

A few minutes later, a small troop of authority figures appeared and, in an instance, ushered all the budding exhibitors and their creations out of the reception doors and towards the main entrance to the hospital, leaving Howard, Samuel and his quivering mother and the gangly-looking receptionist in a contrasting silence to the hustle and bustle of moments ago.

'Howard Jones!' the skinny girl at reception called out. 'If you'd like to go through, Dr Morris is waiting.' Howard sloped out from behind the plant and headed towards the corridor. As he passed Samuel's mother, she coyly offered him a mortified smile, which he ignored with fullest contempt.

'Right Howard,' Dr Morris said as Howard sat down opposite him. 'Well, I don't know if you're aware, but this is actually your penultimate session, young man.' Dr Morris looked better than he had last week and was fairly dapper in attire. Howard took note of what seemed to be a rather expensive three-piece, navy, pinstriped suit and a yellow tie, possibly

357

made of silk, neatly arranged against a crisply-ironed white shirt.

'It is?' Howard replied in surprised confusion.

'Yes, Howard. We initially offer a set of twenty-seven one-on-one sessions with a psychiatrist before moving you on to group therapy, you see.' Howard was visibly shaken. He knew what group therapy meant and was distinctly unhappy with the notion.

'Yeah, but, er... what if I need to talk to someone, you know, in private?'

'Oh, don't worry, Howard. You'll still see someone, a... er, a therapy coordinator. You'll still see them once a week, it's just that you'll attend group sessions as well. You'll get to participate in activities such as, erm... let me see... yes, art and weaving, even some creative writing, that sort of thing. It will do you the world of good,' Dr Morris said optimistically. Howard did not answer immediately. His foot tapped irately as he thought for a moment.

'Yeah, but...' Howard began, unsure of what he was going to say. 'What if they don't... understand what I'm saying? What if they... don't get it?' he finished vaguely.

'Oh Howard,' Dr Morris said with a chuckle. 'They'll get enough to know what to do with you alright,' he went on, a large grin spreading across his face.

'Well, how long will I get, one-on-one, I mean?'

'About forty minutes, something like that. A little less than with me, but not much... You'll be fine, Howard, honestly,' Dr Morris said, seeing Howard's dejected look. 'So I

358

suggest you make the most of the sessions you have left. Start as you mean to go on, Howard.' Howard shuffled around in his chair and let out a huff.

'Come on, Howard, you've usually got plenty to say. What's been on your mind this week? What great theories have you concocted for us this time, eh?' Dr Morris was all sweetness and light, any trace of his usual irritability had flown south for the winter. Howard found it slightly disconcerting and was unsure how to react.

'Time,' he eventually said.

'Yes?' Dr Morris replied.

'Time is change, gentlemen,' Howard said.

'It is? Well, yes, I suppose it is,' Dr Morris responded.

'Time is relative to whatever is experiencing it,' Howard said with little enthusiasm. 'Time is a human construct, anyway. Mathematical units based upon physical distances or changes in space, i.e. designated points on a clock, the transition of stellar life or the changing from day to night, the changing of the seasons and so on.' Howard began to find his feet, his rhythm, but was wobblier than usual, less vociferous.

'All are human inventions perceived through observation, formulised in mathematical systems that are transmitted and agreed upon by groups of individuals.' He paused and Dr Morris nodded in response. Howard cautiously continued his lecture.

'Time is merely change in universal life, fluctuating phenomenon. Humans have had many differing calendars usually celebrating important occasions in culturally specific histories.' Howard paused to see if Dr Morris was still with him, he was. Howard appeared anxious.

'The calendar and method of timekeeping that is currently observed is simply a reflection of current cultural, historical and political discourse. The idea of time as an independent reality separate from human constructs is an illusion, a myth. Time and space are relative to whichever life forms experience them, wherever in the universe, but are certainly not bound by human observations from this particular time and space, designating them into specific units of distance. Other life forms in the universe, such as animals here on earth, or extra-terrestrial entities elsewhere, may experience time and space as similar experiences to our own. They would not, however, necessarily designate them either time or space. These are anthropocentric, linguistically-specific concepts. As is all human existence.' Howard stopped and awaited Dr Morris's response, to see if there would be one. Dr Morris paused for thought.

'What about those experiments they've done with clocks and planes and all that,' asked Dr Morris. 'Haven't they proved that time is different at different times or speeds, or something? Something to do with planes, Howard, and clocks? The clocks?'

'That merely proves my point, Doctor. Time differs at differing speeds – and that's just here on earth. How different could it be elsewhere in the universe?' Howard said, still slightly uncomfortable with Dr Morris's newfound participation in his interests.

'So, there's no such thing as absolute time? Or time as a tangible... erm... grand phenomenon?' Dr Morris asked.

'Yes, the reality is that time is infinite, both backwards and forwards, in linear terms. Or in infinite directions in multi-dimensional terms.'

'But you just said that time is relative. Which is it – relative or absolute?' Dr Morris said. Howard thought for a moment before he answered:

'It's absolute in the sense that it's infinite, and relative in terms of its observation at any given time in space. So it's actually both. We are only able to observe it in relative terms. We can conceive that it's infinite, but cannot live to observe it or separate ourselves, put ourselves outside of where we are in time and space. Only God can do that, because God is infinite in time and space.'

'But didn't we create God, Howard, in an attempt to understand what you are talking about. Don't you see, that our minds can conceive of whatever we create, including the words you have just said, including the idea of God. God is its representation,' Dr Morris smiled at Howard and raised his bald brows.

'None of it exists outside of our minds, Doctor. Our minds are how we experience it. Our minds are how we experience God. God is beyond that, though. God is more than we can perceive,' Howard said with certainty.

'Yes, but you are perceiving – or, more correctly, perceive – that now, Howard, or how else would you tell me about it?'

'God is everything we can perceive and all the things that we cannot. It goes beyond what we can understand.'

'Yes, but if we can't perceive it, then how do we know it exists, Howard?'

'So you think that just because we're not aware of something that it can't exist, Doctor?'

'Howard, you said nothing exists outside of our mind.'

'No, I'm saying it doesn't exist for us until we become aware of it, or we create it. They may be one and the same thing, and you are now contradicting yourself as you said that if we can't perceive it then how can we know about it?'

'But that's true, Howard.'

'It is, I agree, but it doesn't mean that it's not there, Doctor. We're just not aware that it is. You know, like over here before we came over here, or there as it was then, from over there... or here, as it once was,' Howard said, nearing confusion himself. Dr Morris laughed loudly for a moment.

'Yes, but because we can perceive that things may exist that we don't know about means we perceive their possibility, Howard.'

'Exactly, Doctor, and that means they can be anything we think they might be.'

'But that doesn't mean that they are whatever we think they are, Howard.'

'It doesn't mean that they're not.'

'Yes, we can believe that the moon is made of blue cheese, but when we get there we find it isn't. The tangible reality is that it's made of rock, Howard. There is a reality out there we just have to discover what it is.'

'Yes, Doctor, humans have gained consensus on many things, but we also differ about many things, especially religion and science. Fundamentalist scientists, like all fundamentalists, wish to destroy all links to the past, all the avenues of influence that might lead somewhere else, away from present dominance or attempts at dominance. Science seeks to severe and destroy links with its past, with religion, just as religion resists attempts by science to rationalise the divine.'

'Religion comes down to belief, Howard, while science comes down to proof. There is a fundamental distinction and only time will tell which is correct.'

'Reality is created by the victors, Doctor. Human perception is shaped by the stories we pass on.'

Dr Morris rested his chin on his hand and allowed it to carry the full weight of his head for a moment, while giving Howard a frank look.

'Perhaps the stories that get passed on are the strongest, Howard, and that's why they survive.'

'The strongest memes, you mean?'

'The strongest what?' Dr Morris exclaimed.

'Memes. Like genes but of culture, of imitation, units of transmittable knowledge, not biological material,' Howard explained proudly.

'I see... perhaps,' Dr Morris said.

'Perhaps those who are most able to impose those memes will be the victorious narrators, Doctor.'

'Perhaps those that will be most able to impose those, er, memes will be victorious because of the memes they adhere to, Howard.'

'Perhaps...' Howard replied quietly. Dr Morris nodded as if he were the purveyor of bad tidings, tidings that Howard should roll over and accept. This jarred Howard greatly and he exploded with rage.

'First and foremost, science will never, *ever*, get rid of religion and probably vice versa. The more you try and get rid of something, the more likely it is to rally and survive – eradication is bad news, Doctor. It usually leads to even more rebellion. So it's war, Doctor, as it's always been, and everybody feels under threat. So everybody's pushing hard, but as long as we, humans, are here then this battle will rage. Peaks and troughs, Doctor, peaks and troughs, but the war continues,' Howard said, leaning forward provocatively. Dr Morris did not even flinch, nor did he bite the inflammatory hook that Howard had grown so used to dangling.

'Those religious loona... fanatics could destroy us all, Howard,' Dr Morris said calmly.

'Religion could destroy us in a conflict over doctrine...' Howard conceded. 'But its resurgence is a backlash, a reaction to scientific-led technological destruction of humanity.' Dr Morris, looking uncomfortable with Howard's point, turned his head away and waved his hand dismissively.

'The fact is, Doctor, that with compromise science and religion become quite complementary... with a hell of a lot of dialogue and patience, sure, each taking from the other and filling in each other's gaps, of which there are many on either side. Science is the realm of logic, and religion transcends the limits of the intellect. The problem is, when one side sets out to refute the other then they become mutually exclusive systems of dogmatic propaganda, each pot-shotting at each other's weaknesses and problems, without wishing to acknowledge their own inconsistencies. It becomes a power struggle and the first casualty is the truth.' Dr Morris was reluctant to accept Howard's point, despite the fact that he recognised its inherent logic.

'Yes Howard, but the fact is that religion cannot accept that science has exposed its mysteries and demonstrated them to be clear-cut, straightforward, measurable scientific phenomenon to which religion has little in the way of response. We now see the world for what it is, not what we want it to be.'

'Doctor, this is the triumph of materialism over spirituality, earthly desires – of the flesh, denial of anything but the material... It is ultimately the denial of God, the victory of Satan, to win denouncers, Satan's ultimate desire. You see, Satan would not bow down to God's creation – man. Man is the pawn between God and Satan, pulled in two, the test to overcome temptation – Satan's forte. Satan is God's test for human kind. Doctor, all great science leads to God. Fundamental discoveries of science lead to something miraculous, that things are intrinsically inexplicable, except by divine creation. In other words, they don't make sense – they're not meant to... it is a test of faith.' Dr Morris shook his head, but rather than his usual despair at Howard's religious leanings, a humorous expression spread across face.

'I think you know me well enough by now, Howard, to realise that I simply do not share your apocalyptic scenario of God and the Devil. It is simply irrelevant to me,' he said giggling slightly.

'Yes, but Doctor, this is about the survival of the species. We are in danger of going extinct,' Howard implored.

'And what makes you think that we shouldn't be! What makes you think that we should be here for ever! Everything has its time, Howard,' Dr Morris castigated, albeit in a light-hearted manner. Howard could not believe what he was hearing.

'Don't you see the inherent evil in what you're saying, in... in what you reinforce with your attitude, your belief?' Howard said, taking his turn to reprimand, though with greater vigour and malice than Dr Morris's rebuke.

'Perhaps,' Dr Morris said candidly. 'But what makes you think that evil isn't a part of it? Don't you see, that evil is as integral to the whole process as good? And that, in the great scheme of things that you are so smitten with, that what 'you' determine as evil may well be an evolutionary impetus that keeps the whole wheel turning, so to speak. If it were all good by your criteria, then it simply could not work. It would, and – let me point out – does, run into problems, evil as you put it. Problems are as much a part of life as solutions, Howard. Life is one big mish-mash of problems and solutions and problems and failures to overcome them. One man's problem is another's solution, and so it rolls on, Howard. Acceptance is what you have difficulty with, Howard, not evil. Accept what is and get on with it!' However, Howard was not in an accepting mood.

'It's about what side you're on. If you just accept evil as being a legitimate aspect then you reinforce it, you ensure that it happens. You have to resist it, Doctor.'

'Well, get out there and resist it, Howard, instead of waffling to me, or preaching to the choir!' Dr Morris exclaimed with mild annoyance.

'What makes you think I'm not, Doctor? I'm doing the best I can,' Howard protested.

'Well then, here we are, Howard. Here we are.'

'It just seems that this built-in evil is so much more prevalent, Doctor, so much easier than any good.'

'And what makes you believe that you would know the difference, in the great scheme of things? Maybe you're the problem, Howard, not the solution.'

'I have faith, Doctor.'

'Well Howard, you are alone on that one in this room, I'm afraid.'

'A man without faith, Doctor, is like a man without a home – destitute. He may be a high-class hobo, he may rent Buckingham Palace, but he is homeless nonetheless.

Sooner or later, this fact comes to light. Without faith, we're dead, we cease to be human. Without faith we simply could not go on,' Howard preached.

'Well, I have news for you, Howard – plenty of people walk around here and get on just fine without it.'

'I don't have any time for atheists, Doctor. They're just as dogmatic as the religious. At least agnostics admit that they don't know – that *we* don't actually know.'

'Most people are not that interested, Howard.'

'That's because most people don't question things very much. To be honest, most people don't really think about deeper questions very much at all. I mean religion, science, and beliefs generally are full of holes, of anomalies; they just accept generic concepts, a basic gist of a belief system, 'cos if you do delve a little deeper, you know, into specifics, you begin to realise how fragile it all is, how nonsensical much of it is. Maybe it's a good thing, in general, stopping to think about how little it all actually fits together and just how precarious life actually is... is...' Howard for once was lost for words.

'Is a recipe for disaster?' Dr Morris offered. Howard did not respond. 'You see, Howard, thinking too much *per se* is not particularly good for you. Over-analysing things can be quite paralysing. You wouldn't step out of the house if you thought about the statistics of it all. You'd be... how can I put it, anthropophobic now, wouldn't you, eh Howard? It could lead to people avoidance, for example, couldn't it? Withdrawal and a ceasing of communication with other people might well be the result of an over-analytical mind, might it not, Howard?' Dr Morris's probing deeply disturbed Howard, who appeared visibly panicked.

'Communication is over-rated anyway,' he retorted astringently.

'But is vital nonetheless, eh Howard?' Dr Morris continued playfully, but without detraction.

'Yeah, well, as far as I can tell most communication is misunderstanding, miscommunication,' Howard intentionally digressed. 'That's half the problem as far as I can tell… that's what I'm getting at, Doctor,' Howard said continuing the diversion.

'What's that, Howard?' Dr Morris replied carefully, withdrawing from the soft spot he had pressed so effectively.

'For example, we as English speakers call this a table,' Howard said pointing.

'Well, Howard, I'd probably call it a desk, but yes – for all intents and purposes, it's a sort of table,' Dr Morris said, a tad condescendingly.

'Exactly Doctor! That already illustrates what I'm trying to say. Already we are splitting hairs over what to call it and we are speaking the same language. In other languages it's something else. It's… what is table in French?' Dr Morris laughed arrogantly.

'*Table* Howard,' he answered in a flawless French accent.

'See *table*,' Howard said, poorly imitating Dr Morris's French accent. 'So far we have table, desk and now *table*... What's French for desk, Doctor?'

'I'm not sure, Howard,' Dr Morris replied, not wishing to continue the French lesson.

'Well, whatever, but we could argue about whether it's a table, a desk, a *table*, *la desk* or whatever. Do you see my point? And that's just two languages that are quite closely related, you know, table and *table*. Imagine how it is between other languages, you know, that are further apart. What I'm getting at, Doctor, is that we are negotiating amongst ourselves just what this thing we call a table...' Dr Morris interjected:

'A desk, Howard. It is actually a desk,' he said pedantically.

'Okay, but do you see what I'm getting at? We call a piece of flat wood with four legs a table and we use it to put things on, you know, eat our dinner or whatever. But some cultures don't use tables, Doctor. You know, like South American tribesmen, they don't necessarily use tables, so they might not even have a word for it. They may never have actually seen one.'

'What's your point, Howard?' Dr Morris said, still in tranquil mood.

'My point is, that the first time a South American tribesman sees a table he may think it's a chair, or he may turn it upside down and hang his hat off one of the legs. In fact, if he came into a room and saw a table upside down he would have no clue, no inkling that that wasn't the way it was supposed to be. He would assume that that was how it was meant to be and hang his bloody hat off it. Do you see what I mean, Doctor?' Howard rambled.

'Sort of, Howard. You're talking about perception, Howard,' Dr Morris said dryly.

'Yes Doctor, perception. Exactly! Now, if we are splitting hairs over this table – or, should I say, desk – then is it any wonder that we, as a species, argue over so much of what goes on around us? We are in a constant state of negotiation as to what is occurring.' Dr Morris did not look particularly convinced.

'Yes, but Howard, we also agree quite easily on things. We agree about what this... desk is for. We could quite easily demonstrate or explain to a, erm, a South American tribesman what a table is and what it's for. He'd understand it remarkably quickly.'

'Yes, but what if he didn't agree? What if he was adamant that he wanted it upside down so he could hang his hat off of it?' Howard continued to blether.

'Well then, Howard, I suppose that would be his choice, wouldn't it?'

'Yes, but what if every time he came over to your house he insisted on turning it upside down so that he could hang his hat off it?'

'Well, I suppose I wouldn't invite him over, would I?' Dr Morris said farcically. Howard burst into laughter.

'What about when you meet for coffee, Doctor? What if it was necessary that you both had to meet for coffee at some café? What then? When there are other people around who could get involved?' Howard went on childishly.

'Well, Howard, if we went to a coffee shop here in the UK then he would not be

371

allowed to turn the table upside down and hang his hat awff of it, would he?'

'Precisely, Doctor. And if you went to a coffee shop in the Amazon you might not be allowed to turn his hat stand upside down and put your coffee on it, would you?'

"Well no, but...' Dr Morris began.

'You see, Doctor...' Howard interrupted. 'It's the perception consensus cycle, the negotiation of perception, the internal and the external with other life forms, particularly humans. It is the creation of reality.'

'Yes, but where does all this get us, Howard?' The light-hearted mood that had emerged came to an abrupt end as Howard's childlike deportment ceased.

'It gets us to Murder Inc., Doctor, to the point where our killing is okay and theirs is not and vice versa. It gets us to the point of *impasse*. It means that humans are doomed to destroy each other and can agree on little for very long. We have reached a dialogic cul-de-sac, at which point communications break down. Then, Doctor, war is the inevitable consequence. Science versus religion, the religious amongst themselves... man versus man... God versus Satan.' The sombre, troubled Howard had once again reared its ugly head.

'Scientific enquiry of a thorough ilk, from perception of the mind to the study of matter, leads to the conclusion that existence is not reality. Indeed, reality is not actually real, experience is illusion and we are the sum of those experiences. Ultimately, we simply cannot tell what is real and what is illusion. For

God's sake, the whole fucking universe is an apparition. Light takes eight minutes to arrive here from the sun, which means we observe it as it was eight minutes ago. The light from Jupiter takes about half an hour. The further out into space you observe from Earth, the further back in time you go. This means that the entire known universe is not as it appears; out there, right now, something else is occurring. What we see is in fact an optical illusion. The reality according to scientists is totally different, nothing is what it seems. We are blind, Doctor; we have no idea what the universe is actually like now, only conjecture, and hence cannot understand the effect it is presently having on us. We are playing a game of catch-up in an incredibly nuanced time frame. We are living on memories, Doctor, memories. Is matter real or is it something else at heart? Are we a mind, electrical imaging in a moving biological entity, or is the mind really a soul, and does that soul lead to God, or is God illusion too? Surely, only God can determine such matters as fact or fiction? Certainly no mortal can.' Dr Morris shrugged his shoulders with disinterest.

'Sanity is consensus, Doctor, to not question norms. But, ironically, sanity or consensus changes over time and is often influenced, sometimes revolutionised, by what are initially considered insane ideas or thoughts outside of the realms of the current consensus or status quo.'

'So you don't believe in reality, Howard?' Dr Morris said reframing the issue.

'It's not so much that. I mean, you can gain consensus on what reality is, you know, in a small group, perhaps one day as a species,' Howard said with a cynical snigger. 'But it doesn't make it so, Doctor. You know, once we had a consensus in communities that there were witches and we burnt them accordingly. Now, in the West, we think that's barbaric, but not so long ago we took human lives on the basis of that particular consensus. Now we've reached another consensus that says it's wrong, or rather that there are no witches – or none that have any power, anyway. Who knows what consensus we'll come to in the future? Reality or realities are mutable, Doctor.'

'Many cultures still firmly believe in witches too,' Dr Morris said agreeing with Howard.

'That just confirms my point, Doctor,' Howard snapped, antagonised by Dr Morris's ever reasonable disposition and his growing propensity towards finding a common ground with him.

'Doctor, if you extend the argument that religion is faith-based or delusion, which it is, you come to the logical conclusion that all human belief is faith-based delusion. It may seem true or truthful, but believing it doesn't make it true, as you've pointed out. Reality, if it exists, is probably beyond our capabilities, or it may be completely relative, i.e. plural, or you can deconstruct it and understand that it is all human, linguistic, semantic, chemical, physic-based construction and is not what it seems – or delusion. Buddhism has been saying that for yonks, but ultimately it means pick your poison

374

or you pays your money and takes yer chances. It's like that Steve Buscemi character in *Con Air* – have you seen *Con Air,* Doctor?' Dr Morris shook his head.

'I mean, I know he's a fuckin' paedo...'

'A what, Howard?'

'A paedophile. A child killer. But what I'm gettin' at is what he was saying...'

'A paedophile is not necessarily a child killer, Howard. It means lover of children. But anyway, what was he saying, Howard?' Dr Morris asked, his voice filled with distaste.

'He's basically saying that if you step outside of societal norms, of set human beliefs and morals, you realise that it's all bullshit. You can take your pick, you can have your own reality, 'cos that's all there really is.'

'What about sanity, Howard? Isn't that important?' Howard clenched his teeth as the rage welled up inside him.

'Sanity! You want to talk to me about sanity! Well, I'll tell ya. Everybody lives in their own little reality, their own little world and, you know, birds of a feather flock together. So they huddle together and gabble at each other, telling each other how sane they are and how mad and off-key all the others are – they're all nuts, not a sane one among em!' Howard barked as he shook with anger.

'And are you sane, Howard? Are you the only sane one among a world of lunatics?' Dr Morris said quietly.

'Don't be fuckin' silly, Doctor. I'm as mad as... as a mad cunt, but so are they. At least I fuckin' know it!' Howard continued irately.

'And who do you gabble with, Howard? Who tells you you're sane?'

'No one, Doctor. No one!'

'Do you think that that is maybe a part of your condition, Howard? Part of the reason why you're in the position you're in?' Dr Morris's voice was low, but unremitting.

'Of course it is, Doctor, but I can't talk to them...' Howard said with disgust. 'They drive me round the bend. I don't get them, they're fuckin' out there as far as I'm concerned!'

'Don't you believe in society, in human relationships? Don't you think they're important for our survival, our well-being? Don't you see, that they are what bond us and keep us going? Can you see that cutting off human ties, meaningful human interaction, is detrimental to your mental health, Howard, and to your life in general?' Howard looked down as he began to grasp fully Dr Morris's point.

'Yeah,' he muttered in resignation.

'You're right, Howard. Reality is negotiable, but that's what human relationships are about. They're about give and take, trust and mistrust, faith and doubt and all the things you talk about and more. That's what makes us human, that's what makes us alive, Howard.' Dr Morris was calm, but relentless.

'Yeah and look at the fuckin' mess we're in, Doctor! Jesus was in despair at humanity and you have to admit he had a point.' Howard again sidestepped Dr Morris's main premise. 'The funny thing is, that it's all true. The paradox is that all views are just as much right as they are wrong and all views are ambivalent. It simply depends on the person.

My reality is as real as yours and so on. The problem is that people want to assert and impose their views on others and the whole deal runs into problems. If Jesus were here he would say one thing to humanity: "Whatever all of you can agree on is true, whatever you cannot agree on is not."'

Howard was going through the motions, but appeared to be flagging for once, as though he was overtired and overemotional. His firewall of defensive aggression was faltering. Dr Morris picked up on Howard's unusually visible vulnerability, but was undeterred, his softly softly approach had slipped under Howard's radar.

'Look Howard,' he said gently. 'The human mind is an amazing thing. We, people, are very suggestible. Our minds deceive us in all sorts of ways. We have many different survival mechanisms. We use very elaborate mental procedures through which we try to cope and process our thoughts and feelings, both consciously and sub-consciously.' Howard grew annoyed at Dr Morris's tact. He did not like his quiet assertiveness – he needed a fight. He preferred wrath any day.

'The fucking answer is infinity!' Howard declared, trying to enflame the situation. 'Nothing and everything! Macrocosm and microcosm, the maths is all wrong! The missing equation is infinity. Without it, without its inclusion, then all calculations will be relative, never absolute! But that is the fucking point! We can never get it all, we are transient! Einstein wanted to read the mind of God – the poor bastard!' Howard let out something close to a mock stage laugh. 'We are a drop in the ocean. We are part of God. God is the ocean and every drop in it, and more! More than we can ever perceive – except... except by being a part of it, we experience it, or God. But we can never, never, through a limited language we call mathematics, fully express what God is! If we seek to humanise God, to anthropomorphise everything we come across, then...'

'Then what, Howard?'

'Then...' Howard grappled for the words.

'Then we'd cease to be human, Howard. We can't see beyond what we are.' Dr Morris leaned forward and locked his gaze with Howard's, his look was patiently worldly and lacked any hostility or anger.

'No, but we feel it, don't we, Doctor?' Howard said, half offering an olive branch, half bear-baiting.

'Maybe some of us don't, Howard,' Dr Morris said firmly, looking further into Howard's eyes.

'Maybe some of us don't want to, Doctor. Maybe some of us are frightened, frightened of what awaits us, eh, Doctor?' Howard said spitefully.

'Maybe some of us are drug-damaged, Howard,' Dr Morris responded plainly, unruffled.

'Or just damaged, Doctor,' Howard said, going for the jugular. Dr Morris sat back in his chair. What would have otherwise been a red rag to a bull became a white flag.

'Well, that would be all of us then, wouldn't it Howard?' he said with a philosophical smile. Howard began vibrating with tension, with rage and resentment, but also sheer terror at his inability to influence the situation and steer it back to familiar territory. With nothing to push against, Howard's world began to spiral out of control. Dr Morris, his centre of gravity, had pulled the plug and tossed him into free fall, his mind sent racing.

'Infinity plus infinity, times infinity, take away infinity, divide by infinity, equals infinity – the fucking answer is infinity!' Howard ranted as his frantic arm-waving began. 'You can stick E equals mc squared or M equals ec squared or any other anthropomorphic abstraction into the mix, anywhere you like, but the answer is still infinity. We are not the be all and fucking end all of it, Doctor. We are not!' he spouted, waving his finger at Dr Morris. 'Infinite particles, infinite strings, whatever you like, whatever denomination you are!'

'Sshhhh! Shush, Howard,' Dr Morris said gently, trying to pacify him. 'Howard, you're becoming manic, okay? And it's not clear what you're saying, alright?'

'What I'm saying, Doctor, is that what seems like the minutest difference, what we would call negligible or mathematically non-existent, such as where a ball might land in relation to where it's predicted to, for example, may to us be so minute as to not really count. But Doctor, in reality, it is as huge and crucially important as the enormous and obvious occurrences that seem so important to us – the slightest alteration changes everything, you just can't necessarily see how!' Howard was talking at top speed and with great urgency.

379

'Just like the subtle shift in brain chemistry, Howard. One small change… and, well… the whole thing's thrown off kilter,' Dr Morris said, still trying to reel Howard in. Howard became infuriated.

'NO, NO NO, DOCTOR! YOU'RE GETTING IT ALL WRONG!' he shouted. 'Don't you see, Doctor, don't you see it? Inside the perfect circle is the perfect square and vice versa!'

'Howard…' Dr Morris started.

'But there *is* no perfect square or perfect circle. There *is* no such thing as perfect symmetry – it's an illusion, Doctor! An optical illusion! When you really measure it properly, nothing in the world, in the universe, is perfect. It's a thoroughly unsymmetrical, imperfect place!'

'Please calm down and be quiet, Howard,' Dr Morris said gently, but firmly.

'It's just relative by comparison, that's all! But superstring theory is supposed to be super symmetric!' Howard began to laugh hysterically.

'Come on now, Howard.'

'Yes, but Doctor, it's the fabric of the universe, it's all about squaring the circle, circling the square. They've been trying since ancient times, but I can do it.'

'Howard, shush.'

'I CAN! I'VE DONE IT!' Howard shrieked, opposing Dr Morris's perceived denial of his achievement. 'It's all just folding, stretching, from inner to outer and back again, so it looks at this time like a rectangle or an oval, it's just elongated – abstracted from perfection, only to be deformed again!' Howard gave another hysterical laugh. 'It's all part of the process. It's all fucking ongoing, never-ending! Fuck their Calabi-Yau, what do they know!'

'Please Howard...'

'The fabric of space and time are comprised of the perfect multi-dimensional spheres inside perfect multi-dimensional cubes and hexagons and triangles, strings, all the shapes you can imagine and more, all distorted, stretched and elongated and compressed, and they are all pulsating back to perfection and then back to distortion again. All of these are joined at points that all contain the same thing, outwards and inwards. It continues. All of these cubes and spheres, spheres and cubes, are both the point of connection for each other and a point in space and time themselves, like cells, links, chains, matrixes of cells, all linked by others – no gaps – the gaps are filled by more! All infinite in the scales, at every point they merge with both smaller and larger repetitions, inside which are simply more. The space between them is both enormous, infinitely so and minute, also infinitely so. They turn themselves inside out and outside in, and it pulsates! All contract and expand at the same time; they all breathe as one, one solid mass of energy – universal energy, a matrix of energy with differing expressions of one solid sameness. It's all connected because it is actually one confused mass. They mould together to form other shapes, other forms of energy, each point varies in frequency – the breathing, the pulsating, the life, Doctor! It's all a living, pulsating, life force, all at differing stages, different points of evolution and devolution, devolution and evolution, form superstrings and beyond – to us and beyond – out there, the infinite universe! Infinite different universes, all different in expression, but similar in nature! All sizes and shapes, all forms are present, alongside the other; inside us are curled-up hidden bits, we are curled-up hidden parts of the universe, which itself is merely a continuation of this process, this expression, this existence!' Howard now fit the bill of the stereotypical, glinting-eyed ranting madman found on the high streets of every major city in the world. He shook his fist, wagged his finger and looked to the heavens for approval. Dr Morris sat patiently, waiting.

'It's all particles emitting waves, waves comprised of particles – a matrix of this. A mutable, interchanging, interconnecting matrix of particles joined by their emitted waves, waves connected at surges of waves or particles. Like kind particles and waves connect with each other while engaging, interacting, experiencing, existing in conjunction with differing frequencies of other like kind particles and waves. A great mix of this creates fields of frequencies that pulsate and affect each other – a living, vibrating matrix of particle wave connections, interconnections and interference or interaction.' Howard's stream of consciousness had taken over, he was on automatic pilot.

'What about here, Howard?' Dr Morris said, raising his voice slightly. 'What about life on earth, Howard? What has this shit got to do with anything?' The words were belligerent, but his tone was not. Howard seemed to hear what he said.

'The particles are here, everywhere. I told you about them, the balls of energy. They get passed around all the time, all day long.' Howard had quietened down, but was muttering uncontrollably. 'They provide a network. They are evolutionary systems of information proliferation. Energy particles passed on sub-consciously to each other. You can put the balls of energy into your mind, it's how we swap minds, talk telepathically, etc. It's why you get the 'appearance' of ideas from 'nowhere', the 'ether' animals do it too, you know, like the birds with the bottle tops – one minute they can't open them, the next minute they can all do it all over the world. They passed the information on. It's the sub-conscious transmission of thoughts of ideas, a sort of semi-telepathy. It's why ideas seemingly spring up simultaneously, or why individuals completely separate from each other work on similar concepts, write, create certain themes – because it's out there in the ether, passed around from person to person, one person's nonsense is another's eureka and vice versa. I see it get passed on, the information, the energy, good and bad. And in the personality swapping I see the shivering child, the little gremlin that possesses us; it goes between person to person, it's a battle to not be consumed with it, so you pass it on. No one wants it and it seems to come out of nowhere, but it's just been passed from person to person; it makes you panic, unable to cope, to look anyone in the eye. It's an information network, but I have full telepathy, the voices are clear now, I know what people are saying. And the sex thing, I can't believe it took me this long to work it out, to see it consciously! I must have been doing it all my life sub-consciously. We're like virtual banobos, and it makes sense, too. They're our closest living relative, we're just a more sophisticated version, we do it electromagnetically. But I see it now, I'm starting to get it, what I must have been doing all along. The extended penis thing, not your actual one, the energy one. Men compete for women, women compete with each other to control the energy, it's what separates winners from losers, all the energy dropping and shooting, you can really crank it up.'

Howard had become extremely agitated and manic. Dr Morris sat in silence, listening.

'You can see it in the statues of Buddha, the hand gestures. I've worked it out – a finger and thumb facing forward, that's feminine, a fanny if it's elongated. If it's big and round it's a dick, and an arse is like a small round version of the feminine one. They're used to temporarily stun your victim, to get what you want. We smell and eat the ones we want, as well as reusing them or putting them on or in our genitals, or some put them up their arse! You can also use these hand gestures as channels for the energy to travel along, like a tube of energy for the ball to travel through, until it catches someone by surprise and they feel the surge of whatever that energy was and was meant for, or they control it and just receive the information. It's just like string theory and quantum mechanics, particles travelling along strings of energy. We can join them up together, directing the particles in the strings from person to person, like a matrix of strings delivering particles of energy, sexual energy, informational energy to each other. It's a network of energy, an informational delivery system, a form of communication and our favourite pastime. In fact, it's pathological!'

Howard looked up at Dr Morris, who sat like a figurine cast in marble, emotionless, expressionless, listening to the remarkable oration being presented to him. Howard looked distinctly unwell; he seemed to be suffering from nervous exhaustion. His hyperactivity appeared to be winding down, but he seemed on the verge of tears.

'You see, everyone has a piece of the puzzle, Doctor, but only I can put them all together. I see it all laid before me.' It was as though Howard's mind was like a light switch, on, off, on, off, a pendulum that swung clearly from one side to the other and back again, back and forth, back and forth, one disposition then the other, an unpredictable and tempestuous vacillation of ascendancy. It was just a matter of when this change took place. Whatever triggered it had its own mysterious built-in clock.

'I am the second fucking coming, Doctor!' Howard announced, the light switching on, the pendulum swung. His wide-eyed expression left no doubt. Dr Morris said nothing. Seconds later, the pendulum swung back, the light in Howard Jones's mind switched off and he began to cry. He wept like an infant. Uncontrollably the tears poured; he wailed and moaned like some kind of grieving ape, as the snot and dribble streamed over his mouth and chin and down the front of his grey sweatshirt. Still Dr Morris said nothing.

'I am disgusted. I am disgusted at what we are, what it means to be human, at what we do, at how we're made, from the tiny nonsenses we get up to, day-to-day, right through to the atrocities, the unique, clever, spiteful ways in which we choose to impose on other life forms, and shit on each other, on our children. What are we? WHAT THE FUCK ARE WE? I can't stand it. It eats at my soul, it eats at my very being – we are depraved – existence is depravity. Before God I am embarrassed. I am ashamed,' Howard confessed through his tears.

After more than ten minutes, Howard's outpour began to diminish. He rubbed his face with both sleeves and, for a moment, seemed as though he might reach across the desk to embrace Dr Morris. He only gave the slightest indication of this, but it was enough. Dr Morris instantly shuddered and pushed his wheeled chair back a few inches away from Howard. Howard hung his head, snivelling.

'I know that you're not taking your medication, Howard,' Dr Morris said, finally breaking his silence.

SESSION TWENTY-SEVEN

Howard was fearful and very apprehensive. He stood outside the door, unsure of how it was going to be, of how he should be in this, the last fifty minutes with his only friend, his only confidant. He rubbed his mouth uneasily, drew in a deep breathe, knocked on the door and went in. Dr Morris stood with his back to Howard, gazing out of the window. He turned slowly as Howard entered and calmly and collectedly sat down behind his desk. Howard stood hesitantly by his chair, a newer green version of the purple people eater.

'Howard,' Dr Morris said with a welcoming smile, 'please, sit down. How are you this fine day?' he continued.

Howard stood motionless for a moment, as though he were afraid that such a simple action as sitting would signal the beginning, the beginning of the end. Gradually he forced his body to obey the command and he eased himself onto the cheap, foam-filled seat. He waited a second before offering Dr Morris an amicable smile in return.

'Erm, hi, er, Doctor, Doctor, er... Morris. I'm, erm, I'm ok... How are you?' he said sincerely, rushing the last part of his sentence out. It was the only time Howard had ever asked Dr Morris this question, and it did not go unnoticed. Pleased, Dr Morris took it as a sign of progress, in some ways a leap of almost epic proportions considering Howard's usual blinkered existence.

'I'm, erm... I'm very well, Howard, thanks for asking,' Dr Morris replied with a mixture of uncertainty and graciousness. 'You seem a little more relaxed than when I saw you last, young man,' he said, despite the fact that Howard seemed as jumpy as a fox with his head in a dustbin. Howard blushed slightly, as though he were a bit embarrassed.

'Erm, yeah, I've er... had some, er, time to, you know... sort myself out,' he said bashfully.

'The important thing is whether you've been taking your medication or not?'

'Yeah,' Howard said slowly.

'I mean, I don't want to play matron to you, Howard. You know, stand over you, foot-tapping and all that. But it is essential that you are,' Dr Morris said comically, but as serious as a heart attack.

'Er yeah, I know Doctor, you're right,' Howard agreed.

'So have you?' Dr Morris said bluntly, so much so that Howard was slightly taken aback.

'Yeah,' he nodded genuinely. Dr Morris caught his eye for a moment before deciding that Howard's response was good enough.

'Okay then, well perhaps we can get on. As I'm sure you're aware, this is your last session with me, but I don't want you to feel like this is the end of the process, Howard. On the contrary, this is merely the beginning; the beginning, hopefully, of a new stage for you, whereby you feel ready and able to open up a little to new people, people who have had similar experiences to your own, people who you may well be able to relate to and, who knows, even develop some kind of relationships with. But certainly people who you will find in a very similar position... in life, to your own. They may be from a variety of differing backgrounds, all with their own story to tell, but one thing you will all have in common is the shared experience of suffering from debilitating mental illness. And so, through the process of group therapy sessions and activities you will, with a bit of luck, be able to move forward with your recovery and come to terms in some way with the difficulties that you all share in one way or another.'

Howard listened patiently, despite the monotonous sound of Dr Morris's over-used speech. 'Yeah,' was all he offered, reluctantly, in return.

'Well, we still have time for discussion. If there's anything particular on your mind, now is the time to share it, Howard.' Dr Morris sat back in his chair as though his work was basically done. 'What have you been up to for the past week?' he said casually before Howard had a chance to speak.

'Well, er, I've been going to the park quite a lot. It's, er... it's nice to get some fresh air instead of sitting in the house all the time, you know. It's full of birds and squirrels and shit. I quite like just watching them, you know... do their thing,' Howard answered, a more relaxed expression materialising across his face.

'That's good, Howard!' Dr Morris said, enthused in an almost pantomime-like fashion, just stopping short of slapping his thigh.

'Yeah, I, er, do a lot of thinking there now, I guess.'

'Well, Howard, watch all that, won't you? The thinking, I mean. Try not to overdo it will you, eh?' Dr Morris replied, toning down slightly his previous exuberance.

'Yeah, but I need to get it all straight, in my head I mean. Then it would be more clear, you know, what I've got to say,' Howard said vaguely as though his brain was a bit on the woolly side.

'Yes, but Howard, your arguments, your train of thought, is incoherent, full of contradictions. It's just not logical,' Dr Morris said. Howard seemed uneasy, but calm.

'Life is incoherent, Doctor. Life is full of contradictions. There is more to this universe than human logic, even a fool can see that. The religious, the spiritual transcends the logical mind. It extends to realms that logic simply cannot comprehend or compute,' Howard said, forcing his enthusiasm for the subject, as much for old time's sake than for making any real argument or great point.

'Do you know what the greatest word in the English language is, Doctor? The most truthful word?'

'No Howard, enlighten me,' Dr Morris said with a hint of sarcasm.

'Paradox,' Howard instantly replied.

'Paradox?'

'Yes, paradox. Life is a paradox. It is all a series of inexplicable paradoxes,' Howard said quite definitely. 'Human logic is the limited function of individual organs, floating in a sea of infinite paradoxical enigma!'

'So does that mean we should just give up, Howard?'

'If you like, but not necessarily. That's my point. It's whatever you want it to be, no more no less. Whatever you want it to be. It just depends which way you look at the whole thing… or little bits. If you're certain it's this way, then you make up your mind it is. If you're not sure, then you're simply looking at it from another point of view and vice versa.'

'So, you've decided it's all relative have you, Howard?'

'If you look at it like that, then yes, it is. If you think it's absolute, then that's what it is.'

'Yes, but what do *you* think, Howard? That's the important question.'

'I think it's both. I think it's everything we can ever muster up, everything we can create, perceive, believe, dream, everything and much, much more… infinitely more.'

'So it's all infinite, Howard?'

'Absolutely.'

'You firmly believe that, don't you, Howard?' Dr Morris said with a conciliatory smile.

'Yes, but I, er… I could be wrong,' Howard admitted.

'Indeed,' Dr Morris replied.

'You know, belief is inescapable,' Howard said holding up his hands slightly in surrender.

'That it is, Howard, that it is,' Dr Morris said cavalierly.

'What I'm getting at, Doctor, what I'm saying is that there is a sequence of events, a chronology from the beginning of the known universe to this very moment, to each of our lives. It is inescapable and, if the unknown

391

universe is infinite, then it has always been going on and probably always will.'

'And what I'm saying, Howard, is that you have to start from now, not the past, not the future, but here and now in the present. It is the only place where you can actually do anything about it all. You need to stop living in outer space, or in some microscope Petri dish, and be here and now in this world, because it's the only one we have right now. Please take it from me, you need to make the most of it before it's too late. You have to start living in the moment, for the moment, it's the only way to get through it all. Face reality, Howard. Face your life and get on with it. If it is all infinite, as you say, all perfectly ordered, but, er... too, erm, complex to predict or understand, then what does that say for free will? That ultimately it doesn't exist?' Dr Morris was speaking with passion and vigour.

'To be honest, Doctor, it seems likely. But, you know, not necessarily. Free will may be part of that infinite order. It may be relative to our existence, very real, or even otherwise, it may not. The point is that it's probably too complex to know or comprehend... I don't know, Doctor. Maybe,' Howard said pensively.

'Well, maybe it's your destiny to get well, to improve your condition and your life,' Dr Morris suggested excitedly.

'Maybe I believe in free will?' Howard responded in humorous rebellion.

'Well, if you believe in free will then you have a choice. There are things you can do, steps you can take, Howard.'

'Maybe I lean towards destiny, Doctor,' Howard said with a mischievous grin.

'Because it's easier?'

'Because it seems likely,' Howard answered without ambiguity.

'Look Howard, maybe you're right about reality, maybe it *is* what we make of it. Maybe the world does just depend on how you see it. Maybe we have a choice about how we perceive it. I mean, if it is all destiny, then why worry? It's going to happen how it's going to happen, but why not assume that it might be shapable, influenceable? That you have some autonomy in it all? If you don't, then you're guaranteed that it'll just happen to you. But if you try, then there's a chance, a possibility. Why don't you work on seeing the good things, on building your life back up? Why don't you concentrate on creating a better reality for yourself?' Dr Morris finished by stabbing a pointing finger at Howard to emphasise his final point.

'I can't create it out of nowhere. I'm not in fucking control of it. I can't make the world different. I can't change the fuckers out there. I can't tell humanity how to be. It's their choice, or their destiny, or whatever the fuck it is. BUT IT IS NOT MY FUCKING FAULT, IS IT DOCTOR!' Howard bellowed in frustration rather than anger.

'No Howard, it isn't,' Dr Morris said softly.

'SO WHY DO I FEEL SO FUCKING RESPONSIBLE, THEN? WHY DOES IT ALL BOTHER ME SO FUCKING MUCH? ANSWER

ME THAT, DOCTOR!' Howard yelled, on the verge of tears again.

'Because that's how you feel, Howard. It's just how you feel. It's okay to feel like that, honestly it is. You're right, all that is not your fault, nor is it your responsibility. But what you do have a responsibility for is yourself, your actions. What you focus on is important, just as important as what you don't focus on, Howard.'

'Look, Doctor, I'm an idealist, I really am. No one's more idealistic than me. The problem is, the world isn't like that, the world is not like that, and I suffer for my idealism!'

'Yes, but don't you see, Howard, idealists play their part. Idealists have changed the world. Many things in this world would not have happened if it wasn't for idealists pushing their ideals and making a difference,' Dr Morris implored. 'My point is, Howard, that reality out there...' Dr Morris pointed out of the window, 'and reality in here...' he said, tapping his temple with his finger, 'are negotiated, as you've pointed out. But the fact is it is a mixture of the two, not one or the other. How you negotiate the two is the most important thing, it determines how balanced you are as an individual.'

'Isn't that passing judgement, Doctor? A biased notion, you know, not necessarily true?'

'Perhaps it's not about the truth, Howard... perhaps it's about survival.'

'Isn't it about conformity to established norms? Control of thoughts and behaviour, Doctor?'

'Yes, Howard. As I said, it's about self-preservation.'

394

'Don't you want to know the truth, Doctor? Nobody seems to care.'

'I'm not sure I need to know, Howard. I'm not sure it exists. Even if it does, I'm not sure I care, to be perfectly honest.' Howard was dumbfounded, speechless. What could he say? Both men sat gaping at each other from their respective perceptive experiential goldfish bowls.

'Howard!' Dr Morris urged. 'So you've unlocked the secrets of the bloody universe, well that's just great, super! So what, Howard! What does it all mean? What does it all amount to? I'll tell you – nothing! It amounts to you sitting in a psychiatric unit partaking in intellectual masturbation with some old git like me! It is a waste of life, Howard, a terrible, terrible waste!' Dr Morris realised that he had never actually given to a client before, never actually offered a genuine exchange of human-to-human emotion or contact before, apart from anger. This was as new for him as it was for Howard.

'You're throwing it all away,' Dr Morris spluttered, 'down the bloody toilet, and flushed out to sea. And for what? To find God? Many search for God, Howard, but most find religion instead. Why don't you wait until you die, then you might find him. But until that day, why don't you stop fucking squandering the life that he gave you?'

'God doesn't exist...' Howard said blankly staring into space. 'And why does he hate me so much?' he finished bitterly.

'Does it really matter whether he, it, exists or not? The point is to value your life, for until you do so you will remain a morose, pessimistic man so full of himself that he cannot see the wood for the trees. It is really not nearly as complicated as you make it, it really isn't! You just need to let go of your obsession to see it all, to penetrate reality and see beyond it, when in actual fact it's right under your flaming nose! Open your eyes and take a good look around. Take a deep breath and smell it, taste it. It's everywhere, Howard, what you look for is everywhere! You have to try. You have to make the effort. You have to go out to people, Howard, take some risks. You can't hide away forever. You have to face the world sometime!' Dr Morris was truly expressing his feelings on the whole matter. The crux of the problem, the main issue at hand, was completely obvious to him and he wished for Howard to understand it implicitly.

'Yes, Doctor, you're right! None of it makes any sense, anyway. I mean, do you really think it was possible to fit even just the insects, all three million odd species, in pairs onto the fucking ark, never mind the other God knows how many other species there are in the world today, and all those that have gone extinct? All that lot, plus some old beardie, his missus and some kids, I believe, onto one wooden boat roughly three hundred and ninety-five cubits in size and ponce around waiting for the flood to finish? It's about as likely as... well, me being the bloody messiah, Doctor!' Howard said, giving Dr Morris an awkward grin. Although he recognised that Howard was deliberately drifting from the subject, Dr Morris returned the smile, shaking

396

his head, not in despair, but at the absurdity of it.

'It would have really stank, too,' Howard said.

'I'm sorry?' Dr Morris replied.

'The ark, it would have stunk to high heaven.'

Dr Morris returned to the more important matter at hand.

'The question I'm putting to you, Howard Jones, is what have you learnt from all of this, this process? Have you learnt anything of value, anything at all?'

Howard thought carefully for a moment, trying to absorb everything that Dr Morris was putting to him in one large indigestible serving. Eventually he found the words.

'That when the shit hits the fan, Doctor, the intellect is no refuge, no refuge at all. It can't save you or help you. All it can do is trick you back into the game, a new angle, a new slant. It's all okay now, 'cos I see oh so rationally where I was going wrong last time. But this time it's all so clear. Silly me... well, sometimes you just run out, run out of tricks, run out of new angles. Sometimes you just have nowhere left to go.'

Dr Morris paused as he acknowledged Howard's point. For once in a long time, perhaps the first, Dr Morris felt some kind of affinity towards a client, this young client. Finally, albeit briefly, they both actually related to each other. They actually had something in common, something that cut across Dr Morris's usual dismissive pomposity and Howard's alienated rage.

'I'm all alone, Doctor, and I'm frightened, all of the time,' Howard said quietly, with surprising honesty.

'It's okay to be frightened, frightened keeps you alive, Howard, on your toes. We're all ultimately alone… but we're alone together, if that makes any sense?' Dr Morris said with a hardy grin. 'Howard, if I can be perfectly frank with you, it's not about how sane or not you are, I mean, harming yourself and others aside, it's about how well you cope with it all, it's about whether you can cope with it at all. Ultimately, it boils down to this fact.'

'What does?' Howard murmured.

'Life does. Life is, by and large, a state of mind. Life is real, Howard. You need to find some meaning in it, some worth.'

These were the final pearls of wisdom Dr Morris had to impart. Howard looked as though he wanted more; he wanted to continue, but it was over. He could tell by the look on Dr Morris's face. Dr Morris leant forward and extended his hand across the desk; Howard slowly reached out and the two shook.

'Nice doing business with you, Howard,' Dr Morris said cheerfully. 'I expect I'll see you around… the clinic that is… Good luck and, er, God bless, as they say,' he went on. Howard mustered a smile.

'I'll walk out with you, Howard,' Dr Morris said, gathering his grey suit jacket from the back of his chair and his briefcase from the floor. He put on his jacket, quickly wrote something at the bottom of Howard's file, closed it and put it in his briefcase.

'Shall we?' he said in a positive tone. Howard left the room with Dr Morris closely following him. As they walked down the corridor, Dr Morris gently put his hand on Howard's back, barely touching him, almost as though the weight of his hand were guiding Howard as they walked.

'Okay then, young Howard. You take care now,' Dr Morris said warmly as they reached the reception area.

'Okay, er... you, er, too Doctor,' Howard replied back as warmly he could. He stood gawping at Dr Morris as though they might continue the conversation, but Dr Morris turned and walked away towards the reception desk. Howard's eyes followed him as he went.

As Dr Morris stood chatting to the receptionist, Howard slowly went through the front door and ambled up the hospital path. Dr Morris took a single glance through the meshed window of the front door as Howard finally disappeared around the bend. He continued his chat with the lanky, young, freckle-faced girl who had been working the reception for a few weeks now. He always made a point of getting to know the receptionists in the vain hope that one of them might stay and actually get to know what they were doing.

'See you in a little while,' he called out pleasantly to her as he made his way towards the opposite corridor to the one he and Howard had previously emerged from. He had no other clients to see, but was hungry and decided to have a snack before embarking on the hour and a half drive back to his Kent home. As he walked down the corridor, he fiddled with his cuffs until they were suitably arranged before turning left into a minor painted brick corridor that turned off from the main one. He followed it to the end, where a fire exit awaited. He pushed down the metal bar and opened the large red door, knowing full well that he shouldn't, but content in the knowledge that the fire exits never set off the fire alarm anyway.

He stepped out onto the street that ran in front of the main hospital entrance. It was nearly Christmas, the weather was crisp and chilly, but the sun was shining brightly. He huddled over slightly as he did up the buttons to his suit jacket, his breath visible as it met with the cold air. Suddenly he noticed something shiny fly past, just above his line of vision. He gave a double take and then there it was again: a small ball of light, less than the size of a golf ball, was jumping around above him. Dr Morris looked up with a start, confused by what he had just seen. He stopped dead in his tracks and visually searched around for the small shimmering ball of whitish light. As he moved his arm, he noticed it fly by again. Then he chuckled to himself as he realised what it was. He then playfully moved his wrist backwards and forwards as the sunlight reflected from his watch onto the metallic sign attached to the telegraph pole on the pavement. With another giggle, he walked up the street towards the sandwich bar.

Howard sat at the back of the top deck of the bus on the other side of the large main road. Looking from the window, he had seen the ball of energy that Dr Morris had caught and then tossed into the crowd entering and leaving the hospital. Finally, it came his way and landed in his lap; he picked it up and hurled it down the bus, towards a woman sitting at the front. He grinned incongruously to himself. The bus pulled away.